Christmas 2004
To Roberta

Alverna's Hope

by

Phyllis Plowman

Phyllis Plowman

authorHOUSE™

1663 LIBERTY DRIVE, SUITE 200
BLOOMINGTON, INDIANA 47403
(800) 839-8640
WWW.AUTHORHOUSE.COM

First published by AuthorHouse 09/18/04

ISBN: 1-4184-8472-5 (sc)

Library of Congress Control Number: 2004095265

Printed in the United States of America
Bloomington, Indiana

This book is printed on acid-free paper.

TABLE OF CONTENTS

PART I

PART II

PART I

CHAPTER 1 - 1982

December. It's a cold, snowy, windy winter day. I'm sitting in my kitchen warming up with a bowl of coffee soup. It don't taste the same since I gotta use sugar substitute instead of the real stuff, but it'll do. I need something to warm me up. See, I just now got home from the doctor's.

It's strange the way we think, ain't? We get this notion in our heads that we're gonna live forever - even when we know everybody else is gonna die someday. Just can't believe it'll happen to us. But the truth hit me full force when I was coming back from the doctor's where I'd just discovered that my body is almost worn out. I ain't gonna make it to a hundred like I thought. When people find out they'll talk down to me and say, **O yes you will,** and they'll be thinking they're fooling me when all the time I know they ain't, not no more.

Do you know how it is when you get older and people begin to whisper instead of talking normal? How there's so much you don't hear and next time you hear things you wish you didn't? Like when my boy had me at the doctor's for my check-up today and they was talking between them. Most of what they said wasn't coming through. Wasn't that I was befuddled or nothing, I just didn't pay no attention cause he's in charge - like I'm able not to take care of myself! Huh! Just because a body gets old don't mean everybody should treat it like it ain't here anymore. I still got the brains and the common sense I was born with, but them young'uns, they forget all that and act like they gotta take over and make **all** the decisions without thinking how it vexes me. It's hurtful it is, to be talked about as if I wasn't there.

Now I ain't dumb enough to think I can do without my family helping me out, especially since my old man's gone. Come to think of it, he wasn't much help these past years, him being sick and all. Matter of fact, for a long time he wasn't all that much help when he was good.

Sad I never learned to drive. And can you believe it, when I was seventy five my man said, "Don't you think it's time you learned to drive? The kids are growed and you don't work no more at the factory, so you don't have that for an excuse." What was he thinking? Why he was touched in the head to even think I'd get out on the road with all them reckless, high-speed drivers, so I have to depend on my kids to drive me around. Of course my next door neighbor, Ivy, she takes me to market and to the beauty parlor - we get our hair done at the same time - then out to lunch, except at eighty-six she ain't all that great behind the wheel, but that's better'n sitting at home all day. Ivy, she chews parsley or breath mints all the time. I've got a notion it's a cover-up from what she nips before she gets behind the wheel, but I ain't taking no chances, don't intend to tell no one that, especially my kids. So far we done ok; no accidents yet.

I sure do wish her eyesight was better, though. When she asks me what color the signal light is, that makes me nervous. Sometimes the colors fade out on me, but at least I remember the red light is on top and that means stop. Yes well, we don't go too far from home. So far, so good.

Getting back to my kids, feeble minded I ain't. It'd be nice of them to remember that and keep me up-to-date about my situation once in awhile. After all, it's my body.

Anyhow, here we was at the doctor's office. Doc mentioned **cancer** soft and low to my boy. Hadda serious tone he did, one I never before heard. See, Doc usually jokes around with me and that's the way I like it. Not then he didn't. He went on in a low tone that's easier for me to hear than when voices get loud and high-pitched, "We won't worry about that now with her diabetes and other health problems."

Of course I acted dumb, just sat there like a bump on a log, not saying nothing, but boy-oh-boy, my insides got all shook up. Still fluttering around in there because of the way they was going on, talking about me like I wasn't even there.

Someday they'll get old too and maybe someone'll take over thinking for them. Ha! See if they like being treated this way. I'd like to be around to see that, but of course I won't.

"No use pursuing other forms of treatment now. Too many other things going wrong too fast," Doc said to my boy.

Gotta admit it, haven't been feeling too good lately - and me being healthy as a horse all my life except for diabetes when I hit eighty - and that wasn't no fault of my own, just the shock over my girl's accident with a shotgun. She was my youngest; in her sixties. All my kids growed up around guns. We couldn't figure out how it could happen. Guess that's why I went into shock and the diabetes hit. Now I have to sprinkle this darn sugar substitute over the bread in my coffee soup instead of the real stuff. Just don't taste the same, it don't. Maybe I should just tempt fate and pour on the sugar and die from that instead of cancer. (Only kidding.)

Anyhow, when I heard the word **cancer,** I figured it's gonna take me real soon. Sure hope so, don't wanna lay around in pain and misery having everybody watch me suffer and acting like they're feeling real bad, putting-on to make me think they care about me more'n they do. Hovering over me like that, why they'll just be a pain in the neck and make me feel worse. Good grief! Maybe I will use sugar after all.

Doc said I could take up to four of these pills a day if the pain gets bad - but that it's no use to go with anything more'n that, at least not yet. My boy sat 'em on the clock shelf for me to reach if I need 'em. But I tell you right now, I ain't gonna take 'em till I gotta. Don't like the thought of getting all doped up.

So now it's up to me to do what I've been wanting to do for a long time.

You see, the going was hard many a time during these ninety years, but I love life, always did; love life to this day. Why I always say the minute I can't laugh and joke around, the minute I can't carry on no more, I wanna die.

Don't know how much longer I got to live but this much I do know, I'm ready to go. You know that old, old hymn - one of my favorites, always makes me cry when I hear it - **'When the roll is called up yonder I'll be there'**. Well, that's where you'll find me, up there with Jesus. That's the important thing. I wish my kids would pay more attention to religion. Worries me to no end. Guess all I can do is pray for 'em. Talking don't seem to help, but I sure do lots of both, talking and praying.

Haven't seen too many good results yet.

Anyhow, now's the time to do what I've just been thinking about all these years

I love my family, everyone of 'em. Every now and then I'm accused of favoring one over another'n and that sure cuts deep. I got weak points but that ain't one of 'em. That one boy of mine was bitter and angry, out-right jealous to the day he died. Just can't understand why he'd think like that cause I'm not that way. I love everyone equal. One never got more'n the others but he refused to let it alone; he wore me out with his bickering and carrying on - such a mean streak he had! Musta got it from his daddy's side. But I never let on how bad he was hurting me. I prefer peace-making and tried my durndest to make him see it my way, but no. Such a mean streak! Seems like there's always one in the bunch to make life hard, but I ain't blaming him alone. The rest done their fair share to try to make life miserable every now'n then. If they wanted to be measly and cantankerous, wasn't much I could do except refuse to go along with it. That's in every family I guess.

Don't get me wrong. We had good times, lots of good times.

All-in-all, it coulda been a lot worse.

But now, take these little ones that're coming on. My, how I love them little great-great-grandkids! For the big family I got there's only three, two boys, one girl. Why just the other day the youngest one come all the way from Ohio to visit his grandma - she lives not too far from me - then come to see me they did. Three he is now. First thing he done was check out my old, oversized wood rocking chair that Pap built. It's older'n me and in about the same shape I am. Guess the little fellow never seen one like it before. Anyhow, he shimmied up, wiggled those chubby little legs and butt this way and that till he got up and turned around in the droopy cane seat that seen better days. It sags something awful in the middle, coming apart a little bit here and a little bit there. No use getting it fixed since I'm gonna die. Let the one who grabs it first and carries it off after fighting over it, let that one take care of fixing it up.

That dear little fella, he grabbed them long, worn-down-to-the-bare-wood, goose-neck arms, then holding on for dear life he swung himself back and forth, back and forth, working to get the hang of that big old rocker. He got it going, was intent on keeping it moving, so me and my granddaughter-in-law talked a spell but I couldn't keep my eyes off the little one, thinking back to when I was the little one getting all the attention.

Yes well, I remember them days just like it was yesterday.

A pillow behind where I was on the sofa fell down and I got this hankerin' to throw it at the little boy just to see what he'd do. After a minute I thought, **What the hun!** and throwed it when he wasn't looking my way. Hit him square in front, not hard mind you, but surprised the dickens outta him. He was looking all around to see where it come from, his dark, brown eyes big as saucers they was. He looked at his grandma and she just shrugged her shoulders as if to say,

I didn't do it. He looked my way and seen me holding my belly that was rolling and shaking from chuckling at what I done; tried not to but couldn't help myself. He off that rocking chair lickity-split, grabbed that fluffy, old pillow off the floor with its stuffing hanging out and swung it at me with all his might. Reaching for another pillow I started in and we had the best pillow fight, the two of us horsing around and swatting it out with each other. You could tell right then and there how we both relish a little horseplay every now and then.

He woulda wore me out except his grandma put a stop to it, but not before we had a couple of real good belly laughs, the first for me in a long time.

Boy-oh-boy, did that feel good! That little guy was snorting and grunting to beat the band, red in the face, wet and sticky all over from sweating that hot, muggy summer day, but the way he hollered and laughed and went on, why he had just as much fun as me. He fell in love with me right then and there, came and gave me a great, big, sweaty hug, not scared of me being a worn-out-old-looking-lady.

Let me tell you, I gotta admire that granddaughter-in-law of mine; everybody else woulda fussed for us to stop right away cause it might be too much for me to take, but she let it go on and put a stop to it only when she seen we was ready to up and quit but neither of us wanting to be the first to give in. Smart cookie she is. Sorta hate to admit it since she's not blood-related. See, for many a year I favored giving blood relation credit over in-laws when good things got accomplished, but I picked up a bit of wisdom with age and come to see that I wasn't always fair that way. Gotta stop looking at my own kin through rose-colored glasses and the rest not. My own, they got some character defects too. Anyhow, I wasn't always fair to those marrying into the family. Well, I might be ninety but that don't mean I can't change when there's good reason, so I give her some credit.

Can't wait no longer. I gotta get started. See, I never told my story because of having all them kids and work and things. Besides, nobody, not one person except this granddaughter-in-law ever wondered about my young life enough to ask; nobody's interested, not even my own kids. Don't they know I was little once and had a life worth telling about?

Yes well, this granddaughter-in-law's been asking me about things that happened long ago, and that got me all worked up inside, so it's now or never. It's written on my heart and I'm not gonna let this story die inside me now yet.

You know what? Last Monday I was reading my Bible - like I do every day - and I come across where in Isaiah it says, **Now go, write it before them. . . and note it in a book. . . .** And, mind you, today in Psalm 78 it hit me again: **Things we have known and heard. . .we will not hide them from children. . .we will tell the next generation. . . .** Don't you think that's a direct word from the Good Lord, telling me to get started?

I do.

I want for everyone who'll listen to hear about this wonderful good man and how he made life for me. He was *allerbescht,* the best of all!

Telling it's gonna be tough. See, my grammar ain't too good, that much I know. (Guess you can tell that by now.) I growed up learning Pennsylvania Dutch and English both, but not good at neither. Didn't get much education. That's my own fault. But what worries me most is will I be able to get the right words from my heart to this paper?

When I was little I loved to talk. Words rolled easy-like off my tongue. A lively chatterbox I was among them who didn't talk much except for Grammy. And I learned to spell long before others my age just because I loved doing it. Even early on I learned to spell words backwards and I can still do it today, not short, little words, but long, complicated words

9

like threshing machine, springhouse, musician, handkerchief; them are just a few. Even so, that's different from putting thoughts on paper and doing it right.

I don't intend to spin any yarns and use words I read in books today that go on and on describing things in fancy terms. Another thing; I can't tell what I don't know. My intent is to tell it like it was, just the way I lived it. Maybe I'll write it like a letter. I know all about letter writing for Mom and I wrote to each other till the day she died; or maybe like a diary. Oh well, I'm just gonna start and see what takes shape. I'm gonna tell my story.

As for words, now take my Mom. She was opposite from me in most things, especially talking. She was a person of few words and discouraged me from talking so much, always scolding me about that. Between her and the way life hit me hard every now and then, - I ain't complaining, happens to everybody - that quieted me down a bit as I got older. Besides, who wants to listen? Most people are intent only on talking, they don't wanna listen. Maybe it made me quieter in my speech but not in my mind. Always talked to myself, still do. Talk to the Good Lord too. I figure he listens even when nobody else does.

Here I go. I'm gonna lay aside my favorite pastime - I just love working whole sheets of long division - and write down what's been in my head and my heart all these years. For sure, it will be my story, my true story and I don't want it to die with me.

And I sure do hope you'll read my story and come to see why I had to write it.

CHAPTER 2 - HOW I GOT MY NAME

Allen Konhaus was a man of considerable prestige in this part of Pennsylvania and beyond, but to the Farley family, we knowed him as the best cigar-maker who gave us work to help make ends meet. Life was hard but we wasn't people to *brootz* and complain. We worked and made do with what we had. See, we wasn't too much aware of what we didn't have till the railroad brought industry and people of all kinds into our neighborhood. We purty much stayed in the same place with our own kind. People comment that the Pennsylvania Dutch are hard working and frugal - matter of fact they often snicker behind our backs and say we're tight-fisted penny-pinching, dumb Dutchmen, holding tight onto what money we got. Yes well, we are thrifty people, that we are. It come mostly out of needing to be.

The old-timers was even meager with their words. Men didn't say much and when they did their women was expected to keep their mouths shut, listen and obey. And that most of them did - listened and done what they was told. Some women, when they look back, say that men's intent was to keep women - and children - from having a good time. But see, it was our way that men had their place and the rest of the human race had their place and it sure wasn't elevated where men's was, no way. When an outspoken woman chaffed about it, spoke up and stood her ground, she was admonished for not keeping her place, not only from menfolk but other women too. We females was hoodwinked into thinking we was less'n what we was. When I look back I see we women done each other wrong by thinking man's way of thinking - that we wasn't their equals and didn't deserve no more'n they handed out to us. Yes well, so old I had to get to grow wiser.

Of course all men wasn't like that, I'm only speaking in general. Pondering it, I reckon these deep, ingrained, streaks of men thinking they was a cut above women come down through many a generation - as far back as from the old country, Germany. But not all was like that. Many was stern, yet kind and open-minded towards their kin.

We was purty self-reliant as a community but as families and individuals we depended on each other to keep life on an even keel. Us Pennsylvania Dutch stuck together. (Now let me straighten you out on this - it ain't the Amish or the Mennonites I'm talking about. They call us **fancy Dutch**, only Lord knows we ain't all that fancy. Our dress and ways may be different but we're all Pennsylvania Dutch stock, different yet the same. Did you know the Pennsylvania Dutch come from Germany? Confusing, ain't it?)

We got our reputation of being standoffish and hard to get to know cause we stuck mostly with our own. Things began to change though. They always do; never stay the same. More contact with the outside world was bound to happen. Many a woman clucked her tongue and shook her head to Mom and Grammy about strangers moving in and trying to change our ways of thinking and living. It scared 'em something awful.

Yes well, they was right, except it wasn't all bad. Lots of good come out of it too.

But face the facts. Most people with a common heritage stuck together then and still do, don't you think? I read in the newspaper about our country being a melting pot of people, but you know, I'm not too sure about that. Wish I had someone I could talk it over with along with other ideas that swim around in my head. These ideas just don't get too far cause I can't talk 'em out with no one. No one thinks I got anything worthwhile to say.

Getting back to the Dutch. As far as money was concerned, Grammy Farley taught us how to best use what we had and always be thankful for whatever come our way. That's how most of our neighbors lived, or so I thought when I was growing up. (It didn't take long to see how greed can get to the best of people, Pennsylvania Dutch or not.)

Oh, I tell you, I can still make do today with lots less than most of you. If I'd be a betting person which I'm not - just saying it out loud I can see Grammy, poor soul, turn over in her grave - I'd wager I could do with $10.00 when it'd take $50.00 of yours to get the same for the money, even with my tithe to the Lord.

See, Grammy taught us no matter what we earned or had handed us, ten percent went right away back to the Good Lord since it was his to begin with. Grammy had Pap take one of his sharp carpenter tools to cut a slit in an old tin can, then file down the rough edges for each of us to drop our tithe money in for our church offering. Would you believe I have that old tobacco tin yet today? Even my kids know what it was used for. I tried to teach 'em what Grammy taught me, but after they left home I don't know if they followed through or not. They never say.

Anyhow, on a cold, snowy, December afternoon, Allen Konhaus, a man of good Christian principles stopped by our house to pick up some cigars that my uncles had ready. He owned a cigar factory way outta town with about twenty hired hands, but he needed more workers than could get to his factory on account of it being too far away for them who had to walk. So what he done, he set up shops in homes. Al put bins, benches and molds in Pap Farley's cellar for my uncles to work, stripping the cured tobacco leaves and hand-rolling the cigars. I tell you, right here and now, I can whiff that wonderful good, fragrant smell coming from the tobacco bins. Smelled much better then when the finished cigars was being smoked. They made an awful stink as far as I was concerned.

This is the way it was with Allen and my uncles: one of the Farley boys, my Uncle John, him being the oldest - still yet in his mid-teens - stacked so many tobacco leaves in the bins, sprinkled so much wine over 'em to keep 'em moist so they

13

wouldn't break up into little pieces during the stripping. Two other uncles, George and Will, helped with the stripping.

Al liked to bring my uncles work because of the way they handled the tobacco in each step of cigar-making. I was about a year, maybe eighteen months old when Grammy'd sit me in a tall chair near uncles' workbench, wrap one of her aprons around me, the long apron strings tied tight around me and the chair back to hold me in, but not close enough to grab anything cause they knowed I would if I could.

Can't say when I began to remember watching them as they worked in a toe-tapping rhythm, but sitting here at my kitchen table, pencil in hand, my mind takes me back as if it was yesterday, and it comes back so good and clear. There was no music but you woulda swore there was by the way they worked. See, each uncle'd take a large, whole, cured tobacco leaf from the bin, hold the stem and pull the tobacco off one side, lay it on the bench on a nice even stack, then pull off the tobacco from the other side making a second pile. Right sides of tobacco leaves went on one pile, left sides went on a second pile - the two was never mixed together. The stems, along with little pieces of tobacco that broke off was throwed in a box to be ground up as filler back at the cigar-factory.

While they stripped the leaves my uncles moved back and forth in a foot-shuffling rhythm they worked out to keep from getting overtaken with weariness; and they'd count. It went like this: 1-Grab a leaf. 2-Pull the tobacco from the right side. 3-Lay it on the pile. 4-Pull it off the left side. 5-Lay it on the second pile. 6-Throw the stem in the box. Then they'd start all over again.

Some of my first words was counting numbers because of my uncles. I watched and listened and moved back and forth in my chair, swinging my feet in the air trying to mimic their moves. It wasn't long before I was counting with them, "1,2,3 . . . 4,5,6". My uncles liked it when I was there to watch; we entertained each other, them with their boyish high jinks that would of never been carried out if Pap Farley was around, me cheering 'em on for more. Don't know how that chair held me in and didn't fall over with me clapping and *rootching* my little *heiny* all around.

Me being down there with my uncles gave Grammy Farley and Mom more time to do their work with me not being underfoot. Wasn't anywhere else I'd rather be.

Once in a while the rhythm got broke up when an uncle tripped or stumbled. All three forgot what they was doing and turn foolish, getting louder by the second till Pap Farley's footsteps could be heard from above as he crossed over the long kitchen floor from where he was sitting in his chair reading the newspaper after a hard day's work. My uncles was grateful they could hear Pap stomping across that long floor right above 'em for it gave 'em time to settle down. My little heart thumped faster and louder in my chest as I sat and waited, all flustered and wound up to see if they'd get back to work before Pap caught 'em in the middle of their tussling, then tear into them about their dad-burned foolhardiness and how they'll ruin the cigars and they better stop this minute if they don't wanna get a lickin' with the belt.

But them uncles, they was quick. By the time he was on the first cellar step waving his finger as a warning and hollering, "That's enough!" in his stern, Dutch voice, uncles was already back at work. They was smart, settled down quick and got back to work cause Pap could dish out some painful consequences if he thought it necessary. Wasn't above him to use a belt or razor strop on 'em once in a great while, but he always made it look like he was swinging it harder than he really was. Wasn't that Pap wanted to hurt 'em, but he hadda let 'em know who was boss and keep 'em in line.

My uncles, they was quick in their expressions too. One minute they was making monkey faces at each other, but when Pap hit that top step, their looks was already serious and intent. All-in-all they worked hard and fast, they did.

When that part was done, my uncles cut the leaves just the right size, then sprinkled so much filler on a smaller inner leaf that was laid on top of the big outer leaf called the wrapper. The bigger the leaf the bigger cigar they could roll. They rolled each cigar up and twisted each end of the wrapper just so to hold the filler in good and tight. Both ends was tapered if they got it right, which they most always did. Last thing they done was place 'em in wooden cigar molds till Al came by to pick 'em up and haul that batch to his factory where the cigars was finished, each one wrapped with it's own special band and clear cellophane.

Al said my uncles did more'n their fair share of making big cigars and always praised 'em for their good work. Paid 'em fair wages, too.

Al, he made the most money on the biggest cigars. When he first started, the cigars was hauled to Baltimore by horse and wagon, later by train when the tracks was laid on the edge of town. From there they was shipped to Chicago, then to Texas. These places was strange to our ears, but he'd go on about the oil boom in Texas and how them rough and tough Texans liked everything whopping big and that included their cigars. None of us knowed much about Texas or how far away it was, only that the men there liked Al's cigars. The Farley household did it's durndest to provide the biggest and best cigars to Allen Konhaus.

Grammy Farley, like everyone else, had great admiration for Al. Why I growed up hearing the story about her and Al and me over and over again; never tired of it, thrilled my little heart every time Grammy told it. Having a good memory, I stored it in my head to pull out and ponder over time and time again. Never tired of it.

Grammy's story - she loved to tell stories, except no one but me paid too much attention - ran like this:

Al - my uncles called him Dapper-Dandy Al when no one else was around to hear for he always dressed fit to kill;

black hat cocked in a jaunty manner on his greased-down, reddish brown hair starting to turn gray, starched white shirt with a black string tie around his collar, and always with a cigar hanging outta his mouth, most times not lit.

Al come by on a cold, windy, winter afternoon to pick up cigars. Grammy showed him this new baby just born.

"What a pretty little thing!" Al exclaimed. "What's her name?"

"*Ach vell*, we *chust* didn't name her now yet," Grammy said over it. Grammy spoke Dutch at home. I growed up with the language but I can't speak it no longer. Only certain words come to mind today.

Then Al said that his oldest was Estella, shortened to Stella.

"We have an Estella, too. It's this little girl's momma," Grammy remarked.

"Estella Ann Farley."

Al went on to say that their second girl was Lillie.

"*Ach vell*, wouldn't *du* know, we have a Lilliemae now yet too."

Al didn't stop there. "Our third girl is Alverna. She is sixteen years old, just now got her teacher's certificate and is going to teach school for the first time." Then he pulled a much wrinkled piece of paper out of his pocket and said all puffed up with pride, "Alverna wrote out for me the words she'll put on the wall behind her desk to keep in mind the way she intends to teach. Look Mrs. Farley. It says, '*My doctrine*' (doctrine means teaching, Al reminded Grammy,) - *shall drop as the rain, my speech shall distil as the dew; as the small rain upon the gentle herb; and as the showers upon the grass.*' Ain't that beautiful? It comes right out of the Bible in Deuteronomy. My Alverna, she's gonna be the best teacher in these parts."

And, of course, Grammy was so caught up with Allen and his school-teacher girl that she done what most Pennsylvania Dutch do. See, babies was named after people they knowed and liked. That's why she talked Mom into naming me Alverna Nell.

Alverna Nell Holtzapple.

Al Konhaus, he was highly thought of by everyone in the county and beyond, yet as he come to be rich, uppity and snobbish he didn't get.

He was just a young pup when he signed up during the Civil War as a bugler in 1861. He was in the thick of the dreadful battle of Gettysburg. He survived unscathed. (This was another of Grammy's stories but I won't get into it right now.) Being the best bugler around he was asked to play *Taps* when the train carrying our dead president, Abraham Lincoln, passed through one of the railroad stations in the county seat. Al, he cleaned up his uniform till not one speck of dirt could be found - still fit him it did, shined his boots so you could see your face in 'em, and blew that bugle with such deep feelings that it sent chills up and down the spines of town folks and dignitaries alike who turned out by the railroad tracks that awful day.

Al claimed this was surely the greatest privilege ever afforded him, honoring his town and paying homage to the memory of our beloved, gunned-down president.

The Pennsylvania Dutch mostly shunned emotional display, but it's been said that tears coursed down many a Dutchman's cheeks without no shame for the loss of this great man that day.

Course I wasn't born yet when Al done this, but people talked about it for years.

Al, he made his people proud.

After the war Al took to teaching school. He enjoyed teaching but didn't like all the extra work required of the schoolmaster, like making sure there was enough wood to heat up the cantankerous pot belly stove in the winter, keeping the school swept clean, shoveling paths in the snow for the students. The pupils was to help out and most did, anxious to ring the bell, clean the chalkboards and step outside to pound the erasers together with chalk dust flying everywhere. But see, the older boys who was strong enough to do the harder and dirtier jobs, they was unreliable cause they often hadda stay home to help work the farms, even in winter. Al's biggest dislike was their pranks; often hadda go after these boys who, after classes begun, pretended they had to go to the privy, one a few minutes right after another'n, then stayed outside to play ball in the nearby meadow or sled on the snow-covered hill behind the school. He hadda bring 'em back in and it took away from his teaching the pupils who wanted to learn. Folks complained he wasn't strict enough, that he shoulda gave them boys a good whipping or two and sat 'em in the corner to shame 'em.

Well, wasn't long that he quit teaching and went into the cigar business which was good cause he married and had five children in as many years. Teaching didn't bring in much money then. Of course big families was common - and five wasn't all that big. Though he quit teaching, Al fought for good education and was elected to the school board where he served until his untimely death. Dignified and well respected Al Konhaus was. He didn't let it go to his head, though. Al got more involved and helped form a town band. Now believe-you-me, them bands was something else back then! Almost every town had one. Only better-off band members took lessons from paid instructors. Some who already knowed how to play instruments taught the ones just getting started. Others was self-taught and learned the music at band practices held once a week, then went home to practice whenever spare time they could find. They may not of sounded the greatest to a trained ear, but people puffed up with pride in their hometown band whenever it performed. Those rousing marches made blood course through our veins feverish-like and set our feet a-marching in place, especially us kids.

I can see Mom and the rest of my family standing along the parade route on one Fourth of July. Before we'd see the band we'd hear it. Soon appeared the flag bearer with the big United States flag unfurled in the morning sky. Right behind him was two marchers stepping high with the hometown banner, **THE CEDAR GROVE BAND** written in big, fancy letters. We'd swell with patriotism for our country and pride in our town and its musicians. I tapped my feet and clapped my hands to the beat of the music. I'd get all caught up in the excitement and thrill of them rare, holiday mornings.

Uncle Will learned the bass horn and Uncle John the trombone because Allen Konhaus dug up two instruments from who-knows-where so Pap wouldn't have to buy 'em. Al promised Pap he'd teach the boys so they could play in the band. He was a persuasive talker Al was to convince Pap to allow that, but Pap said alright and Al kept his word.

Will and John took such a liking to the instruments that they played in the band till they was both old men.

When he picked up my uncles for band practice Al sometimes talked Mom into letting me go along to the band hall. I was too little to play an instrument. I guess you'd say I was what today they call a mascot. All evening I'd watch the band director work with the musicians and I'd listen to their music with feelings that tickled me all over, gave me goosebumps. When practice got bad and they'd need a break, Al'd sneak me a little flag, I'd jump off the bench and march with gross exaggeration to the music, circling the musicians and waving that flag till finally a couple of 'em missed a note cause they was grinning at my antics instead of paying attention to Mr. Schnider, the band director. He was a good man, serious about the music coming out of those practices, but he got a kick outta me too; tried to pretend he was mad at my clowning around, but when that went on he knowed it was time for the band to take a ten minute break.

I love music because of them bands. The tears come to this day when I hear band music. (I just can't help it.)

Bands and Sunday School picnics; there wasn't one without the other. Back then these *celebrations* was the social get-togethers of the summer. In the picnic grove children played games near the band pavilion, whooped and hollered and flitted around as the band performed. There was peppy marches for cakewalks where everybody, young and old alike formed a big circle and walked round and round until the music stopped. Some of the grown men was too high and mighty to join in. Then there was always them self-righteous biddies who didn't know how to have a good time, clucked their tongues about how the devil had hold of everybody taking part in such goings-on.

The Sunday School Superintendent, the most important person in the church next to the preacher, always had the honor of picking the winning spot during the cakewalks. No one else, just him. Now listen to this: One time there was an awful stink. Some folks suspected the spot that day wasn't picked until after the cakewalk was over; it got around that Mr. Superintendent had a particular person he wanted to win so he waited till the music stopped, then strutted to where this purty lady was - a married lady yet - and claimed her as the winner, handed her the cake, took her arm and walked her back to the bench where she'd been sitting.

If only they both wouldn't of looked in each other's eyes that way. If only they wouldn't of sported such lovey-dovey grins, then maybe nobody woulda thought nothing of it. But they did.

Did he honest and truly not choose the spot till the music stopped? Most people wondered if this could be so. Most growed suspicious.

Now don't get me wrong, most superintendents was outstanding, God fearing citizens, but like human nature is, once in a while a superintendent wasn't Christian-like the way he wanted people to believe. He maybe used that position to his advantage, swaying certain ladies who didn't know their own minds into indecent behavior. When that one come along, Mom couldn't let it alone and fussed about it all the way home. Till the day she died she never forgave - I won't repeat his name though he's long gone to his reward, left town soon after he was caught with a married woman, of all places between the old, wheezing pump organ and the altar. Can you imagine? - and him being a Sunday School Superintendent!

The other guilty party humbled herself, repented in front of the congregation and asked for forgiveness. Grammy and Pap said that took courage and she should be pardoned but they knowed a few outspoken ones wouldn't look at it that way. Her man, he stuck by her but in the end they moved away when they couldn't no longer take being snubbed and disgraced by the self-righteous, do-gooders in town. Mom, along with other holier-than-thou folks quoted what the Bible had to say about adultery, but when it come to forgiveness, they somehow or other forgot that part. The scandal had the town buzzing till some new, juicy gossip come along to replace it.

Mom wasn't one to trust people a great deal to begin with. Me, I didn't care about gossip and I didn't understand her reason for griping. I just cared about grabbing her hand or Grammy's, maybe both, and stepping high around that circle, hoping more'n anything else in the world to win a cake - even if it was one Grammy or Mom baked. Oh, what fun!

Hymns always ended the celebrations. You see now, the Dutch, well, I already said most don't approve of expressing their emotions. That may be, but this parting of the ways at the end of a wonderful day with goings on that didn't occur too often, well, feelings did run purty high. Closing hymns was like music from heaven with the people singing - some warbling more than singing but it didn't matter - and the band playing. Emotions deep inside was unlocked and this was one time when a big sigh and a few tears was tolerated, even expected.

Then it was time for families to pack up their left-over vittles, dirty dishes and tired, grubby kids in their wagons and buggies and head for home while there'd be enough daylight so they wouldn't have to light their coal oil lanterns to guide their way.

Yeah, Al Konhaus was well respected and did a lot for the town!

Life hasn't changed much after all these years. Lots of good things and lots of bad things happened then just like today. The way I see it, folks just can't live in peace and harmony and let alone what don't belong to them. In spite of what come later on, I hold   Allen   Konhaus   in   high regard to this day. He was a good man even though a lot of people was of the opinion he left 'em down. But that's another sad story, not for right now.

CHAPTER 3 - THE FARLEYS

Grammy and Pap Farley's house was close to the edge of town that wasn't yet much of a town. Fields and patches of woods lay behind the house. In a little while houses started springing up along the road. Come the day when Grammy's house would be more towards the middle of town than on the edge. There was fruit trees around, not enough to say it was an orchard; all kinds of fruit for good eating almost into the next growing season. Apples especially. Tart, juicy, Smokehouse Apples; they was my favorite; Mom dried 'em for *schnitz'n knepp*. Ain't seen any around for many a year.

Concord Grape vines growed a-plenty off the back porch and down one side of the long back yard. The arbors made nice, shady spots to sit and play under on summer days till August when the yellow jackets appeared to sting the deep purple grapes for their juicy nectar. We'd keep our distance till time to pick bushel baskets full. Boy-oh-boy, we got stung more'n once, especially when we forgot our work gloves. Grammy's remedy for bee stings was to dab mud on the welts to draw out their poison. Worked good, it did.

People all around said Eliza Holtzapple Farley put up the best grape preserves in the county, not to mention her wine and juice. And oh, her grape pies, they was the best, *allerbescht*! She got more company towards the end of September after the grapes was picked and put up, even though others had their own grape arbors. People gave the excuse they just stopped by to say hello, but we wasn't fooled. And Grammy, she could never turn no one away without offering them something she made from her grapes.

There was a big plot for the garden with vegetables that seen us through many a winter. Potatoes, carrots, red beets, turnips, string beans. . . . Vegetables that didn't need canned was stored in bins in the cold cellar. Cabbage too, except most of it was used to make sauerkraut that was stored in large crocks. Parsley, dill, and other herbs was hung and dried at the back of the stove. Bunches of onions hung from the ceiling of the closed-in back porch off the kitchen where it was cooler. Grammy and Pap had no animals of any sorts, just a pig or two for butchering, and chickens that kept us in eggs and many a wonderful good chicken dinner. Slippery pot pie was my favorite next to Grammy's tasty fried chicken if it didn't get too brown which was the way Pap liked it best. Fried real-dark brown.

As I sit here in my kitchen with thoughts of them days flying through my head, I think, oh, my! What I wouldn't give to go out and cut dandelion greens to cook with vinegar like Grammy did in early spring. That was our spring tonic; strengthened the blood with all that iron in it. My mouth waters just thinking about it. Grammy'd put on her old gardenin' coat when it was still cold and blustery, bundled me up, handed me a dull knife and drug me to the yard and fields to cut baskets of dandelion before the blossoms appeared. (I didn't mind being drug along. Matter of fact I savored it.) When the yellow heads appeared the taste got strong and bitter. We liked it early, before that. But I wouldn't dare do that now! No Sireee! Them people in agriculture, do they know they're ruining the good earth with too much fertilizer and poison weed killers? We tilled the ground proper-like for it to yield crops and all; we used limestone which was plentiful and good for the soil.

Grammy even made wine out of the yellow dandelion flowers. She taught me to pick only the wide open blossoms. She pressed them in a big crock in the springhouse. That smell I could do without but others enjoyed it.

Nothing went to waste by Grammy. She studied - not by books, she didn't have many. The almanac, of course. Everybody had *The Farmer's Almanac*. Also by observing nature, and what she learned from generations before.

She growed plants and herbs and roots in her garden for medicine, sometimes got wild ones in the fields and woods. She doled out home remedies since doctors was scarce and only sent for in emergencies. Cedar Grove didn't have a doctor at first. One hadda travel from York. It was such a distance a body coulda died till the doctor showed up. If desperate, some mighta called in the old hex that lived in a dirty, dilapidated shack hidden behind a grove of trees on the outskirts of town. Powwow was practiced too.

One remedy Grammy always kept on hand was lily leaves in whiskey - killed what was ailing you faster most anything else. Still have some in my cupboard today.

Wouldn't be surprised if some people used it the wrong way and it killed 'em instead of curing.

Grammy worked long and hard, yet always kept her pleasant, ready-to-lend-a hand disposition. A good grammy she was. A good mom, wife and neighbor too.

Pap Farley, William was his first name, he was a carpenter and builder by trade. Wasn't very tall - most Dutchmen wasn't - but lean and wiry he was. Always smelled like seasoned cherry or walnut or some other hardwood or pine. See, there was too many mouths to feed on his boyhood farm, so it was decided that in order for the rest of the family to survive, William and two brothers was to be boarded out to learn a trade. He felt fortunate to be apprenticed to an uncle who trained him with strict discipline in a trade he liked, learned good and worked all his life.

He didn't believe in bragging, but sometimes Grammy needed a listening ear; mine she could trust not to spill the beans when she spouted off about her pride in Pap. I woulda cut my tongue out before I woulda told on Grammy. I craved her stories, wanted to hear everything she had to say.

Pap Farley, he was a stern Dutchman, so he thought. That was the way Dutchmen was supposed to be. His name was William and that's what folks called him. No nickname for Pap. He was hard-working and honest as they come. He believed in work before play and declared more'n a little play wasn't too good for nobody.

Pap left his uncle's business when he and Grammy married, moved into town when only a couple houses was. He set up shop in the back for his trade. He was busy for sure. Customers sought out Pap for his good quality work that lasted. They showed him the greatest respect cause they was fearful he might turn their business away. Some people he would if he didn't like or trust 'em. Not too many though.

Like all Dutchmen, my pap was the undisputed authority in the household, no question about that. He ruled the roost. No one opposed him. When he spoke we listened. His word was law. It was all right for me and my uncles to have fun and carry on, but when he had enough, all Pap done was stick his pointer finger up in the air and shake it as a warning - and that settled that. We quieted down right away.

He always had a quiet smile unless he was deep in concentrating on his work, an unruffled contentment coming from deep inside. You hadda get to know him before you'd pick that out about Pap. It wasn't easy for most folks to see that behind them dark brown eyes that could bore right through you if you did something to his disliking. Thick, strubbly eyebrows he had; his long, narrow, leathery face was lined with deep creases from hard work and the conviction that it hadda be done right. He had a large, hooked nose with hair growing out; outta his ears, too. His mouth was hidden by a wiry moustache and beard speckled with sawdust and woodchips that he combed out each evening before supper. Sounds like the way I describe him, he wasn't too good-looking. He wasn't. Our family wasn't known for its good looks, none of us. Mom was the purtiest.

From little on up I knowed for sure Pap had a soft spot inside that gruff exterior. He just wasn't one to show it right off. If anyone could reach it, it was me. I loved Pap and it was my nature to challenge his reserve, to make the corners

27

of his mouth curl up into a broad smile. Most time it worked, sometimes not.

Now don't get me wrong, Pap was never mean. Stern, yes, but never mean and hateful. There's a big difference between them two things. And to be truthful, I think Pap didn't wanna be as strict as he come across but he felt he hadda prove he was boss. Besides, that's the way most men was (and a lot of 'em still are today, sad to say).

One way Pap showed he cared - and hardly anyone outside our family knowed this about him, wasn't talked about beyond the front door so's not to ruin his reputation. It was when the *poopies* hit. Oh, my! When they hit one person in our household it didn't stop there. Everybody got hit. Such a running back and forth to the privy in the back yard. It was then Pap took down the cast iron fry pan off the big hook in the pantry wall. It was so round it covered two burner plates on the cook stove, that big it was. After it got good and hot he spooned in a big splotch of bacon grease that splattered all over the stove top as it melted down. Such a noise it made. But it was a good noise for we knowed what was coming. He'd stir in flour till real smooth and brown it got. The trick was to not to let it burn which could happen real fast on the old cook stove. Only once I remember that it got hot too fast and burned. That was one time a few choice words outta Pap's mouth come without no warning. He surprised us so! Mom's hands flew up to her mouth in disbelief. The rest of us sat there closed-mouth and dumbfounded. Grammy run to the stove and grabbed the pan handle with a thick rag. The black fry pan was so heavy she could hardly hold it. She hurried outside to dump it out and clean it up.

I couldn't help myself; started to giggle at what was happening. My uncles was flabbergasted that I dare laugh at Grammy and Pap. That started off Lilliemae. The rest, well, they just couldn't help themselves. Nervous laughter filled the big kitchen. Pap looked shocked, was taken aback by our high spirits. Not knowing what else to do he stepped outside to help Grammy clean the pan so we could settle down. We was quiet when they appeared in the kitchen for him to start a new batch of Brown Flour Pap. One thing for sure, Pap never let the flour burn again.

After the bacon fat and flour was browned just right he poured in milk and a little sugar, all the time stirring till it thickened just so. Mom and Grammy dished out a bowl for each of us. That Brown Flour Pap was the best ever. Now we'd get clogged up, the *runners* fast gone.

Now, how many men would do that if they was all gruff and crotchety?

Every now and then I'd whisper to Grammy, "I wish I'd get the *runners* so Pap would make Brown Flour Pap." It was that good.

Grammy, she'd laugh at me - but I was serious. It was *allerbescht*!

Pap said grace at every meal. Never missed. I'd follow along in my mind, learning every word and the way he pronounced each one - the same way every time. This was his prayer: *Kind and merciful HEAVENLY FATHER!* (He'd boom out the heavenly father part which made me wonder if God was hard of hearing and he wanted to be sure to get his attention.) *THANKS be to THEE for sparing us another hour so that we can gather round this table. BLESS these provisions so they will strengthen our bodies. SAVE us through CHRIST. Lead and guide us through this life. AMEN!*

Of course Pap prayed in Dutch just like he talked Dutch at home but I don't remember the spelling so I just put down the English version. Pap would be disappointed in me not remembering.

Another thing: I was spellbound about Pap and the way he ate peas. He'd scrape his knife blade on his plate till was full of peas. He'd bring that knife straight up, level to his mouth then tilt is so they'd slide off; never missed his mouth, never! I watched with my jaw hanging open like I was the one attempting to catch 'em in my mouth. Every time

I waited for just one pea to slide and miss. Never did. Pap, he knowed I was watching and hoping for a pea to slip off. I could see the twinkle in his eyes as he ate them peas. One never went astray. Never. Not that I seen anyway.

My Grammy Farley was Eliza Holtzapple before she married. Now a different story she was. She was short and plump to say the least - said she too much liked her own cookin'. Soft on the outside but strong inside, the way you hadda be to make it back then. I took after her in looks; wide forehead, broad nose that turned up just a bit at the end, hazel eyes, lips pursed downward.

Family pictures don't show many smiles, yet when I think of me and Grammy Farley, that's what I think of - our affection for each other and the smiles we exchanged. Grammy was the one that gave me the hugs my nature needed but seldom got from the other Farley's cause showing affection was generally thought to be out of place. Even when I wanted a hug from Grammy I knowed when **not** to go after it. If it was only the two of us together - and seldom was those times but, oh, so special - she'd sit me on her ample lap, hug me tight and tell stories about the family. I listened hard to not miss a word she said and stored everyone of 'em in my head and my heart. This must be why my memory's sharp and clear to this day. Oh, I tell you, I cherished Grammy! Our times together I loved.

My uncles, vigorous and lively, didn't let Pap's solemn reserve get to them just yet except when he was around. He instilled fear in their hearts along with a great deal of respect. And me, well I was always friendly and outgoing, never tried to be any other way, much to Mom's disapproval.

My mom, Estella Ann Farley was their oldest. She looked like her mom but took more after her dad in outlook, only come across harder on the outside because that's the way she was on the inside, hard as could be. Hard to understand, too. Only once in a great while did you see Mom loosen up with what little softness there was inside. Never smiled much. Always quick to grumble about family, neighbors, the church, the conditions of our little town. Mom's nature was like vinegar. It was easy to shrivel up around her. From little on up I recognized how different she was from the rest and couldn't figure out why.

It took a long time for some answers to come.

After Mom there was Lilliemae, John, Will, George, then Purd. Purd was only a little bit older'n me, coming a bit on behind Grammy's other'ns. Never left me forget he was the oldest of me and him. He lorded that over me till he died. I left him get away with it cause I felt sorry for him. Purd, he wasn't much to look at; bow-legged, pigeon-toed, skinny as a rail and gawky all his short life. A little slow in the head. Yes well, I couldn't stand the way he was teased so bad, so I bent over backwards to be nice to him. We was good friends as long as he got his way with me, so I spoiled him and gave in to him.

Grammy was a storyteller, a good one too. There's one story I loved to hear over and over. It was about me. I was too young to remember when it happened, but Grammy imprinted it on my venturesome spirit. When I think of it, why it's like I'm living it all over again. This is her story:

"*Du* started walkin' before *du* was one year old," Grammy'd say with pride.

How it was, I had this favorite spot in the big kitchen where was one chair that was heavy and solid, didn't tilt over when I'd pull myself up. I'd walk so many steps to the big oak kitchen table. There I sat down, crawled back to the sturdy chair, clambered up and walked to the table again.

As they watched, my uncles would tell me to turn around and walk back when I reached the table. "Don't crawl, walk!" they'd holler in Dutch, slapping their knees in aggravation.

31

I wouldn't.

This got to be a bedtime ritual. After a while Uncle John began counting the ten steps it took me to get from my favorite chair to the table. Soon I could count ten steps. They thought it couldn't be that I could talk the way I could and count. I'd count out the ten steps as I walked, then sat down, crawled back, climbed up and again started walking and counting ten steps.

Next thing, my uncles tried like all get-out but couldn't make me say *eleven*. They watched and laughed. I was happy for this attention and played right along till Pap shook his finger and said, *"Enough!"*. That was all it took for us to quiet down.

One time my uncles was there watching me do this and got cross cause they thought I could say *eleven* but wouldn't. Pap Farley was sitting in his rocking chair after a long workday when all this commotion got to him.

"Ya, ach vell now!" he said over it as he shook his finger. "That's enough! Let her alone. You're houndin' her to say *eleven*. When the time comes, she'll say *eleven*."

That's all it took. John, Will and George was downcast from being scolded and knowed to stop right then. I was looking at the floor and could only see them and Pap out of the corner of my eye.

"Eleven," I said.

My uncles tried to hold back but couldn't. They rolled on the floor holding their sides that hurt so bad from laughing, they snorted. Why they could hardly breathe! According to Grammy I just stood there looking at the floor, serious as could be. Even Pap chuckled against his will. To make it appear that it didn't strike him funny, he cleared his throat with a big harrumph as if something was stuck in there. Taking it further so we'd think he wasn't paying the least bit of attention, he pulled out his thin but sturdy pocketknife that was always hooked onto the end of his long, silver watch chain, the other end clipped to a button hole that held his suspenders to his waistband. He opened it slow and deliberate-like and started scraping and cleaning his fingernails. But he couldn't hide his amusement at this altogether; the corners of his mouth turned up higher and higher through it all.

Of course, Grammy never told that part of the story in front of him. He wouldn't of liked it at all.

The day ended with Grammy remarking, "*Kumme* Alverna, let's to *bedde* go now yet, ain't?"

I counted the steps it took to reach Grammy - all eleven of 'em.

Mom and I lived with her family. The way it was, my uncles told me I never had a daddy, that the crows laid me on a stump and the sun hatched me out, but they'd never say no more. It bothered me not at all when I was little, but when I got old enough to think for myself and seen other girls had a daddy, well, it wondered me so. I didn't push it too far cause the way I seen it we was one big happy family. I was with my uncles and Aunt Lilliemae. My grandma and grandpa was Mom and Pop to them, and they was always Grammy and Pap to me.

That's the way it was with friends and neighbors too, working together, helping each other out where we could. We was thrifty with our money but we was bighearted with our time, reaching out even when time was just as important as money.

CHAPTER 4 - THE HOLTZAPPLES

The Farleys and Holtzapples was related and lived not too far from each other. Their farm was one of the first outta town past us. We visited back and forth, especially Grammy because she was one of them, a Holtzapple before she married Pap.

"*Ach vell*, we have some spare time so let's be goin' to the Holtzapple's for a little visit," she'd say.

When I heard that I'd get excited and dance to a tizzy cause that meant I'd maybe see all the Holtzapple boys. They liked me, took time to stop what they was doing to horse around with me. There was three of them brothers and I was taught to call them uncle, all except for one. What was so strange, they always admonished me to call him only by his first name. As I got older it wondered me so. After all, he was one of them, a brother, you know. Why couldn't I call him uncle like the rest?

It didn't take long to learn when to keep my mouth shut cause there was certain things no one talked about. But me, I loved to figure things out by talking and listening and pondering. In this case though, little as I was, something inside told me to be quiet. Besides it was too much for me being so young to work it out in my understanding.

My Grammy and Pap Farley took me to the Holtzapple's a couple times when I was just a mere baby. The first time I remember being there was this one evening when they sat me on the floor covered with a thick, dark, hand-braided rug made from leftover scraps of wool that wasn't fit to be used for nothing else. In it was little bits of bright colors here and there but was made up mostly of dark browns, blues and blacks. The women's fingers was busy with mending, and their mouths flew while catching up on news. The men sat back behind the stove talking. That's the way it was; men usually kept apart from the women. Didn't include them in conversation, at least not often.

What I noticed as I watched, was how the women was smart enough to talk between themselves, yet all the time listen to what the men was saying. The women learned what was going on by listening to the men while they was in their own conversations. After I caught on to what they was doing I watched in fascination. It tickled me so! Once in a while the women'd get mixed up between their own talking and the men's conversation and reply to what the men was saying when they wasn't supposed to be listening in the first place. Getting caught in their blunder, their faces turned red from embarrassment. Heads dropped and purty quick they'd get back to their mending.

Yep, the ladies was darned good at doing that - and no wonder. They hadda be just to learn what was happening in the county. Pap and old man Holtzapple, I don't think they really cared too much if the women done that. They wasn't so rigid and untouchable like some men. They just sat back behind the stove cause that's the way it was always done.

One time we was there, and Dan Holtzapple come in and seen me sitting there.

"Who have we here?" he asked, surprised and pleased, speaking Dutch as the Holtzapples done at home.

He leans down, picks me up, throws me up in the air. I fly back down free as a bird, arms outstretched towards his work-hardened hands that'll catch me, gurgles of laughter escaping my throat. Next he holds my hands and swings me around in circles. I loved flying through the air that way. Dan, he was the only one who done that to me. After awhile he sits down, puts me on his knees, bounces me up and down while holding my hands and swinging my arms around in rhythm to little dittys he makes up as he goes along. He is having the best of fun with me. I'm enjoying every minute of his attention. We're both catching our breath when his mom gives him a scolding.

What she said I didn't understand. Her voice was shrill and high-pitched and the Dutch I couldn't make out, but her tone was a scolding one, that much I knowed.

Dan, now I could understand what he said. In a voice strong with feeling he held me at arm's length, looked at me with big, dark, brooding eyes and said, "Ich wish to Gott . . ., " then stopped. He hugged me tight against him, sat me back down on the floor. Stomping outta the house he looked back at all of us and hollered, "Things could be a whole lot different than they are now yet, you know!"

Didn't know what he meant, but I never forgot that. Dan, he was my favorite uncle on the Holtzapple side. Him and Uncle John Farley was pals together while Joe Holtzapple and Uncle Will run around with each other. Lawrence, he wasn't too friendly with any of my Farley uncles. Never seen too much of him around. He was ok, just a bit too sullen and short-tempered. Seems like every family has one like that.

The next time we went to the Holtzapple's I was a little bit older and could even take more in. The dear, old woman looked awful old; humped-back, bent over she was, face flushed and wrinkled, her nose crooked, off to the side. Her hands and fingers was all twisted and gnarled, her veins puffed out dark purple. She was mending and with her boys she had lots of mending to do. Her fingers wasn't working too good, and see, when Grammy could help with anything she always did. So Grammy, she took up mending with the old woman while they talked. I watched these two dear old people and noticed how much faster the needle in Grammy's fingers went, but she worked low at the table to not make it noticeable. Grammy was kind, never made herself look better than the next person.

Every night Pap read out loud from the Bible. He called it the *Goot Buch*. Sometimes Grammy did too, but mostly Pap.

Well, lots of them scripture words I didn't understand, but every now and then some words come alive, like one from Isaiah that said *everyone helped his neighbor*.

"Fits my Grammy and Pap," I thought to myself as I learned this new connection between Bible words and loving deeds. Grammy and Pap matched up to them Bible words with the Holtzapples and every neighbor and friend, even outsiders. I stored them words in my memory so I'd never forget how wonderful good to others my Grammy and Pap was.

To this day, ninety years later, it still bothers me that I never learned the first name of the dear old Holtzapple woman. Her man's name was Enoch. I can still hear Pap Farley call him that, but that dear old woman's name I never knowed. I hold that yet today against my mom and Grammy and Pap. They coulda told me. Maybe they figured it mighta been the start of me finding out more'n they wanted me to know.

You read in novels about main characters being beautiful girls and ladies with pale, soft, skin, small noses turned up just so, full, pouty lips, and eyes like liquid pools that melt a man's heart right down to nothing - and all that topped with long, thick, shiny, curly hair. Same with the men: tall, strong, handsome. Why it just goes on and on.

Can't say that for the most part about the Pennsylvania Dutch. Mostly there was long, hooked noses, thin lips in shut tight mouths, broad foreheads, hair pulled back flat and tight to keep it out of the way of work, features that didn't bring out the way beauty is described in fiction stories. Wrinkles and sun-burnt skin showed up early from hard, outdoors work. Of course we all wasn't ugly, but on the whole, we wasn't attractive folks.

It was even worse for Enoch Holtzapple and his wife.

I loved people, was patient when I heard bits and pieces of stories since that's the way they usually come out - in bits and pieces. I stored in my memory what I heard. It took me years to piece the Holtzapple story together in sequence, but I did.

Enoch was just a young boy when somehow or other lye got splashed in his eyes and scarred his face something awful. Most of his sight was ruined. In spite of that he never wallowed much in self-pity, growed up on the farm and took over the family homestead when his pa died when he was just a young lad. Worked the old dirt farm like you wouldn't believe.

No one expected with his condition he'd amount to much (he didn't), never figured he'd find a girl to marry. There they was wrong; he did. Got hooked up with this young woman whose old man beat and abused her something terrible from little on up. She wasn't much with looks after years of beatings - that's why her nose was pushed over to one side. She appeared frail, looked older than she really was.

But with his poor eyesight, looks didn't mean nothing to Enoch and though it appeared she married Enoch to get away from her pa and he married her cause no one else would, the two got along just honkey-dorey. Grateful for each other they was. Raised a strapping family of happy, healthy, good-looking boys through it all. Much more'n folks expected outta them.

I often wondered if that's how Enoch and his wife woulda looked if such misfortune hadn't overtaken them so young; tall like their boys instead of bent over, good looks instead of scars and deformities, healthy instead of so sickly and weak.

When I got to know them Enoch was bent over as much as his humped-back wife. His condition worsened so that when he died, it was said the undertaker hadda break his back to get him to lay straight in the coffin. For the first time in fifteen years or more, people seen Enoch's face as they passed by the pine coffin in the Holtzapple's front parlor.

Them two people had gumption, that's for certain. A strong faith they had, too. Worked hard all their lives with little to show for it except their love between them and their boys. Somehow or other they made do. Their homestead was on the side of a purty steep hill where after many a year most of the top soil had washed off. Below was a stand of woods that the boys played in when little and hunted when they was old enough to handle a shot gun.

All in all, since no one had a smooth and trouble-free life, things appeared purty satisfactory for the Holtzapple family. The boys was the kind any mom and dad'd want. Patrick was their oldest. I learned about him through Grammy.

"Patrick was a good-looker from little on up, but he wasn't sissified or nothin' like that," Grammy told me once. "Girls liked him but it never went to his head. Why even their mommas liked him even though he had nothin' in the way of worldly goods, *chust* good looks *un* first-rate behavior!"

According to Grammy, Patrick was tolerant and uncomplaining, one reason the older Dutch folks liked him so much. He worked long and hard on the farm, never pushed his load on his brothers' shoulders like older brothers sometimes done. All that farming and odd jobs he picked up here and there made his muscles ripple with strength. To top it off, Patrick was kind and friendly. Mommas admonished their boys to behave like Patrick Holtzapple. That caused hard feelings at first. Being jealous they turned against him. Made fun of him behind his back and to his face. Stuck together they did, tried to make Patrick fight. He took it without turning on 'em and before they knowed it, they come to be his buddies.

"*Du chust* couldn't help likin' Pat, he was that good a kid," Grammy speculated.

Yes well, believe you me, I'm not adding nothing to these stories. Only what Grammy told me.

Grammy recalled a day that started out like every other. "Patrick was muckin' a *schtall* in the big barn - nothin' outta the ordinary for him. Only this time, somehow or other," Grammy sucked in her breath, swallowed, then went on, "the big horse got spooked - later they reckoned it mighta been a snake. Patrick got shoved hard against the *schtall*. Knocked the breath outta him, couldn't get outta the way before he toppled over. The horse reared up then trampled that poor boy with his front hooves. Joe was workin' nearby, turned *un* seen the whole thing. Couldn't do nothin'; it happened too fast. Dan *un* Lawrence was outside workin', heard Joe's bloodcurdlin' scream, ran inside the barn; too late they was. *Chust* like Joe, they wasn't able to help Patrick. *Ach vell*, couldn't of done nothin' if all of 'em woulda been right there, happened that fast."

Listening to Grammy, my bottom lip quivered so. I wanted to cry my heart out but she went on; I swallowed my sobs so I wouldn't miss nothing she said.

"Enoch *un* his wife heard all this commotion. Both knowed somethin' bad happened. Holdin' on to each other they hobbled out to see what was causin' the uproar in the barn.

Patrick's brothers was stopped short at what they seen. There Patrick lay with a terrible head wound, face smashed in. Walkin' onto the scene no one woulda knowed it was Patrick. Then the boys went into action. Got the jittery horse outta the way, locked him in another *schtall* makin' sure the bolt was tight, then pulled Patrick outta the barn. While they was doin' all this, they couldn't hardly hold themselves together. Then they seen their ma *un* pa. They'd both been through lots of bad times, yet when they took in this grisly sight, this was the worst. The whole family, sick as dogs they got, throwin' up their breakfasts right then *un* there.

Young Dan was sent runnin' into town for the doctor that *chust* now put an office in Cedar Grove where he practiced medicine a couple days a week. The other days he was in York."

Grammy sniffed into her hanky as she relived the gruesome story. "Dan, just little then, he run down the street like his pants was on fire, hollerin' at the top of his lungs, 'help,

40

help!' all the way to Doc's. I run out to stop him and find out what was goin' on but he clawed his way outta my grasp *un chust* ran towards the doctor's office. Doc heard this *un kumme* outside, seen what a terrible state Dan was in, grabbed his bag *un* Dan, throwed 'em in his buggy already hitched. Doc knowed whatever it was, was bad, so took off he did *un* got outta Dan what happened as they raced up to the homestead.

People who seen Dan runnin' *un* heard his uproar got curious *un* followed Doc to the farm to see what was goin' on *un* how they could help. After Doc seen Patrick *un* checked him over to be sure, he ordered some men to go get the undertaker, told others to help with the chores inside *un* out, said the women was to go home *un* prepare food. He asked Grammy to stay the night *un* persuaded Uncles John and Will to hang around for a couple days with the boys. Next thing, Allen Konhaus shows up. Doc asked Al if he'd take over and see that the family'd get the help they needed for as long as it took. Al was more'n glad to take over. He pulled out a pencil *un* pad from inside his coat pocket *un* went to work. Al was good at organizin' people, *un* he did," Grammy sighed as she attempted to shake off the bad memories.

"We sure live in a *goot* town," she went on. "*Ya*, we hadda *goot* doctor. We hadda *goot* undertaker, too. *Un* Al Konhaus, what woulda this town done without him, ain't now yet?"

Was times like that no one envied the doctor his work. Not H.A. Briggs, the undertaker, either. But everyone was grateful for them men and Al.

Oh, to think after all them earlier troubles the Holtzapple couple went through, then to lose a son like Patrick at seventeen. For this family it was almost too much to bear. Took a long time for them parents and brothers to come around; they did, but a lotta life went outta Enoch and his

41

wife. The Pennsylvania Dutch seen things like that happen in every family, most times considered it best not to linger in grief too long. Get over it and move on. But folks was extra understanding; they come from all around to help out one way or another'n till the Holtzapples was able to get a grip. Town folks and neighboring farmers never gave up on 'em even when it seemed to be takin' an awful long time. Them two people aged something awful that next year.

I can still hear Grammy remark, "The Holtzapples come to say that the goodness of people, their faith in the *Goot Mann un* their other boys stickin' by 'em was what kept 'em from going *unner*. If only it woulda stopped there."

Now what did she mean by that? Was I gonna hear another story? Yes, I was.

Emory was next-to-oldest Holtzapple boy - I never knowed him neither. "Happy, fun-loving if one ever was. Never topped Patrick on looks though. Not that it mattered, *chust* somethin' people noticed about them boys," Grammy thought out loud.

Peeling potatoes after I scrubbed 'em, she went on. "Emory loved music *un* the outdoors. Once he found a beat up old guitar on a junk pile *un* taught hisself how to play. Joe liked Emory's music and bartered so many hours work for a banjo somebody had for sale. He learned to pick *un* follow after Emory when he strummed the old guitar. Sometimes a string'd break *un* Emory couldn't afford a new one right away but it didn't discourage him; played without till he got another'n.

Took a bit better'n a year for them boys to start the music back up again after Patrick's accident. People'd stop by, some bringin' fiddles, mouth organs *un* such. John took his bass horn and Will his trombone. *Ach!* Such a mix. Whoever woulda thought they'd *kumme* up with such lively tunes playin' together like that? Others was there to sing, dance or just visit out on the rickety porch that swelled with young'uns, so many they poured out onto the front yard. Such music *un* fun *kumme* outta that old homestead on Saturday nights when folks, after evenin' chores, took time for some lettin' go. Them that showed up brought extra sandwiches *un* homemade root beet *un* cookies to pass around cause they knowed the Holtzapples didn't have much though they'd of gave all they had. Music *un* company cheered 'em up. For that they was grateful.

This was a good place for Saturday evening socials even though some rowdiness was likely to come about now *un* then. Not much though. The Holtzapples was too much respected for neighbors to bring shame *un* dishonor on 'em. Some kids'd get testy and try to push limits no matter where they was, but few hardly never did with the Holtzapples. They remembered Patrick and who it was that raised him. The young'uns themselves kept the crowd under control. Any troublemakers, off they'd be sent."

"Where was the old Holtzapples while so many people was around?" I asked.

"Enoch's cronies come around to play checkers or a card game in the back kitchen while the young folks milled around out front. Some of the girls, as they passed around sandwiches, noticed how Enoch couldn't hardly read the numbers on the playin' cards. His eyes was bad for sure. They got the idea for to make a big deck of playin' cards. But who? Who could do it? Will and John knowed. They approached Lilliemae and George who was good at drawin', asked them if they'd come up with a set. But they'd need heavy paper. Maybe Allen Konhaus had some. They asked. He *kumme* up with *chust* what they needed. Not only paper but extra scissors and pencils and brushes and red and black paint. They worked every spare minute for two whole weeks, cuttin', drawin' and fillin' in with the paint. Ended up with an oversized deck of big numbers *un* designs just like a real deck. When Will *un* John handed it over to the men one Saturday evenin', why they was bowled over at such a good idea and all that hard work. Now Enoch could see right along with his buddies to join in. The other men didn't complain about them extra large cards. They mighta not admitted it, but their eyes wasn't all that good either. Enoch's wife didn't mind the card playing - some church folks thought cards *un* music was the work of the devil. She didn't believe that but she made sure no money was ever exchanged in them games. 'That's when the devil comes in *un* takes over,' she'd warn. 'No gamblin'll ever take place in this *haus*.' It didn't. There was never no gamblin' at the Holtzapple farm.

When it got what it was late enough to call it a day, the Holtzapple couple sent the visitors on their way. If they lingered too long the old woman got out her broom, walked through the crowd *un* shushed 'em away good naturedly. And that's the way the gatherin' broke up."

That Holtzapple family! Meager circumstances, yes, but it was their warm welcome - and the behavior of their boys - that shone through and overshadowed what they didn't have. Never heard a bad word about them Holtzapples.

As I recall Grammy's next story, her words still bring tears that dribble down my cheeks.

"Emory's favorite place was out in the woods. Coon huntin' was what he loved best of all next to his family *un* his music. Had the best coon dog in the territory he did. Buster was the best of 'em all. Many an older man was jealous of Emory's way with his dog.

Ya, Emory, wiry *un* lively as all get-out, was late one afternoon gettin' ready for a night of coon huntin' with his buddies. Out in the woods he went first. He'd climb a tree *un* rub it over with scent. How this surefooted young fella lost his hold *un* slid down was a puzzle to everyone who knowed him. Jagged, broken branches stickin' outta the tree trunk that he used as footholds to climb up, they tore into his legs and crotch, shredded his pants and skin to almost nothin' as he went down. He grabbed after the trunk to catch hold *un*

44

slow hisself down. Didn't work. Tried to swing away and push off from the trunk. Didn't happen.

Emory managed to get home by crawlin' *un* pullin' hisself along, a bloody mess from gettin' all mangled up like that. Scent, tree sap, splinters, bark, leaves and dirt got in his open wounds. Nasty injuries he had. His brothers held him down while his mom cleaned him up. His moans turned into screams as she smeared strong medicine concocted from herbs *un* roots on the insides of his mangled legs. Was the same what most people made use of till they got hold of the doctor. It was Joe who went after Doc that time. It was Doc's day to be in York, so Joe borrowed a buggy to go after him. It was after dark when Doc arrived. He didn't have nothin' strong enough stop the infection; he didn't have no such medicine like they do today to kill germs.

They wondered about powwow. *Ach vell*, Doc - he was a *goot* man. Most doctors woulda balked at it right off - figured it wouldn't work. But he didn't wanna discourage that hurtin' family from tryin' anything. The powwow doctor come in. His incantations and treatments didn't take.

Turned into erysipelas, it did. Poisoned Emory's skin *un* blood. Was a long, cruel, agonizin', excruciatin' sickness. His ma *un* pa *un* brothers sat around him, pale as death themselves, helpless except to hold him down as the second boy struggled, then died.

Patrick suffered no more'n a couple seconds.

Emory did.

You think people'd get use to sickness *un* dyin' *un* grief *un* pain, but no.

The music stopped for Joe. Forever. He put his banjo away, never touched it again. People cajoled him to play. It *chust* might ease some of the hurt. But Joe, he wouldn't. He *chust* couldn't. He couldn't pick his banjo when Emory wasn't besides him strumming his guitar.

Emory's mom *un* pa made it through another dreadful calamity. *Ya*, they lived through it but their hurt, it never went away. *Ach,* purty beaten down they was," was how Grammy said over it.

Folks asked one more time why good people gotta suffer so bad. Closer than ever the family growed, but the music stopped. They sorta drawed into themselves even though people tried to help out. Grammy said you could see the hurt in their eyes. It stayed with 'em the rest of their lives - that is if you coulda seen Enoch's eyes. Even when Enoch and his Mrs. could come to say they was glad they had them boys for so long and the ones still with 'em, but the hurt remained.

Left was Daniel Joseph and Lawrence, good boys all.

Mighty uneasy when them boys left the house was their parents, wonderin' what was gonna happen next.

Yeah, you might make it through things like that but you never get over it. The hurt, it never goes away altogether. It never did with the Holtzapples. It never did with me neither.

As for Grammy and Pap, I wonder so. Did they carry remorse with what went on between them and the Holtzapples that one time I come to know about? Probably not. They most likely thought they did right by them. They was related, you know.

That was the stuff I learned along the way as Grammy told me her stories. But getting back to the visit with Grammy and Pap when I was just little:

The Holtzapple woman, as she and Grammy sewed, said she wished she had somethin' for the little girl - meaning me - but she didn't know what. She didn't have no toys or nothin' for me. Then her eyes lit up as an idea come. With bony fingers all bent and knotted, she threaded a blunt needle with strong, black, thick carpet thread and tied a button on one end. As she come to pick me up Grammy hurried to help her, knowing the old woman couldn't handle me herself. Together they sat me on the table between where they was on the bench. A whole pile of buttons was poured on my lap.

"*Ach vell*, now *du* can sew too, *du* can sew buttons now yet, ain't?" she wondered so out loud, happy she found something for me to do.

Oh, the thrill in this little girl's heart as between two old women I was on and on putting these buttons. I had a good start till I come to one that wouldn't go on the needle.

I leaned ever so close to that dear old woman and showed her the button. "This one won't go on," I said.

"*Dumpkoff!* That's a *dumm* button," that dear woman fussed in Dutch as she sorted through the pile to find a fancy button that'd fit my needle. She had several cigar boxes full since buttons was never throwed away back then; mostly brown or black, some gray and dark blue. Red, green, bright colored ones was few and far between. I searched through my lap for the purty, colored ones.

When Grammy and Pap was ready to go home I had ever so many buttons on the thread, pleased with my work.

"*Ya, vell*, what to do with that now yet?" the Holtzapple woman pondered. "*Ach, Ich* know what we'll do. We'll put everything together, *un* when *du kumme* again, *du* can put more buttons on."

I loved that dear woman. Her bad looks didn't cause me no fear for I looked right past 'em into her heart and seen how beautiful she was inside. And I knowed she cared about me.

That was the last time I ever got to the Holtzapple farm.

She died then. I can remember that time real good. It was soon after when Mom started helping out at the Geesey farm, and I was back and forth between the two places - the Farley's and the Geesey's.

After all these years it still hurts what was kept from me for so long from my Grammy and Pap Farley, my mom and my uncles, even my uncles on the Holtzapple side.

CHAPTER 5 - MOM

Estella Ann Farley was my mom, the oldest of Grammy and Pap's children. She lived with them when I was born. As long as I can remember, Mom always kept her thick hair parted in a smooth straight line down the middle and pulled back from her face. She tied it with an old scarf while working at home. On special days - like church or market - she wore a wide grosgrain ribbon instead of the scarf. She frizzed her bangs which was the fashion of her day, the only vanity I ever seen in my mom.

When she was young yet, in her early twenties, her hair turned snow white. Then she left the bangs grow out and pulled all her hair back into a bun. Although she had her mom's looks, she was more natured like her pop; reserved, quiet, but much more sullen and sour. There was a distance in her, a deep, powerful sadness far down inside that often come out and hurt others for what I could figure was no reason at all. But I loved her just as dear as I loved my uncles, my Aunt Lilliemae and my grandparents.

You'll say I couldn't of remembered this, but I did. Still do to this day.

Soon I'd be turning three. Mom took an old dress of hers to make a new one for me. Almost two years too big it was, but that's the way we wore clothes then, big to start so you'd get plenty of wear out of 'em. I wore that dress many a day till I outgrowed it. She dug around in the attic and found some old lace to trim around the hem. Extra pleased she was when she found some wide, white lacey ribbon that had turned yellow with age. She bleached it back to white and starched it stiff, stitched it under the dress collar keeping extra long strings hanging down in front to tie into a purty bow.

48

While she was working on this she got distracted with a holler from Grammy who was out back hanging up wash. It was my misfortune that day for being such a curious child. Mom laid the scissors close to the edge of the table. Now I knowed these was forbidden to me. To touch 'em was asking for big trouble but it was too tempting for nosy Alverna. In my mind there was never no thought that I couldn't put 'em back right where they was after I checked 'em out before Mom come back in the kitchen. I snuck quiet as could be to where they was, leaned over the bench, stood on my tippy-toes, stretched with all my might, reached up and grabbed 'em with both hands. They was bigger and heavier in my little hands than I could of imagined. Almost knocked me over when I pulled 'em down.

I studied them, concentrating with all my might to get the hang of working it. I was leaning over in strict concentration. I opened the scissors, snipped it shut.

Holy Moses! I watched in disbelief that turned to terror. Wouldn't you know, right in front fell away a big clump of my long, dark hair. I watched it fall to the floor. I was flabbergasted. Coming to my senses, only as if in slow motion, I tried to put the scissors back on the table. My hands was clammy wet from fear, my insides shaking worse than being in a buggy on a bumpy, dirt road. Nervous and trembly as all get-out I was. The scissors slid off the edge of the table and clattered to the floor. In a panic I grabbed my clump of hair and was trying to stick it back on the top of my head when I saw Mom's shadow. She come to see what the noise was. One look at her and well, I knowed for sure I was in for it.

Grammy heard this too and come running. When she seen what happened she figured I was gonna get punished bad. She tried to make it better for me by fussing a good deal with relief that I didn't jab the scissors in my eye or cut my head instead of just my hair, I snipped that close. That was Grammy for you. She tried to soften Mom's anger.

It didn't work. Mom, hands on hips and rage in her voice right away hollered at Grammy: "*Du* always cover up for

Alverna. *Du* spoil her!" she went on, outta control. *"Ich* don't have no say over raisin' my own *bobbel.* It's up to me for to make her pay the consequence. *Du* stay out of this *onct un* for all!"

Who was more surprised, Grammy or me, I couldn't say. See, I never heard my mom talk to Grammy like that. It's good Pap wasn't there - for Mom's sake I mean. He wouldn't of put up with it. Grammy covered her ears with her hands as she smarted in pain and astonishment at Mom's torrent of anger. Turning white from shame she backed out of the kitchen into the yard to finish hanging up the wash, but not before I saw her mouth quiver with hurt - not only for herself but for me cause she knowed what I was in for. Tears was already slidin' down her cheeks. There was fear there too. She knowed I was gonna get an awful hard whipping.

My blood turned to ice, my heart froze with fear - and the rest of me, too. Only my eyes moved as I watched Mom comin' at me.

They say curiousity killed the cat, but that day my curious nature almost got me killed. Mom was not feelin' kindly at all towards me. See, to make matters worse - if that was possible - Mom set up an appointment in York to get my birthday picture taken - and I'd just cut a chunk of hair right off the top of my head. We'd walk the half-frozen, muddy streets (it was winter) to the trolley station unless Pap or Uncle John could get away from work long enough to hitch up the wagon and drive us in. Mom was hoping we didn't have to walk and get cold and muddy, all befussed in the winter weather to get our pictures taken. The trolley, pulled by a team of big, strong workhorses would drop us off where the studio was in the big city. Years later a trolley run by electricity would take over, but not just yet.

I stood there and waited, every nerve and muscle in my little body squeezed stiff. I couldn't move. Couldn't even swallow. Drool was running from my mouth; I was overcome with alarm. Mom moved in a slow, deliberate manner to me, leaned over, grabbed my wrists with one hand and held tight as she pulled up my dress with her other hand so hard she ripped a big gash in the skirt, and whipped my *hiney* the worst ever. Red welts come out wherever she struck. Still holding me by my wrists she drug me up the stairs and all but throwed me onto the bed, shut the door and there I stayed the rest of the day without no company and no supper. I loved to eat but it didn't matter much right then. My bottom was stingin' too bad to care about food. Had welts for a week, I did.

Laying in bed I got upset with myself. What a bad girl I was to make Mom so mad. I hurt Grammy, too, the way she teared up. Why did I have to be so nosy? Why couldn't I be the good little girl Mom craved? I wanted to bawl my brains out but figured I better stay quiet the rest of the day. It wasn't hard to be still. When I moved just a little bit the pain shot up the backs of my legs, over my *heiney* and traveled up to my neck that was stiff from Mom jerking me around. I knowed I was in for more if Mom heard anything outta me. I reckoned another licking on top of the first one would maybe be more'n I could take. I pushed my pillow over my face so she wouldn't her me simper in pain and disgrace. So mad I was for being such a bad girl.

All because I wanted to work a scissors by myself.

Listening from my bed during supper, well, it was awful quiet out there. Pap and my uncles knowed I was being punished. Mom told 'em why. But they figured there was more to it than what Mom said cause it was easy for them to see Grammy wasn't her usual cheery self. That night and for the next couple days she was pale, rigid, closed-mouth. No way was she gonna tell Pap just how awful Mom acted up. If she did, Mom would sooner or later find a way to get back at Grammy through me. Grammy, bless her heart, wouldn't take that chance.

I was in a tight spot, too. I wasn't my bubbly, perky self for a week, first of all from worry what I might do wrong so soon after my unforgivable sin with the scissors. Parts of my skin was so tender it felt like it was peeling off my back and

51

legs. My muscles so stiff and sore that I couldn't of been bad if I wanted to. And oh, even when I felt better I tried so hard to be a good girl.

Pap looked at me with worry but said nothing. A peculiar feeling that I couldn't altogether form in my mind came to me that Grammy and Pap blamed themselves for Mom's stern way of behaving and didn't know how to make things better.

Pap, he never found out how his oldest girl tore into her mom that day. No one was dumb enough to tell him that, but he knowed his Estella was in a fit for days, and his wife was moodier than he'd ever seen. The appointment with the photograph studio had been set up and there was no way to get it changed. Weary from the tension and strife in the household, Pap tried to smooth things out and said for Uncle John to borrow a horse and a buggy from our good neighbor, Miss Hoff, and take me and Mom to York. Uncle John welcomed the change and was glad to travel into York where he'd have some time by hisself to walk around and explore some of the bigger stores, an uncommon event.

Mom fixed up a big white ribbon to cover my bald spot where stubby bits of hair was beginning to grow out. The red welts was mostly gone but Mom's anger hung on all this time and my hurt stayed sharp. Riding to the city in the buggy between Uncle John and Mom, he teased and joked with me, tried to cheer me up, something I usually found nothing short of delight in, but it was hard to smile that day though I tried. Only it wasn't a real smile. Uncle John and Mom seen it wasn't. So did the nice man, after using every trick to pull a real smile outta me without no luck, took my picture with a sober face. That only made Mom all the more fed up with me.

I let her down again. I wondered so if Mom truly cared how I felt or was it that she just didn't want people to think she wasn't a good momma cause her little girl wouldn't smile.

With her dark mood things was purty bleak around the Farley household for more'n week. Then something happened to put the worst of that behind us.

Distant relatives of Grammy's had a baby and they come to fetch Mom to do the work. People was always going back and forth helping each other out even though it meant extra work for those left behind. See, someone else - on top of their own work - hadda fill in for the one who went to help out. But that's the way it was. Seldom was anyone turned away when help was needed. Frugal, yes, stern, maybe, but the Dutch was generous when it come to helping others out. Anyway, the Farley family was - and lots of others, too.

People who didn't understand or know much about us called us dumb Dutch. Yes well, if helping others made us dumb, that we was. Mostly we didn't pay attention, just went on living out the Ten Commandments as best we could, sometimes slipping but for the most part aiming for the straight course.

Everyone was relieved to see Mom go. Grammy hugged me, told me stories, let me help her with chores, touch things Mom never did. Pap loosened up a bit, didn't scold my uncles for their good-natured noise and rowdiness that'd been absent for some time, now reappearing. Oh, how my wounded heart welcomed the warmth and affection that'd been missing with Mom so mad. With my little body almost healed, my spirit was mending too. We all had a little bit of hope for peace in the coming days.

John and Lola Miller lived right across from the people with the new baby where Mom was. Lola would go over still and see what a wonderful wash and cleaning my mom done. She wondered how such a young girl was so good at all that. She didn't know Grammy and how Grammy taught her girls to do things right.

Lola made it her business more often than usual, because of Mom, to go to the neighbor with the new baby and one day questioned her. "Estella, what are you going to do after you leave here?"

"Go *heemet* to *mudder un vadder. Du* know *Ich* got a little girl there."

The next thing Lola asked Mom was, "Can you milk?"

"*Ya, Ich* can milk. Never much *goot* at it, but *onct* we had a cow and *Ich* done the milkin'."

Nothing more was said until Lola went and got her sister, Annmarie. Between them they talked, then asked Mom whether she'd try to help their mother who was getting up in years. Her legs was swelled so big that she could hardly get down anymore to milk. Dropsy it was, they said.

All my mom hadda do was milk and help in the house. The Old Lady'd skim the cream off and everything like that. Their brother, Ben Geesey, was the youngest, the only brother in their family. He never married, lived there with his mom. Took over the farm single-handed when his pa died. His sisters had married and moved away and he was too busy to milk with all the other work.

Well, when Mom was done helping out the woman and her baby, she went home and told this to Grammy and Pap. They told my mom, "*Du* can try it if *du* want."

Next thing, Annmarie and Lola got together and come in a fancy buggy for to take Mom to see the farm and talk to the Old Lady and Ben. Afterwards they all agreed that this was the best way to go.

Mom went.

I missed my mom but the time I spent with Grammy and Pap and their kids without Mom was filled with joy and happiness. Peace prevailed.

Everything worked out fine till one day the Old Lady and Mom got to talking and the Old Lady found out that Mom had a little girl. That was that! The Old Lady scolded - and she couldn't speak a thing in English, only Dutch - "a *bobbel* belongs with its *mudder!*" (I know Dutch when I hear it, but I can't speak it no more, only certain words I remember.)

The Old Lady wanted to see this baby. Of course that baby was me, only I wasn't a baby no longer. When Mom said my name was Alverna Nell, well, a surprised and befuddled look from the Old Lady come but she didn't say nothing right away. She was purty sure I hadda be the baby named after her granddaughter, Alverna Konhaus, the schoolmistress. Can you believe?

When she told Mom that her daughter, Annmarie, was married to Allen Konhaus, and Alverna was her granddaughter, why Mom could hardly believe it either.

As soon as he found out, Allen would over and over remark to everyone he ran into - and he ran into alot of people, the nature of his business and all, "Can you believe it? That young woman who named her baby after my Alverna, now she's helping out my wife's momma."

Pap and Grammy took me over and when I got there - now I can still see everything the way it was. It's just as plain as if it's right here in front of me today. The Old Lady wrapped her huge, blubbery arms around me and all but suffocated me with a big, bulky hug and said, *"Ach, mei Gott,* what a beautiful *bobbel!"*

Here I thought she'd say something about the way my hair was growing out so funny-like, but she didn't. Didn't even notice.

She sat me on the floor and handed me a glass marble with a sheep inside. It belonged to the Old Lady's children and she always fetched it out for little ones to play with. It became my favorite toy for many a year.

Well, they got to talking but Pap had work he promised to finish up that day. He and Grammy took me back with them because they didn't bring no clothes for me along. They promised they'd bring me back if the Old Lady wanted me - and of course she said she did.

It was like this: I'd go there a couple weeks, then my uncles got homesick for me. Purd was only a little older'n me so he didn't mind me gone cause he got more attention from his mom when I was at the Old Lady's. Then I'd go back to Grammy's for a spell. Oh my golly, after awhile the Old Lady'd get homesick for me, so back to the farm I'd go. This went on till I started school. I hadda stay at the farm then, but I still went back and forth in the summer.

Wherever I was, I was happy.

CHAPTER 6 - GRAMMY'S RICH NEIGHBOR

I like my kitchen. Red and white it is, real cheery. Enough windows for the sun to shine in, and on cloudy days the big heat register in the black and white block linoleum floor - the only heat in my little house except for the smaller vent in the bathroom - shoots lots of warm air onto my slippered feet, then travels all the way up my body. Feels good. My blood mustn't be coursing through my veins like it used to; I'm cold most the time.

Yes well. Such is life. Had my insulin shot and my breakfast, so now I'm ready to write some, except what I just read in my Bible sorta got me discouraged. It's in Ecclesiastes: *"Of making of many books there is no end. . . ."* That sure is true. Lots of books out there. Maybe I should up and quit right now. Who'll wanna read my story? Maybe no one. Well, maybe one, the granddaughter-in-law that's been urging me to do this. She called yesterday, wondered how I was coming along. Did I need any help? Do I need more paper? Can she come and sharpen my pencils? That gave us a good laugh. She's intent on learning more about me, wonders so about this person or that one she heard me talk about. Gets me to thinking about what I remember about them. Yes well, guess I'll keep on writing. After a bit, I'll take a break and work on long division. Yeah, I love to do long division. That'll get the blood flowing through my brain so I get back to writing my story down.

Soon after Grammy and Pap got me to the Old Lady's the first time to stay, she and Mom was in the big kitchen baking bread.

I knowed what a dough tray was, that I knowed. Charlotte Hoff, a neighbor who lived down the street from Grammy and Pap had a dough tray. In her own bewildering way she was a good friend to Grammy. I got that backwards; Grammy was a good friend to Charlotte Hoff.

Grammy and me was often at Charlotte's when she baked her bread. So wonderful good it was, why just smelling it made your mouth water. Charlotte always shared her crusty-on-the-outside, solid-on-the-inside, delicious white bread with the Farleys every time she baked. That was about the only work Charlotte done, not because she had to, just outta her love for baking bread. Didn't do no work, mind you, just baked bread.

Charlotte was rich, didn't need to do nothing. She was a maiden lady and had lived with her parents and her brother, Horace - he never married neither. Them three was dead and buried by the time I was born. I only knowed Charlotte. That was one wealthy family, believe you me. They owned most the land the town stood on and made their money by breaking the untillable land up into plots and selling them. Pap would of liked to have bought some but didn't have the money. H.A. Briggs, the town undertaker and builder bought blocks of plots, and built houses street by street, often asking Pap - and when my uncles got big enough - for them to help. With them and his own boys he'd get one street built up with houses, sell 'em real fast since more industry was coming to Cedar Grove mainly because of the railroad. Then he'd buy more plots and start all over again.

By that time a town council was formed and laid out the town on paper. H.A. had those plans and built according to how he and his son Walter decided which houses to build where. That family was probably the richest after Charlotte. You wouldn't of knowed it though. They never much changed their way of living from the time when they become wealthy.

Getting back to Charlotte, she never had no worries regarding money. She didn't live high on the hog, but out of necessity hired a bachelor handyman by the name of Mr.

Burns to keep the house in good repair inside and out along with the yard and garden. He worked cheap but was good at what he done. When he had inside work to do, Charlotte never left him outta her sight. She didn't much trust people. She was tight with her money, had the reputation of a tight-wad, just like her daddy.

Being around her quite a bit, Grammy seen that Charlotte, deep inside, was a kind and proper lady, she just never learned how to let others see that part of her. Charlotte would ask Grammy about the reliability of people and their work, for even though she trusted almost no one else, she trusted Grammy with her life. Lots of times things come up when no one was around except Grammy. She was always there for Charlotte. Grammy'd never take money for helping her out though she sure coulda used it. Most times after she got back home, Grammy'd find a bill or two tucked in a sweater pocket she carried with her to Charlotte's and hung on the clothes horse standing inside the front door while she worked. Charlotte sneaked it in there when Grammy wasn't looking. See, she wasn't all that tight as people made out.

The one thing Grammy never turned down was Charlotte's bread. It was the best, *allerbescht*! Besides, Grammy was left with the mess to clean up. Charlotte liked to bake the bread, but after it was in the oven she left everything else sit.

One day when Charlotte needed help and sent for Grammy, Mom was in bed with one of her sick headaches. Grammy, not knowing what else to do, took a chance and drug me along. She thought Charlotte'd send both of us back home till Grammy'd be able to go by herself but she had to chance it since Charlotte was expecting her. She forewarned me. "Don't *du* dare touch nothin' in Miss Charlotte's house. Not none of her antiques, not the china or what-nots *un* bric-a-brac that's all over the place. Maybe Charlotte will like *du* if *du* are *goot*. But for sure she will send us home right away if *du* touch even *chust* one little thing."

My, oh, my! I was so excited! This would be my first visit to Charlotte's. I couldn't take it all in what Grammy was warning me about. My excitement didn't do nothing to calm Grammy's nerves.

Charlotte looked a mite exasperated when Grammy explained about Mom, but she left us in. Grammy sat me on an old horsehair davenport, shook her finger as a warning with all the sternness she could muster, reminding me to listen and sit still.

For some reason I knowed one slip-up would keep Grammy from taking me with her ever again so I braced myself to hold back from wanting to walk around, explore and touch. In the cool, darkened living room I seen how different Charlotte's house was from where we lived - the overstuffed furniture, pleasing-to-the-eye, well thought-out clutter, the pictures and paintings on her walls. Shelves of books, magazines laying right in front of me on the coffee table. Glory be! What temptation was before me that morning. How I wanted to pick up those wonderful magazines filled with words and pictures and turn the pages, but the best I could do was concentrate from where I sat to take in the pictures on the covers. Charlotte, it appeared she didn't even realize I was there after Grammy sat me down. Wasn't that she liked or disliked me. She just mostly ignored me. Too much into herself Charlotte was.

Yeah, I forced myself to sit still with only my eyes roaming back and forth. There was so much to look at and ponder over, why I thought I'd never see it all. That's why I was a good girl. I was determined to go back to that living room till I seen it all. I clenched my fists, sat stiff as a board. When it was time to crawl off the sofa and walk home I couldn't hardly move. Every muscle in my body was froze rigid. But, after that first visit Charlotte told Grammy, "You may bring Alverna along with you when necessary as long as she behaves like the good little girl she was today."

Oh, was my heart thrilled! I knowed no matter how often I went there, even if I had to sit on that horsehair davenport the whole time, it'd take forever to see it all.

I must tell you, never was I jealous of Charlotte Hoff and what she had. I didn't want what Charlotte had, I just enjoyed being there, looking here and there while Grammy did what was expected of her. Not then nor anytime in my life did I want too much more'n what I already had. What I had, it was enough. Often I'd say to myself the words I heard coming out of Pap's mouth again and again when he read from the old family Bible: *My cup runneth over.* Mine ran over with joy and happiness for who I belonged to and what I had.

I can still see Charlotte sitting at her writing desk near the only window that had the blind up and the curtain pulled back so she had natural light to write with along with the light from her antique oil desk lamp. With pen in long, slender, white fingers that never seen hard work, she wrote neat, beautiful words on perfumed writing paper that I could smell from where I sat. Near her desk was a painting table that held more paints and brushes than I could count, and next to that was an easel with a canvas on it. I never seen such stuff anywhere like that.

Year round Charlotte painted what she seen from her window. Her pictures was the purtiest. Of course I didn't have other ones to compare them to cause I never yet seen paintings like that. But even today I remember them as the purtiest I ever seen. The colors flowed into each other with a light, airy look. Attractive they was, just like Charlotte musta been long ago.

She never gave away her paintings, hung them on every wall in groups that brought out the best in each one. Grammy secretly admired a picture of pansies, coral bells and lilliesof-the-valley nestled in a flower bed next to a garden wall that Charlotte painted so real-like. Grammy, she never said nothing to nobody about it, but I could see the admiration in her eyes whenever she spied it. Grammy tried to hide it for she wouldn't never want people to think she coveted, but little as I was I seen the longing inside her.

Charlotte was always dressed to the nines. Everything matched, even her long cotton stockings and high heeled shoes with fancy buckles of grosgrain, cut steel or bakelite that could be switched when it suited her. On her face was way too much powder; her cheeks was bright circles of red; eyebrows penciled in too wide and long and dark; bright red lipstick melted down in little lines from her mouth. Grammy said, "It's her eyes wearin' out. When she was *yung* she done it *chust* right." That and not enough light in the house made Charlotte not see how poorly she looked. Yet, from a peculiar person like Charlotte, it wasn't too surprising; you sorta got used to it, expected it.

The same brooch with a big brown stone in the middle always covered the top button of Charlotte's dress. She told Grammy more'n once it was a *15 carat honey topaz mounted in genuine 24 karat gold with tiny seed pearls set among enameled filigree*. Oh, I didn't understand them words as she described the brooch, hinting to Grammy that it come from a beau of long ago, but I loved to hear her say words we never spoke at Grammy's. I said them over and over in my mind until they was memorized in my brain.

I can still hear Charlotte's voice the way I first remembered it, sweet and low almost like soft music. The last couple of months I went with Grammy it was more high pitched; she was growing old and feeble. Some days I thought she cackled instead of spoke. But I remember most her low, soft voice. Her parents had sent her to 'finishing school,' she lightheartedly told Grammy, to make her a 'lady of propriety with fine moral upbringing'. Smiled in a mysterious way when she said it, like she was far, far away, living a life of long ago. What a difference there musta been between that world and the one she was living in now.

Even though I didn't know what them words meant then, it was easy to see the difference between her and us. I treasured being able to sit there and let my soul take in the quietness and beauty of Charlotte's house. But see, when it was time to go home I was just as happy to return to Grammy's house that was filled with a big family and practical, everyday stuff I cherished that Charlotte didn't have.

Charlotte seldom left her house except for about four months during our long, cold winters. (We had long, freezing-cold, deep, snowy winters back then.) She spent them in the biggest and best hotel in York where she was safe from the dangers of winter weather. She conjectured she might get snowed in her house and to just think of all the things that could go wrong and no one there to help out. It relieved Grammy when Charlotte set out for the hotel around mid-November.

Charlotte was waited on hand and foot by the hotel staff since years ago her papa helped finance this much-acclaimed new building. Gossip trickled out that she wasn't much of a tipper, but the bank that had charge of her funds seen that extra was turned over to staff that doted on her. This was supposed to be a secret, for if Charlotte had found out she had obtained such a reputation, she might not of gone back. Being the loner she was she never did learn about it, just everyone else.

Writing letters was Charlotte's way of keeping in touch with her few friends. Her only surviving relative was a distant niece who stopped by when Charlotte needed help with making sense of her finances. When Grammy'd say to Mom about Charlotte's niece being there, Mom just snorted through her nose and said the only time she come around was to take Charlotte's money, not help Charlotte keep it straight. Grammy'd just shake her head over Mom's thinking towards other folks, but only when Mom's back was turned so she wouldn't take note of it.

But I did.

Sometimes one of my uncles run errands for her but it was always Grammy who delivered the goods. Charlotte was fearful of people, especially men. She handed out the smallest change she could get away with without losing what help she needed, but no one believed Charlotte wasn't knowledgeable about wages. She just acted ignorant. Grammy accepted the coin or two for her boy, never holding back none for herself.

This peculiar neighbor was getting up in years, a bit feeble in the knees. Once I heard Grammy mutter with a wistful note in her voice, "In the head, too.". Charlotte kept her doors locked tight and her windows nailed shut. Once Grammy asked her if maybe she should have a house key in case she fetched something for her and Charlotte couldn't make it to the door. You might guess Charlotte was too proud to use a cane. She arranged her furniture so she could get to her front door by holding onto one piece of furniture, then step and grab another'n and so on till she made it to the door. But Charlotte wasn't gonna give Grammy no key, just told her that there was one window on the second floor that wasn't never locked, the one the big old willow tree hid from view. Her niece was the only one who knowed that and now Grammy. She wasn't to tell another soul.

Yes well, Grammy never did tell. At least not till it was necessary. And wouldn't you know, she asked Charlotte at a time when soon after it was helpful to both of 'em. That was one time Grammy proved what a good neighbor she was.

You see, in the cool of the early summer mornings, Charlotte could be seen on her screened-in front porch - if you knowed where to look for her behind all the grown-up shrubbery - in her favorite green wicker rocker covered with colorful flowered cushions that her niece ordered for her outta the Sears-Roebuck catalog. She was practically outta sight behind the wisteria vine that crawled up the porch rails and climbed over the eaves. It was her ritual to have her breakfast of an apple or banana - not both - with toast and coffee at her white, round, cast-iron table with a glass top covered with a tablecloth that matched the cushions of her rocker. Same breakfast every day. Never varied. When finished, she moved to the rocker to read her Bible and newspaper if the weather was fit. After she drank in the sights as she rocked, she went back into her house to spend the day.

One hot summer day Grammy looked towards Charlotte's front porch. This was the second day Charlotte wasn't out. That did it. Grammy was worried, determined to find out where Charlotte was. She come up with a reason to knock on Charlotte's door. I was allowed to sit on the front porch step next to Mom who'd come for a visit from the Geesey farm, and watch as Grammy took a jar of grape jelly for her neighbor. She knocked.

No answer.

She went out back and knocked.

No answer.

Grammy rattled the door knob as loud as she could. The door was locked. There was no sign of Charlotte. Grammy peeked in the window with the curtain pulled back, banged on the glass. Nothing.

She couldn't see in. Charlotte's easel blocked her view

Grammy walked out back again, looked up at the second story window, brooded over it, then come after Uncle Will to lug Pap's tall ladder to Charlotte's house and lean it against where the unlocked window was. The branches of the willow tree tangled in the ladder and Will's temper was growing short along with the heat before he finally got it in against the house. He wanted to climb up, begged Grammy with all he had in him to let him climb the ladder, but Grammy said no, if Charlotte seen a man come in her house she'd have a heart attack right then and there.

Will said something to Mom, but she couldn't climb that ladder. She got dizzy standing on the first rung; was up to Grammy to do the climbing and crawling in the window. Uncle Will tried holding the ladder steady, but he was awful hot and bothered at what his mom was up to. He knowed what his pa'd do to him if for some strange reason he happened by and seen Grammy on the ladder. Will woulda got a good talking to about being a man and then maybe a couple swats with the razor strop. Of course Pap wasn't around; he never woulda left Grammy climb like that.

By this time I had snuck up to Charlotte's trying to keep outta Mom's view. She was so caught up with fear and agitation for Grammy she didn't notice me at first. When she did, she was too shook up to say something.

Fighting the willow branches that slapped after her while she climbed, Grammy inched her way up in her long, bulky dress and petticoat that made the going purty treacherous. Uncle Will was having fits and though Mom wasn't doing much better, she grabbed the ladder to help steady it and told Will to get ahold of hisself or their mom would fall off that ladder from it shakin' so hard.

Finally, Grammy made it to the window. We held our breaths - yes, me included - as she pushed on the window. It wouldn't budge at first but she didn't give up, banged against the swollen wood frame with the flat of her palms, then her closed fists to loosen the old paint that held it tight. Uncle Will and Mom looked at each other aghast! They was on pins and needles worrying about Grammy. Even though the ladder shook like crazy, Grammy wouldn't give up. Pounded till she got it loose. Next she pushed and pushed till the window was up high enough for her to squeeze through. Just barely. I stood there jaws clenched shut, hands clamped together pleading to the Good Lord to keep my brave grammy from falling.

She finally disappeared inside head first, feet in the air. A moan come outta Will. He was beside hisself for not forcing Grammy to stay on solid ground and him climbing. We heard the curtain rod pull from the wall before we saw the curtains tumble on Grammy's backside. Ripping noises was coming from the second floor as Grammy untangled herself from the rotting curtains.

Honest to Pete! It woulda been funny if we wasn't so scared. Grammy stood at the open window with curtains wrapped around her and called down she was ok. She was gonna look for Charlotte. I followed Mom and Uncle Will as they left go of the ladder and run around to the front of the house. We watched and waited, waited some more for Grammy to appear, wondering what in the world was taking so long. Will was ready to go climb the ladder hisself thinking Grammy was in there hurt, but just then Grammy hurried through the front door holding the hanky over her face - the one she always had stuck up her sleeve. Gagging and coughing at the same time, in a shaky voice she managed to tell Will to hurry off to get the doctor and the undertaker. "*Ach du leiber*! Might as well get 'em both," she gasped.

Grammy, outta breath, grabbed at Mom to keep from falling over, then with great effort told how she found Charlotte sitting at her writing desk, pen in hand with head slumped forward. Her face and hands was bluish black and there was juices leaking out her nose and mouth. Trying to take in what she just seen, she went on. "*Mei Gott!* The smell is so bad."

We understood. That smell already saturated Grammy's clothes in just the short time she was in there.

We stood there. Mom and Grammy paced back and forth waiting for the doctor and H.A. Briggs to arrive. No way was Grammy going back in that house till the men come and no way was Mom gonna go in at all. When Will come running back to tell Grammy they was on their way, she made him take the ladder and put it away before Pap got home. She was gonna downplay what she done so Pap wouldn't get mad

67

at Will for not taking over better. She warned Mom and Will to not say more'n was necessary to Pap. She looked down at me and said, *"Un du, du* little chatterbox, not a word to your Pap! *Ich* will handle that."

I nodded.

After he looked in on Charlotte and was hit by the smell of putrefying flesh, Doc figured a heart attack took her that quick maybe two, three days before. The warm, moist air in the closed-up house started Charlotte's body to break down purty fast. The doctor said he'd get in touch with the niece and was more'n happy to give H.A. permission to take Charlotte and do what needed done.

Charlotte's funeral was the same that her parents and brother, Horace, had. A better one you couldn't buy. The dark mahogany coffin - none priced higher - was the talk of the town till something better come along to chew over. Only thing was, people didn't get to see the inside, or Charlotte. H.A. said she wasn't fit to be viewed.

Charlotte's parlor got aired out and cleaned up neat and tidy for the funeral. Grammy helped the niece. Mourners - if you could call 'em that - come to check out the coffin and the house as much as to mourn Charlotte. Everyone oohed and aahed over the flowers on the coffin lid - red roses, dozens of 'em with little white flowers tucked in around. One of the garden ladies said it was *Baby's Breath*.

It was nice that some people remembered why they was there and remarked that it was good that poor Charlotte didn't have to suffer, dear soul.

Charlotte's niece inherited everything. She told Grammy, in confidence, that cash was stuffed under the mattresses, all through the house in cans, boxes, jars, bottles, shoes and clothing. She couldn't throw or give away one thing before checking it out for fear of throwing bank books, stocks, money or jewelry out. Then she looked at Grammy in surprise and said, "My goodness, Eliza. What am I saying that already you don't know? Why you helped Aunt Charlotte. You seen all that stuff. And you never took none, did you?"

Grammy just smiled and said, "*Du* know *Ich* wouldn't."

Now see, all this time Grammy knowed every inch of that house and what was in it, every nook and cranny and the way valuables was laying around. Only Grammy never mentioned it and she never touched nothing except to give 'em a good dusting now and then.

Charlotte's niece was quite a bit more bighearted and generous with Charlotte's money - which now was hers - than Charlotte was. Grammy was paid good to help clean the parlor and close off the rest of the house so people couldn't nose around. Mr. Burns helped too.

After the funeral when she hadda go back and tell her boss she was quitting her job, the niece wondered if Grammy'd stop by and keep on till the cleaning was done, when she had the chance, that is. She even gave Grammy a key. Wouldn't you know, even Mom hadda smile about that.

Grammy cleaned behind locked doors. Mr. Burns stayed on and kept away neighbors who stopped by hoping to get in, even offered to help. Grammy pretended she didn't hear. Kept on cleaning, she did. Grammy accepted what money Charlotte's niece paid her knowing she done more'n her share of hard work. Besides, Grammy realized this woman had enough to keep her the rest of her life, even two lifetimes.

The day eventually arrived when Grammy was finished, stored away the extra cash she had earned for a rainy day.

Whatever cash and furnishings she wanted and carried outta the house, the niece didn't report to the bank that had charge of Charlotte's estate; that way it wouldn't be taxed. The bank wasn't fooled. They knowed what she was doing but figured the bank would get enough with handling the remainder of Charlotte's bank affairs and estate. The niece had time enough to take out what she wanted. The bank was thoughtful to consider their customer as much as itself, ain't now?

One thing Grammy never suspected was the surprise Charlotte Hoff - long before she died - had planned for Grammy. It wasn't discovered till after Charlotte passed over, just the way she intended it. What happened was when sorting through Charlotte's artwork, the niece come across the painting Grammy always admired. Stuck in the back of the frame was Grammy's name in Charlotte's beautiful handwriting. Another paper said, "Present this note and painting to Eliza Farley.

We all crowded around in wonder and excitement as Grammy opened the envelope. This is what she read : *Eliza, I see how much you admire my watercolor of the flowers against the garden wall. You never asked me for one thing, you accepted very little, but my-oh-my, you are such a generous lady. You gave me so much. You are honest, hard-working and kind. Now that I'm gone (I am or you wouldn't be reading this), I want you to have this painting. I know you will cherish it. Don't tuck it away to protect it. Hang it where you can see it every day. Thank you for being my good friend and neighbor. Someday I'll see you in heaven. Charlotte.*

It was too hard for Grammy to hold back. We seen the tears of joy slide down the furrows in her wrinkled cheeks and chin and drop on the front of her dress as she slipped out back to have a good cry. (See, Grammy proved the Pennsylvania Dutch had feelings even if we wasn't supposed to show 'em.) Nobody went after her. We stayed indoors and gave Grammy the space she needed to sort through what Charlotte done. Beyond the open back door we heard her blowing her nose again and again. After she pulled herself together, she come back in. "Gotta get at the dishes before it's time for *bedde*," she said, acting like nothing considerable happened a short time before. She shoulda knowed the dishes got already done.

That only flustered her more. Not knowing what else to do, she picked up the old family Bible, sat down and rocked. Didn't read it, just sat there holding it on her lap.

Even Mom was weepy over that. I shed some tears, tears of joy for Grammy, tears of sorrow for Charlotte Hoff. We all went to bed that night happy at Grammy's good fortune.

See, that proves how right I was when I always believed deep down what a good person Charlotte Hoff was. That made me all the more sad for all the good things Charlotte coulda enjoyed in life, only locked herself away and didn't. She just never learned how to let loose.

Can you see why I loved my Grammy and what she stood for? And best of all, Charlotte recognized that in Grammy too.

Wouldn't you think it'd of helped if Charlotte was to loosen her purse strings a little bit more while she was alive? But no.

Here's why I say that: One day while Mom was helping Grammy put up some grape jelly, Mom seen her shaking her head and clucking her tongue, so she pressured her to say what she was laughing at. Grammy remarked that she was thinkin' how Charlotte told her onct how the preacher come by her house for his yearly visit and kindly suggested for her to put the church in her will. "Not that you'd deprive anyone you intend to name in your will, Miss Hoff. But perhaps you'll consider a charitable sum that would help the church."

Well, that didn't go over too good with Charlotte. Grammy went on how Charlotte snickered as she told her that aside from her weekly offering she gave an extra $5.00 to the church every Christmas, knowing it was taken not too kindly by the pious preacher. Charlotte didn't like anyone suggesting she share her money with them, not even a man of God.

In the end we seen that Charlotte did relent. She left a sizable donation to the church specifying it should be used for a new organ. Not that she'd been in church for ages to hear the old one wheezing and going on, but Grammy told her once how bad it sounded. Wearing out, it was.

A large, solid brass sign, real dignified, with Charlotte's name beautifully inscribed on it was attached to the new instrument where it faced the pews so worshippers would be reminded every Sunday who contributed this exceptional pump organ to the sanctuary, whether they wanted to be reminded or not. All in all though, I imagine Charlotte was best remembered for her strange and out of the ordinary vocabulary and behavior.

We missed Charlotte but didn't mourn her overmuch. Grammy said Charlotte was where she never more need fear the real or imaginary dangers she faced here on earth. Maybe it was for that reason that the Farley family - if the truth be told - missed her bread as much as Charlotte, God rest her soul.

All except Grammy, that is.

Pap hung Charlotte Hoff's painting on the parlor wall for Grammy. Most times Pap got Uncle George to help Grammy around the house with little jobs, but it seemed he understood how much this picture meant to Grammy. He hung it hisself, just for her. Watching Pap gave me the idea how much he thought of Grammy. He loved her, just didn't show it too much with words. But I could see the other ways.

Pennsylvania Dutch or not, what a shame to be so puffed up with pride that you couldn't never show your true and tender affections. Hogwash!

Of course, I filled the bill every now and then, just like the rest, so I better watch my tongue.

The soft beautiful colors of the painting didn't altogether fit in with the rest of the faded, practical belongings in their house, but it hung there as long as them two lived. A bright spot in more ways than one, it was.

CHAPTER 7 - THE FARM

In the big farmhouse kitchen, Mom and the Old Lady was kneading dough. More flour was there than I ever seen at Charlotte Hoff's place. The Old Lady'd grab a sizeable hunk from the big portion, sprinkle flour all over it and punch it this way and that, every now and then sneaking a look my way.

I'd been put on a high chair that was pushed against the table. Leaning over I was, chin in hands with elbows propped on the table watching the Old Lady, my eyes glued to what she was doing with all that dough. Over that Ben come in. Ben was the Old Lady's son, her youngest and the only one at home now yet. I suspect he was too curious to work outside that day with a little stranger in the house. Even though I was purty young I sensed there was a need for him to see what was going on, even wanting to be part of it, only not sure how to fit in. He musta figured he'd come in, stand back, and watch. The Old Lady told him to just now look how different it was when him, Annmarie and Lola was at the table while she was working the dough. "*Ich* had to fight with *du* three all the time cause all over the table *du* had flour, ain't now? *Chust* look at her sittin' there *un* she don't move," she remarked, hardly believing a child could sit so still.

"*Ich* see," was all Ben said.

The Old Lady finished all that, then Mom hoisted the big dough tray to carry back into another room.

Next, a most glorious thing come about, so wonderful good it was! I seen Ben standing near the door at the porch like he'd been waiting for something. He walked my way, stood close to my side, but not too close to scare me. We regarded each other for some time off to the side, not direct.

Then he walked around where he looked at me straight in the eyes and I looked right back at him.

"*Ach vell* now, *du* seen all that, Snip." (From that day on he always called me Snip.) With a broad, friendly smile that couldn't no way hide under his big red moustache, he asked, "Now, are *du kumme* with me to see the guineas, the turkeys, the geese, the ducks *un* everything?"

See, there was this great big farm you know, and I wasn't used to all that, but there I was, no more'n three years old. I was ready to jump outta my chair - didn't wanna miss nothing. His arms reached out to me and I reached back. Next I was lifted into the arms of a great big robust man with the rosiest cheeks I ever seen in my whole life.

I looked him over careful as he picked me up with calloused, strong yet gentle hands, arms bulging against shirt sleeves wet with sweat even though the air outside was cool. As red as his moustache, that's how black was his hair. And oh, how his eyes twinkled with high spirits and good intent. I just now cry when I think of it, so special a time it was. I looked deep into those eyes and he looked straight into my soul. Both of us knowed from that minute we was special to each other. I right away loved him with all my heart and I knowed he felt the same way about me. There was never no doubt about it. I committed to my heart that time forever.

You say to yourself that this is Alverna's imagination, she don't remember all that. Let me tell you for sure, everything that happened that day almost ninety years ago is printed on my heart and mind .

Me forget it? Never!

Just think! Ben Geesey was the person that kept me on the right course during my young life. He gave me a little bit of hope when hope was hard to come by. Maybe it was him that kept me from becoming mean and bitter and hard like Mom. He was the best of all, *allerbescht!* That don't mean it was a straight and easy path for none of us to walk. Many a time the going was rough. How we made it through like we did was only by the grace of God. Yep, God put Ben in my path for my good.

He carried me outside and I right away felt safe in the strong, sturdy arms of this stranger. We headed in the direction of a big red barn that needed fresh paint but never got it as long as I remember. The first thing we come to was a great big wooden pump with a long wood handle but I had no idea what it was. He lifted that handle with his free hand - he still held me in the crook of one arm, and glory be! Water come gushing out.

"Oh-h-h-h!" I went.

"See the *wasser* go down in the trough. That's where the horses *un* cows *un saus* get their *wasser* to drink."

He pumped a long time for the troughs to get filled up. I didn't mind. Watching the water run into all the troughs was spellbinding. When done with that he swung open a door and walked us into the pig pen. I never even seen a live hog then yet and they had lots of hogs there, but what caught my eye was a momma *sau* and her baby pigs. Them little ones was crawling all over their momma. I clapped my hands with delight, almost jumped out of Ben's arms as I took in them little ones drinking.

"*Ach*! Hungry little critters, ain't now yet?" Ben laughed as he watched me looking 'em over.

In my excitement I pointed and counted, *One, two, three, four, five.* His strong arm tightened around me with surprise and pleasure as I counted those baby pigs.

There I coulda stayed to watch them greedy babies drinking but we moved on, pulling the gate shut behind us, all the while explaining to me he didn't wanna take no chances for the pigs to get out. Then, still wearing his high, black, gum shoes, Ben stepped into what I come to learn was the dung yard. With his long, loping stride we come to a big door. He opened it and said, "Them two big, black mules in the *schtall* are Bully *un* Kate." When he said Kate's name, the mule turned her head, looked at us and brayed.

"See, she knows her name. Are *du* want to touch her?"

"Oh no-o-o-o!" Frightened, I buried my face in my hands, turned and hid against his big, broad chest. Never had I been so close to so many large animals before - or such a big man. It wasn't long before Ben helped me overcome any fears I had.

We went deeper into the barn. He was going to skip the next door, but me, I was nosy. Losing my bashfulness real quick I pointed to it and declared, "You didn't open that one. What's in that door?" I wanted to know.

"*Ach vell, du* little Snip! *Du* must see everything now ain't? *Ich* will tell *du* there's not much in there, *chust* the corn *un* hay *un* things we feed Bully *un* Kate *un* all the animals with."

That was all right once I knowed. I trusted him. Whenever he spoke his words rang true, even when they hurt. Of course he never intended to hurt without cause; the hurting part was meant to teach me, to help me understand and grow.

Once when he showed me a Bible verse about speaking the truth with love, I reckoned it was referring directly to him. I think it was the truth Ben spoke and the caring way he spoke it that helped me accept what come along in life, for I faced many a hard time without always caving in or growing bitter. (Some Sundays in church I heard the preacher preach about how God never lies. Them times I thought of Ben and wondered if he was maybe God cause he never lied.)

At the next stall was two doors in one, an upper door on top of a lower door; one part you could swing open while the other stayed shut. (Boy, was I learning a lot that day!) Ben swung open the upper door and into the dark stall I could see an outline of a horse. When he turned the handle on the bottom door and swung it out wide - my glory! - a great big, chestnut horse come out. Only I wasn't paying much attention to the big horse. My eyes was on her *hootchie*. Oh my! You couldn't believe how excited I was then! All these

77

mommas with their babies. I woulda sprung right out of Ben's arm if he wouldn't of been holding me good and tight.

"The big momma horse we call Pet," Ben told me. "She's been with us a long time."

"What's the *hootchie's* name?" I wanted to know. I loved babies of any kind.

"We didn't give her no name yet, but if *du* come *un* stay with us, maybe *du* can give her a name," he said like that.

Pet walked right to the water trough to drink and the baby was at Pet drinkin'. We followed them outside and Ben shut the gate.

"Oh, Petty," I squealed and clapped my hands with delight. "You don't know what for purty baby you got, she's so purty. Red, just like you she is"

Ben studied me a minute then said, "*Du* are right, Snip. Pet never seen her *bobbel*. Pet is blind."

Well, I didn't know what to think. I couldn't take it in for I didn't know what blind was.

He stepped closer to Pet so I could touch her. All the while he talked to her quiet and gentle-like so she'd stand still. As I petted her she turned my way. I coiled against Ben in horror! Here Pet's great big eyes was all covered over with black. Now I knowed what blind was. It hurt me so bad to know she couldn't see. Right away I began to cry, oh my, how I cried. I sobbed so hard I thought I'd retch. They even heard me in the house.

Ben talked to Pet and patted her. "*Du* better go back in your *schtall* now." Pet and her baby walked into the stall. Ben shut the doors, then headed back to the house.

The Old Lady right away wanted to know what in the world happened that I bawled so. Ben explained. Mom was looking at me disappointed, as if I done wrong by crying. I knowed she was upset with me but I just couldn't keep the tears from running down my cheeks.

As I rubbed my eyes with my balled up fists to wipe the tears away and hide my shame, Ben pulled from his pocket his big red handkerchief and was drying my tears and wiping my runny nose. "My goodness," I thought to myself between hiccuping and sniveling. "My uncles hand me over to Grammy or Mom when my nose is running and here this big man's wiping it with his own hanky."

That showed me for sure how much he cared about me!

"*Ach, mei Gott* in *Himmel!*" The Old Lady went on. "That little girl'll go a long, long way."

And here I am yet today.

The dough tray was back on the table. Mom was rubbing six loaf pans that seen a lot of wear with a greasy rag. The Old Lady'd grab a hunk of dough, pat it and shape it just so till she was satisfied, then she'd slap it into one of the greased loaf pans. By now I had settled down. Ben sat me back at the table. I watched, not blinking an eye for fear I'd miss something. Touch a thing I dare not. Mom wouldn't want that. I didn't want her to get mad and send me back to Grammy's just now yet when there was Ben and the Old Lady and so much new stuff to learn about here.

I tried to please Mom, honest I did. It was just that my friendly, outgoing nature made it hard. But I kept working at it. I sighed. If only I wasn't so much full of chatter and energy.

Just like that, almost quicker than I could blink, the Old Lady up and grabbed a piece of the dough, sprinkled flour on it and throwed it right in front of me. There I sat. I looked at the dough, then at the Old Lady, then at Mom. What should I do? I wanted to touch it, but Mom wouldn't look my way, just kept shaping her loaf. I couldn't figure out what would please her.

Ben saw his mom do this. "*Ach, vell* now Mom, *du ferhoodled* her! *Du* scared her!"

His mom said to him right straight out, "*Ich* think how it was when *du un* the girls was little. *Du* into everything got. She *chust* sits there *un* looks."

79

The Old lady, with much difficulty because of her heavy bulk, *scrootched* down the bench and moved to where I was, handed me the dough and showed me how to work and shape it into a loaf. At first I touched it with one finger only, not knowing what to expect. My finger made a hollow spot in the spongy dough and I shrunk back thinking I ruined it. But instead of scolding me, the Old Lady took hold of my wrists and slid my hands around in flour that lay in piles on the blue and white checkered oilcloth spread out over the table, then showed me how to shape the dough. Wasn't long till I got the hang of it, dipping into the flour and shaping it by myself. I woulda sat and worked it all day but the Old Lady said, *"Du* know what? We're gonna bake the *brodt un* after it's baked we're gonna *kumme* in *un* spread *lottweirich* on it *un du* can *esse* it." I had no idea what *lottweirich* was, but I was ready to tackle anything that came my way with the Old Lady and Ben. They was making it real easy for me to have a good time, wanting to stay.

At that then she asked Ben if he showed me where they bake the bread.

"Nee. When *Ich* go out to make the *feier Ich* will show her then."

He took me out where the outdoor bake oven was. I sat way back where he put me while he made a roaring fire.

Ben come and stood by me and said, "It'll soon settle down into hot coals *un* then the *brodt* we'll put in. We'll go in *un* help carry the *brot* out. Carry your own loaf *du* will." As we went back to the house, this time instead of carrying me he stood me down next to him. Together we walked, my little hand swallowed up in his big one. Oh, how good and grown-up I felt. My insides was glowing from happiness. When we got to the porch steps he stepped behind me, took both my hands in his and holding 'em above my head he half-lifted me up as I climbed the steps one by one onto the porch. Heaven couldn't of been any better than this for I felt loved in a way like never before and I was accepted for just the way I was. I didn't have to be different around Ben, I could just be me. Oh, glory!

Mom and the Old Lady was ready for us. All this time Mom stayed quiet, said nothing. I think she was fearful I'd spoil things and she'd have to go back home to Grammy and Pap. My young mind saw this as her chance for adventure, to see new things and meet new people in spite of long hours and hard work waiting for her. She loved her mom and dad but she felt restricted being around her kin day in and day out. I was doing my best to please Mom, for her own good - and my mine, too.

Before I knowed it I was carrying my very own loaf pan, one arm wrapped around it so tight I could feel its rolled-under edge digging into my side beneath my dress. Ben held my free hand so I wouldn't trip on the hard-packed dirt path. They got the five remaining loaves to the big outside oven and Ben put them inside, laid mine in front and shut the door. After awhile the Old Lady come with her - I called it a shovel to get under the pans and straighten 'em out. I was sitting where Ben sat me. Leaning forward I peeked the far distance into the open oven and started counting, "One, two, three, four, five, six."

"*Ach, mei Gott!*" the Old Lady sputtered. "Why she can count, now ain't yet?"

I saw the corners of Ben's mouth turn up in a grin for already he knowed I could count from the baby pigs. Even Mom looked proud then.

After the Old Lady turned the loaves she come and sat down beside me till the baking was done. Mom went back to the kitchen to clean up.

When they was ready, my loaf come out first.

After my loaf cooled a bit the Old Lady knocked it outta the pan, tore too big a piece off, dipped it in the apple butter dish and shoved it in my mouth. So that's what *lottweirich* was! Sweet, sticky-brown, apple butter. It got all over my face, even up my nose. It tickled me and I giggled as I wiped it off, getting some on my hands and dress sleeves. The Old

Lady cleaned me up with a wet rag and dried me with her apron that covered her ample bosom and belly.

Mom woulda fussed something terrible if we'd of been at Grammy's, but here she said nothing. I come to understand she was under the Geesey's authority and figured she had no say of her own there so she stayed quiet in spite of wanting to scold me to no end. That'd come later. Right then she musta been worried I'd get spoiled and out of hand. She didn't take in the fact it was Ben and the Old Lady at the Geesey's, just like it was Grammy at the Farley's, giving me enough freedom to keep my strong, outgoing nature from becoming rebellious and outta hand.

That dear Old Lady. I can still see her nearly toothless smile that lit up her whole face. Almost ninety years later and I can still see her yet. Short and plump she was, so round in her middle and on down to her feet, each leg almost as big as me. It looked as if she fell she'd spring back up again - like those round plastic toys weighted in the bottom and filled with air in the top part that they make today, the kind that bounce back up when punched down. Her gray hair - what little there was of it - was pulled back in a bun. Her face had wrinkles galore all over, the skin lined and saggin' with years of hard work. Chin whiskers too. Long hairs growin' out her nose. And them brown, plaid felt slippers - never seen any other covering on her feet. Oh my, that dear Old Lady. I loved every inch of her and she loved me too. She always said of me, "This little girl'll go a long, long way, this little girl will now yet."

And here I am today now yet. I wonder so what the Old Lady'd say if she could talk to me after all these years.

Yes well, I never got to name the baby horse. Wasn't long till it got sold.

CHAPTER 8 - THE OLD LADY'S BREAD STORY

After we ate my loaf all, Ben went back outside to work. Mom had more work to do so the Old Lady took me aside, sat me next to her and told me this story about bread and the war.

"*Ich* always bake six loaves of *brodt* at a time. One day when *Ich* was bakin', two *menn* come around *un* smelled the *brodt*. They didn't leave till it was done, then dumped all but one loaf in a bag *un* went off."

"Oh, they was bad men!" I shuddered.

"*Nee, nee!*" she went on. "They wasn't bad," but more she wouldn't say.

I just couldn't get it in my head why she didn't think they was bad taking all the bread but one loaf. My Grammy Farley was generous to a fault and would give anything to anybody for the asking, but for someone to just up and take, why that was another matter. And my mom, now she woulda put up a terrible fuss, maybe beat 'em off.

Later that evening Mom milked, stored it in the springhouse and started making supper. I was sitting there on the floor rolling the marble with the sheep inside, rolling it back and forth, back and forth when all of a sudden I missed the Old Lady.

"Where'd the Old Lady get to?" I wanted to know.

"*Ich* guess *du* played her out this afternoon. *Du* was gabbin' too much *un* she got tired *un* had to go to *bedde*."

That was my mom for you. She blamed me for wearing the Old Lady out when more'n likely it was all the baking she done. But I didn't know that then, just accepted the guilt Mom plopped down on me.

I sighed. I was feeling bad about what I done to the Old Lady to make her so wore out; sat there thinking about her and her story. Ben was in his chair reading the newspaper while Mom got supper ready. I could tell he was studying me from behind his newspaper but I didn't let on.

"*Wass iss*? Are *du* got homesick for your Grammy *un* Pap?" he wondered.

I felt warm inside that he cared enough to ask after homesickness. You see, in my heart I knowed he loved me just as much as I loved him, but still I said nothing.

"*Ich* know *wass iss*," he went on. "Cookie, the *katz*, got your tongue."

Cookie was laying there and when Ben said her name, she went, "Meow".

It hit me then that the animals knowed when Ben was talking about them. They loved him too, just like me. I couldn't help it. I throwed back my head and laughed.

"*Nee*, by golly, *du* got your tongue now yet. Now, *wass iss*? Don't *du* feel *goot*?"

"Yes, but I'm thinkin'."

With a deep chortle he went on, "*Ach vell* now, if that ain't somethin'! *Du* thinkin'. It's *goot* somebody around here thinks, now ain't?"

Then we laughed together, but not Mom. She just kept fussing over supper.

Before we sat down to eat, Mom took supper upstairs to the Old Lady, so I went on to tell Ben about the Old Lady and her bread story.

"Did she also tell *du* that she'd hide some boys when *menn* like that come around?"

"No she didn't say that, she just said about the bread."

He told me then, "It'll be a long time before *du* can read that there, but that was when the Civil War was on. When them kind of *menn* - they was called foragers - come around they took whatever was in their path, whatever they thought they needed to help win the war, *un* especially *yung menn* if they thought they could fight. My momma didn't mind them takin' *brodt*, but boys too *yung* to fight was another thing."

That made me laugh and he wondered what I thought was funny. I told him about my uncles at home, how they'd fight, scrapping with each other till Pap Farley'd put his hand up and shake his finger. "Enough!" he'd say and that quick it was settled.

That made Ben laugh too, but he went on, "Wasn't nothin' funny about the war. Fightin' in the war was a different kind of fightin'. Brothers fightin' brothers to the end; soldiers always hungry. That *mann* took the *brodt* to feed 'em. When Sim Reichard comes around - that's my momma's *bruder,* he stops here every now *un* then - he can tell *du* about the war till *du* can read about it. He's a fine *alt* gentleman. He had his one eye shot out in the war *un* now he's got a glass eye."

Well, that got my attention and I wanted to hear more but by now Mom was back down and got out our supper on the table. While we ate there was no more story telling about the war or anything. It appeared disagreeable to Mom. As soon as supper was over Mom said, "*Ich* think it's time for *du* to go to *bedde.*"

Word soon got around that Estella Ann Farley was helping out at the Geesey farm and her little girl was there too. I overheard Mom tell Grammy that Ben appeared pleased with her work and he was telling this to everyone he knowed.

Ben, he was well thought of around them parts. People respected him for the capable way he worked his farm, his honest dealings, his true character. Quite a few got curious about what was going on out at the farm and the Old Lady got more than the usual visitors. Frank Weaver who owned the general store, one day stopped by. He was so taken up with me he told his wife, Laura, about this smart and purty, little girl at Ben's that sings so good. She wanted to see me, so, Frank brought his whole family to visit. Laura and Mom got to talking and come to be purty good friends, that is for the little Mom cared about making friends. Timmy and

I was of one age and I can remember how we'd sit on the floor and roll the glass marble with the sheep back and forth to each other. Poodle, he'd sometimes get between us and swat the marble with a paw. Timmy and I, we'd acted as if we was scolding Poodle while we laughed and chased after the marble, seeing' who could reach it first.

What happy memories!

CHAPTER 9 - POODLE

Poodle was a big, old woolly dog, mostly gray. His legs was spindly for what a fat body he had. He looked like a poodle but wasn't. That was just his name. Poodle was my companion at the Old Lady's. He took the place of my uncles who played with me at Grammy's. I was always chattering, mostly to Poodle cause he was my friend, always beside me with head cocked and ears perked up like what I was saying was real important. The big farm had people around now and then, but other times it could get lonely for a little girl that liked to talk. I loved Poodle.

The Old Lady told Mom, "Don't be scared about Alverna. Poodle kept other kids safe *un* he'll see Alverna through now yet, ain't Poodle?"

See, it didn't make any difference where I was, Poodle was with me. If Mom looked out and seen Poodle she knowed I was nearby. If she seen me, she knowed Poodle was nearby.

One of my chores after I got to the Old Lady's when I was still purty little was to clean the spittoon - smelly, miserable work if ever there was, but I done what I could to help Mom out. Besides, I liked being outdoors; so much to see. Sometimes I'd get side-tracked and forget what I was doing, then Mom, so provoked, would scold me good. I tried real hard to be good for Mom. She had a bigger load to carry with the Old Lady getting more wore out. Mom's work begun at sun-up and went most days till dark.

Most men chewed tobacco back then, spitting long trails of the foul-smelling, black juice across the room, sometimes hitting the spittoon, other times hitting the wall or the floor. The spittoons needed emptying too often to my way of thinking except that it got me outside where I loved to be the most. Mom would only have to look at me and point to the spittoon. I went for the rag hanging in the pantry, wrapped it around the big, brass container stained inside and out, and headed to the toe of the dam where the water ran in just a trickle. Poodle trotted along side of me. I dumped out the rancid tobacco remains, rinsed the spittoon out again and again till the water ran clean. Next I wiped the outside with the rag till the black come off and the shine come back. After that I hauled it back up the worn, dusty footpath to the house. There was so much to see and get into down there and I wanted to stay longer than Mom most times thought reasonable. She often accused me of being a troublesome child, but I did the best I could with my lively nature that longed to explore and check everything out.

I figured no matter how hard I tried, I'd never be good enough for Mom. I appeared to shame her, but I tried. Oh! How I tried to listen. The trouble was I didn't know what to change to make it better for her and for me. Nothing worked, nothing made it any better. I always fell short.

All the fowl had the run of the yard then, but it was the gander who lorded it over anything that got in his way. One day, two geese and the gander was nearby when I was heading down the footpath minding my own business on my way to clean the spittoon. For no reason I could gather they come after me. The gander lowered his head, stretched out his long neck, hissing and a going on something terrible; wings was spread out wide, flapping like crazy, feathers a flying everywhere. He come right up to me and grabbed the rag in his long beak. I tried to pull it away but he just kept shaking his head in all directions and wouldn't let go. I got scared and finally let loose since he was winning the tussle. I hollered, "The gander's making a snoot at me and I can't empty out the spittoon." Nobody heard me. No one except Poodle and he was as scared of the gander as me. I run from the gander, sat down under the weeping willow tree with the spittoon. Finally the big bird dropped the rag and waddled out of sight. After awhile I got brave enough to take the spittoon to empty and wash out. When I was done and looked up, here I spied a goose egg laying in the deeper water of the dam. I wanted that goose egg and I knowed I could get it by reaching into the water. It didn't look deep at all.

Mom warned me to stay away from the dam except at it's toe, but I wanted that egg. In my excitement I forgot what she said. I sat down the spittoon and marched to the water. Poodle saw what I had in mind so he come between me and the water. He pushed me back and wouldn't let me get near no matter how hard I tried. It was the only time I got mad at Poodle, tried to push him away, but he wouldn't let up.

When I tired of this, I gave up and took the spittoon and the rag back to the house. Mom had that look on her face that said I took too long, so while I was wiping tobacco remains off the wall and the floor with the wet rag, I told Mom about the goose egg.

The Old Lady was sitting in her favorite rocking chair and heard me say this. "*Ach, nee!* Poodle won't let *du* get close to the *wasser*. His job is to keep all kids away from the dam. He will look out for *du*. Poodle won't let nothin' bad happen to our little girl."

The Old Lady leaned heavy on one side of Mom and used her cane with a fancy carved handle Ben whittled for her to keep her balance as we walked back to the dam. So slow they made their way down the footpath while I skipped ahead and pointed the goose egg out. Mom fished it outta the water with a bent stick laying nearby and carried it back to the house in her apron.

When I seen how deep the water was from the stick, being mad at Poodle melted away. I learned Poodle was keeping me from falling in the water and maybe drowning. I loved Poodle all the more, if that was possible.

"*Du* know what Alverna?" cackled the Old Lady. "That egg's gonna be yours for breakfast tomorrow morning. *Du* will get the *oi* for sure!

I could see Mom's face fall but she covered up her disappointment real quick. It hit me she was hoping to use the big egg for something she had in mind; maybe cookies or a cake. But because the Old Lady said so, she made me the egg next morning under watchful eyes. As I was eating it, relishing every bite I could tell there was just maybe a little jealousy in Mom that it was me that got the egg and not her. But I reasoned in my head that Mom had plenty of eggs yet from the hens. But no way was I gonna bring it up to her face.

The Old Lady took pleasure in watching me eat the goose egg as much as I enjoyed eating it. I offered Mom and the Old Lady some but the Old Lady said no, it was only for me. That made Mom turn a bite down too.

It was the best egg ever. It sure filled me up full.

See, no words of that kind ever passed between us - some things just wasn't talked about - but the Old Lady seen how Mom could be towards me. She tried to soften my puzzled hurt by taking up for me, only without letting Mom know just what she was doing.

That Old Lady - she was such a grand Old Lady. And Ben - he was a wonderful good man - *allerbescht*!

The night after Mom retrieved the goose egg outta the dam, I was telling Ben how the gander and geese come after me.

"Maybe it was because *du* was gettin' too close to that *oi*," he suggested.

Ben, he helped me understand so much.

I don't know who enjoyed it most - Mom, Poodle or me. One thing the three of us loved to do together was blow bubbles. Mom didn't have much spare time, no one on a farm for that matter did. We all worked hard to make a go of it. Us Pennsylvania Dutch had hard work built into us. But once in a great while Mom would mix some water and homemade soap in the red rimmed granite wash basin. She'd sit me and the basin on the porch then plop down on the other side of the basin. With our feet dangling over the porch she'd hand me an empty wood spool, then dip one end of hers into the sudsy water. Lifting it to her mouth she blowed through the other end real slow and careful to make stream after stream of little bubbles that sparkled rainbows of colors as they floated off the porch. I watched, then dipped my spool and followed after Mom. Mom kept a clean wet rag next to her to wipe the soap that hit us in our eyes and stung like all get-out.

Now and then Mom said let's see who'd blow the biggest soap bubble. I wanted Mom to stay happy like she appeared then, so I blowed into my spool too fast so they'd come out small or break up before coming to be bubbles. Mom thought I was too dumb to slow down. She never knowed this was my way of letting her blow the biggest bubbles and making her happy, being the winner and all.

Poor Poodle! He'd stand on his long, skinny legs, cock his head in puzzlement as he watched the bubbles come outta the spools. In no time he'd swat after them with his forepaw, then jump back in surprise when they'd break. Mom and me, we laughed at the way Poodle looked.

Them was good times the three of us had together.

I loved it so much at the big farm. It was home to me when I was there just like Grammy and Pap Farley's was home to me when I was with them.

One wonderful good thing was in my favor. Since Mom was at the farm, Grammy was more open with me when I was at her place. Hugged me more often, smiled more, opened up and told me stories I never tired listening to. So many there was. Yep, it was as if Grammy was free from some past sadness that no longer had her tied down. It not only freed Grammy up, it gave me time to be myself without being afraid of Mom's constant disapproval.

See, I knowed Ben and the Old Lady loved me, but I seen they kept a certain distance about my liveliness unless Mom was out milking. Then they got a kick outta my noisy pleasure and delight in simple things and didn't think wrong of me to be so full of life. But they seen Mom didn't like it so much. They wondered if she might take it out on me behind their backs. With Grammy and Ben and the Old Lady loving me the way they done, I knowed that there couldn't be all of me that was naughty and not fit for nothing. They made me feel I was worth something and kept me on the right track. Besides, it gave me a little bit of hope that someday Mom would love me like that.

Poodle and I was sitting on the farmhouse porch to play with stones I collected. It was an Indian Summer day when the beautiful colors of the leaves was peaked. My heart was content. There wasn't a happier child in the whole, wide world.

Poodle was snoozing when Ben come from cleaning the stable; hot and dirty he was, all covered over with sweat. Watching him walk towards me, he seen me sitting there and I noticed a smile come over him that lit his whole face. An idea come to him, I could tell. I just didn't know what the idea was, but I seen it just then pop into his head. When he snapped his fingers, that told me something good was about to happen.

"*Du chust* stay here *un vait* now yet. I'll be back in a *minutt*," he said so jolly.

That woke up Poodle. He made sure I wasn't moving off the porch, then shut his eyes again.

There I sat and waited for whatever Ben had in store for us. It'd be a wonderful good adventure, that I knowed.

Ben come back down the path with two long rye straws from his rye crop. Climbing up the porch steps, he pulled a chair over and stood me on it next to the cider barrel. Poodle lay his fore paws on the chair seat trying to take it all in. Handing me a rye straw Ben told me to lean over, stick the straw in the cider and suck.

"Are *du* suckin' through this now yet?" he asked.

We didn't have to wait long till I got the hang of it. When that wonderful good cider hit my tongue, I nodded and sucked away. When he seen I was getting cider, he stuck his rye straw in and joined me. There was the two of us drinking cider and laughing at ourselves when Mom heard this commotion and come out from the kitchen to see what was going on. She stood there at the screen door, wiping her sopping wet hands on the wrap-around apron that protected her dress from the stove that spattered grease all over her as she fixed the meals.

I can see her now. So resentful she come across. With hands on hips, she tried to stare us down. Ben and me, we kept the straws in our mouths and our eyes on the cider barrel. When she seen we wasn't payin' her no mind, she shook her head in aggravation and warned Ben right off, "If that girls poops herself, *du* will be the one to clean her now yet!"

Ben, wiping cider off his chin with his big, red hanky looked at me. "*Du* won't poop in your pants, will *du*?"

Not ever wanting to do anything that went against his grain, I said, "No, I'll go to the privy."

We'll *chust* see *onct* now yet!" Mom protested as she turned and stomped back to her work.

After we was clear of Mom, Ben took his rye straw outta the barrel and *spritzed* me with cider, then Poodle. We laughed. Poodle yelped. I tried to *spritz* Ben back but got more on Poodle than him. Before we headed back into the house to face Mom, Ben took me around to the back where there was a pump for water. He filled the dented, old wash basin that hung on a long, rusty nail on the back porch wall and cleaned us up real good before we went in for supper. When he was done with us he throwed the basin of water over Poodle. The poor dog yowled and shook all over.

My-oh-my, what fun me and Ben had! Ben made me feel safe in ways that nobody else come close to doing. I loved everybody in my big family, but him, he never caused discord

93

(well, maybe only once or twice), and that made me love him all the more. Where others spoke in ways I couldn't figure out, Ben always made it plain for me. He made life good. Grammy and the Old Lady and Poodle come in next. They helped me to understand the Good Man who lived in heaven better. Lots of folks went to church, read their Bibles and quoted from it but come across so stern and strict, never much happy nor getting any pleasure outta their days, judging others in ways that wasn't very nice. Was this the kind of little girl the Good Man wanted me to be?

Then there was Ben, Grammy, the Old Lady and Poodle who enjoyed who they was and looked for good in things; took pleasure in life, they did. I leaned towards their ways, striving to be good and happy, living the way they done.

Now take Mom. She was strict with me but I loved her just because she was Mom. She worked hard all her life. Seldom did she relax and let go just a little. Too much she seemed so sad and somber, rigid, unbending. I just couldn't figure out why.

Oh, when I just think of it - how pieces of Mom's anger fell into place as time went on and I understood better.

Mom never left me get close when she was making lye soap, all the ingredients coming right off the farm. She got real crotchety then, afraid I'd get burned from the lye. I stood at the far end of the kitchen with Poodle laying next to me. We watched as she heated the lard and strained it through cheesecloth laying over a crock to get all the fryin's out. She mixed the lye with cold water in a big kettle, then real slow tipped the edge of the crock that held the cooled-but-not-yet-hard lard into the lye water. Mom stirred it with a wood paddle with holes to get it good and mixed. Ben made that paddle special for her to stir till it was ready to be poured into molds. It took forever for Mom to do the stirring. If she accidentally splashed some, or get her fingers against that mixture while she poured and stirred, they'd blister and burn, look sore and ugly for days.

One time she was stirring away and got distracted. When she come back to stir, the water had all come to the top and everything else got hard underneath. She couldn't throw this stuff away so she had to work it and pound it to get it to come out right. By the time she was done she was wet all over with sweat, so wore out she swore it'd never happen again. It didn't, either.

I stayed back then, was real quiet. Didn't move. I didn't want Mom taking it out on me - or Poodle.

CHAPTER 10 - THE OLD LADY

One afternoon when I was at the farm, a rainstorm come up. Real quick! The weather was terrible with lightning that wouldn't stop flashing, and thunder that kept rolling on and on. Mom was cooking supper when Ben hurried in, water running off his wide-brimmed straw hat, clothes soaked clear through. He looked a fright. He told Mom to put everything away quick and to keep away from the stove.

"*Ich* don't want *du* usin' no knives, no forks, no nothin' as long as this storm is on."

I seen that Ben had a special affection for Mom. He was kind and gentle, never asked more of her than what they talked over when she first come to the farm.

When the Old Lady heard Ben say that, why she got even scareder than she was before - and she was always scared outta her wits when it come to thunderstorms. Right away she jumps outta her rocker faster than I ever woulda believed she could, grabs me, then half-carrying, half-pulling me she moves towards the stair steps using all of what little strength she had. When it dawned on me what she was doing I went along with it so I wouldn't wear her out too bad. We got inside the stairwell and she slammed shut the stair door. Outta breath and panting hard, she hauled me on her lap and shook with fear as she heaved her apron over our heads to cover us - from what I couldn't imagine because already we was in total darkness, darkness you could even feel, if that's possible. Outside it was storming all get-out. We could feel the damp from the storm pushing in against us hard, even feel the deep, thick, wet darkness behind the door. Between all that and the Old Lady squeezing me, I couldn't hardly breathe. She held me tight as she shivered and shook from fright, her breath coming fast from rushing in on the steps and from fear. Her heart was thumping through her chest hard and quick as she held me tight against her. The only way I knowed to calm her down was to pat her hands as she continued to squeeze me till my insides hurt. The Old Lady, although she was the one that hated and feared the thunder and lightning, made out like she was protecting me, that I was the one who was scared. Only it was her all along.

When the storm was over we come out. Ben scolded his Mom in Dutch for that's what they always talked between them. *"Mudder, Ich* don't want *du* to act like that. *Chust* listen now yet! If the forces of nature is supposed to get *du*, why they can strike *du chust* as quick in there on the steps."

But she couldn't see that. Little as I was, I wasn't dumb. I knowed what she was up to and I played along with her because I didn't wanna make her feel worse after Ben's scolding. I stood right by her and held onto her - my small arms stretching partway - that was as far as I could get 'em - around her oversize waist until her shivers left up.

After all that then, Ben told me what this lightning was and what this thunder was. "A *Goot Mann* lives in *himmel un* uses the clouds for his chariot to ride over the skies. Every *onct* in a while he has to use his whip *un* that makes the thunder. *Ich* read about that in the *Goot Buch*," he assured me. "And the *goot* prophet Isaiah predicted that someday the Lord will come in his chariots like a stormwind."

It was still raining yet but the sun come out. Ben took me to the door looking for a rainbow. "The *Goot Mann* shoots his arrows and that makes the colors of the rainbow."

This wonderful man would explain things to me so I could reason them out in my mind and understand. It made everything all right with me.

Some people believed playing cards was the devil at work. They wouldn't touch cards, frowned on them who did. On a rare evening when Mom was done her work, she and the Old Lady and Ben played cards then. Casino, mostly.

I'd sit between Ben and the Old Lady on a chair stacked high with pillows. The Old Lady let me hold the cards they didn't need right then. "*Ach vell* now, don't bend 'em," Mom would warn me. You could hear the threat in her voice.

I wouldn't.

The Old Lady, she'd look at what cards I was holding and whisper what was what, only her voice wasn't quiet, she just didn't realize how loud she spoke. It provoked Mom cause they wasn't supposed to know what was in there but she said nothing. I seen how Mom felt about this. I didn't want her to be mad at me, so during times when it was just me and the Old Lady before supper, I'd get the cards, sit with her and go over 'em. I soon learned them and the Old Lady didn't have to tell me no more. She'd pat me on the shoulder. "*Ach*, such a smart girl. *Du* will go a long, long, way. *Ya, du* will."

That way Mom wasn't so provoked when they played real card games. I was secretly pleased that I kept Mom from getting mad at me.

One Sunday evening - well, the Old Lady didn't like that they'd play cards on a Sunday. Any other time she said ok, but she refused to join in and play on Sundays. This one Sunday evening Ben talked her into it. Grudgingly she did. They was playing Casino.

After awhile, without no warning, we heard noise out on the porch. We thought at first it was one of the Heindels or some other neighbor stopping by to visit. The Heindels spent a lot of time at the farm. They lived just one farm over. Mom'd get so put out with 'em. She said they talked about nothing but money. It worked on her nerves.

Only this wasn't the Heindels. It was a strange sound. One we never heard the likes of before. Didn't sound human. More like a four-footed beast. We heard this at the door like it was trying to open it but couldn't.

Poodle was laying at our feet. He stayed put, didn't get up and go to the door with a welcoming bark like he always done when company'd come. He growled like I never heard before - a low, ominous snarl, not like Poodle at all. We looked down at him and seen his kinky, wooly hair stand straight out - something we never before seen from Poodle. The growl turned to a frightened whimper; he put his forepaws over his eyes like he was scared beyond belief, shying away from who or what was out there.

We looked at each other. Mom and the Old Lady was puzzled, then alarmed. This wasn't no neighbor out there. I sensed danger and got scared too. Never before did I quiver with such dread. How can I explain it? I felt in the air something evil, something wicked coming to get us. Goosebumps come all over me, the hairs at my neck stuck straight out as if they was electrified.

Didn't appear to bother Ben. At least he didn't let on it did. "*Kumme* on in, " he hollered. Footsteps on the porch again. Footsteps like we never before heard. Shuffling at the door.

But no one come in.

We wondered so what was going on, growing more anxious by the second. The Old Lady begun shuddering. Mom, scared stiff as all get-out, was trying to calm her but not too much doing a good job.

Ben was agitated, told us to calm down. "Somebody's playin' a joke," he went. He pushed back his chair. I was glad he was so big a man for I was sure his size would scare anyone off. Yet I was nervous for him. I didn't want nothing to get him.

He went to the door, looked out, didn't see nobody or nothing. He started outside. Mom's muffled voice was quaking. She warned him not to go. He hushed her up, went out the door. We listened to his footsteps as he walked around the porch, then stepped down into the yard. Then we couldn't hear nothing. We looked at each other. Was he was gonna walk down to the spring house and barn and look around? We all just wanted him to come back inside.

We was so afraid. Who was out there? At first we just sat motionless. Then the Old Lady come to life and started to gather up the cards. Mom caught on to what she was doing and helped. She moved fast, but when she got hers together her hands shook so bad she dropped them and hadda start all over again. I pushed the ones in front of me over to the Old Lady.

When footsteps was again heard on the porch it was Ben. Come back in he did. "Nothin' out there. No footprints, no nothin'. Musta been the wind."

"*Ach, nee.* It's an evil sign, a bad omen. *Ich* told *du* playin' cards on Sunday ain't right. Ben, put them cards away right now or somethin' bad's gonna happen," the Old Lady squawked.

Ben didn't argue. Didn't agree, but done what his mom said.

We never did find out what it was all about. We didn't never play cards no more on Sundays. Not never again.

This is the way it was: I'd go back and forth, back and forth between Grammy and Pap Farley's and the Geesey farm. Wasn't long that the Old Lady was growing more feeble. She couldn't hardly get around no more which meant Mom was working harder'n ever. An old upholstered rocking chair that worked like a glider with springs and coils that moved back and forth smooth as butter, was at the end of the kitchen set up for the Old Lady to spend her days. Next to it was a good-sized table with socks to be darned, clothes to be mended, thread or coarse yarn to crochet with, things like that to occupy herself if she felt strong enough and wanted to. Ben laid his newspaper and almanac there when he was done reading 'em, but about all she could see was the big headlines. Mostly she sat and rocked and watched Mom keeping busy and me learning to take on more chores or playing with the big glass marble. Poodle laid by her when he could keep both of us in sight. She seemed content most of the time, only once in a while she'd complain that she was a nuisance and why didn't God take her since she wasn't no good for nothin'. Mom just clucked her tongue. Ben scolded her when she talked like that, and while I wasn't altogether sure what she meant, I'd pay her extra mind to try to keep her happy so she wouldn't go away with God or anyone else.

When her girls and their families come to visit the Old Lady - which wasn't too often - they'd bring real homemade candy from The Prowell's Candy Kitchen. Besides them treats, Mom made sure there was plenty for the Old Lady to snack on; there was baked goods and sweets of all kinds. Her favorite was Molasses Pie. See, after Mom was done making pies, she took the leftover pie dough, slabbed it with butter then poured molasses over, rolled it up, sprinkled cinnamon on top and sliced it to bake along with her pies. The Old Lady'd pop a piece of the sweet, sticky crust in her mouth, the molasses dripping off the crust onto her fingers or her favorite shawl she had wrapped around her. Mom wouldn't say nothing to her about it, just take the wet rag laying next to the Old Lady and wipe away the molasses wherever it landed. It was a balm to my tender soul to see Mom and the way she showed kindness to the Old Lady. It was more'n she showed most people.

How I longed for Mom to be kind to me like that, gentle instead of rough. How I ached to get a kiss or hug from Mom.

Was too much to expect from her, it was.

Mom always had something simmering on a back burner of the cook stove, the wonderful smell traveling all through the house. No one never come that wasn't offered some of what was in the big kettle. Didn't get turned down much that I remember.

Young as she was, Mom gained good standing for the exceptional way she done things - especially her cooking, but cleaning and washing and other things too.

Black was creeping up the Old Lady's feet and legs as she sat there day after day. When they got the doctor out once, he seen the sweets but never so much as hinted to Mom that maybe the Old Lady should cut back on 'em. Later Mom wondered if it wasn't diabetes the Old Lady was suffering from along with her other ailments and why didn't the doctor say something. Mom hadn't thought it through earlier cause she was busy just keeping after what needed done with milking and taking care of the house and garden.

I was devoted to the Old Lady and spent as much time by her chair as Mom allowed. Poodle laid next to her rocking chair but was always alert to both me and the Old Lady. You'd never think so, so quiet he was, but just let one of us move and right up he got. It was getting harder for him, too. He was growing old, just like the Old Lady.

The Old Lady enjoyed when Poodle and me was with her. Before, she had such a busy life that filled almost every hour of her day. Now her days drawed out. She got discouraged by her failure to keep after. I tried to give her back what she was missing by talking to her about what was going on outside, and showing her my picture books Ben had got for me. I made up my own stories from the pictures when they was too hard for me to read. She minded but tried not to show it when Mom *shussed* me away from her chair.

See, Mom accused me of wearing the Old Lady out. Not only that but she blamed me for eating her candy. (I seen Mom more'n once help herself to that candy when the Old Lady was in bed, but I never did. Wouldn't of dared. Even still, the Old Lady never minded one bit who helped themselves to what was hers.) Of course Mom never said any of this in front of the Old Lady. Believe you me, them sweets was tempting as all get-out, but much as I wanted to, I never touched 'em unless the Old Lady pushed some on me. She knowed I liked sweets as much as she did, and she had me take my fill when Mom wasn't watching us too close. I trained myself to not never reach after any without permission.

Eventually the Old Lady got so sick they hadda put her to bed. The stair doors was kept open so we could hear when the Old Lady needed something. Every now and then she'd call downstairs, "Al - wer - nee! Fetch me some *wasser.*"

My legs was too short to climb the dark, steep, narrow stairway yet, but Mom took a dented old tin cup - the Old Lady's favorite - and she'd go to the pump at the sink and fill it half full of clear, cold water that was pumped in right from the spring. She showed me how to take it up the steps. Each step was narrow front to back, and steep up and down, so the only way I'd get up to the Old Lady was to sit and lean against the back of the step and push myself up one step at a time. I'd sit the tin cup one step up for that was only how high I could reach. Though there was hardly nothing for me to hold on to, step by step I moved myself and the cup up till I made it to the top. When I got there and looked down at how high and steep I just finished climbing I couldn't hardly believe I done it on my own. So's not to get dizzy and topple down I'd crawl away from the top stair step as fast as I could, then reach for the cup of water to take to the Old Lady.

Mom warned me each time before I'd set out, but not loud enough for the Old Lady to hear, "Don't *du* dare tire her out now yet or I'll learn *du* a thing or two!" I listened to Mom cause I knowed I was in for it if I didn't. Mom was strict, a whole lot stricter than Ben or the Old Lady.

Into her room I'd walk, feeling so proud inside, so happy to stand on tip-toe and stretch out my arms to hand the Old Lady her tin cup of water. Then, real quiet I'd crawl onto the chair next to the bed so Mom wouldn't hear any scraping noise below to make her think I was bothering the Old Lady.

After taking the cup in shaky hands she'd sip it greedily; most of the water run down the creases at the corners of her mouth, down her neck and onto her flannel nightie and the bed clothes if I didn't get the rag fast enough there to wipe it.

"*Ach vell*, it tastes so *goot!*" she'd say.

I'd wrap her worn, black shawl tighter around her shoulders to keep the chill away. We'd sit and talk a little bit, then her eyes would shut and her head would slump back on her pillow. I'd lean over quiet as could be, take the cup away and brush the hair - what little she had - outta her eyes. Mom took time to comb back the Old Lady's hair but *rootchy* she'd get, then the pins loosened and tumbled out. In no time her thin, *strubbley* hair fell down onto her face and into those dark, twinkling eyes that was getting covered over just like Pet's. When I first looked in her eyes I could see Ben belonged to her because his was the same - twinkling with merriment no matter what was going on right then and there. I didn't dare hug her like I wanted, she looked too poorly, but I laid my little hands over her cold, blue, swollen, liver-spotted ones, patting and rubbing them gently to warm them with the tender affection I felt towards her.

Even as little as I was I could see the change, how drawn and gray was her face, her eyes hollow and sunken with black circles, her skin hanging loose, the red and black blotches on her arms and hands that was always cold, how her body didn't work no more like it used to.

I'd sneak back downstairs - going down was just as hard as climbing up - so's not to wake her up.

This I did whenever she called. I loved her and wanted to help her and Mom however I could.

One day then, Grammy and Pap come in the wagon to fetch me back home with them.

Before I went I asked Mom, "Who'll see the Old Lady gets water when I'm gone?" Mom said Ruby Heindel was coming for a couple days to help out, and between 'em they'd take care of her.

My uncles was sure happy to see me again and prodded me about happenings on the farm. At times it seemed there was people around a lot, yet hard work from morning to night had a peculiar way of keeping us isolated at other times, so any kind of news beyond our own stoop was welcomed. After my uncles got what they wanted outta me, Purd, who was mostly ignored by his older brothers, he'd get me to pay attention to him and because I pitied him, I would. He liked to lord it over me, letting me know that he was older; bossed me around whenever we was together. I mostly let him.

Aunt Lilliemae, friendly and happy-go-lucky, didn't have much to do with me just then cause she was taking an interest in young men. Most of all I loved to be near Grammy and help her when she'd let me. It seemed I was there longer'n normal, but one dreary, rainy Saturday afternoon, Mom and Ben come and got me. It didn't seem so dreary anymore when I seen Ben.

When I walked into the farmhouse, first thing I seen the stair door was shut. I went right away to open it, standing on my tiptoes, reaching for the glass door knob and asking, "Why is that door shut? If the Old Lady calls we can't hear her."

Mom and Ben looked at one another so quizzical when I questioned them. They didn't know how to tell me, so Mom said just like that, and I can hear her now, "*Ach vell* now, the Old Lady ain't here no more."

"Where is she?" I asked not believing.

"She died *un* we buried her yesterday."

Just like that she said it.

I couldn't hardly take in what Mom was saying, but that was my mom for you, getting right to the point. Mom never taught me about things, just blurted 'em out as they happened. I didn't know for sure what she meant, just that something was terrible wrong. The Old Lady wasn't here.

Here, what happened, Mom and Ben had put me at Grammy's so I wouldn't be around when the Old Lady died.

Now don't get me wrong; little as I was I had went with Grammy a many a time to the cemetery where she fixed up a grave here and a grave there, and I knowed people was buried there but I couldn't get it in my head about it cause I never seen nobody die. Our elders just took those things as they happened, almost never talked 'em over that youngsters understood, didn't even talk about 'em when we was around. Little kids growed up learning about these things only if they was smart enough to pay attention or if they was directly involved.

Well then, anyway, Ben said to me, "Are *du* remember when she picked *du* up off the floor and hid in the stairs when the storms hit? Remember when *Ich* told du about the thunder?"

"Yes, I remember. That was the Good Man driving his chariot over the sky."

"*Ya, vell* now, the *Goot Mann* has got my momma. He's got my momma right now."

"If he's got her, why'd they put her under the ground?"

Not understanding dying, it hurt me so bad. That was the hardest thing in the world for me to understand. Questions flooded my mind. I didn't understand yet that dead meant never coming back again. I wondered so if she was afraid being all alone in the grave, or if she'd be able to come outta the ground when she woke up. Ben went on to tell how it says in the *Goot Buch* that when *du* are absent from the body *du* are present with the Lord, and that meant her body was put in a coffin and buried in the grave and she wouldn't never come back, not ever again. Then he went on to tell me that her soul, the part of her that loved me and him and Mom, the part that thinks and talks and feels was the part of his momma that went to *himmel* with the *Goot Mann*.

I broke down then. I cried and cried. Great big sobs took away my breath. I couldn't help it. It was like I got hit in my stomach and all the air was blown outta me. My heart was broken. Here I come back to the Old Lady's and she was gone. I just couldn't take it all in. She should be here with us, not with the Good Man in heaven. It was like I lost a part of myself. Why did the Good Man take the Old Lady? I bawled till Mom and Ben got scared I'd get sick.

"Now don't cry," Ben begged. "Tomorrow we'll hook Pet up *un* the buggy. Then we'll go *un* show *du* where we buried her."

I sat and hugged Poodle who looked like he was sad and lonely too. And old.

After I got done crying, the pain in my heart was so deep I couldn't eat supper. For the first time in my life I didn't wanna talk. I needed more details but knowed none would be in the offing, so I just shut down in misery. After Mom put me to bed I couldn't sleep even though I was tireder than ever before. I was confused. I wondered if it was my fault. Did they send me away because I was bad and made the Old Lady sick? Was I troublesome and wore the Old Lady out like Mom said? I got cross at myself; maybe it was my fault she died. If I'd of listened more to Mom maybe the Old Lady'd still be here. Why couldn't I do things right?

I hoped the Old Lady knowed I loved her and that I didn't run away when she needed me. They made me go to Grammy and Pap Farley's. It was their fault. If they'd of left me stay and take her water and sit with her the Old Lady'd still be here. She'd still be alive.

It was on a Sunday when we got to the cemetery. I saw this mound of new ground where the Old Lady was buried. It started way down deep inside and come up, a cry of anguish and despair. I began to blubber. Inside me was a confused and somber heart, a shattered spirit. Ben begun to snivel as he picked me up and that started Mom off. Yes, not even Mom with the hard, sharp edges she put around her heart to keep the world out could hold back the tears. And my-oh-my, how I sobbed. We all stood by the grave and cried. It was better we cried together because then I knowed they was hurting, too, just like I was hurting. I felt a bit kinder towards Mom instead of letting my thoughts be so harsh towards her, even when I loved her so much.

On the ride back to the house my imagination went to work and I figured even though Ben said she wouldn't, maybe the Old Lady'd come back again. Day after day I watched and looked for her, but she never did.

After a while Mom told me I better not take advantage of the Old Lady dying to make people feel sorry for me. She accused me of being lazy and stubborn. That was because I tried to shut off my feeling's and cried only on the inside. It didn't work. I was hurting so bad from the Old Lady not being around anymore, and now more'n ever I wanted Mom's approval.

Something deep inside said I'd probably never get it; didn't keep me from trying. See, I always had this little bit of hope she'd change and love me.

CHAPTER 11 - ESTELLA AND BEN

We went back to the house after we come from the cemetery. Two of Ben's nephews, Chance - that was John and Lola's boy, along with Howard who was Al and Annmarie's son, come from town and was milling around there, not knowing where we had went. They got tired of waiting around and was in one of the Konhaus's fancy buggy, just then pulling out.

Chance hollered, "We're leaving Uncle Ben, but you're gonna get more company after a little."

"*Ich* thought that much," Ben said but he didn't explain.

Over that it wasn't long till two of the Konhaus girls came down, Lillie and Stella.

"Uncle Ben, you're in for it. We're here and we're gonna do all we can to help and see you through. You're in for it, you know."

"*Ich* expected that much," was all he said.

"We know things are gonna be rough, but we're here to help you out. We don't want you to have to sweat it out alone."

That was all that was said. I had no idea what this ruckus was all about, but with the Konhaus and Miller kids coming around, it was easy to see something was going on, I just didn't know what.

It wasn't long till a buggy come with two of Ben's sisters, Annmarie and Lola. I was sticking with my mom. The surprising thing was she didn't push me away like sometimes. Lola come right over and stood by Mom. Lola was always the friendly one, real kind and ladylike. She knowed more hurt than some, so she understood what Mom was in for.

There wasn't many people Ben didn't like or get along with, but one he disliked awful much was Lola's husband,

109

John. He owned a cigar shop like Al but added a fancy gift shop with all sorts of things that went with cigars or any kind of tobacco: ash trays of colored glass, brass or tin, little ones and big; ash tray stands of brass and wood; swanky cigar and cigarette holders, plain and fancy match holders, cheap and high-priced spittoons, tobacco tins, pouches, you name it, he had it. Cigars and their accessories was big business with the good limestone soil all around to grow tobacco in. His was a thriving business where local folks earned extra money. He bought the things they carved, stitched or hammered to sell in his shop, but only if it was the best quality. The blacksmith was good at fashioning spittoons out of brass and other metals he had on hand.

John bought these things dirt cheap and shipped them all over the country pulling in big profits for hisself, all the time making people believe he was doing them a big favor, paying 'em not nearly as much as he shoulda for their top-notch work. That's what vexed Ben so much. Seldom did he come down hard on other people but Ben held that against John, also called him a lady's man, said that one of his many shortcomings was droolin' over anyone in a skirt. John paid more attention to other women than his own wife. Folks all over the county was familiar with John's weakness with women. It shamed Lola to no end. This didn't sit good with Ben. He owned up that his sister lacked for nothin' in material things but knowed for sure that she wasn't happy, reason bein' her husband didn't treat her right.

Lola, she thought she was getting the best of all worlds when she married John, but after a couple years of marriage with as many kids as years, things went from bad to worse. It was hard for the family to swallow when they seen how John made fun of his wife in a sneaky sort of way. His words carried double meanings, so if it was brought to his attention that maybe he was hurting his wife by such talk, he raised his eyebrows in mock surprise and assured everyone around that he was truly being misunderstood.

Ha! The only person he had fooled was hisself.

In time this wore Lola down to a frazzle. When John seen she was ready to break down from the heartless way he mortified her, that quick he'd turn around and act nice and lovey. He'd indulge her with expensive jewelry or send her on a shopping spree to convince her just how good he was to her. He finagled her into thinking that she hurt his feelings to think such mistaken things about him. It was at times like that Lola doubted herself, got confused and thought maybe she was going mad. Could John be so revolting as she'd think him to be, then turn around and act like a generous, loving provider? Was she making too much of what she thought was his cruel behavior towards her?

Ben compared this heartbreak to a man danglin' a carrot in front of his donkey to get it to do what he wanted, but never the donkey gettin' the carrot.

Everyone who loved Lola felt downright helpless. She was in a bad way, but no one could prove - or depending on who it was, didn't want to - just how wrong John treated his wife.

It was almost unheard of for a woman to divorce her man, but once when Lola was at the end of her rope and went to talk to a lawyer, John got wind of it (probably from the lawyer) and showed just how dangerous, controlling and hateful he was. Having no regard for Lola's feelings he threatened her, warned her he'd do something to her she wouldn't like if she ever tried anything like that again. Hinted there was no telling what might happen to her, and maybe she'd never see her kids again; went on to say it was hard to tell what might happen to them too.

Lola stopped fighting. Too afraid she was. She accepted her lot and did the best she could.

It was understood that some family members - no one ever mentioned names, too risky for them brave souls, it was - tried to help Lola out but soon come to see how John had his bases covered. The Justice of the Peace, lawyers, police, magistrates, any kind of legal help wasn't available when it was sought after. Why wouldn't they help?

111

Everyone in the family, much to their sadness, come to understand what a powerful person John Miller was, how he used that power for evil instead of good. It come to be knowed that John Miller wasn't above hurting anybody who got in his way.

None of Lola's family was a match for him, not even Al Konhaus. They come to see that John believed he had a right to anything he wanted and he'd get it no matter what it took. Oh, John could hide that part of him real good. He came off smooth and charming when it suited him. He appeared above reproach first off, fooled a lot of people with his deceit - even people that shoulda knowed better. When the tables turned and they got burned by his evil misdeeds, only then did them folks keep away from John Miller. Even with his corrupt reputation, no one appeared able to stop him. Common knowledge was that certain folks was either scared of John Miller or was working for him. Lola hadda live with that all her life after he showed his true colors. She put up a good front for many a year - to protect her kids, she'd say to Ben. He was the only one she trusted enough to talk to without it getting back to John.

Yep, but the day come when the outwardly wonderful John Miller finally got what some said was coming to him, what he deserved. If John woulda used his smarts for good, it coulda been a lot better for everybody in the county.

Annmarie and Lola was different as could be even though they was sisters. (When I growed up and understood Lola's situation I often thought maybe it shoulda been Annmarie married to John. They probably woulda done each other in soon after the marriage and saved everybody a lot of heartache.)

Anyway, Lola stood with Mom while Annmarie stayed away from them and hauled in on Ben about him and Mom living in the house now that the Old Lady was gone. She raved and carried on so, insisted Estella hadda leave this very day. I seen her fuss before, but this was more'n all that. She stewed something terrible. I got upset because this fussing had to do with the two people I loved most, my mom and Ben.

"What are you gonna do now? To have two young people like you living together, you know how people'll talk. What will they think?" Annmarie wanted to know.

"Ya, un verdammit!"

Well! I was almost shocked outta my britches! I never before ever heard Ben say a bad word. On rare occasions I heard my uncles say that word when Pap Farley wasn't nearby, but they'd wouldn't of dreamt of saying it when he - or anybody else - was around. This strong talk meant things was not good, but I had no idea why. I remained quiet, trying to sort this out.

"Since that new preacher come to town, everything's gotta go for him, now ain't? He don't think about nobody else or anything else. That's what I think about him *un* the town gossips!" Ben said not in the gentle, jovial way I come to know Ben.

Then his niece, Stella began, "Uncle Ben, I said we're gonna stay here so you're not alone."

"Ya? Vell now, *chust du vait*! What are *Ich* supposed to do?" Ben went on, gettin' agitated beyond reason, his big round face gettin' redder and redder by the minute. He was good at stayin' self-controlled, a virtue he prized, but now his self-control was worn thin.

"Are *Ich* supposed to choke her off now after all these months she was here doin' all this work?"

Now it was Lillie's turn. "Uncle Ben, I told you we're gonna stick by you while the going is rough. If that means that one of us has to stay with you until you get somebody to do the work, we will."

It appeared to me that Stella and Lillie was standing up against their mom.

"My," I thought. "What brave girls to speak up against their momma's rage." My respect for them swelled greatly.

Annmarie butted in, ranted and raved on and on but couldn't get nowhere with Ben. Lola just stood by Mom like she was protecting her. Of course I didn't know what this was all about, but right then and there I loved Lola even more.

Didn't have much affection for Annmarie though.

Finally Annmarie said, "Well, something's gotta be done and we're not leaving here until it's settled!"

"Ok," said Ben with a matter-of-fact shrug. *"Du kumme* down, Annmarie *un* do the milkin'. *Du* work at all the stuff she done. Then she can go."

Ben wasn't no dummy. Annmarie thought herself a lady of refinement and high society and wouldn't of thought about coming back to the farm to do that kind of work. Ben knowed for sure she'd never come back. Never! Annmarie thought she was a lady.

Huh! She sure wasn't acting very classy that day. Too bad she couldn't see herself for what she was.

People like that never do.

Nothing was said for a bit.

Annmarie got madder. Walking back and forth, stamping her foot, huffing and puffing she went on. "This isn't right, Ben. People will talk."

Clinging to my mom's leg, I wondered what was so important for people to be talking about. Mom was distracted. She didn't even seem to know I was there.

Ben got madder, red-faced, sweating something terrible in the Sunday clothes he wore to the cemetery.

"Un du, Annmarie, *du* will be the first to talk!"

Annmarie didn't like that. She turned to Lola. "Lola, come here," she fussed. "We can't get no headway here."

Lola, lady-like, calm and quiet - now there was a real lady - said something to her brother that I couldn't make out.

Ben just said, "That's up to her," and pointed to my mom. "If she wants to stay, she stays. *Ich* don't give a *verdammit* what anybody else thinks!"

Just that way he said it.

"If not," he said more calm and resigned as he pointed to Lillie and Stella, "*Du* two can stay *un* do the work."

Mom stood there like a *dumpkoff*. She didn't know right what to do or say. But then Lillie and Stella, they talked with Mom.

"Estella, Grandma always thought a lot of you. You know the ropes and everything. Please don't make us stay here alone because we don't know about milking or anything."

"All right," Mom said. "I'll stay. At least I'll stay till *du* can get somebody if *du* want me to."

"That's all *Ich* wanna know," said Ben.

Lola and Annmarie went and the two girls stayed.

Ben and Mom took me over to Pap Farley's again and told them all about it.

I overheard Mom say to Grammy that she knowed Lillie and Stella didn't intend in the first place to stay there alone and do that hard work now yet. They wouldn't know where to start, not being raised to do it.

Still, I didn't know the gist of what was going on, only that bad feelings was all around. But, oh, I remembered. I can see it all right now before me. My memory was good. Still is. Not only am I saying that, but people always tell me when I talk about the past, "Alverna is right. That's the way it went."

Pap Farley said he thought that was the way it would go, "But *du* two have to know what *du* wanna do."

Ben finally said, "*Ach vell* then, we'll let Snip here, but we'll be back for her."

115

CHAPTER 12 - MOM AND POP

When they fetched me back to the farm after several days, Ben said to me, "Now don't go in the *haus* with your momma. *Du* stay out here *un vait* till *Ich* put Pet *un* the buggy away. *Ich* wanna show *du* something."

I wondered what in the world was going on, but I stayed and waited for Ben. I was so happy to be back at the farm again even though I come to realize I'd never see the Old Lady again. I missed her so bad.

When he come back he took my hand that got swallowed up in his over-sized, work-roughened one.

When I look back I can't find the right words, I can only say it this way: his love washed into the deep places of my soul and cleaned away any bad feeling's that might be lurking inside, not too many or too often mind you, just every now and then. Pure happiness I felt inside as we headed down towards the spring house and the lower porch, hand in hand.

"*Ich* want to show *du* something. *Chust du vait un see.*"

He didn't have to show me anything. Being with him was enough.

"My goodness," I thought. "I've been down here many a time. What does he wanna show me that I never seen here before?"

He led me down farther and when we neared the lower porch at the spring house I saw, oh, the wonder of it! There hanging from the biggest limb of the old cherry tree was a brand new, wonderful good chain swing with a board seat. He made that swing just for me. I just stood there and gawked. When I finally tore my eyes away and looked at him, he saw how he surprised me and made me happy. "Now *du* can swing while your momma strains the milk *un* puts it away. *Un du* can drink all the milk *du* want."

How loved I felt just then. And how I loved that big, burly man.

He was pleased to see how happy I was.

Oh, when I think of all that warm milk I drank then right after it come from the cow.

Couldn't do it today.

"Climb up," Ben urged, but hard as I held onto the chain and tried to jump up, I couldn't land on the seat. I was too clumsy. He finally lifted me up and pushed me. The feel of his hands against my back, well, I was in glory land.

It was time to go back to the house for the supper Mom was fixing.

We washed our hands on the back porch where Mom had filled a basin from the outside pump. When we went in, Mom asked me, "What did *du* see, what did *du* find, Alverna?"

"Oh, he put a swing up, he put a swing up, he put a swing up!" I tried to explain and went on and on, spilling over with joy as I danced and twirled around in the big kitchen.

"*Ach vell, du* like it, ain't now yet?" wondered Mom.

"Oh, yes, I like it, I like it all right. You bet I like it!"

"Are *du* got happy?"

"Yes, I am happy."

So that's the way that went. Nothing more was said just then.

We ate supper, then I helped Mom put the dishes away.

After Mom got me ready for bed that night, Ben said, "Now *Ich* want to tell *du* something else." Just like that he said.

Oh boy! Another surprise? Only it didn't make any difference what he said cause I loved him so much. He always made things right. He was such a wonderful good man. A*llerbescht!*

"What would *du* say if *du* go to *bedde* tonight *un du* have to sleep alone?"

I looked at him in puzzlement. "Why?" I wanted to know.

"*Ya, vell* now, *Ich* will tell *du.*" He paused, looking for the right words. Then he simply said, "Your momma *un Ich* got married."

"I don't know what married is."

Your momma *un Ich* will sleep together, but *du* will sleep in the same room in the other *bedde.*"

"Well, if I'm in the same room I don't care."

See, what they done was they had went and got married, then come and got me. Now I understood what Pap Farley said to Ben when they was talking. He shook Ben's hand and said, "If there was any *mann* I'd want my daughter to marry, it's *du.*" Though I still didn't get the whole gist of it I knowed it was a wonderful thing my grandpap said to Ben that day.

When I was put to bed that night I couldn't go off to sleep right away with all the excitement of the day. With what noises I heard coming from the big bed, later I come to recognize that maybe it was a good thing Annmarie come to the farm that day and fussed like she did, for as far as human nature goes and what little bit of next-to-nothing I knowed, my mom and Ben mighta already been at what Annmarie was making so much fuss about.

But I didn't care about that. What I cared about was we was together. It woulda been better if the Old Lady was still there, but this was the next best thing.

How I lingered over Mom's words when she asked, "Are *du* got happy?" She asked me if I was happy. Maybe that meant Mom loved me after all. Oh, how her question gave me just a little bit of hope.

The next morning at breakfast, Ben said, "Now, Snip, with your momma and me married, I'm your new poppa. I'm your real poppa now. Will *du* call me Pop?"

"Oh, yes! Yes I will," I promised.

That day Ben Geesey became my pop. Now I had a real daddy.

He liked it when I called him Pop as much as I like saying it.

Happy, yes I was happy.

And that's the way it was.

Pop was a big man, well over six feet tall and pushing more'n two hundred fifty pounds. Cooking for him and all the men who come to help at the farm started Mom getting heavier too. Not only that. Her hair started losing it's color. Before long when she was still young yet it turned pure white.

One hot summer morning Mom was baking sugar cakes. Pop went out to shave - he always shaved out on the back porch in the summer, then rubbed his teeth and gums with salt to clean 'em. When he come back in the kitchen he tapped Mom on the shoulder and pinched her on her rear end. He got a kick outta doing that, especially since she got so heavy there.

She looked up from her baking and said, *"Ach, mei Gott!* A wasp stung *du!"* She didn't realize for a minute, but when she looked right, his moustache was gone. Pop shaved off his heavy, red moustache due to the heat. He'd let it grow back in the fall.

"Ach, du dumm ox!" she admonished him as she swatted after him with the big spoon that was rimmed with cookie dough. He laughed and went back to the basin to clean cookie dough off his shirt sleeve.

My pop, however things went he always tried to make a good time out of 'em.

Before Mom went to the Geesey farm, she and I walked to Sunday School and Church with Grammy and Pap Farley's

119

brood, the Holtzapples and other neighbors we met on the way. Old Mrs. Holtzapple - and Enoch for that matter - never went much cause they was all crippled up and couldn't walk far. Sometimes Dan and Joe stopped to walk with John and Will. We lived a good mile from the church and we walked on Sunday mornings and again late Sunday afternoons. We'd head home before dark so's we didn't have to light the coal oil lanterns to see where we was stepping. If dark hit early they'd get lit. That was a happy time with families, friends and neighbors strolling together, talking along the way.

When I was little we walked almost everywhere. Everyone took turns carrying me until I'd squirm to be put down. I'd run ahead a little bit, hopping over the ruts in the dirt road, then turn around to watch 'em as they walked together. My little heart would puff out with joy as I'd watch and wait for 'em to catch up.

See, at first it was because all around me was one big family that I didn't realize during my early days that I didn't have a daddy.

The church bells rang as we walked to the little Reformed Church surrounded with some buggies and wagons, a handsome carriage or two. People milled around to catch up on the latest news before they went through the bright-red door of the church. The graveyard was in the back where Grammy'd go and fix up some graves every now and then.

From little on up I always knowed there was a God - a kind, old man in the sky handing out lots of good things. With Grammy and Pap, Mom and my aunt and uncles - and now a pop in Ben - this *Goot Mann* made me feel special. I didn't have the words then, but in my heart I believed he was looking after me with tender kindness. Never talked out loud to God when others was around, but I did when I was outside and 'twas only me, and then at the farm, Poodle. From where I played under the willow tree I look out over the golden fields and rolling meadows that turned into green woodlands with soft purple hills beyond. These was beautiful gifts for me to prize, and that I did. In my heart and sometimes out loud, I'd say "Thank you, Good Man." Poodle's head would cock in a queer fashion, staring first at me in puzzlement, then looking around to see who I was talking to. Not seeing no one, his head went down on his forepaws for a light snooze. Poodle never slept so sound that I'd get away from him. That's the way I thought about God, too. Him and Poodle was my friends to my child's way of thinking. I always knowed there was a God, no doubt about it. Thanked him for Poodle too. Yes, I did.

Pop hooked up Pet and the buggy for Mom and me to go to Sunday morning church, but seldom did he go, only once in a great while. He was no church man, but if ever there was one that got to heaven, I know he did.

Camp meetings was a different story to Pop. Whenever there was a camp meeting, that's where he wanted to go. They was held in big open picnic groves that got filled up with people from all around when the news about them spread. This was one time it didn't matter much which church anyone belonged to, lots of different churches was represented, not just one. Hours of preaching and singing and praying and weeping, that's what camp meetings was - a place to let loose things we kept inside too long. The Pennsylvania Dutch most often held their emotions in, but the music and the preaching outdoors in the evenings stirred feeling's from deep inside. I watched and listened. It wasn't hard to tell the difference between tears of joy while the preacher spoke about heaven, or tears of sorrow listening about the work of the devil. At every camp meeting we was warned by the preacher to repent and change our ways so we wouldn't end up in the fiery brimstone of hell. Sometimes I'd feel the fires of hell creeping up, they made it that real. It was scary all right!

Now and then the Holy Rollers heard about the camp meeting and joined in. They went beyond the *amens*, *hallelujahs* and *praise the Lord*, and took to shouting in strange languages and falling over, more'n what most Pennsylvania Dutch took stock in. Such behavior was embarrassing to our kind. It was looked on as shocking, almost unchristian you know, but it was generally accepted that camp meeting was for everyone if to be there they wanted. Mostly though, the Holy Rollers didn't come around after the first service. They grumbled that the crowd wasn't spirited enough, that our ways of worshipping was too somber, too grim. Thought we was next to heathen.

Well, if they come looking to convert people to their religion, they found us purty tough nuts to crack, they did.

One afternoon Pop told me, "Snip, we're goin' to camp meeting tonight so *du* better lay down *un* take a little nap or on your momma's lap *du* will be all *nacht*."

I couldn't have, oh, I couldn't have slept that afternoon if they tied me down I was that excited. Poodle and me was out on the porch where I was to be resting, but every time I'd hear a noise like dishes rattling or a broom sweeping, I'd get up and wanna help Mom. She got exasperated with me but wasn't up to her usual scolding cause she was excited about camp meeting too.

Finally it was time to head on out. The preaching was mostly more'n I could understand. After a bit I'd wander away from the message. My favorite pastime was watching the people, but when it come to singing, I paid attention then; joined in with gusto. Oh, what joy and happiness to be in such a wonderful good place with my mom and that wonderful good man I called my pop. My heart soared with joy. Life was *allerbescht,* the best it could be.

Before darkness settled in we headed home.

Mom and Pop was usually *het* up after a camp meeting, but this night they was both on the quiet side.

Not me.

My mind went every which way as I sat in the buggy between them two. Watching how Pet pulled us and the buggy, I got to thinking about Pet and her being blind. Getting sleepier by the minute, I asked as darkness began to take over, "Pop, with Pet being blind, how can she find her way?"

Pop showed me the harness he put on - I seen Pop oil the harness time and again so it wouldn't rub Pet sore - and the bit in her mouth, how he guided her with it. "But," he went on, "she knows so much she can go straight ahead. There's not a road around here Pet don't know. *Ach vell* now, *Ich* could set back without using the reins *un* she'd get us back safe *un* sound. Pet *un* me work together *goot*, ain't now yet?" he asked.

Contented, I laid my head on my mom's lap and fell asleep. Don't remember being put to bed that night.

When I think what happened to Pet later on when the going got rough, why the tears still come thinking about that poor animal.

The morning after camp meeting - I can see it all now. Done with my morning chores, I was sitting on the floor rolling the glass marble with the sheep inside when Pop come in. I wondered what Pop was doing inside so early - couldn't be done working outside yet. When he went straight to the clock shelf that meant only one thing - music! Pop kept his green mouth organ there on the old clock shelf.

"Oh boy!" I thought to myself. "We're got music."

I loved it so much when Pop played his green mouth organ, but it was never in the morning, only at night before bedtime. Many a time in the evening Mom would say to Pop, "Why don't *du* play a little bit?"

I was happy when Mom said that cause she seemed more calm and settled down when Pop played.

Pop would get Mom to sing something, then he'd work it out on his green mouth organ, playing till he got it just right to suit him. Pop played while Mom sang. I'd join in if it appeared it was all right with Mom. This was the most beautiful music in the whole, wide world, thrilling my heart till I thought I was gonna burst with downright happiness.

Pop had a song on his mind that we sang at camp meeting the night before.

Though he tried to do his outside work, he couldn't with the song going round in his head. It worked on his nerves so he reckoned he'd come in once and try on the green mouth organ to see whether he could get part of it together. He was going over and over it when I recognized what he was trying to get. I sat humming while he played. "Hm..hm. hm.. hm.hm..hm.hm..hm.hm..hm..hm...."

Pop stopped and looked at me dumbfounded.

"*Du* little snip, *du*. Are *du* know *wass iss*?" I can hear him say it yet.

"Why sure."

"*Ach vell now. Wass iss?*"

"That's *Standing on the Promises*."

"Where'd *du* learn that?" he wanted to know.

"We sing it sometimes in Sunday School."

"*Ya? Vell*, sing it now!" he sputtered.

All I knowed was the chorus, so that's what I sang. It wasn't long he got the drift of it and was playing it on his green mouth organ. Mom was in the cellar working and she heard this going on up there and she come up and wondered what it was all about.

He just looked at her in disbelief and said, "*Ich* couldn't work, had that song on my mind. Couldn't get no work done. Thought I'd *kumme* in *un* try to get it together on my mouth organ, *un* here this little Snip sings it for me."

He asked Mom if she knowed all the words.

"Sure."

"*Ach vell*, sing it for me!"

Mom sang the verses until he got that part together. When he had it worked out, he played, Mom sang and I joined in the chorus. I was sitting on the floor holding my marble with the sheep inside, singing my heart out, when outta the corner of my eye I seen Pop reach inside his shirt pocket and pull out his big, red handkerchief. I turned just a little so I could see what was going on. There was Pop, sitting on the bench and playing *Standing on the Promises* with his green mouth organ, trying to wipe away the tears coursing down his rosy cheeks with the big red handkerchief that was always stuck in the pocket of his bib overalls. There was Mom, sitting and singing with tears streaming down her cheeks. And there I was wondering why in the world they was crying. It was such a wonderful good song and it was such a wonderful good time. *Allerbescht!*

Of course I later on come to grasp the reason for Mom and Pop's tears. See, I cry when I'm happy and I cry when I'm sad. That day them tears was happy tears coming from my momma and poppa.

CHAPTER 13 - THRASHING TIME

Thrashing time was a busy season for everyone. I'll never forget this one time when four men was helping Pop thrash. Pop had oiled the thrashing machine and I watched from afar-off how the horses was hooked in the thrashing arms and that was the old horsepower. The way the arms went around in a ring and started the thrashing machine up fascinated me. The wheat was fed into the thrasher and out come the grain one way, the other way come straw which was gathered and taken to the straw shed. Men helped each other out to harvest the crops, bringing along their teams of horses and mules.

The manpower it took at certain seasons wasn't needed all year long, that's why farmers helped each other out with harvesting. Pop always said how the rich soil gave us wonderful good crops because of our way of taking good care of the ground.

It was the way for women too, helping neighbors out when there was a need. They had their own work, houses to keep up, children to look after, gardens to plant and small livestock to tend; they milked, mended, cleaned, cooked, baked and sewed. Mondays and Thursdays was washdays cause somewhere way back, the idea was planted in their minds that to wash on Wednesdays brought bad luck. Grammy baked almost every day for her big family. Mom didn't but she baked enough that her and Pop put on lots of weight. She had one room shut off that stayed much cooler then other'ns and that's where her pies and baked goods was kept to stay fresh. They didn't last very long, though.

Pop liked to sneak up behind Mom when her hands was busy at the stove and pinch her backside which there was a great deal of. Mom acted like she was gonna' hit him over the head with what kettle she was using to cook with. I'd get besides myself, hold my breath thinking she might, but she never done it. Pop just laughed.

The men was helping Pop in the fields that day. At dinner time they had washed up where Mom put extra wash basins on the back porch and at the outside pump; some dunked their heads right in the rain barrel at the corner of the house to get the dust outta their beards and mouths. They wanted to enjoy Mom's good cooking.

They was at the table eating. Tillie and Mary Godfrey, Pop's nieces, helped Mom during thrashing time. Their mom was dead this long time so the two girls lived with Aunt Jemima, a sister to Pop, and her husband, Earl. Jemima was a lot older than her sisters, Annmarie and Lola, too busy on the homestead she and Uncle Earl farmed to interfere in family life at the Geesey's and make trouble like Annmarie, the uppity town sister.

This time of year the flies was extra pesky. Couldn't keep 'em out. Mom took a long, thin, sturdy tree branch and wrapped thin strips of newspaper around it for Mary, since she was the tallest, to walk up and down the length of the long table behind where the men was sitting. The table had all its boards in to make it long enough to hold all the workers. Mary went up and down swinging that fly chaser back and forth. It helped keep the insects away from the men and off the food as Mary swung it above their heads as they ate. It took a toll on Mary's arms it did. She struggled with that branch, heavy with paper, to keep it moving back and forth all dinner long, but she loved her Uncle Ben and admired my mom. She was determined to do her job right no matter how tired it made her.

Tillie was one of Pop's favorite nieces. Matter of fact, all his nieces was his favorite. He loved each one, especially loved teasing Tillie. She was waiting on the table, filling up the dishes as soon as the men emptied 'em. She was reaching over Pop with a big bowl of squirrel potpie when Pop just

127

said over it, "Tillie, *du* smell *chust* like them horses *un* mules we was usin' in the *feld* today."

Poor Tillie. She was so embarrassed, sniffed all around at her clothes to see if it was so.

"*Onkel* Ben! *Du* hurt my feelin's sayin' such a thing! *Ich* don't smell like your stinkin' animals!"

"Why Tillie, are *du* not got a nose to smell through just like them animals do now yet?"

How the men hollered and laughed. Then Tillie laughed too.

Just then the idea come to Pop for me to sing for the men. When he come to fetch me, Mom sent a stern look his way and warned. "*Ach*, now, don't get her started!"

At the back of the big kitchen was a table with wings where Mom kept her kettles and hooks and such things on. Pop swung up a wing, bolted it upright, sat me down on it.

Pop just said over it, "There's Alvin, he *chust* got married, ain't, Alvin? *Ich* want *du* to sing that song for him."

"You mean the marrying song?"

"You know what I mean, Snip."

Such fun, my pop!

Mom was exasperated with us. "For goodness sakes!" she fussed from where she was at the stove.

I sat there with a wide grin, swinging my legs back and forth and slapping my hands together to get the rhythm going. I began to sing:

A cross-eyed baby on your knee,
A wife with a wart on her nose.
Ain't it funny if you got a lot of money,
But you gotta wear second-hand clothes.

And they just hollered and laughed about that there. My mom sang those songs when no one was around but me and I'd pick 'em up from her.

Lance Mellinger, a kind neighbor who was helping Pop that day said, "If my kids had a voice *un* could sing like that, *Ich* think I'd have 'em singin' all the time."

Mom just shook her head in vexation. Pop, he just grinned and told me to sing about the cowboy.

Take me down to the graveyard and lay the sod on me,
For I'm a poor cowboy and I know I've done wrong.
Then play the pipes slowly and play the drums lowly,
And play the dead march as you carry me along.
Take me down to the graveyard and lay the sod on me,
For I'm a poor cowboy and I know I've done wrong.

Lance said over it, "We ain't never got music when we're thrashin' at other places, ain't now yet?"

The men laughed and wanted more. Pop said one more and Mom just shook her head again. She was too befuddled with slicing the fresh Shoo-fly and Montgomery pies and two kinds of cake - chocolate and walnut - then pouring a fresh pot of coffee for the men to finish off their meal to protest too much.

And me, was I having the best fun. Yes indeed. And Mom couldn't stop it with all that company there.

Into a tent where a Gypsy boy lay,
Dying alone at the close of the day.
'Need I must perish? My hands will behold,
Nobody ever the story has told.
Tell it again, tell it again,
Salvation's story repeat oe'r and oe'r.
Tell it again, tell it again.
Till none can say of the children of men
Nobody ever has told me before.'

With that the men got up from the table and headed back to the fields. Pop helped me down. Us girls and Mom started to clean up after them. Took all afternoon, it did.

One time Grammy was at Secrist's during thrashing season helping May Secrist cook, serve and clean up at mealtime. That time May sliced only enough bread so that each man got one piece and no more. That was a big mistake. Almost sinful, it was. See, the men always worked hard. Thrashing time was no exception. Well, a couple of the men asked Grammy for more bread while she was serving at the table. They was just getting started into the meal and they'd need more bread to sop up the leavings on their plates when they was through. So clean them plates would look, just like they was washed clean. Poor Grammy! She was embarrassed. She knowed the men shoulda had more bread but she didn't wanna throw it back on May, making her look bad even though it was her own doing. She just put her head down, shrugged and busied herself with other things so she didn't have to answer. By golly, when Pete Secrist went for more bread and found out there was none, he tore into May for not giving the men as much bread as they wanted.

"That'll never happen again," Pete warned her.

May shoulda knowed better, but, no, she showed herself to be stingy and tightfisted. Started that meal off on the wrong foot. What was she thinking? Was her own doing she come by a bad reputation. Being a bit regretful for what she done coulda helped her save face. It woulda been forgot and put aside, but no, she never admitted to what she done, even hinted around that some of the women helping out that day ate her bread before the men come in for dinner. Didn't mention names hoping each woman would look with suspicion at the rest, but nobody took that to heart.

When the men come in for dinner, the women didn't eat till the men was all done and back at work. Oh, maybe if a finger got stuck in the potatoes or gravy while serving, that finger'd get licked off but that's as far as it got. None of those women woulda helped themselves to bread before dinner and they all knowed what May hinted at wasn't true. She was the one looked upon with suspicion from then on. The women, they still helped out at the Secrist's, wasn't much choice about that; but they all stuck together so none could be accused of any wrong-doin' when they was there.

Be sure that May always had enough bread from then on, thanks to Pete.

CHAPTER 14 - THE BEST DADDY IN THE WHOLE WIDE WORLD

This morning the sun is streaming in so nice and bright through my kitchen window above the sink so I decided to get out my magnifying mirror and tweezers to pull out some bristly chin hairs, so long they get. Seems like the hairs on top of my head are getting thinner while hair's growing long and stiff other places I don't want. This getting old is for the birds.

That tweezers got me to thinking of a time long ago.

Pop made himself a tweezers. He was handy like that and made a-many of his own tools, repaired 'em too when they broke. Sitting in his rocking chair this one time he called me over to his side and said with such a somber tone in his voice, "Now Snip, *Ich* want *du* to take this tweezers, *un* if *du* see any white hairs on my head, why *du chust* yank 'em out." Through this sober sound I heard a suspicious echo of humor. Was he was just joking with me? I wasn't certain.

I was a small child, spunky but small, so spunky that whenever Pop asked something of me I'd do my best to find a way to carry it out. I decided to go along with his request. He handed me the tweezers in the same somber way he spoke. My fingers was just so little that I could barely squeeze it shut. Looking at it I was reminded of Mom's scissors I once held in my hands and ended up causing so much damage and pain.

I went to work. Pop had black hair, lots of black hair on his head, but the big moustache that covered his upper lip and ended in a slight curl on each side was red as red could be. There I was, walking from one side of his head to the other looking for white hairs and I could hardly squeeze that tweezers shut; tried with all my might, but wasn't strong enough get the hang of it.

Finally Mom had enough of this and fussed at him, *"Ya, du* tell her to pull the white hair out *un* every time she pulls one out, *du* get ten more."

Just like that Pop jumped up and scared me outta my wits.

"Are *du* think *Ich* will?" he teased. "Then don't pull anymore out, Snip."

Just like I was pulling any of 'em out. Such fun my Pop!

And that's the way he'd carry on with me and that's the way Mom would on and on fuss, but it never got Pop down. He was always conjuring up some kind of fun for the two of us. He would of liked Mom to join in more, even encouraged it with his fun lovin' ways, but Mom, she had a melancholy look about her most the time. It softened a little bit when they was first married, but always she remained mostly brusque and harsh.

But my pop, he was better, better, a whole lot better than most real daddies are to their children. There wasn't a man that coulda treated me any better than he did. Pop, he was *allerbescht,* the best of all.

One time - oh, I'll never forget this, we had two enormous big walnut trees. The one walnut tree at the big red barn was full of walnuts but they never amounted to nothing, just stayed little with no walnut meat inside. I'd be out there, Poodle and me, and I'd pick them walnuts up and make a little pile here for the house and a little pile there for the barn and other piles for the livestock. Then I'd make a row and pretend that was the path from the barn to the house and the other outbuildings. I was by myself and played like that. Mom often said over it that she never had to worry about me because Poodle kept me safe. Where Poodle was, I was. Where I was, Poodle was. He was a wonderful good playmate.

It was haying season, a time I loved. Men came with their machines and scythes to help Pop, then Pop'd go to their places to help them. They moved together in an even row with long swinging strides, tossed the hay in yellow heaps for the wagons to carry them from the field to the barn. It was a wonderful sight.

This one year Pop hooked Pet in the hay rake. Some men was soon coming to haul in the hay. He went to rake the hay up. The last round he went to make, the seat didn't stay on the hay rake. He got off, and here what happened the nut had come off the screw. When he put Pet away before he was finished, Mom wondered about this. He told her what happened then said, "*Ich* will rake that last round together with the wood hay rake." She offered to go help him out knowing how important it was to get this done, but one thing about my pop, he never left Mom go out and work in the field.

It was a day or two later when I was playing with some walnuts that was laying around. Pop used to say to let me play with 'em because they wasn't no good anyway. Now and then Pop picked up a pile that I gathered and he'd throw 'em against the tree. Then he'd say I'm to try. Well, I couldn't hit that tree no matter how hard I tried. I wanted so bad to make Pop proud of me, but I just couldn't hit the tree. I was too gawky, took after my Mom that way. He'd laugh, but not a laugh to hurt me. It was a laugh that said he loved me even when I hit everything but the tree.

This particular day I was piling these walnuts around and I found the nut off the hay rake. I run right in the house, Poodle right alongside of me.

"I wonder whether this is what Pop wanted," I said to Mom, showing her the nut.

Pop was coming in from outside and heard me.

"What's she got?"

Mom said, "*Ich* believe she's got what *du* need."

When I showed it to him he asked, "Where in the world did *du* find that, *du* little snip, *du*?'

133

He realized then that it come off the hay rake when he first started, but the seat stayed on until he had everything raked but that last round.

"*Goot* for *du,* Snip. *Ich* won't need to go now *un* get a whole new screw *un* nut made. *Du* saved me a lot of time from runnin' around."

An afterthought came to him. "Are *du* wanna do somethin' for me?"

Ha! When he said anything to me like that I was in my glory. I woulda done anything for my pop.

"Follow me. *Kumme* down here."

See, the big red barn was, then the big wagon shed, the corn crib beside the wagon shed. Below was a great, big, long platform with stone walls around and a roof ready to cave in. Three sides was open. On there Pop always had all his tools laying.

That's where we went. He picked up a spike that was all bent.

"*Du* know what this is?"

"Sure. It's a nail."

"*Du* know where that goes? There's an *alt* bucket. Somethin' we can't fix no more, that'll go in the bucket. *Ich* want *du* to straighten everything out on here for me - all the wrenches *un* everything."

I got right away to work. If there was a nail he could straighten, I'd put 'em together. I laid the wrenches side by side, the saws together, all the tools with their kind. I finished up that job after a couple hours. When he seen me away from the platform he asked if I was finished already.

"Yeah."

Hardly believing, he come and he looked. He seen I finished and the job was done right. I knowed how pleased he was when he gave me a great big bear hug. I was happy all over. He sure did love me, yes he did.

He said to Mom when she come out to milk that evening - of course he talked to her in Dutch, "*Ach vell*, now look at what she's done. Now she's my right-hand-man. *Chust* look at how she fixed everything up."

Mom just said over it so sober like, *"Un* how long will it stay?"

Pop just grinned.

When it come time for Pop to trim the grapevines - we had so many - as busy as he was and as hard as he worked, Pop always took time to hunt a nice long vine or two that wasn't knotty for me to jump rope with. He done that every time he trimmed. Mom would put her hands on her hips in exasperation and scold him whenever he found things like that for me to play with.

"Du will kill her yet!" She fussed

"Never mind. She's doin' all right," was all he'd say. And I was. I was a happy-go-lucky child, able to content myself with the glass marble, walnuts for toys, a grapevine jump rope, Poodle and Cookie the cat. Mostly I didn't know no different. Oh, some children had real toys, but not enough for me to think I was lacking any. I was happy with what I had.

One springtime when the weather was warming up, we was sitting out in the back yard under the big mulberry tree. I wanted to go barefoot so bad but Mom only said, *"Ya, un chust* like the Mellinger girls will *du* be. When *du kumme* for your shoes *un* stockings, one shoe's here, another'n there, *un* the same with your stockings."

Mom felt strong that the Mellingers was too lax towards their kids; they never could find nothing when they went looking for it. She made sure this wasn't gonna happen with me.

Pop said, *"Du* go barefoot only when *du* hear the first whippoorwill"

135

Now, I'll never forget this as long as I live - no sooner he said it, sitting together under that tree we was, and here comes the haunting cry of the first whippoorwill of the year.

"*Haerkumme*. Come hear," Pop laughed. "First *du* have to turn a somersault."

I never could turn a somersault and he knowed it; always went on my side. And I did that day too, hard as I tried to go over right. But Pop, big and heavy as he was, he went over his head and turned a perfect somersault. We all laughed together, even Mom. And that made Pop laugh even more.

Now I could take my shoes and stockings off, but there was some things Mom never allowed.

She warned me, "*Du* may take 'em off, but know where *du* put 'em so when *du* get up in the morning *du* can find 'em."

Yes, the Mellinger girls did have one shoe here and one shoe there, stockings somewhere else. That was one thing my mom never allowed. Never bothered Susie's momma too much. She held her kids accountable to find 'em when they needed 'em or go barefoot - or bare whatever. Such a going-on it was at their house with all them kids till they found their shoes and stockings - and other things - but after much rushing around with laughter and in a frenzy, searching here and there and everywhere, they was sooner or later found.

I always sat my shoes and stockings to the side of the stairwell. They was well outta the way where no one would fall over 'em but where I'd always be able to get to 'em when they was needed. Mom taught me good there.

Pop come in one day. "Hey, *du* know what? It won't be long till we'll soon have fresh cherry pie on the table."

Mom wondered where in the world was cherries ripe.

"Them over at the road are gettin' ripe fast. In a week or so."

We had early cherries but there was only one tree that I could get up in. The other'n was too far from the fence for me to climb up.

One day a couple weeks later, Mom wondered about the cherries.

"Are *du* got time to pick cherries?" She asked Pop. "*Ich* got about an hour's work yet in the cellar, then *Ich* can bake pies."

"*Ich* got about a half hour's work in the barn now yet," Pop said.

Mom got the bucket, tied the hook on it, sat it on the table. She went back into the cellar. Pop went back to his work in the barn. I pick up the bucket, walk over to the tree, climb the fence, all the time holding the bucket. I grabbed the lowest limb of the giant cherry tree and throwed the hook over the branch, crawled up into the crotch of the tree, crawled out to where there was cherries and started picking. Some went in the bucket but they was so good that more went inside me.

Picking away I was when all of a sudden I hear Pop holler - in Dutch, of course, "Where's the bucket?"

"It's over here in the tree and I'm with it," I hollered back.

He come over and seen me.

"*Du* little snip, *du*, How are *du* got up there?"

"Crawled up."

"Them ain't so ripe up there. The ripe ones are all on the outside where the sun hits 'em."

"Yeah, but I can't get to 'em."

"All right. *Haerkumme*. Come down. Now take care *du* don't fall."

I handed him the bucket and heard his voice echoing back out of it as he looked in and remarked, "By durned, *du* are got some already in the bucket."

He hung the hook on a limb then reached to me.

"Hold onto that limb. Now watch yourself."

I held on to the limb as he inched closer.

137

"Now, on my shoulders get."

Standing on his shoulders I picked cherries, holding a limb with one hand to steady myself, Pop moving the bucket from branch to branch as we went. Big as he was, Pop moved easily around the tree so's I could pick what cherries I could reach. When the bucket was full he got another'n and we moved on to the other tree that was too big for me to crawl up in and we picked some of them on the outside too.

"Mom'll be surprised," Pop whispered to me, "but we won't tell her about them that ain't quite so ripe."

Neither of us ever told her that I was up in the tree either. She never asked. It was our secret to this day. All these years and this is the first I'm telling it.

I washed and seeded the cherries while Mom got ready the pie dough.

We was finishing up supper with warm cherry pie and milk. Every once in a while Pop looked at me with that merry twinkle in his eyes. He'd wink and say, "Sure tastes *goot*, ain't?"

The joke was on Mom; she never knowed how the cherries was picked.

And you know what? It probably won't even make my kids chuckle what Pop and I done. If they read my story, that is. They'll say, "Mom, you're touched in the head. You didn't climb that tree. You just think so."

"Don't write your story," they say.

"I must," I come back. "It says in the Bible book of Esther *'that these days should be remembered throughout every generation'*. I want to pass on my days to you."

They'll just shake their heads at what they think is my imagination. Maybe they're afraid I'm writing about them and the dumb things they done over the years. Yep, that's what they must think. Only I ain't. Just about me and Mom and my wonderful Pop. He was *allerbescht*.

I gotta write about this wonderful good man before I leave this good earth.

Bet they won't read it though.

138

Purd was with us visiting one time. It was locust year, full of 'em everywhere. At that time we had a chicken yard and that's where the ducks was. Purd and I, we was catching locusts. As fast as we'd catch 'em, we'd laugh and run with those locusts tickling our hands, then throw one after another to the ducks. They'd gobble 'em up as fast as we throwed 'em in. And, Lord, here we lost I don't know how many ducks. More died than lived. No one was sure why these ducks died, but Pop thought out loud they got too many locusts to eat.

Purd, of course he didn't wanna, but I'd not take no for an answer; we hadda tell Pop how we fed the ducks all them locusts.

Only not when Mom was in earshot.

"*Ach vell,*" went Pop, lookin' so downhearted and discouraged. He didn't scold us cause he figured we didn't know no better. But Purd and me, the two of us knowed them dead ducks hurt Pop in the pocketbook. He worked hard to keep us going, and Mom did too. We let 'em down.

Purd said, "If only we'd of knowed that, we wouldn't of fed 'em like that."

"*Ich* didn't know *du* two was doin' that," was all Pop said. I was so filled with remorse that I tried extra hard to be good - at least for awhile.

That year there was so many black snakes around. I remember it real good cause I connected it with the summer after I started school and could recite the ABC's backwards faster than my classmates could recite 'em forwards. I was alone so much of the time and worked out things like that to keep my mind busy.

That year we had a turkey acting purty strange. All the fowl - chickens, ducks, turkeys, geese - had the run of the yard then. It was before Pop built a chicken yard. This one turkey would go every morning. A little later it would come back and call and call and call.

"Somethin's the matter with that turkey," Pop noticed. "Don't know *wass iss*. Makes no difference, somethin's the matter with it."

Then he teased me a little bit by asking, "Will *du* be afraid to go *un* watch?" (He knowed better. Wasn't too much I was afraid of.)

"No, I won't be afraid to go watch, but I don't know what I'll find."

Next morning I went and I watched. The turkey was way down in the wheat field and I was way up. I could see the wheat move so I followed the turkey like that; couldn't see the turkey, just the wheat moving. Wasn't long till the turkey turned around again and headed back the way it come.

"Now," I said to myself. "I'm gonna go look."

I followed the path through the wheat field the turkey took and my Lord! Here was a great big black snake coiled on the turkey's eggs. Then I run. I run home a flying and stood in front of Pop to tell him what I found out.

"Now I know what's the matter with the turkey."

"*Wass iss*?" Pop wanted to know.

"There's a snake on her eggs There's one egg rolled down outside."

Pop scratched his head. "*Ach vell, Ich* don't know *chust* what to do about that. If *Ich* shoot *Ich* could get the *schlang*, but *Ich chust* might ruin all the turkey eggs too."

Mom said, "If *du* let the snake on, when the turkeys hatch out it'll be liable to *esse* 'em, *du* know."

Pop thought the snake would eat the eggs before they hatched but Mom didn't, so he took his rifle and went to where I told him.

When he come back he said, "By dog! There was the *schlang* layin' *chust* like Snip said." Then he said how he whistled, the snake put its head up and he shot. The snake rolled off the eggs. With one shot Pop blowed its head off.

Some of the eggs was cracked already for the turkeys to hatch. Pop didn't know what to do so he let things go like they was. Next day I watched the turkey head down through the wheat field but she didn't come back. I snuck down as close as I dared without her spotting me and by golly, here she had sat on the eggs. For a couple days I'd go and sneak a look at the turkey. Glad I didn't run into any snakes. Finally one morning she come back through the wheat and had seven little turkeys, only seven out of thirteen eggs. When I said to Pop about the number, he reminded me: "Snip," he went on, "If it wasn't for *du*, there wouldn't of even been seven *bobbel* turkeys now yet. What *du* done was *goot*. *Du* help keep us goin'."

Oh, my pop. He was so good. *Allerbescht*!

Mom was baking sugar cakes. So soft and spongy they'd come outta the oven, high in the middle sprinkled over with sugar, a little brown around the edges but not burnt, good for dunking in coffee or milk, only you couldn't keep 'em dunked too long, they'd fall apart to nothing. Pop and I liked 'em sitting out a day or two to get hard, then we dunked 'em to our heart's content.

She gave me two for each man that was working in the fields with Pop and a bucket of fresh, spring water, so cold it hurt your teeth to drink.

"*Ach vell* now, hurry! Don't play around that the *wasser* gets warm till *du* get there or *Ich* will learn *du* a thing or two now yet!" Mom warned.

She knowed sometimes I forgot what I was to be doing and got to playing. But I listened to Mom that day. I went to the field right away. I gave the men the sugar cakes and water. They wanted me to eat some, but I said I ate before I come down.

As the men sat down to eat and drink, Pop said, "Snip, go *un* get the whetstone at the fence *un* we'll sharpen the scythes *goot* before we start again."

It took me so long and he hollered and wondered what was the matter.

"I can't get it," I answered.

Clate, one of the men with him scoffed - accusingly like Mom woulda - "Now don't tell me *du* can't reach that now yet. Do what your Pop says *un* stop your whinin'."

Most men didn't take any back talk from children or understand 'em like my pop. Clate was unmarried, didn't have none of his own - at least that we knowed of - so he was sharp with me right off.

"I can't. It's a snake there."

Pop and Clate, they both jumped up and come with the scythe. That long, shiny black snake was a monster, rounder than I ever seen, as round as Pop's upper arm. Pop right away cut the snake through. Next, oh, it was dreadful! The front part of that big black snake slithered off the fence and headed straight towards me. In my mind the snake was coming to get me. I got so scared that I turned and run back, blubbering and hollering to beat the band. Scared outta my wits I was.

"It won't hurt *du* now no more," Pop said. "It's *dod*."

It took some convincing even on Pop's part for me to after awhile believe it .

When I got back to the house Mom seen the dirt streaks on my face from the tears I cried.

"Uh huh! *Du* got a scolding. *Du* didn't get there in time *un* the *wasser* got warm *un* they scolded *du*, ain't now yet?"

"No, it wasn't that; was a snake."

"Now don't lie!" she said right away and come after me like she was gonna hit me. (That was my mom for you.) "Don't lie! A *schlang* didn't get after *du*!"

Mom wouldn't let me tell her how it happened but I broke in, "I ain't fibbing. Pop cut a snake and it come after me."

"We'll see. When they *kumme* for dinner, we'll see *onct*. If *du* lied *du* will get the worst lickin' *Ich* ever gave *du*."

They told Mom what happened when they come in. Pop hadda chuckle, but not in a way to shame me. "It did look as though the *schlang* was slitherin' right to her. She run till it stayed layin'. She run and she cried."

Clate backed him up.

142

Only then did Mom believe my story. It wondered me so if she was sorry when she heard the truth, maybe wanting me to fib so she could punish me. She was so quick to scold. Without explaining and teaching me, she expected me to know and do everything the first time right.

I thanked the Good Man, who to me was an old man with a long, white beard in heaven, for my wonderful Pop. He was *allerbescht*.

Clate was all wound up. He seen his dream unfolding before him. See, he'd been putting money back to buy hisself a new pair of boots. He had his eye on 'em for a long time now. And Pop, he done his best to help Clate get ahold of them new boots, paid him extra for his help. Wasn't long Clate come around wearing his new boots. Paid all the way $5.00 for 'em. A goodly sum it was. Claimed these was the best you could buy. We admired them and believed.

There was a mulberry tree there in the yard a whole lot older than Pop was. A great big tree it was with branches bigger than some other tree trunks around the farm. The mulberries was as big as my little finger. Oh, such wonderful mulberries! When they was ripe people come from all around to pick 'em.

Relatives was coming that afternoon for mulberries. Pop said, "*Ich* got the ladder."

Right away Mom scolded, "Of course! For her! No wonder *Ich* get them sick headaches."

"*Ach vell, Ich* can't go up." Pop was too heavy. His big size was getting to him, holding him back from some things he'd been used to doing all his life.

"*Un du* won't go up," he said to Mom. When my mom got on the lower rung of a ladder she got dizzy already. That's why she always said she don't know who I took after.

Pop put this ladder up. Me, I had no fear of climbing. I grabbed the stained, granite berry bucket, climbed the ladder, jumped onto a limb and started picking mulberries. The bucket was half full when I hear the limb crack.

"*Ich* don't know whether it's safe," Pop called. "*Du* better turn around *un* hurry down."

As I turned to come down, the limb cracked one more time.

"*Schprung!* " Pop yelled.

The limb went crashing down and took the ladder with it.

"Jump!" Pop was hollering when already towards him I was jumping. He reached out to catch me and I almost knocked him over cause I had hold of the bucket and no way was I gonna let it go. As he caught me, the almost filled berry bucket was between him and me. It hit him smack-dab on his forehead, sent him reeling backwards. He stood his ground and managed to keep from falling over. My golly days! There wasn't one mulberry spilled out of the bucket. Not one mulberry.

Mom hauled Pop over the coals as he almost keeled over, wiping away at the tender spot on his forehead. She made him hold a cold rag on the duck egg-size bump it left there. Worried she was but wouldn't own up to it.

Mom had a hard time handling our adventuresome natures. My, how she fussed. "She'll get killed yet. She'll kill herself yet." She was so cross she woulda smacked me real good if Pop wouldn't of been right there to keep her from it.

Pop was a wonderful man. He was so different. Mom was right away to hammer and scold where Pop tried to get under the thing and straighten it out right. Mom used to say to him, "*Ya, un du* are makin' a regular tomboy out of her."

"She's doin' all right," was all he'd say.

Pop, he was the one that set me on the right course, yes he was.

When all the relatives come that afternoon they picked buckets full of mulberries just off that one broken limb.

Tillie, Pop's niece said about that dear, poor, old mulberry tree.

"*Un* it's the last mulberries it'll ever give," Pop warned.

He was good as his word for he had some farmers come and help him saw it down. Clate come, wearing the boots he was so proud of.

It coulda been a terrible calamity. See, while they was cutting up the wood, here when Clate swung his axe one time he missed the limb and the axe blade cut right through his boot into his foot. Blood spurted out everywhere. The men drug him onto the back porch and managed to pull the boot off. He was hollering and screaming something dreadful. Pop thought it was from the pain but come to find out Clate was more worried about his boot than his foot. Mom went right away to her medicine cupboard, pulled out a bottle, the one with lily leaves soaking in whiskey and poured some of its contents over the wound. They hauled him into the doctor, too. Sewed it up, he did. Said Mom done the right thing pouring that stuff over the wound till he got there. Killed alot of germs, it did.

Clate was laid up for maybe a week, I'm not real sure just how long. With all that time on his hands he took to cleaning the dried blood and dust from inside and outside his boot, then sewed where it was sliced open with a narrow leather thong. No one ever woulda believed Clate could manage such fine stitching, but he done a mighty good job closing the hole in his boot that was his pride and joy. He stitched the same design on top of the other boot to make 'em look alike. Took quite awhile for the swelling to go down enough for him to pull them boots up, but once he did, it was almost like they become part of his skin. Clate sure did like them boots.

CHAPTER 15 - MY DOLL BABY

Mom always put a plate out for me every Christmas and Easter, and oh, how I looked forward to it. On it was an orange and some candy - the real clear toy candy at Christmas, chocolate candy at Easter. That was one thing children always got for Christmas - a plate with an orange and some candy. If they was lucky like me, at Easter too.

On the night before Christmas Mom said to me, "*Esse* all your *sobber*, then maybe there'll be something *goot* on your plate when *du* get up in the morning. Or maybe there'll be two *gross* pieces of coal that bad kids get."

Didn't know why Mom said that. She was a good cook and I ate heartily for my size. More times'n not I'd empty my plate without no scolding.

At that then, Pop came in and heard this. He always got a kick outta teasing Mom and one way was grabbing her backside and giving it a good pinch - Mom got heavy and there was lots to grab. Whenever he done that I knowed he was in an extra good mood. He teased her and asked, "*Un* what will be on my plate?"

Mom came back with, "It might *chust* be a *gross* chestnut burr."

Next morning on my plate with the orange and candy was two big hedge apples. There couldn't of been anything better cause I loved to pick 'em up and roll 'em in my hands and smell 'em - they smelled so wonderful good!

Pop come downstairs and when he looked, there on his plate was a great big chestnut burr laying. Now I didn't know why, but oh, my, how they got a kick outta that and laughed about it all through breakfast. It was so good to hear laughter and feel the happiness. I laughed right along. Mom was in a good enough mood to share her coffee soup with me, even let me tear up a slab of bread in a little bowl and sprinkle on it a spoonful of sugar before she poured over it the coffee and milk. Nothing never tasted better cause we was so happy that morning. Them was good times we had together.

The year before I started school - I was five - I wanted a doll baby so bad for Christmas. When Christmas morning was, I went to the table and there laying next to my plate with the orange and candy was a package. Of course I figured right then and there I got my doll baby. My, was I happy! My heart almost jumped for joy outta my chest! Mom was right there in the kitchen fixing breakfast, so quiet as could be I snuck up to the table, reached up and pressed the package, my heart pounding and palms sweaty from excitement.

My enthusiasm died as soon as I touched it. "It's no dolly, it's too soft," I moaned under my breath. It was such a let-down that in my throat come a big lump. I couldn't swallow. Trying to settle down I took a deep breath, pulled the package off the table and opened it up.

There was a pair of rubber galoshes and legging's, a couple years too big for me then yet. I just couldn't help myself. Trying to choke back the tears I begun to snivel, then the tears run and wouldn't stop. I began to cry out loud knowing it'd cause trouble. I just couldn't help myself.

Mom got cross right away and began to hammer on me and scold.

Pop was coming downstairs when he heard Mom at me and me crying.

"*Wass iss*? What ails *du*?"

Choking on my words I hiccupped, "I didn't get no doll baby."

"What are *du* got?"

I told him.

Pop, big as he was, leaned down and looked me in the eye and explained.

"*Ach vell* now," he said. "*Du* will be startin' *schul* one of these days *un du* will have all the snow to go through. Them leggin's *un* them galoshes will help out a whole lot."

147

After he explained things like that it sunk in and made everything all right.

My wonderful pop, he was so different. So good and kind he was.

In a stern, hard voice Mom said to him - she was saying it more and more all the time, "*Ach*! *Du* are spoilin' her, makin' her a regular spoiled brat."

"She's doin' all right." was all Pop would say back.

Later that day, Sim Reichard, the man with a glass eye - he had his eye shot out in the war when gunpowder hit him right in the eyeball - come to visit. Young as I was, Sim would tell me war stories. I'd sit and listen, spellbound. He could never say much in English, only Dutch, but I could understand him, yes sir! Most times, that is. Didn't matter. I liked being next to him, listening to his stories. Anyhow, Sim seen I wasn't my usual peppy self and he wondered about this. Pop told him how I wanted a doll baby but didn't get one.

"She's gonna get her doll," Sim, with a shake of his head said just like that. I heard but didn't pay much attention cause why in the world would he care about a little girl wanting a doll baby.

He only stayed one night and the next day he went to his daughter's house. She lived in York. He come back soon after that, walked in the house, came over to me and handed me a purty box almost as big as me. I wasn't used to being handed something like that. What should I do? I looked at Mom. She wouldn't look my way, busied herself at the stove. I searched Sim's face to know what to do. His grin showed a mouth of broken, yellow teeth. Nodding his head at me and the box I clumsily tore open the lid. Oh, my! Oh, glory! There lay a beautiful doll, the most wonderful thing I ever seen. I turned breathless with surprise. I never seen such a doll like this before - all dressed up so nice and purty she was; had on a long, light purple dress with white, flocked flowers, a full, frilly white petticoat that made her dress stand out, pantaloons underneath. I lifted her out of the box and pulled her to me. My very own doll baby. I sat down and put her on my lap to look her over. Her black patent shoes had shiny, little buckles on stockinged feet. She had long, yellow curls, was perfect in every way. Her blue eyes opened and shut; rosy cheeks she had, and her smiling lips was purty pink. Oh, the wonder of it! I looked at Sim who was grinning from ear to ear, taking note of how happy he made me.

"Is she for me to keep? Forever?" I asked, still not believing.

"*Ya. Ich* know *du* will love her *un* take good care of her."

I just loved my new dolly. I carefully touched her cheeks, not yet believing she was truly mine, then her lips, her eyes to see how they opened and shut. Mom, watching outta the corner of her eye seen me do this and almost hissed at me - not within hearing range of Sim and Pop who was now talking with each other, "If *du* punch out her eyes, that's what *Ich* will do to *du!*"

I was taken aback that Mom would think I'd hurt my dolly. I pulled her to me and hugged her tighter, carried her with me all day. We rocked on the big, old rocking chair and I showed her my books. I showed her to Poodle and told him I had another best friend along with him. Poodle just looked and cocked his tired, wooly head. At suppertime I sat my dolly on the rocking chair while I ate so I wouldn't drop no food on her.

I didn't give her a name right away, but I mulled over what it would be. I was the happiest girl in the world and would take my time to give my new doll baby a name that suited her.

That night when I was getting ready for bed and had my doll baby with me, Mom took her outta my arms, rather rough I thought, but I convinced myself it was only till I got into my nightclothes. But that queasy feeling in the pit of my stomach proved my sixth sense was working right. Instead of handing her back to me so I could tuck my dolly in bed with me, Mom took her and slammed her down hard, high up on the bureau next to my bed.

That night I lay sick at heart, fearful that Mom wouldn't let me hold my doll baby ever again. There was no sleep in me. As I lay in the dark trying to take in the form of my dolly high on the bureau, it was then I decided to name my doll baby, Hope. When Pop - and Grammy and Pap for that matter - read from the Bible about hope, it come to me that hope had something to do with wanting but not yet having. Well, I got my doll baby but now I couldn't hold her. All I could do was hope I'd soon be able to again take her in my arms. Yep, Hope was my doll baby's name.

My fears in the night proved true. Mom never left me hold her. Never! My doll baby just sat there. Only could I see her sit up there so high when I went to bed before the oil lamp was outened. I didn't dare fuss or Mom woulda hid her in a drawer where I couldn't see her at all. Oh, how my empty arms ached to hold my doll baby.

It was a Saturday in October, 1898. In a couple months I'd be six years old. This day they put me down to Mellinger's and I was told to stay there till they come for me. It was getting towards evening and I figured it was time for me to go home.

When Carrie Mellinger started supper, I said so anxious, "I must go."

See, I didn't know nothing about nothing, and the only thing I worried about real good was the scolding I'd get from Mom if I didn't get home in time for supper.

Lance Mellinger saw how worried and strong-minded I was to go home. He said, "*Du* stay right here till they *kumme* for *du*. Then if they want to whip *du* or anything, then they got me to whip."

Carrie and Lance was the best neighbors, but they didn't know how mad my mom could get; they didn't know my mom like I did, of that I was sure.

See, this day they knowed what it was going on but I didn't. Nothing was said to me.

It was good to eat supper with that big family - seven children in all they had . Before they ate, everyone bowed their heads and Lance prayed a blessing. They was good Christian people, and more'n that they wasn't afraid to show affection. During that then the food was kept on the warming shelf above the old cream colored cook stove to keep it hot. It smelled so good it kept me from being intent on the prayer although I bowed my head and closed my eyes. But my mouth sure did water as the inviting whiffs of delicious food traveled up my nose, yes it did.

What a happy time around that table. The older girls helped their mom set the table and put the food out. During dinner the talk was lively. Each family member, no matter how young, was allowed a time to say what was on their mind as long as it was suitable for all ears and didn't hurt no feelings.

Supper was over so I helped Susie with her chores. All her brothers and sisters was fun-loving and didn't hurry with their chores maybe as fast as they shoulda, so of course, I went along with that. I never had so much carefree fun with chores at home. Nonetheless their work got done in good time.

Susie was my pal. We growed up together, we had our sicknesses together - measles, mumps, chicken pox - why the two of us even have a chicken pox scar in the exact same spot at our left eye brows. Susie and I sat together in school and everything.

Uncle John Farley was at our place and he come down with the lantern since it was dark already. Him and Lance and Carrie stood outside talking, then with me in tow he headed back to the farm. As we made our way through the fields and meadows it wondered me so what was going on.

Uncle John, as we walked along would sing, "Oh, joy! Your momma's got a surprise!" But that's all he'd dare say.

When we got in the house, Ruby Heindel was in the kitchen and I didn't see Mom. Ruby and her twin sister, Coral, them two girls was something else I tell you; lots of fun but a bit snippy, too; about the same age as Mom. Coral wasn't there, only Ruby.

"Why are you here?" I wanted to know. "Where's Mom?"

Ruby told me Mom was sick in bed and she come to help out.

Pop come down the steps and said to me then, "*Ya,* Snip, *kumme* with me. We will to go upstairs to your momma."

I was more'n worried cause Mom never got sick except for them terrible headaches. Other'n that she seldom had an ache or pain and considered them that did just a bunch of sissified *brootzers*. And now here was everyone acting strange with Mom in bed.

I went up those steps lickity-split. My gosh! Oh my goodness! I never had an inkling. I never woulda guessed. When I hurried into the bedroom I stopped short. Could it be? I seen two babies lay. Oh, boy! I was in my glory. Now I had babies and how I loved them right off.

They filled my heart with joy, happiness and a little bit of hope.

You see, people'd come and visit us still that had babies. One time Lance and Carrie Mellinger come up when Gertie was a baby and Lance knowed I liked babies, so he asked me did I wanna keep her.

"Can I, Mom?" I was overjoyed to think I could keep that baby.

"All she does is bawl," Lance warned. But she didn't cry once while they was there. They knowed then there was babies on the way at our house, but of course I didn't. See, them things wasn't talked about in front of children then. Why I seen all kinds of animals being born and eggs hatched out but I never connected them things with real babies coming into the world.

When they wrapped Gertie up to take her home, my heart broke. "I thought you was gonna let her here," I whined.

They didn't. Just chuckled and took her along home.

I didn't see nothing funny about the way Lance changed his mind. Not at all.

Now, when I seen them two babies lay on the bed near Mom - Pop said a boy and a girl - I was in my glory! I just couldn't keep away from the bed. I stood and looked and looked. No way would I thought of touching 'em just yet, much as I wanted to, but I could picture myself rocking one, then the other'n. I had my own babies now and I adored them. Lance could keep Gertie and it wouldn't bother me none at all no more.

When Ruby helped me get ready for bed it showed me how sick Mom was. Mom never left nobody do that except Grammy. I worried about Mom but fell asleep happy as I looked up at Hope and told her under my breath that someday I'd show her my babies and we'd all rock together.

Grammy and Pap come for me next day. For the first time in my life I didn't wanna go back with them. I didn't wanna leave my babies. I wouldn't leave. I pouted. I begged them not to take me away from my babies.

But then Pop said over it, "*Ich* know *du* wanna stay here with the *bobbels*, but Ruby's got so much on her with the milkin' *un* everything. She don't have time to comb *un* fix your braids *un* everything."

Finally I went along with Grammy and Pap. I stayed one week.

When I come back, one baby wasn't there.

"Where's the other baby?" I wanted to know. They told me the little girl died.

I stopped in my tracks. At first I was shocked and speechless. Then I started shaking with anger and hurt. Never did I talk to Mom and Pop like this before, but resentment got the best of me and right off I accused them. "See, if I'd of been here I could of held her and rocked her and made her better, you know."

My heart ached so bad that this time the tears didn't let loose right away. Instead a deep rage inside grew as I tried to sort out how my baby sister could die. Lots of babies died back then but I didn't know that, I only knowed that one baby was gone. I didn't even get a chance to know her. It was the second time they pushed me away and didn't let me in on it till it was too late. First the Old Lady and now the girl baby. I felt like I was robbed of two people I loved with all my heart. I coulda kept her alive you know, loving her and rocking her. But no, they didn't listen to me and now she was gone.

I was inconsolable. In bed that night I looked up and seen Hope sitting where Mom slammed her down so long ago. I still had Hope. If only I could hold her and tell her what happened. But only there did she sit high on the bureau staring straight ahead. She looked desolate too. I wanted to ask Pop to get her down but something held me back. If he woulda turned me down I'd of learned right then and there he didn't love me like I first thought. Then for sure I'd shrivel up into nothing. I didn't dare take the chance. I just couldn't chance it, hadda keep on believing he loved me so.

As cross as I was I begun to settle down for I didn't wanna bring Mom and Pop more trouble and worry; the only way I wouldn't take it out on them was to blame myself. It was my fault. I was the guilty one. I shoulda insisted on not going to Grammy's. I shoulda stayed to help with my babies. The anger was so strong it left me speechless, the one who was never at a loss for words. I crawled inside myself, quiet on the outside, but screaming noises raged on and on in my head.

Next day I didn't talk about her. No one did, not even Ruby who was still there helping Mom. Busy she was. Tried to lift me out of my moodiness, but when I refused to oblige she left me alone after she got me dressed and my hair combed, humming as she worked away. I didn't even ask if the little girl had a name, and they didn't say. I wanted to know all about her. I wondered so if they buried her next to the Old Lady but I was too hurt, too proud, too stubborn to pursue it with Mom and Pop. Besides, I didn't think they'd tell me more'n what was already spoken.

I maybe coulda been spared a lot of sorrow if I'd of been told the truth, but things wasn't that way with Mom. Pop was awful quiet and said almost nothing for days, just like me. I felt so alone. And lonely.

Sometime later it dawned on me that Pop's silence was from hurting too. Besides, the baby boy needed lots of attention. He was named Albert Franklin Geesey. Mom gave him the Albert - she thought Albert and Alverna sounded good together - and Pop named him Franklin after Mr. Weaver, a good friend who had the general store in town.

Albert was sick, just like the little girl, but he pulled through. The way it went was the doctor said to put him on a bottle right away. They hadda put so much milk, so much wine water, a little bit of sugar and things like that together in his bottle. The only other thing he dare have for a long, long time was the whites of an egg beat up stiff. Mom used the yolks for cakes and puddings, things like that, never wasted nothing. That's the way Albert growed up until he was one and a half. Then he dare have a little bit of this or a little bit of that, but not much of anything and his milk.

How hard my mom hadda work!

As I watched Mom work at trying to feed him I'd sit and wonder so, "How awful it is that Albert can eat only things like that and I can eat anything." I pitied Albert to no end.

I look back and think of how puny Albert was. But then I think too, "Yeah, but after all, Albert lived to a much older

155

age, a whole lot longer than our pop." (I'll tell more about that later.)

When he got older and was able to eat more, Albert and I shared everything. See, when Pop went to the store for certain things we needed, Mom always made a list: chocolate, sugar, rice - not much. I 'd always be sure to remind Pop, "And a bag of candy for me."

Pop would take butter and eggs to exchange, sometimes a duck or chicken. He'd say to Frank Weaver at the store, "My little girl said don't forget to fetch a bag of candy."

Soon after Albert was born Pop said when he was getting ready to go to the store, *"Ach vell,* Snip, should *Ich* fetch one bag of candy or two?"

"Albert's too little to eat candy, but you don't never need to get two bags. When he's old enough I'll share my candy with him."

I seen Pop turn and take his big red hanky outta his pocket, wipe his eyes and blow his nose. Why, I couldn't understand till years later when Mr. Weaver told me how Pop at the store told him what I said. Mr. Weaver said that even then Pop was so touched that he used his hanky to blow his nose as he was telling him about it.

Frank Weaver told him, "You have a wonderful family, Ben,"

"Ya, Ich got a wonderful family. *Ich* am pleased with my family, that *Ich* am."

But you see, that was the way we growed up. What I got I always shared with Albert; what Albert got he shared with me.

One time Pop hadda go to Hoover's mill and he took Albert along when Albert was purty little yet. Ethel Hoover gave Albert a banana, a rare treat back then. She thought he'd tear it open and start eating it right away but he sat there in the wagon and held it just so to keep it from bruising.

"Give it here. I'll peel it for you," said Ethel, thinking he was too little to start it.

"No, I'm savin' part of it for Alverna."

Well, Ethel couldn't get over it how Albert wouldn't eat the banana till he could share it with his sister. She run back in and got her mom and told her about this. She just couldn't get over it! "The first thing most kids'd do was eat it before they hadda share. This little boy, he's savin' part for his sister." Ethel took another banana out for Albert to give me. Still Albert waited till he got home so we could eat our bananas together. And they was delicious.

Only once I almost hated Albert for that terrible injustice he did to me when he was still yet purty little, but old enough to know better.

I eventually forgave him - but I never forgot, not to this day.

It took me a long time to get over it.

See, what happened, Mom took Albert upstairs with her when she had her work up there to do. One day Albert was fussing more'n usual even after Mom sat him on the bed with the glass marble. When he throwed it on the floor I grabbed for it so it wouldn't crack or chip. Albert didn't know about the marble like I did. Someday I'd tell him about it and the Old Lady. In the meantime I slipped it in my pocket to hide and keep safe.

Mom was at the end of her rope with Albert. Not knowing how else to settle him down she took my doll baby down off the bureau and gave her to him, probably thinking it might keep him quiet for a spell.

I was taking the chamber pot to empty when I seen Mom give my doll baby to Albert. My heart started thumping like mad. If I got the pot emptied and cleaned, maybe since Mom gave my dolly to Albert she'd let me hold her too. I hurried to finish up, making sure the pot was extra clean so's not to upset Mom more'n she was with Albert's whining. Done, I started climbing back up the steep stairs, not an easy thing to do worrying with that big, heavy chamber pot. Almost at the top I was when a strange, sharp, cracking noise like

I never before heard come from the bedroom. Something was terrible wrong. But what? Did Albert fall off the bed and hurt hisself? Did Mom let something fall? I rushed into the bedroom and what I saw stopped me in my tracks. I gasped in wretchedness, almost dropped the pot.

First off, I couldn't believe it. Nevertheless, it happened. Albert, in a fit of temper, took my doll baby and swung her around and bashed her head against the iron headboard.

How could such a sickly little boy get the strength to do that? There I stood in horror looking at parts of my beloved doll baby, her china head and hands shattered to bits and pieces. But no more shattered than my spirit. Her beautiful, long yellow curls lay on the floor tangled with shards of glass. Her body was caught between the wall and headboard, feet sticking straight up, one shoe on, the other'n in Albert's hand. It was like in slow motion I watched him throw that little black shoe down off the bed as he plopped on his tummy from throwing my dolly baby around.

Albert just lay there, his beady, brown eyes now wide open, staring fascinated at what he done.

I looked Mom's way, still not believing what I seen.

As the truth dawned on me, I desperately hoped for some sympathy in Mom's eyes and her meting out some harsh punishment to Albert. Hands on hips she looked so provoked, but not at Albert. She said nothing.

I seen it then. She had no understanding, no sorrow for me. My heart sank. I could see what was coming. She pointed to me, then the broom.

It was up to me to clean up the pieces of my beloved, broken doll baby.

I sat the chamber pot down with great care and deliberation because what I wanted to do right then and there was slam it on the floor like Albert slammed my baby on the rails of the headboard.

Denying it could really happen and thinking maybe I could put her back together again, it didn't take long for the truth to sink in. Again. I was now convinced my dolly couldn't be fixed. I pulled her headless body out from the headboard and felt so sick I thought I'd throw up. I gagged as the tears started. The hurt cut deep. My pain was so dreadful I thought I'd collapse right where I was and never get up again.

With my doll baby now lost to me forever because of Albert's uncalled-for behavior, something inside of me snapped. I determined to fight back. I'd not let Mom and Albert see how overcome I was. I stopped crying; figured if they seen they couldn't hurt me by what they done with my doll baby, they'd never on purpose try to hurt me again. But, believe you me, I was hurting like I never hurt before except when the Old Lady died - and my baby sister.

Off the bed and floor I took all the time in the world to collect the countless bits of my doll baby, every now and then deliberately looking at Mom to see if she might show the slightest unease for my pain and sorrow.

She didn't.

I begun to lay the pieces carefully on a newspaper Mom spread out on the floor, hardly caring if she disapproved of the way and how slow I was cleaning up. I wanted her so bad to scold me so I could talk back to her. Not a word she said. A flake of glass splintered my finger and the blood ran. Good! I wanted to bleed. Maybe if my hands hurt my heart wouldn't ache so bad. Gathering pieces of broken glass, I laid them on the palms of my hands and clenched my fists tight. As the blood oozed out it would show Mom and Albert what they done to me. I smeared my blood-stained palms and fingers over the white flocked flowers on Hope's light purple dress.

Albert just laid there, quiet as a mouse, taking all this in.

When every last piece was cleaned up, Mom went to wrap the newspaper around my ruined dolly but I stepped in between her and the newspaper to finish the job myself, not caring what she thought. Let her swat me. It didn't matter. I couldn't hurt more.

I wrapped Hope up gently as my blood smeared the newspaper all over. Mom reached to grab my hands to look at the damage I done but I pulled away before she got a strong hold on me. She left me go. She looked like she was gonna hit me. I didn't care. Let her.

She left it pass.

I hoped my dolly would understand that I loved her and with my blood was giving her a part of myself before I hadda dump her in the woodstove. Working away, I wiped my bloody hands on my dress, an intentional wrongdoing. I walked close to the bed. Stock still I stood close to Albert, stared him down while holding the wrapped up pieces of my doll baby. I wanted him to see my bloody hands. Albert never seen me like this. He knowed I was furious. He stared at me, frightened, eyes as big as saucers ready to pop outta his head, quieter than I ever seen. I would of wiped some of my blood on him but I didn't dare go that far.

"Now," I said as I walked outta the bedroom, braver than ever before. "You can get your work done, Mom. Albert's quiet. He's settled down."

Downstairs I went, walked to the woodstove. Before I put my ruined doll baby inside I laid the newspaper on the floor and opened it again. I looked for a sharp knife and cut off a blood stained piece of what a couple minutes ago was the beautiful dress of my doll baby. Next, with the same knife I sawed off one yellow curl that wasn't too filled with broken glass. I was gonna take her shoe, too, but Albert touched it, so I didn't want it. I stuffed 'em in my pocket with the glass marble to later hide somewhere from Mom, but first I hadda wrap up the paper and what was inside and stuff it into the fire. I didn't close the fire door right away, instead, I watched my dolly go up in smoke. Some of the smoke poured out into the room, a terrible smell. "Good!" I thought. "I hope it stings Mom's eyes and makes Albert sick."

After I washed my hands I put the pieces of Hope and the glass marble in a damaged cigar box Uncle John gave me a long time ago. I'd have to find a place to hide it but my mind wasn't working that clear just yet. I'd find a good hiding

160

place though. Maybe out in the corner of the barn where Mom never went.

My spirit was crushed.

What I said to Mom about getting her work done was the last words I spoke for days.

Mindless, I carried out my chores. My hands festered. Splinters from Hope stuck in my hands and fingers. I didn't care. I hurt so much all over that my infected hands was of no concern to me. One morning Mom made me straddle a bench, then placed a basin of warm water with Epsom Salts in front of me, stuck my hands in to soak the soreness out. I left her do to me whatever pleased her, all the time shutting her out. I was like a rag doll. Didn't pay Albert no mind either.

That was one time I won the battle of wills. My hands stayed in the water the way Mom put 'em. I sat like that till the water went cold. My upper legs dug into the bench. Soon I couldn't feel my legs and feet. They went to sleep hanging down. My arms froze into rigid stumps. My hands got cold, my fingers turned wrinkly and blue. Mom thought I'd pull 'em out when I couldn't take it no longer.

I didn't move.

When she heard Pop step up on the porch she hurried over to me, pulled my hands outta the water and dried me off. She stood me up but my legs was asleep and I buckled down onto the floor. She woulda left me there except for Pop coming in. She then pulled me over to the Old Lady's rocker, sat me down. Mom got good and scared I was gonna die from grief. There I sat till supper time when the blood returned to my legs. I roused myself to set the table.

Pop seen that the salts brought some glass pieces to my skin's surface. He went and got his tweezers, held my hands tender-like. Looking at them tweezers and remembering the fun we had with 'em, I almost broke down then. Instead I got back my resolve, stiffened my back and let my hands go limp as he pulled some splinters of Hope from my hands.

Pop, he said almost nothing through all this, didn't ask me what happened. I'm sure he and Mom spoke about it but I don't know. Maybe Mom didn't tell him the whole story. For awhile he stayed outside most the time, busier than usual. Young as I was I felt he didn't know how to deal with this between Mom and me.

He knowed better than to try to humor me when he come inside, knowed I wouldn't have no part in that. The reason why he never stood up for me and my dolly I'll never know, but that hurt bad. Whatever it was, the secret died with him.

The closest he ever got to acknowledging my hurt was one evening. Mom was getting Albert ready for bed, Pop was sitting in his chair, wearily thumbing through his worn Bible like he was looking for a certain place. He musta found it, paused, then read out loud: "A proverb. 'By sorrow of heart the spirit is broken'." He looked my way for a long pause then shut his Bible. Looking dejected and all washed-out, he slowly pulled himself outta his chair and climbed the stairs, weary and worn-out.

I almost hated my brother and my mom. I worked long and hard at forgiving them, but for a long time I didn't care, didn't want to.

I eventually did forgive 'em. But I never forgot.

Hope was gone except for one yellow curl and a tiny piece of dress. That was all I had left. Just a little bit of Hope.

Never got another doll baby. Never wanted one.

CHAPTER 16 - CLASSMATES AND NEIGHBORS

One of the school teachers was friends with Pop. When I was only five, Charl Hoffman, the *schulmeister*, knowed how I could say my ABC's and everything. Why, I read the whole Tom Thumb book through before I went to school. And I spelt words - long, complicated words like *alphabet* - backwards. This was one way I passed time when I was helping Mom with tiresome chores. Pop taught me ciphering too. The older I got the more I enjoyed working out long division. It got so I could work a problem that was as wide as a sheet of paper sideways. Still do to this day.

Charl stopped by to talk to Pop about some school matters since Pop was on the school board. "Ben, please let me take Alverna along tomorrow morning when school starts," he begged.

He had too many scholars to begin with, but I'd of fit in a whole lot better than some of them who was the right age. Pop said it wouldn't go, parents would accuse me of actin' too big for my britches and point the finger at Pop himself for usin' his position as a school board member to his own advantage.

That settled that. I didn't start school until I was six, but I loved to learn and Pop helped however he could. Mom, too, sometimes.

After the Old Lady died, Pop was the head of the family. His Mom was the authority when she lived, now it was Pop's turn. He sought out Mom's advice and listened to her reasoning more'n most men who was too pig-headed to pay attention to their women. Pop listened and at times even took her advice. Mom's problem was she never got over being around men from little on up whose word was law and whose authority was never questioned, so she held back more'n Pop wanted. She wasn't never used to women being valued for their opinions. Pop tried to help her see her importance but it was an idea too hard for Mom to grasp. It was ingrained in most women to not think too much and voice their opinions only when asked.

Now take me for instance. When I was in my early teens I thought I was more broadminded than Mom, but the time come which proved to me I wasn't not much more better at standing my ground than her. But I'll get to that later. Maybe.

Romance novels and mystery stories usually have happy endings. But not always history books. Maybe I'm mostly writing history cause I can't promise everything here has a happy ending. But history has good parts, too.

When I started school I made friends with all the kids my age, even older ones.

Liza Peters was a classmate who had a whole handful of warts, just her left hand. Rough and bumpy and ugly was her hand, all covered over with warts. Twice as big as her other'n. When we'd play games at recess none of the other girls would take her hand, just turn up their noses, make a snoot and jump back if Liza got too near. Liza, she'd just stand back and hang her head.

I pitied her so bad.

"Come on Liza," I'd say. "I'm not afraid of them warts."

When the others seen I wasn't gonna give in, she was allowed to join our games but only if I'd hold the hand that was full of warts. It did feel awful strange but I never let on.

When I told Pop about it he said, "If only *Ich* could get to her, *Ich* maybe could try for 'em - think *Ich* could get rid of 'em." But Pop, he never got the chance to powwow Liza Peters' warts.

And that's the way it was with Bill and Martha Hartman. They was Dunkards, wore plain clothes. Martha wore a little cap on her head that only Dunkards wore. Them at school wouldn't bother with Bill and Martha cause they dressed different. The brother and sister stood back and watched the rest of us play, all the time wanting to join in. Well! I couldn't take that. I'd coax 'em till finally they'd join in. When the rest of the kids seen I wasn't gonna' give up on 'em, they let 'em play too.

Pop was proud of me that way. He'd say, "*Du* will get your reward, Snip, *ya, du* will now yet. The *Goot Buch* says *du* will reap what *du* sow *un* it looks to me like *du* sow the *goot* seeds."

Pop, he made me feel good about myself. He made things better for me since Mom's stony heart coulda made me mean and bitter.

It always snowed every winter back then, and everyone hooked their sleds onto the backs of others and that's the way we'd sled down the hill on the north side of the schoolhouse during recess. Some of us didn't have sleds, maybe just a piece of tin or cardboard that we made do. Most of the time Bill and Martha wouldn't join in, just stand back and watch. They was shy. Then one day Bill come to school pulling his sister on this wonderful good sled, the best we ever seen. What happened, their dad went and made it for them. When everyone seen what a wonderful fast sled they had, then the rest hooked three or four sleds onto Bill and Martha's because it gave the fastest ride. Then Bill and Martha was all right.

Even kids can be mean. When I think of things like that and how greedy and mean people can be, they sure can be nasty sometimes. Yeah!

Pop would tell Mom and me. "Let it go. People who are greedy are never got satisfied. They *esse* their hearts out because there's always somethin' to be greedy *ebaut*." I could let it go but Mom wouldn't. Things like that stayed with her and she'd stew over 'em, seldom get over it.

Now take Opal Heindel, for instance. Opal - she was my age - had warts and Pop powwowed for 'em and they went away. Opal would cast it up to me over and over in a sing-song voice, "Your Pop powwowed my warts but he never powwowed for you."

I never had warts.

Opal was natured to want me to think she had something over on me. She was always like that, but she got it honest from her family. She hounded me about it, wanting me to beg her to tell me how Pop powwowed for her warts, but I wouldn't. I already knowed. Finally it got the best of her and she broke down and told me anyway.

"Your Pop brought this round potato, smoothest I ever seen." Opal began. "He pulled out this sharp knife (it was the one he used only to powwow with, only Opal didn't know that; I did), real sharp it was, and sliced that potato clean through the middle. He rubbed each half back and forth over my warts all the time repeatin' strange words I never before heard. He then took them potato pieces and buried 'em under the rainspout."

"Opal," he said to me. "Believe the warts will go away. If *du* believe, when the potato rots away so your warts will . They'll be all gone."

"In three weeks my warts no more was. Feel my skin, Alverna. Momma says it's as smooth as a baby's behind."

It was.

You see, the Heindels had one farm behind us, so Opal and I walked to school together. Mr. Heindel, Bill was his name, wasn't so bad, but his wife Pearl, didn't want nobody to get ahead of 'em. Their twin daughters was Ruby and Coral, then two boys, Hunter and Stone. Then Opal.

Now Opal was different from the rest. She was bought by the Heindel family. They bought her from her mother who visited the Heindel's every now and then. Opal called her real mother, Aunt Phoebe. Though I heard Mom and Pop talk about this between 'em, Opal and I, we never talked about this lady being her momma. Things like that was only talked about behind people's backs.

Hardest thing for me to understand was why the Heindel family bought Opal. She didn't appear out of the ordinary. Matter of fact she was big and clumsy, not purty in any way. Mom once said they got Opal cause they needed an extra hand to help Pearl with all she claimed she hadda do. Pearl, she took sick purty often, but Mom wondered how much of her sickness was real and how much was imagined. Mom thought Pearl was on the lazy side.

Folks today don't think things like that happened back then, but they did. Some people hadda do things maybe they didn't wanna do just to make it in the world. I heard Mom telling Pop about all this and how this Aunt Phoebe would fetch Opal clothes when she visited. They wondered so if maybe it was out of guilt for selling Opal. Maybe that's all she could do for her. Anyhow, Opal dressed a whole lot better than me. And if she did work hard for Pearl, at least she got lots of nice things. But Opal was sorta lazy. Got outta doing whatever she could.

Remember Sim Reichard, the man who got his eye shot out in the war, the man who got me the doll baby? One other time he got me this beautiful book-bag. Sim knowed something happened with my dolly cause he never seen it when he come around. He asked me once about it and I just hung my head and sulked, said nothing. Sim never again asked. He took a liking to me and I liked him back, not just cause he got me things I never woulda got any other way. I liked his stories that got me all wound up inside. I listened to every one of 'em. He was kind to me, but not too nice in front of Mom cause he knowed she was afraid he'd spoil me. Besides that, she was suspicious he'd tell me things I shouldn't hear, bein' so young and all.

It was like a game they played when Sim was around. He'd try to get me with him to tell stories and Mom would be keeping near so she'd hear what he was saying. But Sim went only so far and respected Mom's feeling's cause he didn't want her to get too cross and take it out on me when he wasn't around.

Sim made certain Pop was around when he gave me the book-bag, figured at least that way I had a chance of getting to use it instead of Mom sticking it away somewhere.

I didn't need to bring books home cause I got 'em done in school, but well, I was tickled with my new book-bag and carried my books home cause it made me feel good.

Opal saw this right away and when her family found out I got a book-bag like that, well, not wanting anyone to have something better than their Opal, it wasn't long till she had one just like it except hers had a fancy gold **O** - for Opal - on the front.

Of course when she stopped in to show it off to Mom and Pop, it didn't go good with Mom, but Pop would say with a soft, quiet voice, "Don't say nothin'. They'll get their reward now yet."

It snowed long and hard them winter days so I got a lot of wear outta my rubber galoshes and leggings. I walked one and one half miles to school. Opal stopped at the house so we could walk together. We was the same age, she born in May and I in December. She lorded it over me because she was older'n me and thought herself smarter'n me. Anyhow, Pop showed me how we could cut off a quarter mile by coming through his corn field, so that's the way we walked.

Opal tried to make trouble between Susie and me cause she was jealous of our friendship. Susie and I seen straight through her, knowed what she was trying to do so we made a promise to each other to never let her break us up. Wasn't a hard promise for either of us to keep.

Opal always had ways of scaring me, and she did her dirty best. While we trudged single file between the corn rows, she walked behind, trying to scare me by making these awful choking noises in her throat. When I turned to see what was the matter, she'd holler and laugh, pointing her finger at me and making' all the fun in the world. Oh, Opal enjoyed herself that way, she did.

One day Susie and me was eating our dinner at school. Opal come up and said, "Are you got candy in your bucket?" She meant the candy we got at Christmas, the real clear, toy candy.

"Yeah."

"Let's keep it and eat it on the way home."

So that's what we done. We was coming down through the corn rows and Opal started making deep, throaty noises. I had caught on to what she was doing and I just said over it without looking back at her, "Yes well, Opal Irene Heindel, you ain't gonna scare me this time, no sir-eee."

I kept on walking but she still made these noises and when I couldn't take it no longer I stopped and looked around. My Lord! There was Opal, holding her neck, blue in the face. Blue as could be! Here this candy went back in her throat and stayed sticking.

I was almost home so I begin to run. I run hard and fast cause I knowed she needed help and I didn't know what to do. I run. She run too and tried to grab me, but she stumbled over a corn stalk and fell down. I heard her fall so I turned around and here what happened the candy went down her throat when she hit the ground.

Helping her up she fretted, "Oh, Alverna, you run away from me. I'll never, never make you scared again. I promise I'll never make fun of you no more."

She said she was going along in to tell Mom and Pop what happened.

Mom seen us coming. "Somethin's the matter. Opal's comin' along in. Look out now yet, somethin's up."

"Wass iss?" Pop asked when Opal come in.

169

Opal explained what happened.

Now Mom shook her head and scolded Opal right away in her sternest voice. "Serves *du* right!"

Pop didn't. He just said over it, "Opal, *du* know everybody gets paid back one way or the other for things they do. *Du* scared Snip here so much. This time *du* needed her *un* she run."

"Yes," I chimed in. "But I run to get help. She was blue in the face."

When Opal realized why I run, she whispered, "Mr. and Mrs. Geesey, I promise that's the last time I'll ever scare Alverna. I'll never ever fool her again." She couldn't hardly talk for her throat was so sore from the candy sticking in and going down whole. She couldn't hardly eat anything for a couple days.

Opal's older twin sisters, Ruby and Coral come over in the evening and they said what she told them. "We didn't know she made it like that for Alverna," they said. "It'll never happen again."

Pop would always say, "Have your fun now yet but at nobody else's expense."

And that's the way I do to this day.

All this sure didn't stop Pearl from taking advantage of Mom which made her madder than ever. See, the Heindel's, like most farmers, went to market to sell their extra produce. Any extra we had, why people knew what good stuff Pop raised and how Mom tended her garden so they'd come right to the farm to buy the spare.

Pearl stopped by our house one time and saw what nice, solid turnips Mom had from her garden. "Let me take some to market and sell them for you," Pearl offered Mom.

The first week Pearl paid Mom for the turnips Mom sent, but the next week when they come back from market Pearl said that the turnips didn't go and brung back wrinkled turnips, not nice at all. Mom never sent them kind of turnips to market with Pearl Heindel or anyone else and wondered if they sat in the sun they was so droopy. She throwed 'em into the slop bucket for the hogs. That same day a neighbor stopped by and she noticed the nice, solid turnips laying there Mom had just pulled. Mom told her how Pearl Heindel said they didn't go at market.

Well, that lady was purty sure what was going on so she went to market the next week and come back to Mom and put a bug in her ear - told her she seen people buying nice, big, fat turnips right and left from Pearl, but there was wormy ones there that didn't go. Didn't take Mom long to figure out what Pearl was doing. She was selling Mom's turnips, keeping the money and passing the scrawny ones back to her.

Mom made sure Pearl Heindel never got no more of her turnips - nothing would she send with Pearl after that.

"All she thinks about is money," Mom complained. See, there was a time when the Heindel family was at our house to visit. All seven of 'em. They got to talking about dreams. Ruby was saying how her last dream was that wherever she was - she couldn't remember where - there was this big pile of money, but whenever she tried to reach after it she couldn't get none. Not no matter how hard she tried, 'twas always just outta her reach. Pearl piped in, "When you see money like that in your dreams, put your apron on inside out, then you'll get rich."

When the Heindels left and was walking back to their farm, Pop chuckled. Then he asked Mom, "Since when do maiden ladies wear aprons to *bedde*?"

Mom looked puzzled for a couple seconds, then busted out laughing at the joke. That made us all laugh, but before long Mom was back in a stew to think Pearl only cared about herself and what she could get by cheating like she did.

Pop said, "*Ach vell* now, let it go. The *Goot Buch* says that *'the wrongdoer will get paid back for the wrong he's done.'* That goes for Pearl Heindel, too."

I purty much got along with all the schoolkids; except for this one older girl - her name was Adelaide Shorts. A rough girl. She acted like she knowed it all.

I think it was all a big front. She built herself up by tearing other kids down.

When Adelaide talked it was more like hollering, pointing fingers at and making fun of everybody who didn't think like her. She was a hard one to get along with. Susie, Opal, me and the rest of the girls our age steered clear of her. As long as we stuck together we didn't feel too bad about the way Adelaide poked fun at us. Her bullying made us stick up for each other. Strength in numbers is what they say. But if she ever got one of us alone and tore into us with her harsh words and nasty threats, we'd quake in our shoes and sometimes pee our pants, that spiteful she was; scared us all to heck.

One cold winter day Adelaide come to school with only one arm in her worn, heavy, hand-me-down coat that was slung over her other shoulder. Couldn't stay warm that way in weather like we was having. Opal noticed it right away and wondered so about it, but no way was any of us gonna bring it up and aggravate her. Here, when she took her coat off, her right hand was wrapped up, so swollen she couldn't of pushed it through her coat sleeve. We didn't stare too long for it'd make her mad for sure, but we just couldn't hardly help ourselves. Another thing; there was a burnt smell coming through the rag that covered her hand. The room got hushed. Everyone of us there that morning knowed something awful bad musta happened to Adelaide. Her face was all tear-streaked, her eyes almost swolled shut; her hair fell down into her eyes and over her face so it wouldn't be so noticeable. Only it was.

Mr. Hoffman, the schoolmaster had her off to the side trying to get out of her what happened while we was working the lessons he just now put on the board. There was usually three kids to a bench. Opal, Susie and me sat together. The thing was, Opal was so big we hadda squeeze together on the short, narrow bench, not an easy thing for us three.

That morning we was so intent on Adelaide and Mr. Hoffman talking, that when Opal went to sit down she hunkered too close to the edge of the bench. It coulda been a terrible disaster when the bench tilted and Opal landed on the floor with a big thump that shook the whole school building. Susie, on the other end, flew a couple feet in the air as her end of the bench went up. I watched her fly up but couldn't help her out. Being in the middle, I slid down and landed on Opal. Boy-oh-boy! Was we ashamed, and ever so scared at what Mr. Hoffman might do to us! We committed an intolerable infraction in the classroom, a fair reason for punishment. As we picked ourselves and the bench up, red-faced and flustered, there was snickers from around the classroom before the kids covered their mouths with their hands. All of 'em woulda been laughing out loud if it wasn't for Adelaide. We got scolded read good, but Mr. Hoffman knowed how we was nervous and upset about Adelaide so he let it stop there. He was purty befuddled hisself. Thank goodness! If Mom woulda got news of that, I woulda been in real trouble.

We overheard some of the older girls talk at lunch, all the time pretending we wasn't listening. Here what happened, Adelaide was tending her little sister and twin brothers who was just beginning to crawl and climb while their Mom went to the cellar. When Adelaide went after Raymond, Richard crawled over to the cook stove and burned his hand when he grabbed at it to pull hisself up. When their Mom rushed up and seen why he was screaming, right away she blamed Adelaide for not watching the boy, pulled her over to the cook stove and laid her hand right on the hot burner plate. Reaching for a clean rag she wrapped up Adelaide's hand and sent her off to school.

You could tell all day how bad Adelaide was hurting even when she tried not to show it. It woulda been easy to think, "You're finally getting some of your own medicine, Adelaide," but I pitied her so bad in spite of her meanness. So did Susie, but not Opal. Of course Opal, being overweight and clumsy, she took more of the brunt of Adelaide's scorn than Susie and me - although we got our share. Opal, she looked at it different than us, sorta looked glad at Adelaide's hurt and shame.

It didn't change Adelaide none. She was all her life grouchy, rough and hardhearted. Maybe we all woulda been like Adelaide if we had a momma like that.

CHAPTER 17 - AUNT LILLIEMAE

One time Mom got one of her sick headaches, couldn't even stand up she was so dizzy; throwing up, that sick she was. I was looking after Albert by myself. Mom taught me most of what she done around the house and with Albert so I could help her out. Ruby Heindel had just stopped by on her way to town and seen how sick Mom was. "I'm gonna stay and help out till you're feelin' better," Ruby told Mom. She put Mom to bed and sent me to the Heindel farm so's I could tell Pearl what Ruby was gonna do. Opal wanted me to stay with them but Coral said she'd go to town in Ruby's place and drop me off at my Grammy's house. Pop was working in the barnyard when Coral and me stopped to tell Pop this. He welcomed their help and said I should pack some extra clothes in a sack, that I could stay for a couple days. I was used to Mom getting them headaches. So sick for a day she'd get. I didn't worry too much about Mom for I knowed Ruby'd stay and help her out with Albert and the milking and other work. And me, I was relieved, ready to visit Grammy and Pap again.

Like I said before, I was back and forth between their house and Pop's, even after Pop and Mom married.

The morning after I got there, Grammy was on her way to help out a sick neighbor. She told her girl, Lilliemae, to kill a chicken, defeather, clean and cook it so it'd be ready to make slippery potpie for supper when she got home. Grammy said I was to help. Lilliemae was in her teens, fun-loving, lighthearted about life when she could get away with it. I often thought I musta got some of her blood in me cause I was a happy, cheerful child much like her. With Grammy gone she'd do what she was told, only she'd do it in her make-believe, play-acting, entertaining way. Her goal was someday to move to a big city and become an actor. Where she got that idea no one knowed for sure, but Grammy and Pap told her right off that they didn't wanna hear any such talk. "Get them sinful thoughts outta your head, girl," they'd say. "They is wrong as all get-out. No more talk like that!"

Lilliemae performed her chores like it was a school play. She done exaggerated movements with her arms and hands, a purposeful stride and a strong, clear, stagy voice since Grammy and Pap was gone. I mimicked her as we stoked up the cook stove and put water in a great big boiler to cook. I was taking great pleasure following after her and doing what she told me, - that is, till Lilliemae caught the chicken.

She said I was to hold it at the head while she chopped it off.

With her standing there holding the chicken and the hatchet, and pretending she was on stage, I got scared that she'd forget what she was doing and chop off my hand instead of the chicken's head.

"No," I squealed, refusing to go that far. "My hand you'll chop off instead of the chicken's head."

With wounded dignity she held its head while I held the legs. "Now, when I chop off its head, you let go," Aunt Lillie instructed me.

She swung the hatchet from above her head, chopped. I let go. The chicken flew off the chopping block and started running around and squawking like crazy.

Here, Aunt Lilliemae didn't chop the head clear off. Right away we run after the chicken with its head hanging off to the side but not cut off altogether.

"Catch it Alvernie"' Aunt Lilliemae hollered, forgetting all about acting now. "If it goes in the woods we'll never find it and Mom'll be mad at us."

Aunt Lilliemae was upset. She was running after this chicken with it head hanging over but not cut off and bawling all at the same time. Of course that started me off too. The two of us was chasing it to beat the band till it finally got stuck in some dead branches. There it fell over dead.

176

Uncle George, he was coming around the back of the house to get some tools Pap needed from the tool shed when he seen this. He just hollered and laughed at us. "You two was running around like chickens with your heads cut off more'n the old chicken was," teased George after we pulled the dead, limp chicken outta the rubble. By then our tears turned into hysterical laughter.

We finally come back to our senses. Lilliemae and me, we got the chicken cleaned, but by that time the water was all cooked up so we hadda heat more.

"Don't tell Mom," Aunt Lillimae warned me and begged Uncle George.

When Grammy got home and seen how the chicken was all bruised up, she wondered what happened and we hadda tell her then.

"*Ach vell* now, *du* two. I oughta give both of *du* a *goot* lickin', ain't now?" But she didn't. She just said to wash the dirt streaks off our faces from crying so bad. She got to work to make do with the chicken. Grammy told her boy to keep quiet about this at supper time. "It's not that *du* never done nothin wrong," she reminded him.

Lilliemae and I, we was nervous wrecks, sure George was gonna' tear into us and make fun of us at supper but he said nothing. Sure did have a big smile on his face while eating the potpie. Pap - he was so glad to see me when he come home for supper - knowed something was up but didn't question us. He usually liked to be kept up-to-date about happenings with his family, but with all the commotion that went on now and then, there musta been times he figured the less he knowed the better off he was. This was one of them times.

Lilliemae and I, we stayed nervous for a long time cause we was purty sure George would blackmail us, make us do for him something he'd not wanna do, then say he'd tell on us, embarrassing us to no end. That was one time I was ready to go back to the farm real fast. It turned out he kept quiet. My respect for Uncle George swelled cause he never tortured us about that till we was all adults and able to laugh over it.

You hear about these things but never think they'll happen in your family. This one did to us: Aunt Lilliemae had a beau, not a local boy. A good looking fella with more education than most people around here. Gordy worked for the government, had a high faluting position, at least according to Gordy. His job was to test the amount of alcohol in whiskey at distilleries and make sure all distilleries, no matter how big or small was paying tax on the whiskey that was made. There was a big one on the edge of town and many more small ones within so many miles. He rented a room at Sadie Burkholder's boarding house, staying in town for a couple of weeks every now and then.

Like cigars, kegs of whiskey was loaded on wagons and hauled to Baltimore or Philadelphia by teams of workhorses and returned with goods for the shelves of the general store or stuff the blacksmith or others needed for their workplaces. The time come when they was shipped by train but not then yet. Anyhow, that's how Gordy happened to come to town. One day he ran into Lilliemae while she was in the dry goods store looking to buy fabric and thread to make herself a new dress.

Poor Lilliemae. She fell hard for Gordy. He was a charmer for sure; nice turned-out appearance, a smooth, slick talker from Philadelphia. When he was in town Lilliemae'd have him for supper if Grammy said it was all right. Lilliemae helped more with the cooking then. She wanted to impress Gordy. He liked Grammy's cookin' better'n Sadie's at the boarding house, so he fussed over Grammy and Lilliemae both, complimenting them more'n Pap and my uncles ever done, probably in hopes he'd over and over get invited back. During dinner he entertained us with stories about his so-called dangerous work. We figured he might be stretching it a bit. We was a bit leery of strangers moving in or passing through for they often bragged about how notable they was and what good deeds they accomplished and the hardships they put up with on our behalf, as if we was to bend over with gratitude. Them kind didn't much fool us; made us suspicious, all except Lilliemae. Gordy'd tell us how his work was important and he was in great demand, for according to his boss, no one could do the good job like he done. His territory covered hundreds of miles and that's why he traveled so much. He used whatever transportation he'd find to get to them distilleries off the beaten track - train, horseback, mule, bicycle, anything; in all kinds of weather.

Sometimes he'd speak almost in whispers, laughing at getting run off and shot at when he got too close to small stills where moonshiners was fermenting their own mash. Gordy - being the nice fella he was, according to Gordy - didn't wanna turn backwoods moonshiners over to the authorities, mean as they was when anybody got too close to their stills. He saw how they was struggling to hold family together with what little bartering or money they'd get for their home brew. Feeling sorry for them he just looked the other way and run. "Anyway, most of them moonshiners can't hold a firearm straight, too full of their own whiskey, they is."

Pap told him he was all wrong about them kind not bein' able to shoot straight and he better be more careful in his work. Pap knowed how them backwoodsmen in the hills could handle a weapon of any kind, that he did.

Poor Lilliemae, she'd gasp in fear and terror at what might happen to her Gordy.

One day I overheard - not intentional, of course - Uncle John and Uncle Will talking. They wondered so if maybe Gordy was accepting payments, sorta like bribes from some moonshiners and distilleries to keep quiet about how much they was turning out. When Uncle John said that he better be careful or he'd end up being shipped out dead in one of them barrels or maybe buried in the woods, well, I had to sneak away from hearing more. My teeth began to chatter and the hairs on my neck stood straight out in fear and excitement. See, by now I knowed what 'dead' meant.

Young as I was I found Gordy a mite puffed-up. His adventures was fun to listen to but I could tell they was way blown out of proportion. Pap, too, had that certain look that said something wasn't just right about Gordy. Said nothing mind you. He could hide his feeling's from lots of people, but not from me.

Gordy didn't come around often, but he and Lillemae seen each other that way for two years. He declared his love for her and spoke with longing for the day when they'd marry and settle down.

Well then, wouldn't you know, Lillimae got in the family way. When Lilliemae told Gordy - all excited she was, sure they'd get hitched right away and move to the big city where life was bound to be exciting, even a bit wild. And yes, she'd miss her family but she'd visit when Gordy traveled here to work. Lilliemae also reasoned that if Gordy wanted to move to town near her family, that was all right with her, too. Whatever Gordy wanted. She was so happy.

Yes well, wouldn't you know it? That quick the sly bugger slunk away and never come through town again.

Pap mentioned Lilliemae's predicament to Al Konhaus; figured Al maybe had the means to find out something more about Gordy Tanner. Didn't take long for Al to find out that he lived in Philadelphia with a wife and two boys.

Gordy, he never come back to see how Lilliemae fared and what for child theirs was, a boy or girl, nothing.

So much for big city silky charm, smooth talk and good looks.

As brokenhearted as she first was, Lilliemae accepted her lot, gave up wanting to move away and get famous. Nevertheless, she always stayed a bit theatrical and dramatic. That's how she was. She never denied it. It was in her blood. Poor Grammy. She couldn't never figure where it come from.

Lilliemae and her little one, Lester, lived with Grammy and Pap. Lester, he was a handsome boy who favored his dad in looks, but it ended there. Lester was natured to be kind and honest and that's the way he growed up.

When he was three, Lilliemae married a man who loved her, loved her flair for laying it on thick which sometimes drove others to aggravation, and just as much loved Lester. Treated him as his own, he did.

That's why it was so hard to take what happened later when Cleo and Homer, their twins, was born.

CHAPTER 18 - LENNY DELLER, POP'S GOOD FRIEND

There's only one time in his whole life that I know of that Pop didn't make it right - except for my dolly; that makes it two times. It was when I was hickling around and Pop noticed this. He checked my foot, seen a stone blister so big it covered the bottom of my foot. Musta happened when I was tending the cows. Right away Pop goes out to the dung yard for fresh hot dung to spread on my foot. He wrapped it with clean cheesecloth to hold the smelly stuff in place. I sat on the porch that scorching, humid, summer day, leaning against a porch rail trying to catch the little breeze that was coming around the west side till Pop was ready to clean off my stone blister.

At that time Sandy Kemmerly come visiting. Sandy had plenty of money and wore lots of nice clothes. Somewhat uppity Sandy was; thought he was better'n most folks. He liked Pop though - everyone liked Pop -and come around every now and then to spread the latest gossip, hoping to hear some he could pass on to the next person he run into.

Pop wondered out loud to Mom sometimes where Sandy's money come from. No one was sure just what kind of work Sandy Kemmerly done. He hung around John Miller enough for it to look like them two was caught up in shady dealing's, but nothing could be proved. Sandy, he was good at changing the subject when he didn't wanna talk about something brought up to him. Pop was overly cautious about what he said to Sandy.

Wasn't long that Lenny Deller happened by while Sandy was there. The men sat in the shade of the porch, forgot I was there. Hard as it was, I tried to be quiet and stay outta the way so's I could hear what they was saying.

Lenny and Rosemary had a big family. There was Gracie, Mark, Thomas, Charity, Eve, Faith, Rachel, Joel, Leah and Paul. Rachel was my age. Mom said there'd probably be another'n be comin' on soon. She was right. They ended up with sixteen in all.

Lenny didn't have much of a farm, wasn't his to begin with. The stone quarry Lenny worked at owned farms all around the quarry. Men who worked the quarry was allowed to live on these farms as long as they worked the land while working at the quarry. With his boys helping out, Lenny was able to make a go at both jobs. In time he'd get one promotion after the other at the quarry till he was up there purty high. But not yet.

Lenny, he was a wonderful good friend to Pop. He helped him and us out so much. A good man he was.

Sandy didn't like Lenny Deller cause Lenny was Catholic. That day, right there on the porch, Sandy, smart-alecky as ever made a spiteful remark to Lenny - something about Lenny having an empty plate except for kids. See, the Dutch word for plate is *deller*.

Well! That got to Pop. He stood up straight and tall and serious looking, towered over fancy Sandy Kemmerly who was sitting down just then. Pop remarked over it that he'd rather have a *deller* with not much on it than an empty dish.

Boy-oh-boy, that hit Sandy right in his pride cause he knowed Pop was referring to him as the empty dish. He got mad and walked down the lane in a huff, dust swirls flying and coat tails flapping.

Lenny slouched there, shoulders hunched, hands in pants pockets; mortified he was. "*Ach* Ben, *Ich* made trouble. *Ich* don't wanna come between *du un* Sandy. Besides, he was right. *Ich* don't got much of nothin' but my wife *un* kids, but *Ich* got all *Ich* want."

Yeah, it was a hard life for the Dellers but you'd never know it by them. They was a happy bunch. If only you coulda seen 'em at Christmas time, why they was a joyous family. See, the quarry handed out presents for every boy and girl whose pa worked there; sent 'em home with the men the day before Christmas and gave the men Christmas day off. Each year was the same things wrapped up for the kids - chocolate drops in a box decorated with holly leaves and ribbons, a pair of mittens and a scarf. One year they'd be black, the next year red. Never any other color. Now you'd think them Deller kids was getting the most wonderful presents in the world, even when they knowed what they'd be opening year after year. Course they got good use out of 'em, too. And wouldn't you know, some of the kids at school - though they didn't have much more - made fun of 'em wearing theses presents from the quarry owners. Them Deller kids never let that drag 'em down. They was grateful as all get-out for them presents. A nicer bunch of kids you'd never meet, just like their ma and pa. Not one of 'em was mean or spiteful, at least none that I knowed.

Pop talked to Lenny as he checked my foot and cleaned the dung off my stone blister then opened it with his razor. Boy, did the pus fly out then! He said, "*Ach vell* now, it makes me so cross when Sandy blows off that way. Not everything that shines is gold, Lenny. *Du* are the kind of friend and neighbor *Ich* want."

You could tell with them few words from Pop how Lenny, when he headed back home, stood up straighter, walked with a little more pride - not too much - and a bounce in his step cause of the way Pop treated him. Pop made him see he was more important than money and clothes and vanity.

And Pop never did make it right with Sandy Kemmerly.

If I make Pop out to be perfect, he wasn't, but a good man he was. One time - and to this day I never learned why Pop did it, but he hit Bully the mule at its jaw and made its nose bleed. Mom was on her way to the barn to do the milking and seen this. It bothered her and she said something about it, but Pop told her to never mind, she had enough to tend to inside and the milkin', he'd take care of the outside. Mom didn't let things like that go by too often, mostly pursued it till she got to the bottom of whatever it was, but this time she seen the bad mood Pop was in. That was something we hardly never seen in Pop.

Mom, this worried her; it troubled me too. You could tell Pop wasn't hisself. He knowed he done wrong to Bully. That made him all the more crabby.

That night Mom put Albert to bed. I climbed in next to him, then her and Pop settled down. We was all asleep when we got woke up to a dreadful racket of glass breaking.

"*Wass* in the world was that?" Mom woke up screaming, jumping straight out of bed. I sat up, swung my legs out over the edge of the bed, ready to grab Albert and run. Albert was so scared he pulled the blanket over his head, cowered there.

Mom lit the coal oil lamp. Then we seen what happened. Here, Pop went and punched his fist right through a window next to his bed. Scared the daylights outta Mom and me and Albert.

Albert started crying. By this time Pop woke up. After he was awake right and seen what he done, he said to Mom how it was good he was turned that way in the bed cause he'd of hated to think how she'd look if he'd been turned her way and hit her in the face like that.

Mom knowed it had to do with the way Pop hit Bully that day, but as far as he was concerned that was the end of it. Pop wouldn't talk about it even after he broke the window; next morning Mom took cardboard and fit it into the window, stuffed rags around the sill and frame. Never did get new glass back in.

CHAPTER 19 - POWWOW AND HEX

When Pop was on the school board, he come home from the meeting one evening and said to me, "It's too late now to take this broom over to Knaub's *Schul. Du un* Opal can take it over on Saturday. Opal knows where it is cause her one married brother lives close over there."

"Oh, Alverna!" Opal wailed when I told her. "That one place we have to pass has so many dogs. I'm afraid!"

When I told Pop this he took me aside. "On the way to Knaub's *Schul,* say this," and he told me what to say over it as we walked along. Then he went, "When *du* get there, them *hunds* won't hurt *du* or Opal."

That made it all right. I trusted Pop with my life.

I didn't say nothing to Opal. As we took turns carrying the broom, I repeated them words over and over under my breath. *Hound, hound, keep your nose to the ground. God made me and thee, hound. In the name of the Father, Son and Holy Ghost.*

Opal knowed something was up but couldn't get nothing out of me. With all them times she tormented me with her mean tricks, I decided this one time I'd keep quiet and give her back some of her own medicine. She didn't like it one bit.

When we heard dogs in the distance barking and howling something awful, Opal got skittish as all get-out and wasn't gonna go no farther. She was holding onto my arm for dear life and held that broom in front of her to protect herself from them snarling dogs. I started repeating them words out loud. When we seen them dogs - five in the yard - they had shut up. Not one barked, not one!

Opal, her eyes went wide open in surprise and her mouth dropped in astonishment. She couldn't understand it! After she got over being speechless she prodded me with questions, then threats, but I kept my mouth shut about the whole thing. We made it to Knaub's School and delivered the broom. Same thing happened on the way back. Then I told her what Pop said to recite to keep us safe so no dogs wouldn't come after us.

That was the only other time besides Opal's warts that I knowed for sure that Pop powwowed. I heard talk every now and then so he musta done it on occasion. See, people who powwowed was looked on as gifted healers, a supernatural gift granted by God. Witch doctors that practiced hex - or black magic - did it for harm. Hex was different from powwow.

My Pop, he was a wonderful good man, the *allerbescht!* He never woulda harmed a soul.

One thing Pop didn't believe in was hex, a witch and a curse on a person. Pop said, "Anyone who believes in that is already *ferhexed.*"

Mom believed and told Pop why. She told him a story about what happened to her mom, my grammy. *My momma always has people stoppin' by the haus. She welcomes everybody, never turns no one away. This one woman, Mrs. Sterner, somehow got to know Momma and come around quite a bit for awhile. Whenever she left, Momma'd get sickly as all get-out, end up in bedde the rest of the day.*

Phillip Brown, a good friend of Mom un Pop's was there one time when Mrs. Sterner was. After she left he tipped off Momma. 'Eliza, don't let this woman in your haus ever again! She don't mean well by du. She is a hex!'

But Mom, she had a hard time believin' it. Besides, she couldn't turn no one away, isn't her nature. Phillip got good un perturbed at Mom after Mrs. Sterner's visits cause she ended up sickly every time. He come to notice Momma wouldn't prevent the hex from comin' in, so in aggravation he insisted that Momma lay a broom across the doorway. Witches won't never cross over a broomstick. Ach vell, Momma done this when she seen her comin' one time un wouldn't du know it, Mrs. Sterner at first didn't come in. Fidgety as all get-out she was. Finally she picked up the broom un purty much hissed at Grammy, 'Guess the wind knocked this over.' Momma pretended she didn't know what happened, she didn't let on she put it there. When the woman left, wouldn't du know it, Momma hadda go to bedde for the rest of the day.

Another thing ebaut Mrs. Sterner, she always sat in the same chair. Phillip Brown noticed this un wouldn't take no from Momma for her to draw an x unner the chair seat. She agreed if he'd scrawl it on for her. He did. The next time she come she'd not sit in that chair, she sat in another'n. So next thing they did was to put an x unner every chair. Well, when she come one time, the witch wouldn't sit down. Nervous-like she said, 'Eliza, Ich can't stay but Ich was wonderin' so about them wonderful cucumbers du growed. Might Ich got some seeds to plant?'

Phillip Brown had forewarned Momma. 'This woman will ask du for seeds from something du planted. Don't give her any or du will soon be buried as deep as she plants the seeds.' So Momma - as much as she was against tellin' a lie - got goot un scared enough that she fibbed un told her that she didn't have none, that the cucumbers rotted before she got some.

Mrs. Sterner got outta there in a huff un never come back again.

A couple weeks later Momma run into Mrs. Sterner at market. 'Ach, mei Gott, your arms un face! What happened?' Momma asked in alarm. The woman was all scratched up somethin' terrible.

'Ach vell, chust a katz,' Mrs. Sterner said as she hurried on without stoppin' to talk. When Mom seen all them scratches she rightly believed this woman was a hex. She told this to Phillip Brown when she seen him. He said that every hex has a cat and the cat scratched her cause she didn't get no seeds to plant. 'But the cat won't hurt no one else, just the hex.'

My mom told Pop, "That much Ich know un that's why Ich believe a person can get hexed."

Pop listened to what Mom hadda say. He didn't outright agree but he shook his head, his way to let her know he was pondering' it. Mom and I we both could see he was thinking deep.

CHAPTER 20 – THE CELEBRATION

I was eight years old and this I remember like I'm living it right now.

One bright and glorious Saturday morning Mom told me as I was doing my chores, "Today's a celebration at the church grove." (Picnics was called celebrations then.) "*Du* can go when your chores are got done."

Along with camp meetings and parades, celebrations was the best get-togethers of the summer. People worked for days to get ready. They'd come with dishes and kettles and wash baskets full of all kinds of things to lay out on the tables for to eat.

My chores got done with a great deal of speed though time seemed to drag on and on. Nevertheless, I chided myself to be careful and do everything right or Mom might change her mind, make me do 'em over again, or worst of all, not let me go. When I got done, glory be! Mom said, "*Du* can go now, but tell your pap to let *du* know when it's 4:30 so *du* start for home, unless *du* are supposed to go along back with them."

So happy I was. I went skipping out our dusty lane, on down the long, winding, hilly road. It was a long walk to the church grove, three miles at least. It was much longer than from Grammy's house which was in the opposite direction. I worked up a sweat as I set out but nothing was gonna dampen my spirits. I was going to the celebration! I'd see Grammy and Pap and friends I didn't see much since school was out for the summer.

I got there early, outta breath from hurrying so. A tree stump was there for me to sit on and catch my breath while watching the road as I looked for Grammy and Pap.

There was always one stand that sold ice cream and soda pop at the celebrations. I never bought nothing since Grammy always brought enough food and drink to last all day, but hardly any money. Mom didn't give me none either.

That was all right. I didn't need nothing from the food stand even though ice cream woulda tasted good after the hot trip from the farm.

Next thing what happened, you just won't believe it! Here I seen one of the Holtzapple men walking purty fast towards me. As he come near he spoke to me in Dutch *"Ach vell*, look now who's here. Too long a time did *Ich* get not to see *du! Du* come up to the stand. *Ich* want to set it up to *du* - anything *du* want."

I was caught unawares. It was like a bolt outta the blue! I was never offered anything like this in all my life, never yet had a drink of soda pop except for Grammy's homemade root beer. And I was just thinking how so dry was my throat. Did I hear right? Did he did say anything I want? Some ice cream would hit the spot too. Boy-oh-boy, I was in my glory as I jumped off the stump to head up to the stand with him as he reached out to take my hand.

Over that, Miriam Stonebraker, his girlfriend - she wasn't his wife then yet - jumped out from behind a big tree and started hollering - more like screeching - in Dutch. I jumped, so *ferhoodled* I was. Lawrence pulled his hand from mine. I fell backwards over a big tree root sticking outta the ground as she hollered, "Lawrence, *du* get away from that girl this *minutt. Du* know she ain't your kid!"

So shamed and red in the face I got from falling and her hollering like that. "What is going on here?" I wondered so as I hopped back up fast, brushing the leaves and dirt off my dress. When I looked up there was Lawrence giving me one last look, then turned and run like a whipped hound scurrying away with his tail between his legs. Of course I didn't get no ice cream or soda pop, nothing from Lawrence Holtzapple. Heck, no!

I took it all in. I sat back on the stump looking around, hoping nobody else seen all this. I didn't spot no one, but you never know who's lurking around and watching. I waited. I studied about it. Still, I wasn't sure, I didn't know. But it stayed in my mind, stayed in my mind all day.

Finally I seen Pap's wagon with Grammy and the whole gang come. Boy-oh-boy, the whole gang! What a good day this was gonna turn out to be. I run to meet 'em and help carry their stuff to a shady spot where a couple tables was already pushed together.

Grammy was so glad to see me she gave me a big hug. Now I don't wanna appear selfish for wanting more'n what I had, but oh, how I woulda welcomed a hug like that from my mom. Never got one. She wasn't the hugging kind. Now I was big enough that she didn't have to help me get ready for bed; I could brush and braid my own hair, so every year it was like she was drawing more and more away from me. The closest she come to touching me in a long time was last winter when I took a bad chest cold and she rubbed my chest with a mustard plaster. She didn't rub gentle and her hands was rough but that didn't matter; them was Mom's hands. I relished that and it only made me long for her touch other than the occasional smack when she got so put out with me. Times when I was so filled in my heart with love for all things that I wanted to run and put my arms around her waist and squeeze her tight and say how I loved her. Well, I knowed better. The way she held herself apart told me I better not. Anyhow, this day I hugged Grammy back and was glad for that. I could tell Pap was glad to see me, too. With a big grin he said over it. "Mom, *chust* look who's here." Then he asked, "Are Estella *un* Ben got here now yet too?"

"No, I come by myself. Tell me when it's 4:30 so I can start for home."

"*Du* goin' home? *Nee. Du* are goin' down with us," Pap said.

Of course that settled that.

Susie come with her family, so spend the afternoon together we did, running from table to table to find other kids to play games with and skip to the music. Oh, what joy and happiness!

When supper was over and the band played hymns to end the day, we all sang *Blest Be The Tie That Binds,* then *Abide*

With Me Fast Falls The Eventide while we packed up to head home.

When we pulled up at Grammy and Pap's, like always I helped empty the wagon, carry things into the kitchen and put 'em away. Grammy made a fire in the stove and put water on to heat while I put the dirty dishes in the sink.

Later on I was washing the dishes; Grammy was drying. Pap was there and two of my uncles.

"Alverna, *wass iss? Wass* the matter?" Pap asked. "*Du* seem so quiet. *Du* are not your peppy, happy self. Don't tell me *du* got homesick."

"No, I don't got homesick." I stood there thinking what I should do or say. I finally blurted out, "But something strange happened today while I was waiting on you."

Everyone stopped what they was doing, looked my way. I could feel all eyes on me waiting to hear what was to come next. So I told them.

"Lawrence Holtzapple come down and wanted to take me up to the stand. He was gonna set up whatever I wanted. Anything, mind you; as much as I wanted. We started down. Just like that, Miriam Stonebraker jumped out from behind a tree where she was hiding; was watching us all that time she was. She hollered at Lawrence, told him to get away from me, to get out of there, that I ain't his kid."

I saw Grammy and Pap look at each other. The blood drained out of Uncle John's face. Uncle Will's jaw dropped open; looked like his eyes was gonna pop right outa his head. He swallowed hard. That minute it dawned on me that they knowed this since the day I was born. Did they figure that I'd never find out?

'Twas Uncle John who spoke up first. Croak is a better word as he said over it, "Alverna, we told you this long time that you never had no daddy, that the crows laid you on a stump and the sun hatched you out."

Pap just put his finger up and shook it. "That enough! *Ich* don't wanna hear that no more."

193

"She's eight years old. *Ich* guess we can tell her," Grammy said.

Then they begun to tell me.

"*Ach vell. Ya*," Grammy said. "Lawrence is your real pop. Your pap *un Ich* wouldn't let your mom *un* Lawrence marry since they're cousins. His mom *un* pop agreed with us."

I stood, froze to the spot, my hand in the dishwater, right away thinking that Ben was my pop and I didn't need or want another'n. But I wanted to understand more. I looked at each one there, then at Pap and asked, "Why did that matter that they're cousins?"

"We seen already that sometimes offspring from when cousins marry ain't *chust* right," Pap said, "*un* that can make problems to *yung* people *chust* gettin' started."

"Is something wrong with me?" I questioned.

"*Ach*! Course not!" Pap said. "We wasn't sure before *du* was born *un chust* figured it best if Lawrence *un* your momma didn't marry, that your momma keep living here with us. It all come out all right so no use worryin' yourself about it no more."

So.

That's what that meant then.

I wanted to know more but Pap let it be knowed by his manner that this talk was over and done with. And it was.

In bed that night I lay thinking. Lawrence better not try to come between me and the pop I had now. Pop, he was much better'n Lawrence Holtzapple, that's for sure. I didn't want things to change for us. I wondered if Pop knowed Lawrence was my real daddy. For sure I wasn't gonna bring up the subject when I got back to the farm. I knowed in my heart Pop wouldn't send me off now that I knowed who my real daddy was, but laying in the dark, alone and confused, fretful with unanswered questions flying in my head, believe you me, fears and doubts kept me awake most the night. It was my pop's love that gave me that little bit of hope that everything would turn out okay.

My mind couldn't form ideas real clear, but as I look back, what come to me first was, maybe this is why Mom's often so cranky and hurtful, why them headaches come on real sudden now and then. Did she never get over not marrying Lawrence Holtzapple? Did I bring her more hurt and shame by being born while she wasn't yet married? Aunt Lilliemae's little boy didn't have no daddy and Aunt Lilliemae got over it - eventually. She didn't bear no grudges that made her go off and sulk all the time. And Uncle Dan, he not too long before married a cousin. I heard Mom griping to herself about it one day, but thought nothing of it till now. Was Pop gonna have to suffer Mom's standoffish ways forever cause he wasn't her first choice? That thought hurt more'n all the rest put together. Sleep wouldn't come during the long night as I pondered all these things.

Towards morning, all of a sudden it hit me. And they never said. They never told me. Enoch Holtzapple was my other grandpap. The dear old woman that gave me a needle and thread to sew on buttons when I was just a mere little girl, the crippled old woman I loved with all my heart was my other grammy. And they never told me. I never knowed. And now she was gone. Dead and buried.

Yes, it was a long night. I didn't sleep none. My thoughts never left up.

The next morning it was like the particulars I learned the day before at the celebration and then later at Grammy's didn't make no difference to anybody at the Farley's. Not a word was brought up about it. Everybody tried to act like it was a regular day, that nothing changed. I said little. Pale and worn out I helped Grammy like always. Otherwise I kept to myself. When something was said, it was either quieter than normal or louder than usual. Trying to pretend nothing earth-shattering happened the day before, they was. Only it wasn't working. For the first time in my life I seen that every soul in that household was anxious and uneasy. A lot of sidelong glances come my way from everyone at the breakfast table. I didn't give no one any comfort. They didn't deserve it, keeping this from me all my life. My uncles, not knowing what to say or do, got outta the house as soon as breakfast was done and over with. Pap went off to his work shed like he done every morning. I seen a worried look on his face but I didn't give him no reason to feel better. Every now and then it appeared Grammy was gonna speak up. I'd look her way, she'd pause, then stop herself.

Finally I stood next to Grammy to let her know I had something to say. It was only her and Aunt Lilliemae and me in the kitchen. As far as Lilliemae was concerned, I couldn't fault her too much, but, yes, she and Grammy, especially Grammy, needed to know how much I was hurting. With head down, staring at my feet, I decided to be brave. I looked at my grammy that I always loved and trusted, looked her right in the eyes and said, "I always wondered so why I loved down deep in my heart the crippled, dear old woman right from the first day I seen her." I swallowed hard, then went on. "You coulda told me, you know. You coulda said Enoch and the dear old woman was my grandparents. I never had a chance to call her grammy like I call you. You coulda told me."

Grammy hung her head. A tear slipped down her cheek. She just nodded in agreement but said nothing.

At least now she knowed how I felt.

Lilliemae was gonna scold me for talking to Grammy like that, but Grammy just put her hand over Lilliemae's mouth. Then Lilliemae kept quiet.

It hurts to this day that I never had the chance to call dear old woman, Grammy to her face. It mattered that much. But I never had the chance.

'Twas a month later. Pap come to the farm in the wagon to take Mom and me to Grammy's to help her out for a day, stay the night, then into the next afternoon before he'd take us back to the farm. Albert was along too. Ruby was gonna come down to the farm and milk for Mom that evening and next morning. We'd be home in time for the evening milking.

We was putting up the grapes. While I was washing bunches of grapes galore - baskets of 'em - Grammy, in a whisper that meant it wasn't for my ears, only her whispers I'd make out since they was purty loud, mentioned to Mom that Lawrence and Miriam went and got married. They was living on the Holtzapple farm, probably'd take it over and let the old man live out his days there. He couldn't do nothing no more. Mom stayed quiet, said nothing, just stirred all that much faster the pot of jelly her and Grammy was working on. Grammy comprehended she made a mistake by telling this. I watched as she bit her tongue and pursed her lips tight so's not to say nothing more about it.

Not till the hot grape juice, not yet thickened, spattered out over the kettle and hissed as it hit the burner plates and made purple splashes on Mom's apron did she realize what she'd been doing. She slowed down her stirring but her lips stayed pressed together real hard too.

"Uh-oh," I thought. "Another'n of Mom's headaches'll be coming on."

When I seen Mom act like that I couldn't believe she thought more of her cowardly Holtzapple cousin than Pop. She was doing just what she accused me of so often - pouting cause I didn't get my way. I understood now that Mom wasn't never gonna forgive or forget. She was wronged and didn't get what she wanted and she couldn't let it pass like Pop'd tell us every now and then. "*Chust* let it go." More'n that I could tell Mom intended to make everyone else around her pay for her misery. My mom, oh, I was so put out with her then. Why, oh why, couldn't she let herself be glad for her good fortune with all that she got? So much good was hers. Of course I couldn't say nothing. Neither could Grammy. She already said too much.

CHAPTER 21 - CEDAR GROVE

The little town where Pap moved when he married Grammy was first called Caesar's Cave. Grammy told me how the name come about. It was a story about a freed slave that managed to make it this far north after the Civil War. He happened across a little cave at the stream that flowed nearby and set up a place for him to live. He never bothered nobody, purty much lived off the land, scrounged around, kept outta sight as much as he was able, figuring white people wasn't gonna accept him.

She told me how Caesar made do: He had a patch for a garden, gathered wild berries, paw-paws, other fruits and vegetables, edible roots, all sorts of things. Snared rabbits and squirrels, wild ducks, whatever could be ate; scoured the dumps to make a go of it. See, people, most times when they gave up housekeeping, loaded their belongings in a wagon and dumped 'em in an abandoned quarry hole, a gravel pit, or in the woods.

(Wanna stop here and say this happened to me once long after I was married. I come down with the flu and we was getting ready to move. My man, he took everything he didn't want and hauled it off to a dump. Me, I was too sick to salvage what I wanted. That was hard for me to take cause there was things he throwed away that was important to me. But that's the way it was back then. Uncle George, getting up in years by then and plagued with rheumatism, he found out about this and went and brought me back the family Bible, some books and my Mom's letters I kept in an old cigar box all these years. The Bible and books made it through, but Mom's letters, already yellow, brittle and worn from reading them over and over looked like they'd been deliberately dumped outta their box. They was ruined. This gave me a set-back. I took sicker than just the flu and was downhearted for a time. George seen this and went back to the dump to see if he'd find more; he wanted to lift my spirits; came back with an old tobacco pouch inside another cigar box. This was the one most precious to me. It was where I hid the marble with the lamb inside, the torn, bloody piece of my doll baby's dress and her one yellow curl. And the ring when I couldn't wear it no longer. Oh my! After all them years! Boy-oh-boy, I let down and cried then. Now I had a little bit of hope after getting all that back. I soon got to feeling better. I just never stayed down too long. George, he knowed how much that meant to me. Yes, Uncle George was always good to me, God rest his soul.)

Caesar come to be a fixture, not bothering no one, most folks letting him alone. Or so 'twas thought. See, there was some grumbling and complaining according to Grammy, from some of the backwoods folks that only come to town to barter at the general store. They didn't like the idea of Caesar being around. They was suspicious of him cause he was different; thought much the same about gypsies.

Pap and Grammy agreed that them folks shoulda noticed how different they was cause of their strange ways of behaving - or misbehaving, how they griped about a skinny, little old Negro that looked like he couldn't hurt a fly. They was scared cause he looked different. Wouldn't let it alone. Wondered so out loud about him.

It was Frank Weaver at the general store who got all hot and bothered with them who complained about Caesar when they was outright thieves. See, he always hadda keep a sharp eye out when they come in to barter for some essentials. Merchandise always ended up missing after they left. They was smart and it was too many of 'em for him to watch, even with Laura's help. Frank always found stuff gone after they left.

Most folks felt sorry for Caesar, seen what a hard go it was for him bein' such a loner. Didn't attempt to make nobody's acquaintance. Too scared, he was. Once in a while something'd be placed near the cave to help him out, only never when others was around. It was done secret-like. The Pennsylvania Dutch have good and generous hearts.

"He appeared content," Grammy'd say.

"But didn't he have no family, no one to keep him company or help him out?" I'd wonder so, pleading with Grammy that maybe just one time she seen just one person with him.

"Never seen no one with him. Always alone he was. But there was them who helped," Grammy'd come back.

My little heart almost burst with sadness that in this world somebody'd be that alone. I never coulda took that, being so alone. Time after time I hoped Grammy'd give a happy ending to this story.

When I got older, maybe eight or nine, Grammy finally broke down and told me what happened to Caesar; didn't gloss over the story to make it better'n what it was.

"My John - he was *chust* a purty *yung* boy - come runnin' in one day," Grammy started. " He said Mr. Briggs, the undertaker, was notified to go where Caesar's cave was. John heard the commotion *un* followed along. Oh, the shame of it! What he seen curdled his blood. There was Caesar hangin' from a tree, dead as a door nail. Didn't do hisself in, mind *du*. Wasn't no accident. Mr. Briggs noted it was a deliberate killing, but said under his breath he knowed it'd never be proved who done it. Likely happened at night when folks wasn't around."

I listened spellbound and alarmed as Grammy went on. "The undertaker stood there for a long time looking at Caesar and figurin' out what measures to take. A crowd started forming. Word spread fast. Them that come upon the grisly scene stood behind Mr. Briggs, gawkin', quiet as a crowd could be. No one moved till he sent some boys after the doctor to come out *un* pronounce Caesar dead. See, Mr. Briggs wasn't sure 'twas necessary since nothin' was knowed about Caesar, no relatives to get in touch with about Caesar passin' over into Beulah Land. But he followed proper procedures like always.

Mr. Briggs, he left Caesar hangin' there. He told Pap later he done that to let people see what hate can do to an innocent victim of prey. Besides, he figured it was the safest thing right then, that no one'd bother Caesar's body as long as it was hangin' on the tree."

"He didn't leave it hanging there forever?" I wanted to know.

"Now don't be in such a hurry," Grammy warned. "I'm gettin' to that part. See, while some went for the doctor, he asked your Uncle John if he could drive the Briggs' wagon to town for a tall ladder, an oversize knife or small saw blade, whichever he'd come across first; he told him where to find a couple shovels, said to find someone to help him put a pine coffin in the wagon. They wasn't heavy, just awkward for one to lift in the wagon alone. *Un* a brand new blanket he kept at the funeral parlor near where the coffins was. 'Twas good John was there since the Briggs' boys was at the other end of town buildin' a new house and didn't yet hear about Caesar. John run into your pap as he was heading to the Briggs' place. Pap, he hopped in the wagon *un* helped John pack up the stuff. They stopped for just a couple seconds to fill me in on what was happenin'. John insisted on it or your Pap probably never woulda thought of doin' that.

The doctor was there when they pulled up in the wagon. H.A Briggs got the go-ahead from Doc to cut Caesar down. He laid the new blanket on the ground *unner* where Caesar was, propped the ladder against the tree trunk, climbed up hisself in the clean, fancy dress clothes he always wore, cut Caesar down on his own; hadda let him drop a couple yards. No one stepped in to help catch him except for your pap. John said H.A. didn't ask for no help, but intended to get the job done by hisself if need be. Your pap cushioned the fall and laid him down on the blanket H.A. had spread out *unner* him. Mr. Briggs - everything he done was slow and measured that day. He wanted it to stay on the minds of everyone there for as long as they lived. John watched as H.A. grabbed the shovels, handed one to your pap, started diggin' in the soft ground right near the cave."

Grammy took a deep breath and went on. "At first everyone there was dumbstruck. Could they believe their eyes? Was H.A. Briggs and William Farley diggin' a grave right there near the cave?

John moved in after awhile to take a shovel from their hands *un* shoulder a turn. That went on, the two shovels bein' exchanged between them three. John figured more woulda helped except they was afraid maybe them who done this cruel deed was there watchin' *un* might carry out mischief on them for helpin' out. About three hours later the hole was long, wide *un* deep enough to put Caesar in. Your pap, the doctor, John and Mr. Briggs each took a corner to lift Caesar who was wrapped in the never-used-before blanket *un* laid him in the coffin. By that time H.A.'s boys heard this and come by. With them it was eight in all lifted that coffin like it held gold *un* lowered it in the grave. Before the coffin was covered with the ground *un* altogether buried, Mr. Briggs, he stood at the foot of Caesar's grave, quiet *un* solemn, head bowed, hands over his heart. Your pap, John and the Briggs' boys followed his lead. The crowd was speechless. Somethin' was goin' on there they never before seen. Mr. Briggs recited the Twenty Third Psalm *un* ended with the Lord's Prayer with some of the crowd joining in.

Your pap stepped up to the head of Caesar's grave with a cross he fashioned outta branches where Caesar was hung from when H.A. *un* John was takin' their turns diggin'. He had wrapped a vine growin' up the tree around the cross pieces to hold 'em together *un* pounded it in the loose ground at the head of Caesar's grave. 'That'll do till *Ich* can make one more suitable,' he piped up to no one in particular.

Your pap, he never got around to it. The one he made first off, rotted away.

John remarked proud-like how Mr. Briggs thumped your Pap *un* him on the shoulder as a way of thankin' them for helpin' him out.

He offered to take 'em back to town, so they turned and walked together to the wagon. As they climbed onto the wagon seat, H.A. turned around to the crowd gathered there and said, 'The Bible says to seek good and not evil. . . . We still gotta lot to learn in these parts.'

Then they headed out, not saying another word to no one.

John told me again and again it was a holy, sacred time he spent there by Caesar's cave that day."

"Did anyone ever come around looking for Caesar?" I asked Grammy between sniffles.

"*Nee*. Alvernie, all that's left of Caesar is the line in Mr. Briggs ledger that he showed your Pap one day. It says, *Cut down and buried a male Negro named Caesar. Hung by outlaws and cowards.*

Grammy finished up by telling me, "Alverna Nell, your pap and Mr. Briggs is two of the best men around these parts. Your Uncle John, too. They paid respect to a down-and-out nobody that never caused no one no trouble. That's the way we all should treat others so it never happens again."

She stopped talking then. I knowed she was done with her story. She said all she was gonna say. I stood next to where she sat, my arms flung around her neck. Tears was streaming down both our faces from sorrow for Caesar, for anger at the unnamed killers, and for pride in Mr. Briggs, Pap and Uncle John.

Then it was time to wipe the tears away and get back to our chores.

I woulda rather listened to a happy ending about Caesar, but Grammy always told the truth - except to Mrs. Sterner about the cucumber seeds. At least there was Pap and John and Mr. Briggs and their good deed that I could be thankful for.

The town council, which really wasn't a true town council just yet, only a group of men that headed factories and stores and the bank that opened up for business because of the railroad goin' through, decided to incorporate the town. A name was needed. Nobody wanted Caesar's Cave to be the name of their town. Too much ill repute in that name. Besides, it didn't have a distinguished ring to it. The men, they couldn't agree on a single one, so come up with the idea to ask the people thereabouts to submit names for the new town. The final choice was Cedar Grove. It appeared best suited because of a wide stand of cedar trees at the edge of the Hoff farm. Town folks liked it much better'n the old one because of the shameful goings-on behind it.

CHAPTER 22 - THE BLACKSMITH

The Hoff family had the most land and biggest farm with all sorts of outbuildings that accumulated as the farm expanded. Some sat empty with a run-down look as Mr. Hoff was getting up in years and took on interests beyond farming.

The time come when a blacksmith and millwright was needed on a regular basis since land being timbered to the north brung horses pulling wagon loads of logs past the Hoff place to the saw mill about five miles south of his farm. Many a time a horse needed shod or wagons broke down, especially the wheels. Mr. Hoff seen he could put a couple more dollars in his till to have a blacksmith set up shop in one of the outbuildings, only it hadda be far from the farmhouse so the noise and the heat wouldn't disturb his family. Of course the rumor got around that the real reason to keep it away from the big house was he didn't want Charlotte getting too friendly with any of the help. Them kind was beneath his social standing. Nobody in these parts was good enough for his Charlotte. She was born when it was thought her momma was too old to have another baby. Their son, Horace, was a young man when Charlotte was conceived so she was raised like an only child. Horace had been spoiled, protected, and sheltered from common folk. Now it was Charlotte's turn. Although they wasn't any better'n other folks, Mr. Hoff's money got him to thinking that way. He didn't want Charlotte running into any of his hired hands and strike up a friendship. 'Twas one reason she never married. She was already an old maid - according to Pennsylvania Dutch standards - when her daddy was looking for a blacksmith.

The blacksmith he found, why, according to Grammy, a better man you'd never meet in Jakie Prowell, at least at first. So tall and strong he was, yet quiet, keepin' mostly to hisself. His reputation for good work spread fast and he was soon taking care of the smithing needs of most everyone around. Jakie and his young wife, Esther, lived a good distance from the Hoffs. Many a time Jakie'd worked late into the evening, too late to start for home. He built a make-do partition and fixed up a sleeping area for when he couldn't make it home. That didn't go over so good with Esther. She knowed what a handsome man her Jakie was, figured there was no tellin' how some women might be taken with him once they seen him. She got up her dander thinking how other women always took notice of his muscles that rippled from handling the heavy tools and equipment of his trade. She remembered how she looked him over with interest when she first spied him, so she understood how other young women might take note of her man. After all, she had found ways to accidentally run into him till she won his affection and they married. Yeah, Esther understood all what might happen with her being so far away to protect Jakie from them kind.

When Mr. Hoff got wind of Jakie's wife's displeasure - news like that always traveled fast outta nowhere - and seen the way certain females begun to show up with their papas who wanted work from Jakie, well, Mr. Hoff, he didn't wanna give no romantic-minded, foolish girls a chance for him to turn this bustling enterprise into a disaster, so right away he worked it out with the blacksmith that he'd find a house for Esther and him close by if Jakie'd sell the one he had and put the money in this other'n. Jakie agreed. Took no longer'n a couple months that Jakie and Esther settled into a new house on the one long street that made up most of Cedar Grove. As more streets was laid out and plots was sold, the blacksmith shop come to be situated in a back alley at the end - or beginning, whichever way you come into town - of Elm Street.

Things went good for Jakie and Esther. She had a knack for sewing on the treadle sewing machine her momma gave her, using the brightest materials she could find. She insisted she wouldn't put up with drab. She sewed curtains for her windows, embroidered linens, towels, washcloths, pillowcases and hankies with colorful threads; and her baking and candy-making was outta this world. People never seen the likes of it around Caesar's Cave that become Cedar Grove. She said her candy was made from secret recipes handed down from generation to generation by her Irish ancestors.

Another thing about Esther. The way she put smocking into her clothes was new to most ladies. It caught their eye.

Wasn't long Esther and Jakie started a family. First come Tim, then the twins, Jenny and Lee. When mommas saw what purty dresses Esther sewed for Jenny and outfits for her boys, they asked her to show them how, or better yet, sew clothes for them. Esther wasn't no dummy, didn't wanna interfere with quilting parties or the like, but just maybe she could teach her skills in exchange for, not money, that'd appear too brash on her part, but things women had they could barter with.

Tim was the oldest of the three kids. From little on up he helped his pa. Wasn't made to, wanted to. When too little to shoe horses or the like, he gathered wood, pumped the bellows at the forge, seen his pa had the tools and materials he needed at hand, cleaned up after him, Tim did. As he growed bigger and stronger he worked at the forge forming candlesticks, lanterns, spittoons, any practical gadget he could fire up and pound into a one-of-a kind finished product. Jakie made sure Tim's work was finished right. Them pieces caught the eye of people stopping by at Jakie's shop for repairs and bought 'em up in short order. John Miller bought what he could for his gift shop, only Jakie and Lee was smart enough to sell many without John's help. John didn't like that too much!

What a pair that man and his boy made!

Lee, the younger boy, didn't like smithing, hated the pounding noises and burning stench that went along with it, didn't like nothing associated with the trade. His nose was stuck in a book all day long if he could get away with it. He was smart enough to mind his mom and help with whatever chores she had for him. That way he didn't have to help at the forge. Jakie and Tim was relieved of doing chores at home - except for the heavy ones Lee couldn't do on his own, so it worked to everybody's advantage. Esther kept Lee busy cause she seen he wasn't suited for smithing. Besides, there was plenty for him to do around the house and in the garden since his pa was busy from early morning to most times late night.

Jenny learned all kinds of sewing, embroidery and needlework from her mom in between her chores and schoolwork, but her favorite pastime was cooking and baking. Musta been born in her from her Irish ancestors. When so little she didn't have hardly the strength to lift some of the pots and pans, not even strong enough to open the oven door of their brand new cook stove, she finagled Lee into lending her a hand. He did cause it gave him time to read in between him helping her out. It was easy to tell them two was twins the way they worked together.

Jakie turned his rent money over to Mr. Hoff for the building, then what he had left over he put away to someday own his own shop.

Jakie's good reputation went far and wide. People was coming from a good distance so their repairs'd get done right the first time.

It was common for folks to barter. What some folks bartered with Jakie, well, it got outta hand. See, moonshine paid the debts of folks from the backwoods and hills along with some farmers who had their own stills.

Moonshine come in slow at first. Them bringing it wanted to be sure Jakie'd accept it without causing no trouble since there was problems with moonshiners paying taxes - or not paying taxes - on what they produced. At first Jakie took it home for Esther to flavor her delicious mince pies and other concoctions she and Jenny took to market to sell where they went every Saturday with food and sewing. They brought in extra income for the family that was by now wholeheartedly welcomed by the folks of Caesar's Cave that become Cedar Grove.

Yes well, after some time a sizeable stock of this devil's brew was building up in Jakie's shop since it was more'n Esther could use at home, even after turning some into medicinal purposes. Her cupboard was full and overflowing.

Now and then Jakie'd take a nip while working away. Some people can hold their liquor, some can't. Jakie, big and strong as he was couldn't hold his. Now don't get me wrong. There was other men who drank more'n Jakie and it didn't bother them nearly as much. Jakie was one of 'em who just couldn't drink much till it overtook him. It happened slow, but before they knowed it, the man that was sought after for his fine, outstanding work was turning into the town drunk. Didn't hurt his smithing early on, but he was getting soused up oftener and oftener.

It pained Esther to see Jakie going off the deep end. She got rid of all the temptation at the house, even went to the blacksmith shop and poured it out. Tim watched too. Didn't help. More kept coming in. Once he got hooked, nothing Esther or Tim said or did stopped his drinking. He never did no harm - at least early on - when he went on a binge but people was beginning to talk. Things went downhill for the kids. Even though everyone liked 'em, it was human nature to make fun when someone was down and out. There was plenty of caring folks who felt sorry for that family and didn't say nothing, hoping Jakie'd get turned around. Then there was them that said more'n than they shoulda. Jakie's kids come to be ashamed of their pa and his strange ways of behaving. They quit asking their friends to come by, knowed their parents wouldn't allow it if Jakie was home which was happening more often. Grammy said you could see in their eyes that they was hurt to the core.

It got to where the women that bought nice clothes from Esther stopped going to her house to be measured for a new outfit, most times ordering a matching hat. Her income was slipping and Jakie wasn't bringing home no money . She was grateful people still bought her stuff at market, at least just yet.

When Esther seen Jakie either couldn't or wouldn't give up the drink, she threatened him real good, gave him one last chance to quit the drink or throw him out and lock the doors on him. After so many warnings, that she did.

What a downfall for such a promising family.

Jakie spent nights at the make-shift living quarters at the blacksmith shop after Esther locked him out.

Mr. Hoff, he done all he could to get Jakie to quit the drink, threatened to throw him out. He didn't carry it through cause Jakie did good work drunk or not. Mr. Hoff, he didn't wanna lose that extra rent money Jakie was bringin' in.

The worst was bound to happen.

It did.

One cold, winter night, in a drunken stupor, Jakie somehow or other got in the house while Esther was straightening up before bedtime. So quiet he come in that when she seen him, she was bowled over. He reeled towards her. Esther, without thinking and scared outta her wits, ran to her bedroom, bolted the door by sticking a chair under the doorknob hoping it'd keep him out. With the noise he was making she felt certain her children shut themselves up in their own rooms. She listened to him on the other side of the door pleading with her. He promised he'd give up the drink forever if she'd only let him come back home.

She heard that too many times before. Sat on the bed she did and shed silent tears behind the braced, shut door for the man she loved but lost to moonshine.

After what seemed like forever Jakie turned away and started down the steps. Esther and the children musta sighed with relief that Jakie was leaving.

As it turned out, going down the hall he spied Jenny's reflection shining from a window in her little room where she was cowering in a corner, frightened by her pa. She scampered to the hidey hole without first shutting the door behind her. Jakie noticed how much she looked like her momma. Had her good looks and love for bright colors and purty things.

Wasn't long that the gossip was spread all around town. Looking at Jenny in his drunken stupor, Jakie went off the deep end, musta thought he was seeing his Esther of years ago. He lumbered into the room after Jenny. At first she couldn't take in what he was after but when the realization struck her she backed away, screaming in terror. Her brothers heard and rushed from their loft on the top floor to see what was going on. Esther heard too. Numbed and befuddled she clumsily groped with the chair, finally got it pulled away, wasted precious time fidgeting with the door, at last got it open and ran to Jenny's room.

Jenny tried to run out the door but Jakie was bigger, was between her and the door. He grabbed her and pulled her to him. Lee, the littler one who wasn't strong like his big brother but could move fast got to Jenny's room first. What he seen sent his blood run cold but he sprung into action without thinking of the outcome for hisself. Seeing his pa up to no good, he jumped right at him in to protect Jenny

"Stop it, Pa!" he hollered as he ran up to Jakie, grabbing his arm.

One swipe of Jakie's strong arm sent Lee sprawling headfirst into the wall, knocking him out. While that was going on, Jenny got free of her pa. She knowed she'd never get past him and out the door. Though she was scared for Lee and wanted to go help him, not knowing how hurt he might be, she had to think how to get away from her crazed daddy. She lunged to the window, pushed it up and climbed out barefooted onto the frozen metal porch roof wearing only the flannel nightgown her pa tore at when he grabbed after her. By the time Jakie was half out the window reaching for Jenny as she crawled away from him to the icy roof's slippery edge, Tim and his ma was pulling at Jakie with all their strength, both of 'em crying and hollering at him in hopes their noise would bring him to his right mind. Jakie backed into the room swinging away. In the meantime Lee come to, staggered to the wash basin, grabbed it with what little strength he had and throwed the cold water right in his pa's face. Between that and cold air coming in the open window Jakie was shocked into short-lived reason. He bolted for the door. Lee followed behind, watching to be sure he left the house while Esther and Tim begged Jenny to come back in. Only when she seen her pa lurching down the street did she let her ma and Tim pull her back in the window.

Lee was lightheaded and dizzy. While Esther put Jenny to bed, Tim checked all the doors and windows, made double sure the house was locked up tight; even put some chairs under the front and back doors for extra protection. Esther wrapped Jenny in a heavy quilt to warm her up. Lee heated milk for his sister to warm her insides and calm her down, drank some hisself then laid down next to Jenny with a goose egg size bump on the top of his head and an awful headache. They stayed in Jenny's room, none wanting to be alone. They needed each other then as never before. Tim put hot bricks at Jenny's feet, rubbed them to chase the cold away, then made a rag cold to wrap around Lee's head. All night long Esther and her boys huddled on the bed and talked in quiet whispers about what they should do as Jenny lay there, quiet and pale from shock. She loved her pa the way he used to be but the way he intended to hurt her that night was almost too much for her to abide. The boys and Esther, well, their love for that besotted brute died that night. Not really and truly, but that's what they thought then. A sad, sad night it was.

The locks was changed, dead bolts - almost unheard of in Cedar Grove, was put at the doors. And of course the news - probably exaggerated, bad as it was - got out about what Jakie done. He was warned not to bother his wife and kids no more or he'd be run outta town. 'Twas only because of Mr. Hoff and his clout that he wasn't sent packing right then and there. Jakie was watched purty close for a long time, he was.

Tim quit school, couldn't handle the shame. He was a bright boy but getting to the age that many boys stopped going. He figured his mom needed what little money he could bring home. He continued to work with his pa, hard as that was, but 'twas all he knowed. Told his pa he'd be paid cash at the end of every day or he'd quit on him. Promised his mom and told his pa he'd never touch a drop of hard liquor. It made Tim sick to the core to work with his pa and remember what a good man he was before drink, how they worked together so good, how the family sat together in church, how they worked it out to be together for celebrations. He kept a secret burning inside that by helping his pa with smithing - much as he hated the looks of pity that come his way and the contempt shot at Jakie even though his work was still sought out - that someday his pa'd turn around and be the man he once was. Dreams die hard, they do.

Tim was getting to be a good blacksmith in his own right, good enough to cover up for Jakie as more and more he was too unsteady to do his work right. The day'd come when Tim would take over altogether, of that he was certain. So was Mr. Hoff.

Esther took in wash and ironing. The bulky, heavy sadirons was kept hot from late afternoon into the night for her to keep after. Hard work it was for them all. Lee growed stronger as he done heavier jobs around the house, but he never stopped reading; often read into the wee hours of the morning. Jenny helped her mom with the washing and ironing, then carried loads of sparkling clean, well-ironed pieces with Lee back to customers' homes when people wanted them delivered.

Esther was smart. She hung her beautiful embroidery and home made clothes on the wash line along the side of the house where they'd be seen by passerbys, keeping other folks wash out back where it wasn't noticeable. One day she took some of her finest to market in hopes of picking up orders. How surprised and happy she and Jenny both was when that day was over. Tired they was, too. Esther sold her creations and took orders and made appointments to measure ladies for new outfits which left Jenny on her own selling their baked goods and candies.

The more fashionable women in York that had money to spend seen Esther's beautiful work; one by one they searched her out and her business thrived. Eventually she gave up washing and ironing - did her regular customers fuss about that! - and turned her parlor into a sewing room that was good enough for the fussiest woman to enter and get measured for a new dress, or help choose the design and colors for new curtains, table cloths, antimacassars and other stuff. Bolts of material was lined up against one wall, a quilting frame and sewing accessories was off to one side, and at the far end of the room a big, three paneled screen was placed where her customers could be measured in privacy.

Jenny helped her mom with the sewing but her first love was baking and candy-making. She hunted out spices and herbs, experimented with strange flavors that most women didn't have the time to search out or have planted in their gardens. She used her imagination - which every member of this family appeared to have plenty of - to decorate her baked goods and confections with a flair that wasn't usually seen around these parts. This was a waste of time for most women who baked outta necessity. Decorating was a frittering away of precious hours needed for everyday necessities.

Lee helped Jenny haul her delicacies to market where she sold out every Saturday. Some of the women in York had time that wasn't all tied up in daily toil and took an interest in Jenny's homemade, hand-decorated baked goods. Bought them first for their looks, then found out they was tasty and delicious too.

Lee, he roamed the market house when he wasn't helping Jenny, his eager curiosity egging him on to talk to whoever paid attention to him till it was time to help Jenny load up - though there wasn't nothing much to load up - and head back home. Some of the market vendors took an interest in him, looked for him every week, talked to him in between customers. He learned about faraway places and people he only before met in books. He picked up old newspapers, free gospel tracts, whatever he could find to take home to read. People lent him books, trusting him to return them the following Saturday. Everybody at market come to know and admire Lee and his twin sister.

People placed special orders with Jenny and she got busier than ever. She quit school to give more time to her growing business. Lee helped her out by taking orders and shopping for ingredients she needed right there at the market. After a market day they counted the money and figured how much they needed to charge to turn a profit. Nobody made fun of them kids any longer. Lee even gathered staples and ingredients for her while she baked, helped clean up (he didn't like it but he did it) while he shared with Jenny about the things he learned at market. Al Konhaus told Pap them kids was getting a better education than most that sat in school all day. Of course, it wasn't his Alverna that was teaching at the school where the Prowell kids went.

One day after a difficult and trying trip to market in cold rain and wind that took its toll on Jenny's baked goods, Lee come up with a wonderful good idea. Why not take the room next to the parlor where the big window looked out over the street and set up a worktable where people'd watch as Jenny decorated her cookies, candies and cakes. It'd maybe bring in more business right at the house and they wouldn't have to cart all that stuff to market each week, although Lee knowed he'd miss going there.

"Well," he thought to hisself, "I figure I can go off to market without worrying about Jenny and her confections and do what I wanna do." It wondered him so how to handle the matter. When he brought it up to Jenny she was all for it. Together they come up with the idea to sketch posters for his Mom's and Jenny's businesses and pass 'em around market - inside and out. Around Cedar Grove too.

That night Jenny and Lee told Tim and their mom what they was thinking of doing. Esther agreed right then and there it was a good idea; it'd bring more people to the house which meant more business for her, too. Tim said right away he'd help make the cupboards and tables and fixtures Jenny needed to set up a work space.

The whole little town of Cedar Grove, which was growing street by street, stopped at the lighted window to watch Jenny with fast and nimble fingers do magic with her baked goods and candies. Tim made a sign that pointed to the door with the hours when people could come in and shop. Nobody paid much attention to it. If the door was locked they knocked till they was left in. The benches Tim constructed to sit out front and on the side porch was often filled with cheerful neighbors who happened by to snack and gossip a spell.

What fun this come to be, every family member working together except one. That was a sadness that couldn't be glossed over. Jenny had started nervous as all get out, thinking her pa might hang out at the window and ruin her new business. More'n that, even though she still loved her pa but couldn't admit it even to herself, she was scared of him though she didn't let on. Lee sensed this and took over as Jenny's protector, always nearby. He seen how she kept her guard up even though her pa never showed up after the one time he shuffled down the other side of the street looking over at her in the window with bloated, unshaven face and bleary, red rimmed eyes; his chin and lips quivered from drunkenness and shame. The tears run and Jenny couldn't finish up that night, so hurt she was from what coulda been if it wouldn't of been for her pa's weakness for drink.

Esther was every bit as busy as she wanted to be, hired two girls to help with the sewing. But there was certain parts only Esther worked on, that particular she was.

This broken and incomplete family was making it on it's own, everybody happy for 'em, just wishing Jakie could get back to when he was at his best instead of staggering about in drunken befuddlement. He shoulda been home with a family that couldn't let him in to do them more harm. Just couldn't be trusted, Jakie couldn't.

The hurting and shame never stopped. Yeah, Jakie continued to hurt his family, cause he wasn't strong enough to stop guzzling the 'white lightning'. Things went good enough for them to somehow put the bitterness behind them, but never the sadness.

It come to the place where another smith was brought in to replace Jakie. Mr. Hoff wanted Tim to stay on as an apprentice, he was that good. Tim couldn't handle working there with a stranger and without his pa. He left to work in the furniture factory. Edgar was glad to hire him for Tim come up with some unusual ideas about adding certain features to the furniture with his smithing skills. Edgar recognized how several inexpensive add-ons fashioned by Tim made a standard piece of furniture look altogether different - and bring in a couple more dollars.

No one never discovered who was the mysterious backer that seen Jakie had a basement room in Sadie Burkholder's boarding house after Mr. Hoff sent him packing. It was generally thought to be Al Konhaus but that could never be proved. Some wondered so if maybe it was Esther and her kids since maybe they could afford it. No one never found out. Sadie musta been paid good for she never told a soul who it was that covered Jakie's expenses - and that hadda be hard, for see, Sadie was the town's leading gossip, being

217

in a good place to hear the latest rumors. Why she was even seen carrying meals down to Jakie's room when all her other boarders hadda come to the table or not be fed.

At first them who felt sorry for Jakie handed him a coin or two but found out he headed right to town's one tavern. It was come to be understood if you wanted to do something nice for Jakie, the best thing was to give the money to Sadie Burkholder and let her buy what Jakie needed. She did just that. Hankies, socks, shoes, overalls, underwear, whatever he needed she got him without him having to ask.

Grammy said you just couldn't help but shake your head at what Jakie was when he come to Caesar's Cave before it come to be Cedar Grove and how he ended up; you just couldn't help but shake your head.

Every night when I said my prayers I remembered to say one for Tim, Jenny, Lee and their momma and poppa. And I thanked the Good Man for the poppa he gave me - and the grammy who told me stories.

CHAPTER 23 - THE UNDERTAKER AND HIS FAMILY

Mr. H.A. Briggs was the undertaker in Cedar Grove before it was named Cedar Grove. Matter of fact he was one of the men who got together the idea of how to name our little village and then went on to get it incorporated.

Friends and business acquaintances called him H.A., but not us children who was always instructed out of respect to say Mr. or Mrs. or Miss to grown-ups. His appearance was stern-looking; that plus the mystery of being an undertaker, why us kids was scared to call him anything to his face. We quaked in our shoes and shied away from him when we seen him on the street, turned and ran the other way we did.

He was a bit younger than my pap only much like him; guarded reserve and a rather grim appearance. Matter of fact he appeared unfriendly and standoffish till you got to know him, then you found out what an honest, upright businessman he was, a person of authority and good, Christian morals, just like Al Konhaus. He never bragged but you knowed he was behind much of the growth and improvements in our town. His name come up quite a bit at Pap's since H.A. had a reputation of being one of the best builders and makers of fine furniture, and Pap was one of the best carpenters around.

The only item H.A. claimed he had to supply too many of was coffins. "Too many people die before their time," he'd remark in his gruff, serious voice. "Especially little ones." Assembling them coffins by hand, he knowed what he was talking about.

When there was no undertaker in town, some businessmen got their heads together, approached H.A. and asked him to take on that work, him being a man of fine personal character, good business sense and an exceptional furniture manufacturer to boot.

Yes well, there was lots of things for him to think through. First off he wanted to convince his pa to move off the family farm about seven miles distance since he'd need more help in the furniture business. Shouldn't be too hard, H.A. figured, since his pa couldn't keep after the farm with all his sons growed up and moved away with families of their own. None stayed to keep the farm going mainly because it was on lowland, much of it sloping right down to the river; rich soil, but in regular danger of flooding. Healthy, abundant crops was harvested aplenty if they didn't get flooded and washed away. Some good years, lots of bad.

Robert Briggs, H.A.'s pa took right away to his son's request to heart. "Farmin' has me wore out," he complained. "Too old I am for keepin' after the place. I need a change, something different, not so hard."

The farm sold quick to a young couple who was certain they'd make a go of it with their newfangled methods, As soon as they looked over the farm they was right off figuring ways to control the flooding. They believed this was where God wanted 'em to be.

Time would tell.

"Good for them," Robert thought. "That's just what this land needs, young folks with fresh ideas." They worked out the transaction with the new bank H.A. helped get started in Cedar Grove. Robert wished them good luck then packed up to move to Cedar Grove with his wife, Hilda.

H.A. right away added a matching addition to the big, three story frame and brick house he'd built for his growing family. That way the two families would live side by side. Close they'd be but with separate front and back entrances so as not to get in each other's way too much. The house was too big for the older couple, but H.A. liked things lined up nice and even. The extra rooms in his folk's house, especially the cellar and attic could be put to good use as storage for his thriving businesses. Behind the two connected houses was a storeroom, workshop, storage shed and barn.

Even with his boys working with him, H.A. hired extra hands when things got too busy to keep after. He relied on Pap a good bit and some of my uncles from time to time. Finally, he traveled to Philadelphia for a short stay to learn how to preserve the dead. Up until then all he could do was lay 'em out on ice till time for the funeral.

When he got back home H.A. worked hard at his undertaking and furniture businesses and in the next several years built two more matching buildings attached to the two houses, making it four. The last two wasn't to live in. One was a fine-looking furniture store while the one on the far end was the funeral parlor. Most funerals was still held in otherwise seldom-used parlors of the departed persons, but H.A. was planning ahead to the day when more funerals would take place in his establishment. This was a man with keen foresight. With all the outbuildings and such, Mr. Briggs and his establishments took up one whole block of Elm Street.

H.A. didn't dwaddle in life about much of anything. He had two top-notch businesses - with more to come in the future - and a fine family of four boys, one girl.

H.A.'s boys worked right along with him from little on up, first running errands, doing chores, cleaning the buildings and equipment, caring for the horses that pulled the furniture wagon and hearse, all the chores that got them acquainted with the trades. As they got older he apprenticed them under his personal supervision to design and build furniture, then houses; had them helping out with funerals too. That was a family business if ever there was one. They worked from after school till dark with a break for supper and time set aside for study. He wanted in a bad way for his boys to get an education and seen they did. They went to the business school in York after they graduated from the one room school on the outskirts of Cedar Grove.

Mr. Briggs, he gave no thought about what his boys wanted, he chose what they'd do without asking them if maybe they'd wanna do it. They never had a part in decision-making. He just told 'em what was what and expected them to follow through without argument or back-talk. Made for some purty rough times in the family as the boys got older, it did.

Pap said H.A. had good business sense but his sense of being fair was not up to par when it come to his family. He was more of a stern taskmaster than a pa to them boys. Course Pap never said much about things like that beyond Grammy's hearing, and certainly not never in front of us kids unless it slipped out when he didn't know we was in hearing range. When we heard, we kept it quiet, knowed it was to go no farther'n Pap's front door.

It appeared them two Dutchmen come from the same vine, only Pap was a little bit more accommodating than H.A., yeah purty much more.

From little on up H.A.'s girl, Suellen was knowed as the purtiest girl around town. Nice and friendly, too. Don't know if I could do justice to her story. Maybe that'll come later.

H.A. taught his boys how to draw up plans for houses for our growing town. For a start he drew five or six blueprints of single houses, double houses, even row houses. The oldest boy, Walter, was the only one who got a good grasp of this. Wasn't long he was sketching and designing on his own. Good as he was H.A. never gave him full control. He coulda but didn't. Always kept an iron hand over his boy and his drawings. Added or took away, changed it just enough so it appeared it was more his idea than his boy's.

When Walter drawed up blueprints for the butcher shop, the drug store and barber shop, the butcher, the druggist and the barber liked 'em right off. H.A. looked 'em over, suggested they change this or that. Well, nothing was said in front of H.A., but the men all agreed they liked Walter's first drafts the best and told Walter that's what they wanted.

222

Walter agreed to go along with 'em only if nothing was said to his pa about it. It hadda be kept quiet or Walter'd get run outta town by his pa. So, it was settled behind H.A.'s back, a secret joke between the men and Walter for many a year. The respect for H.A. in other dealings kept them from spreading it past their own tight, little group. They knowed when to keep quiet. Besides, they didn't wanna lose Walter even though sometimes he displayed a bad temper. Nobody was sure if it was his inborn nature or because of the disapproving way his pa treated him. He'd take to a bad mood now and then after his pa tore into him time and again for not doing things the way H.A. told him to do. All het up Walter'd get. Sorta explode around all them tools and equipment and building supplies, throwed 'em around, got mean and nasty he did; scared people with his threats, even his own brothers. They learned to back off and let him alone till he got over it. Sooner or later he did. Pap figured that was Walter's way of letting loose his anger and hard feelings he'd kept inside too long.

Anyhow, after the planning, Walter got right in there and helped build them houses from start to finish. People knowed they was getting good quality for their money when their houses was built by H.A. and his boys. Nice looking houses too.

The next boy, David, he fit in best taking charge of ordering tools, supplies and equipment and getting them lined up at the worksite. Of course his pa had to inspect David's course of action on every job.

Pap always said, "*Ach vell*, H.A. trained David real *goot* but never told him he done *goot*. Only pointed out his mistakes. Of which there was few. Hearing H.A., it appeared everything David done was wrong. Nothing could *du* say to change his mind."

David, he was the quiet one. Never had much to say. A loner. Only time David truly come to life was when sure-

223

footed as all get-out he was climbing over the open beams of the roof-tops of a three story house. He showed no fear of falling or getting hurt. His pa warned him he was too careless. It didn't appear so. People was always milling around when a new house was going up and they marveled at how sure and steady David was around all the supplies and equipment no matter how muddled up they got. Come the end of the day, David organized everything neat and orderly to begin next morning. It was something how that stuff could be left at the site overnight with no fear of it being stole. That's the way it was back then. Except when the gypsies showed up; or the backwoodsmen.

Anyhow, rumor had it that Indian blood was in H.A.'s family going back many a generation. David made the hearsay appear true. He looked different from the rest of the family. Bronze skin (course he was out in the sun a lot), straight, black hair (his brothers and Suellen had light, reddish brown hair), high cheekbones, and more Indian features and manners that made it a good possibility. They wasn't seen in no other family member, only David.

Things like that happened back then, only in this instance it musta gone way back cause no one alive knowed it as a fact; no one even remembered how the talk got started. Some people never forgot though and was always bringing stuff like that up. Every so often a passing remark was made about David and Indian blood in his veins. Things, they just happened back then; still do today. David, who looked like he coulda had Indian blood, kept the talk alive because of his looks and his ways.

After he graduated business school, Adam, the next to youngest boy went off to Philadelphia to learn the undertaking trade like his pa. He knowed most of it before he left but his pa wanted him to make it official and get his undertaker's certificate. When he come back, father and son worked the trade together. Adam come to do most the work on the dead in that little room in the back where no one except him and his pa was ever allowed; that was after they stopped working at people's own homes where the funerals was held. Didn't matter that when somebody died and Adam was called out at all hours of the day or night, H.A. seen he helped build houses and do his share of work in the furniture store in between making arrangements and working on the dead. He also handled all the accounts in both businesses, all under his pa's watchful eye.

Where money was concerned, H.A. kept full control. Adam, for all his bookkeeping never signed a check, only his pa who doled out earnings more like he was a bighearted benefactor handing over unearned dollars rather than honest wages them boys more'n earned. It griped 'em, that's for sure. They often swallowed hard and held their tongues just to keep the peace.

Most the time them brothers worked together just fine, but now and then people wondered how come they didn't kill each other with a hammer or saw during a heated spat about what shoulda been done, who shoulda done it, how and when it shoulda been done. But mostly they kept their tempers and gear under control and kept plugging away since that was the Pennsylvania Dutch way of doing things. Besides, they was smart enough to fear their dad and his consequences when things didn't go his way.

H.A., he thought he was fair all around, but his kids had real reasons to gripe.

My kids, they griped about me and their dad too. But without no reason at all, at least where I was concerned. I was fair through and through.

The youngest boy of H.A. and Kathryn was another story, the black sheep of the family; a misfit. See, Kathryn already had her hands full with her growing family and filling in for whenever or wherever her man needed her. She knowed the ins-and-outs of his work as much as H.A. and her boys. Then

Edward was born. It was said he got more attention than the rest since he come a bit on behind. His brothers was taken with this new baby, fooled around with him whenever they could. With the grandparents next door it was believed Edward got spoiled with all the extra attention. But Grammy said that's just the way it was with Edward. Everybody loved him, gotta kick outta him - all except maybe his pa. Good natured this little boy was with bright blue eyes that was always merry, and big grin from ear to ear. From little on up he'd get people to smile back at him, wrap 'em around his little finger. He come to think he was put on this good earth for making people laugh at his high jinks. Used it to his benefit he did

He was an easy-going boy, unruffled by his pa's demands to listen up and behave at all times. Purty much got scolded something awful by his pa. Then his brothers hung back till their pa left and spoiled Eddie all the more. A bit lazy Eddie come to be, especially when told to do something he didn't wanna. H.A. didn't scare this one like his brothers when they was scolded, but Edward paid by not having no supper till he finished the wretched chores his pa put on him. Sometimes he got whipped with the belt, but never with the buckle end. No matter, the boy wouldn't fit into the mold his pa tried to squeeze him into.

Yes well, it was bound to happen. Edward rebelled. Did deliberately what his pa told him not to do, then snuck off and hid till he hoped it'd blowed over. Good at hiding he was; couldn't never be found. Didn't come home till the family got frantic about his whereabouts, then he returned, ready to take what punishment was waiting for him.

No one could figure that boy out except his mother, but she didn't dare say nothing to H.A. after the first time she stood up for Edward. She seen it was no use after the way he flew off the handle and blamed her for spoiling him something terrible. Why, of course it was all her fault!

Everyone was puzzled cause it appeared Edward was asking for trouble on purpose. His brothers come to resent him cause he put his pa in a such dreadful frame of mind and they paid for it as much as Edward.

Grammy ran into Kathryn while she was working in her flower beds one morning. Kathryn, usually calm and levelheaded was all vexed about something. When Grammy asked about her family, Kathryn unburdened her heart. "Eddie's not a bad boy," she sighed. "He's different from the rest. If he gives in to his pa it's like he's gonna lose the person he is inside. He doesn't wanna turn into what H.A. wants him to be, somebody he really and truly ain't. Only now I'm worried. Eddie's fighting against his pa so bad he's gonna forget who he is. Eddie's taking a turn for the worse."

Looked like she was right. Edward Briggs was outta control, foolish, reckless and unafraid. Wouldn't of been no wonder if he got killed doing such dim-witted and risky stuff. People seen how he was behaving and come to feel impatient towards him instead of pity. They wondered so if he was a bit touched in the head, a little crazy, you know. Hardly no one blamed his pa anymore. They figured the reason H.A. was hard on Edward was cause he was trying to get the boy back on the right track.

Edward was like that from little on up. This rebellious boy got hisself into more messes than you'd wanna know about. Listening to Grammy's stories about Edward, why I'd clench my teeth in horror at his pranks. Yeah, but thank goodness, before it was too late, he come to his senses and seen how he was hurting hisself and his mom who he loved more'n anybody. The rest of the family, well he decided he couldn't dwell too much on. Figured the damage was done, nobody'd give him a chance for him to make amends for the way he acted up. All he could do was try to work things out with his pa and brothers and still struggle to be hisself while making it up to his mom and grandparents. It wouldn't be easy. Knowed his pa'd never forget how he tarnished the family reputation, never forgive him. All he could do was try. And that he worked at; real hard.

227

Edward started by applying hisself in school and at home. 'Twasn't hard, he was bright. He ate humble pie over and over again. He done what his pa told him. H.A. laid it on him with hard work, testing how earnest he was about changing his ways. His brothers laughed in his face at everything he done since they was seasoned in the work and he wasn't. Made it hard for him they did. With intent they left the dirty work for him, made it worse by letting things go that under normal conditions - and under their pa's watchful eye - they never woulda done before, then expected Edward to fix it up before their pa come to inspect. His unused muscles ached, his whole body yearned for rest of which there was little. But he didn't cave in and turn resentful which was what they expected he'd do. It took a lot outta him to work alongside his older brothers and pa, but when his anger flared up he poured out his fury into the grueling, hard work. His mom and grandparents was troubled about this harsh treatment that seemed to have no end, but knowed they better not interfere. Their comments was not wanted. In fact, H.A. harbored some harsh feelings against Kathryn, thinking she contributed to Edward's disobedience. He knowed it wasn't his fault; must be hers.

It happened that not only his body got more fit, Edward's mind become more clear and he seen how he could measure up and do all he was told and still, somehow or other, not give up who he was inside. But he knowed he'd someday have to find his place outside his family, that they'd never forgive him altogether or accept him after all the trouble he caused - all except his mom and grandparents, and they didn't count when business matters was involved.

CHAPTER 24 - ROBERT BRIGGS

The way Grammy said about him, I woulda liked Robert Briggs.

H.A.'s dad fit right in after moving to town; jack-of-all-trades Robert was, a happy, agreeable fellow who loved a joke that was often only funny to him. You could hear his jovial laughter rolling down the streets of town. It made everyone around chuckle too. He had a set of strong, powerful lungs and made use of them by funning, but never to hurt another person. Robert loved life and he loved people.

In spite of his joking around Robert was intent when it come to doing good work for his boy. He liked the work too, thrived on it. *"Ach vell* now," he'd go on. "What *Ich* do here, it sure is much easier than the farmin' *Ich* done all my life. Best thing happened when *Ich* come to be here with H.A. Nothing could be better'n this. Now take Hilda *un* Kathryn, they get on so *goot*. We couldn't ask for nothin' more."

Robert - he become a common sight around town, always out amusing people, keeping them in stitches with his funny stories, mostly about his farming misadventures. Robert wasn't tall but he was robust with ruddy cheeks and a comely all-over look. That's the way he was inside, too. When Robert seen somebody could use an extra hand as he undertook his daily constitution around town early every morning in fine weather or not, he'd step right in to help out however he could. Robert never walked away from no one; he pumped water into the troughs, broke up the ice in winter, maybe headed back to a barn to feed some animals, hook up a horse to the wagon to see someone got to the mill or to York. Sometimes he was so helpful he'd get in the way, but nobody griped. Robert become a regular town character, was accepted like he lived here forever.

Once after a long, snowy winter - normal around these parts - the sun come out for a couple days and made the roadbeds - no paved streets then - slick and rutted with deep gullies of mud from melting snow. It felt good for Robert to be out in the bright sunshine on a blue cloudless day in spite of the muck and mud that stuck to his black, rubber galoshes and splashed onto his coarse, work coveralls. He got word there was cargo waiting to be picked up at the train station, so he hooked the two horses to the supply wagon and told David to jump on. A shipment of brand new furniture arrived that very morning. Robert needed his grandson to help load the big, bulky crates onto the wagon. From there they'd take 'em to the storage shed where Edward would unload 'em with their help. It'd then be up to Edward to take hammer and chisel in hand and pry open the containers nailed shut tight, a tedious, miserable job with big splinters from the crates flying every which way to jab through his work gloves and clothing and into his skin causing infection if they wasn't dug out soon enough. No one else wanted that job. Edward, he didn't mind. He looked forward to what he'd find in each crate, taking care not to scratch or damage each piece he unpacked. He looked at it like opening a gift, only he never woulda said that out loud to his brothers. They woulda laughed and made fun, for sure.

Later on everyone said they shoulda knowed better, but that's hindsight for you. Anyhow, a purty steep grade was; the horses was pulling just fine. Later they figured it was maybe from the melting snow and the weight on the wagon that the front left wheel gouged a deep, gaping furrow in the roadbed. Then, oh lordy, when the back left wheel slid into that rut, the load shifted, the wagon started to tilt. The horses strained but the wagon and its load went over. David jumped off the right side and landed on his feet in the middle of the muddy road. Wasn't hurt, not a bit. 'Twas different for Robert. Off the seat he fell, still holding onto the reins. He went down. The front of the wagon come to rest on top of him. David hollered for Edward who was waiting for them.

He heard this commotion and was outta the storeroom and on the scene in no time. When they got the wagon off their grandpa - some said it was a miracle the way they lifted it off of him so fast - and pulled him out from under, not a mark on him could you see. But unconscious he was.

David carried him onto the back porch of his mom and dad's house. Adam was at the desk poring over the books, heard the uproar and in no time grabbed a folding cot he used to transport the dead, helped David get their grandpa onto it and carried him to his bed. With the shouts from the boys, Kathryn dropped what she was baking and Hilda ran from the washing machine. After they got him in bed, David went after the doctor. News reached Walter where he was surveying a plot of ground for the new town hall. He headed home leaving all his equipment right where it was.

Edward started cleaning up the wreckage, borrowed Pap's wagon to load up the crates, a couple at a time. Walter lent a hand when he seen he was of no help in the house. Pap and John and Will and George done what they could, all working in shocked and somber silence after they learned what took place. Everyone was waiting to hear the outcome of Robert Briggs, the town's adopted comedian.

Took all day to get the road cleared, the crates cleaned off and put in storage. Men come from the furniture factory, pulled the damaged wagon by hand over to the blacksmith shop.

One horse hadda be put down too.

Robert had been put in his own bed not knowing what happened. Doc Harrison told H.A., Kathryn and Hilda it was internal injuries and that most likely Robert wouldn't pull through. Nothing to do but keep him comfortable where he was. All they could do was wait and see. With Hilda, Kathryn and Suellen taking turns caring for him, Doc come around every day. Of course the preacher stopped by to pray at the bedside, pleading for a miracle. Robert's other sons and their families come to rally round the injured man. Some stayed in the big house with Hilda to keep her company and help out. Grammy and other women sent food, carried linens and Robert's night shirts back to their houses to wash and then return. Everybody helped that could.

Two weeks went by. Robert hardly moved. One late afternoon he started bleeding from the mouth. Then, he was gone.

'Twas a sad time for Cedar Grove. The thought of no more Robert and his one-of-a-kind stories distressed everyone, especially them who was often the butt of his humor. No more help with pumping or feeding the stock, no more encouragement from a friend who never betrayed a confidence.

H.A., he confided in Pap he was filled so bad with guilt and remorse since he was the one who talked his dad into leaving the farm and moving to town to help out. Then, after all this time, to have this happen.

Carried it with him the rest of his life, he did.

At the funeral parlor, all the town was there still filled with disbelief and shock from losing this kind and generous, warmhearted man. The men folk was silent with grief as they chewed their cud of tobacco faster than ever and thumped H.A. on the back or pumped his hand awful hard not reckoning how bad they was squeezing. Didn't know what to say. Death happened to every family, but with Robert, it was like he belonged to every family in town. David, he pushed everyone away, hung back separate and alone as if to say, *don't come near*. David, he seen what happened to his grandpa, was filled with remorse from the *maybes*; maybe he coulda somehow or other kept his grandpa from falling if he woulda thought of him instead of jumping off to save hisself; maybe he hurt his grandpa more when he carried him to the house; maybe he shoulda handled the horses instead of his grandpa.

David needed comforting but was left alone after he chased everyone off with a scowl. All except Ralph, that is. He was an old fellow past his prime with not much to him. He hung out with Robert on his early morning walks about town. Them two was often seen chewing the fat as they sat at the station watching the trains pull in and out. The day of the funeral, Robert's buddy Ralph walked right up to David. Teary-eyed he threw his arms around the young man and gave him a pint-sized bear hug before David knowed what was happening. Ralph, half the size of David, pulled him to a bench and sat hisself and David down. Them two sat like that, neither saying a word. Just sat there feeling each other's hurt as well at their own.

The ladies hugged Hilda and Kathryn and Suellen with tears streaming down their cheeks. Some said things that comforted, some said things that hurt though they wasn't meant to. Was just hard to know what to say to make it better, even when they knowed it couldn't be made better. Yet they tried.

H.A.'s reserve stiffened up even more. Folks shook their heads at how it was a shame that H.A. had his own terrible grief while having to deal with the misfortunes of so many other people. No one envied H.A. and the kind of work he done.

Robert's wife, Hilda, left her big empty house and moved in with H.A.'s family. Plenty of room there was. The two women and Suellen got along just fine.

Instead of letting it sit empty, H.A. eventually took the attached home that Robert and Hilda lived in and doubled the size of the furniture store - the finest furniture establishment for miles around.

If only Robert woulda been there to see it and help out. He woulda been so proud.

CHAPTER 25 - THE GYPSIES

I don't see gypsies no more. Guess they travel in cars and trucks, or maybe they just disappeared, got mixed in with normal people. But boy-oh-boy, when I was a kid and heard the gypsies was coming, my blood ran cold from fear and excitement.

I didn't get to Grammy's too much after I was ten. Mom and Pop needed my help more'n ever, but late one summer soon before school was to start I was there helping Grammy in the cold cellar - the part of the cellar with a ground floor, cool and damp, a good place to store winter vegetables. I was sorting potatoes, throwing the rotten ones in the slop bucket to take home for the pigs. Purd come running inside all excited.

"Vernie, hurry up! The gypsies is comin', the gypsies is comin'," he hollered down the cellar steps.

I looked at Grammy, yearning to run up and hear more, my heart pounding with excitement. I held back in case Grammy didn't approve. When she nodded for me to go on, I started to race up those cellar steps, then remembered and ran back down for the slop bucket. I didn't want Grammy to lug it up the steps though she woulda. Oh, how I loved Grammy. She understood me just like Pop understood me.

When the gypsies showed up, mystery and thrills and anticipation galore was in store for us and I didn't wanna miss out on any of it. Grammy come lumbering behind me just as excited, only more nervous than me. And for different reasons. *"Wass iss?"* she questioned. "They're here now yet? It appears too late for their comin', ain't so?"

Purd, all wound up said, "I ain't kiddin'. They pulled into the woods between the picnic grove and the train tracks and are settin' up camp right now."

Spine-tingling jitters took hold of us kids when we heard the news. We'd hear stories about the gypsies, wasn't sure

234

if they was true or not, but they scared us to high heaven. Other'n that I didn't know nothing about who they was except they'd come and set up camp for maybe a week every summer. We was warned and scolded about staying away from their camp. "They'll steal the clothes off your backs," we was admonished. Or, "They'll grab you and carry you off."

Us kids couldn't hardly believe such a thing. Yet we was cautious. Being fully warned, we took courage by banding together for protection, then sneak up to spy on their camp. At the last minute courage failed us. We never got too close. We was too noisy to sneak up on anything. Oh, we started out we did, couldn't stay away though we was scared silly to get too close. We was fascinated by the way them groups of strange-looking wanderers with all their worldly goods in carts and wagons pulled by donkeys or ponies with bright, colorful cloth braided in their manes and tails, camped in the nearby woods every year. Bells attached to harnesses jingled in high spirits as the animals trotted along.

That evening we was all sitting around while Pap was reading the Bible. From the book of Zechariah he read, *"And on that day there shall be inscribed on the bells of the horses, Holy to the Lord."* Purd and me, we looked at each other. The gypsies was on our minds and we wondered so if their ponies had them words on their bells. Before bedtime Purd decided that tomorrow we was gonna get close enough to see if our suspicion was true. I took note that Purd said 'we' meaning him and me, for he was too much of a scaredy cat to go look by hisself. He'd be brave enough only with me in front, and him hiding behind my skirts.

The men and women, even little kids, dirty though they always was, you could tell how they loved flashy-looking clothes with bold, bright colors. Their costumes was trimmed with tassels and lace. The girls and women had flowers stuck behind their ears or down the front of their blouses in their bosoms. Their full skirts swirled around their legs as they stepped to the beat of fiddles, tambourines, little drums and other strange-looking instruments, some shaped like gourds that rattled when shook. Lots of jewelry, men and women and kids, all. We'd never seen the likes nowhere else. Of course this was all too good to not spy on.

When they showed up it was like they appeared out of nowhere. So thrilling they was, so full of life. They sparked our imaginations about people completely different from us. I wondered so to Purd how many more different kinds of people was out in the world beyond Cedar Grove that we didn't know about yet. Yeah, on one hand we kids was scared of 'em, wondering if they'd steal us or anything else they'd get their hands on. On the other hand we got as close as we dared, spellbound by these outta the ordinary strangers.

Was they truly that underhanded, always on the lookout to grab what didn't belong to them? For sure, the grownups of Cedar Grove got the jitters when the gypsies come. Fear lay in their hearts for their property and gardens and animals and everything they owned, thinking of the danger not only to themselves but for their widow neighbors and old folks who lived alone and was more vulnerable to be taken advantage of and stole from.

That little was all I knowed about gypsies. I wanted so much to talk to a gypsy girl close to my age. I seen her every year. I'd ask her questions about how they lived and where did they come from and where was they going, what names their donkeys and ponies and dogs had. But I didn't dare. But this one time she was looking my way and approached me as I peeked out from behind a tree. I said loud enough for her to hear, "My name's Alverna."

She called back, "Alverna. That's a funny name. I'm Maribella." Then I ran off.

Maribella. Now I knowed the name of a gypsy girl. Maribella. It was like a treasure for me to cherish. Maribella.

This time, except for the tinkling of the bells on the harnesses, the gypsies was quiet. We never seen this side of 'em before. It even more scared the daylights outta us. What in the world was they up to? The older kids who hid in the dark woods brought word back to town that camp was set up, fires was lit, but a strange, solemn stillness lay all around.

The next morning, several gypsy men followed what musta been their head leader onto Elm Street. Purd was up early with the rest of us, wanting not to miss anything. He was first to see 'em coming. Grammy and Pap was at one window with me between, the rest peeking out others. Troubled, most folks stayed indoors, but eyes glanced guardedly from windows. Some doors was opened just a crack to see out. A couple of brave women was out sweeping off their porches, staying close to the door in case they wanted to move inside quick-like.

The gypsies come by the old Hoff place walking with slow measured steps and serious faces. It wondered us so. We watched. With steady and dogged steps they stomped by Pap Farley's house, not looking to the right or left. I had goose bumps all over. When they was outta sight we all stepped outside to follow them with our eyes. They stopped at the funeral parlor. The chief gypsy man tried to turn the big, round, brass doorknob. It was locked. He banged the Lion's head doorknocker so hard that it vibrated all the way down Elm street. That knocker was a fancy one that fit right in on this important-looking establishment, but woulda been outta place in the rest of the town except maybe for the bank, only banks don't need doorknockers. So sober was them gypsies. Never seen 'em like that before. Every citizen of Cedar Grove who knowed they was here was in suspense.

Mr. Briggs answered the door. All neat and clean he was - like always. His white collar was tight around his neck and a string tie you never seen him without, dressed up in black suit jacket, trousers and shoes, the kind he always wore no matter what work he was at. Grammy kept Pap looking neat and clean as much a carpenter can be, but she often sighed and wondered so just how much washing and ironing

Kathryn Briggs must do to keep after her man and them boys of hers. All those white shirts that needed starched made her shudder. H.A. stepped outside to greet 'em but wasn't long till he opened the door wide and motioned 'em inside.

I was glad Pap was good friends with Mr. Briggs cause them two often had their heads together about the goings-on of Cedar Grove. After the gypsies headed back to their campgrounds and an allowable amount of time had passed, Pap strolled towards the funeral parlor. We was restless, couldn't settle down to our chores - of which there was always plenty. The morning lasted forever. When Pap come back at noontime for dinner we was all ears to hear the news first hand. Here what happened, an old gypsy lady took sick on the journey and died after they pulled in during the night. They come to H.A. for him to help get her buried. He agreed to do what he could but since this was the first gypsy funeral he ever handled, he had no idea what he was in for.

First of all, the gypsies went back to camp and tore it down, not letting Mr. Briggs know ahead of time they'd all be coming to his place to stay for the duration of the funeral. That afternoon everyone of 'em marched into town. The stateliest pony of the bunch - if there was such a thing, they all looked purty straggly - led by the gypsy chief, pulled a cart in which the old, dead, gypsy lady laid. Believe you me, everyone in town managed to be on Elm Street watching. You woulda thought it was Independence Day cause no one appeared to be working. It was even better than a traveling circus though I never seen one, only heard about 'em. H.A. Briggs and Adam was there waiting, took 'em around back. Some of the local boys - Purd for one - brave in numbers, straggled on far behind, then into the alley to keep an eye on things. I wanted to but Grammy said *no way* and kept me under her wing so I wouldn't sneak off.

H.A. took the gypsies - everyone of 'em - to where he kept his coffins. They picked a cheap one which made H.A. thank his lucky stars since he figured he'd never get no money outta them. All this time he was sweating under

238

his collar wondering so what they was gonna do next. The women got busy and pulled out the stuffing that lined the coffin and put in their homespun blankets and rugs to lay the old gypsy lady on. Without so much as asking - they reasoned it was the way all funerals was - they set up camp on H.A.'s property behind the funeral parlor near the storage shed. They went right ahead and bedded their animals in H.A.'s stalls which made for awful crowding of his horses. Cooking fires was started outside, but what surprised the dickens out of him more'n anything was when the whole band of gypsies moved into the funeral parlor and hunkered down until they got their matriarch buried. Everyone took turns tending the animals - helping themselves to H.A.'s fodder - looked after the fires, cooked the meals. They took turns, some outside while others stayed indoors. Most the men slept outside, the only place they was comfortable and used to. The women and kids throwed blankets on the floors. They liked being outta the weather for a change.

Two and a half days they was there till the old gypsy lady got buried.

What a nerve-racking experience that was for the Briggs family. They sure was on edge about what the place was gonna look like when the gypsies up and left. No matter, Pap said H.A. treated 'em no different than his regular families - except he had his boys sneak some pictures off the walls and remove what-nots off the shelves, move the best furniture outta the funeral parlor and make sure certain doors was kept locked real good and tight, and although he didn't make no money off the gypsies, not much was carried off and he didn't too much go in the hole.

Of course most people was suspicious, guarded all they had so nothing ended up missing. Us kids, we daringly walked past the funeral parlor, peeked around the corner to the back, hid behind some bushes in the alley to steal a look every chance we got. We was so eager and curious to see what was going on. Purty much ignored by the gypsy band we was cause we didn't venture too close; never seen inside, just what was going on outside.

When the gypsies pulled out, they looked despondent in place of their usual high spirits. Some gardens had less in 'em than a week before, but all-in-all, no one fared too bad. Many folks - outta the goodness of their hearts and hoping their belongings'd be left alone if they shared - dropped fresh fruit and vegetables, produce, baked goods, all sorts of food off for the gypsies. Nevertheless, the whole little town of Cedar Grove breathed a big sigh of relief when the gypsies was on their way to who-knows-where. H.A. told Pap he was glad he didn't have no more funerals while they was there; don't know what he woulda done.

Them gypsies, they gave us something to talk about for a long time. To this day, that's all I know about 'em. They'd come back every summer, camp out where they always done, go to the graveyard and clean around the grave. If I'd be at Grammy's I'd go to the same tree, peek out and look for Maribella. If she'd catch my eye I'd say, "Hi Maribella, it's Alverna." She'd reply, "Hi Alverna. You remembered my name."

That I'd never forget.

A year or two later my whole life purty much changed so I couldn't take too much an interest in their goings-on.

But I never forgot the gypsy girl named Maribella.

CHAPTER 26 - EDWARD AND FANNY

One day Edward Briggs was in the furniture store chasing the feather duster over the showroom stock, a job the other boys - young men by now but always called *boys* - thought beneath them and passed onto Edward - when his sister Suellen, showed up with her best friend from business school, Fanny O'Rourke. Fanny and her mom drove up in a fancy buggy that people right away noticed wasn't from around here. I was at Grammy's that summer day, outside when the buggy went by. I went inside to tell Grammy. She and I stepped outside to gawk together.

The O'Rourkes lived in Harrisburg, a purty good distance. Suellen'd been wanting Fanny to visit her in Cedar Grove for a long time. When she heard Fanny's mom was looking for some fancy parlor furniture, and even though she knowed there was plenty of it for sale in a big city like Harrisburg, she talked them into a visit and promised to take them to her pa's store.

Suellen introduced them to Edward. He took one look at Fanny and felt an immediate attraction to her. At first glance it was hard to tell why. Terribly shy and backward Fanny was, mostly cause she knowed she lacked purty features of any kind, but Edward, he right away noticed what she was inside. Seems Edward was always looking for that in people since he struggled so long and hard at finding hisself.

Mrs. O'Rourke wasn't at first sure about Suellen when Fanny took her home once for a visit. She noticed that the girl dressed nice, had good manners, but Mrs. O'Rourke was particular who Fanny associated with. She figured Suellen's invitation come at the right time to check her and her family out.

She was surprised and impressed with what she seen - the large business enterprise of the Briggs family in such a little, outta-the-way town. She couldn't even fault the manners of Suellen's family, particularly her mother. "Even the grandmother is rather nice, though a bit countrified," she thought to herself. Everyone in town was protective towards Hilda Briggs since Robert died in that wretched accident, and Mrs. O'Rourke woulda been chased outta town if she had expressed them thoughts out loud.

Mrs. O'Rourke seemed to right away take an interest in the whole family cause she seen Edward eyeing up Fanny and picked up how flustered it made her daughter. Never seen her take an interest in a young man before. For some time now she was keeping her eyes open for a husband-to-be for Fanny who she admitted - only to herself - was lacking an air of dignity and self-confidence. She didn't know why, did her best to instill all those traits in her only daughter, even took her to Philadelphia for some polishing-up, but it didn't appear to help none. A proper suitor might be hard to come by even though Fanny, from a Scotch-Irish background that two generations back climbed up in Harrisburg high society, was a mite too timid and backward to attract young men.

As the day wore on Edward turned his charm onto Fanny and her mother, hoping to get them to like him so he could get to see more of Fanny even though she lived purty far away. Mrs. O'Rourke was pleased with the attention that was paid to Fanny and was working outta plan of her own. See, although she didn't find suitable parlor furniture, she bought several small items she declared was of such beauty and originality that she never yet seen in the large establishments in Harrisburg. Why they'd fit right into her music room. She remarked to Mr. Briggs that she expected Edward to take charge of delivering them on the day they agreed upon. Edward couldn't of been happier.

The pieces could be handled and delivered by one person so H.A. agreed to Mrs. O'Rouke's request, or maybe I should say *demand*. He was a bit uneasy about it though, thinking his boy might do something to ruin his chance of expanding his range of business. Wouldn't you know it, H.A. was too nearsighted to see that it was Edward who was expanding his pa's range of business. Poor H.A. He just couldn't always see things clear, not when his boys was part of it.

Fanny and her mom spent the afternoon at the furniture store and visiting with Suellen and her family. I was out front jumping rope, Purd was on the stoop counting my jumps when I seen the strange looking buggy head down Elm Street towards the pike. I called Grammy and Lilliemae to come out and watch it go by. That was the most exciting thing to talk about in Cedar Grove for at least a week.

A courtship was in bloom. People who knowed the O'Roukes couldn't get over how Fanny blossomed. See, for the first time in her life she felt loved just the way she was. It was thought-provoking for her to take this in since she spent much of her life trying to be someone she wasn't in order to make her parents approve of and love her more. She was tired and worn-out from pretending, and now with Edward's attention, she come to understand what she was doing. She didn't no longer have to pretend, could be her true self, especially around him. That's why Fanny took to Edward. He learned how to use his positive disposition that attracted people to him for good instead of selfish intent. Fanny paid attention to what Edward said and began to see possibilities in herself. "Just maybe I can bring out the real me that'll be good enough for Mom and Dad. Just maybe I can stop being somebody I'm not." Still, it took time to discover who she really and truly was since she had hid her true self for so many years. But she was coming around purty good.

Edward, not wanting to upset Fanny later on or have her think his whole life was easy, confessed to her about his reckless youth, but how he was a changed man. Between 'em they decided it'd be best to not to bring that part of Edward up to her parents.

Edward insisted Fanny was beautiful. She wasn't. Yet, she stood up straighter, spoke out clearer - even though it near scared her to death at first. Edward encouraged her to voice her thoughts and opinions because she was well read and very smart. Before she come to know him, she never woulda dared that, so shy she was.

She did get to be easier to look at. Suellen, a true friend, helped her bring out her finer features.

Edward was getting on better with his pa but wasn't earning enough to give Fanny the things her parents gave her or the life she was used to. Maybe never would. He told her so. She promised it didn't matter, but Edward knowed she had no idea what it was like for her to do without. Still, he got up his nerve, asked Mr. O'Rourke for Fanny's hand. Her father said he'd better talk this over with his wife and Edward's parents before he gave him permission.

Kathryn liked Fanny right off, knowed she'd be good for Edward. When she and H.A. went to visit the O'Rourkes in Harrisburg, the four was in agreement to the marriage except for one thing. Fanny's parents spoke up and questioned Edward's finances. H.A. told them Edward had great promise but got a late start in the businesses. He didn't tell them why, just mentioned that as being one reason his income was purty low. H.A. assured them he'd increase it, just not too much at one time. Edward and Fanny could live in the upstairs of the house that Robert and Hilda had lived where now the first floor was part of the furniture showrooms. He wouldn't charge them rent so they'd get a head start with what earnings they took in.

Mr. and Mrs. O'Rourke wasn't too upset. Secretly, they was glad Fanny got that good a catch. For a time they thought maybe she'd never marry. Besides, they had plenty to give this young couple but they'd keep it quiet and bestow some fine things occasionally without making it seem like they was unhappy with Edward's finances.

'Twas a fine wedding in Harrisburg the O'Rourkes gave their daughter. Wasn't many fancy church weddings in them parts back then. Edward's parents done their share to make it a grand affair. Suellen was the maid of honor, every bit as beautiful as the bride. All of Edward's brothers were all there, and Hilda. She kept her hanky close by for she missed Robert so bad not being next to her. And every member of the Briggs family was happy to see Edward settling down the way a young man should.

Fanny and Edward lived right in the middle of the Briggs' enterprises. Not having enough to keep herself busy, Fanny began to help Adam with the bookkeeping when he got bogged down with other work. H.A. provided her a small income although it went against his grain. Deep down he didn't believe women should earn wages but he hadda go along with it since he didn't wanna get on the wrong side of the O'Rourkes. H.A. had sent Suellen to business school, not so much to find a job but to help with the bookkeeping and maybe find herself a man that suited him. Matter of fact, H.A., he never thought Suellen'd take a job anywhere else except with him. And being his daughter he might not have to pay her at all, consider her work payment for her room and board. Suellen took him by surprise, but I just can't get into that right now.

Aunt Lilliemae and Grammy enjoyed having the young, married couple in the neighborhood. Lilliemae announced they breathed fresh air into stale, old Cedar Grove with their refinement and style. Lilliemae! She never lost her love to perform. Yet, most everyone was charmed by this young couple who went outta their way to talk to neighbors, shop in the local stores and walk to church every Sunday. They sure did surprise most folks who thought they'd be too uppity to mingle with us commoners.

Edward purty much passed his lengthy period of hardship and testing. He was proving hisself with resolve to stick it out and do his best. His brothers, without openly admitting it, now trusted him to not run out on 'em and bring shame to the family, especially since he was married and settled down.

Truth of the matter was, things was looking up all around. The businesses was growing; Edward was a main reason why. See, he had this special way of drawing people to him. His pa and brothers seen it and knowed it but they never woulda admitted it out loud. Just too proud.

Then the day come - it was bound to happen - when Edward got overconfident and made a mistake that woulda been of hardly no consequence except H.A. couldn't abide it.

Adam was telling Edward how a piece of equipment was needed to provide for better funerals. Edward agreed and ordered it without consulting his pa. The day it arrived by train, Adam and Edward hurried to the station to pick it up. As soon as they got it hauled into the storage shed they assembled it and was carrying it where it was needed. H.A. seen this and asked what they was up to. It made him so intolerable mad because he wasn't asked permission to purchase it. He tore into Edward like never before. Didn't blame Adam. Guess he depended on him too much with undertaking. Asked Edward who did he think he was? The boss to be taking on something like that without consulting his pa? So mad he was he told his youngest boy it hadda be returned and the shipping charges paid outta his pocket; if it stayed it'd be paid for outta his wages.

H.A. used the excuse of money. Edward was smart enough to know the undertaking establishment had plenty to cover it, otherwise he wouldn't of ordered it. Adam knowed it too. What it was, H.A.'s pride and strong will got him worked up. Yep, H.A.'s pride was what got in the way. Word got out and soon the whole town was buzzing. Everyone held their breaths for it looked like the young man was gonna be run outta town by his own pa who wouldn't admit his youngest could be a wise business partner.

Edward was sure he was gonna be got rid of so he and Fanny started talking about where they might move to. Philadelphia, they was thinking. But that was so far away. Maybe Fanny's dad could give Edward some leads to look for work in Harrisburg. They knowed Fanny's parents would like that. Yet, they liked Cedar Grove and Cedar Grove liked Edward and Fanny almost as much as it's people had loved Robert Briggs. In a different way of course, but the good feelings about this young couple was all around and easy to behold.

Pap, knowing how proud and stubborn H.A. was, done some conniving and fast, hard talk to persuade H.A. to let up on his boy. Grammy was so proud of her man for sticking his nose in where it coulda got him in hot water. That was one of them times when it was important to do, Pap said, and our family hadda accept the consequences, good or bad. Grammy agreed wholeheartedly. I sensed how important this was to my grammy and pap, and although I didn't get the whole gist of what was going on, the gratitude and respect I felt for them that day has lasted all my life, giving me a little bit of hope.

It come about that father and son purty much worked out a truce, though it stuck in the older man's craw to think his own son didn't cater to him like he shoulda. H.A was too proud, wasn't never gonna let it go altogether.

Edward seen the way things would go, that his dad'd never let up on him and give him the free rein he needed to get ahead. He thought about leaving the family business before things took a turn for the worst, if that was possible. He stuck it out while he looked around the area for work. Wasn't much out there. Then luck had it that there was an opening for a cashier at the bank that opened a couple years earlier and was growing like wildfire. Edward talked to Mr. Hostetter, the bank president. At first he refused to take Edward on since H.A. was the one who bought the most stock to get the bank up and going. Being a business associate, Mr. Hostetter figured it might put a strain on his and H.A. Briggs relationship. But all-in-all, the bank needed good help and Edward fit them shoes. Mr. Hostetter talked to H.A., tried to smooth things over as much as possible so he'd agree to Edward being hired at the bank.

H.A. knowed the finger'd be pointed at him if the news got out Edward wasn't hired, so he hadda go along with it. Sure wasn't easy for him though.

Grudges died hard with H.A.

Another reason that the situation was hard for H.A. to swallow, was the bank office was located catty-corner from H.A.'s house. It was in Mr. Hostetter's residence till a bank could be built - that is if it proved profitable - not that the stockholders thought it'd be anything but. Walter was working on blueprints for a new bank building so they'd be ready when the bank directors called upon him for his know-how.

From his house, H.A. seen Edward come and go to work every weekday. Edward often stopped in to say hello. When his pa seen him coming he'd usually disappear. His mom was glad to see him though, always had something on the stove for her wayward son turned good.

The young couple moved from his grandparent's-house-turned-furniture-store into a small house on the edge of Cedar Grove that was just now put up for sale by an older couple who lived in it since brand new. They wasn't no longer able to stay there and was moving in with a daughter and her family. The house had been built by Edward's pa and brothers. It'd do just fine till the young couple could afford to build what they wanted later on.

Edward, he never faulted his dad to make hisself look good. He pointed out how his pa truly didn't need him, had enough workers to keep things going. "Why, in banking I'll be working as a team with Pa and the rest. I'll show people how to use their money to their best advantage so they can pay off their furniture and homes and funerals in record time." (Money was hard to come by for most folks back then, just as much as it is today.)

Folks was pleased. They come to think a lot of Edward, Fanny too. They breathed a collective sigh of relief when H.A. didn't drive 'em away. Relations between the two men was strained all their lives - which was too bad. H.A. wouldn't give in and patch things up, then one day there wasn't no more time.

I wasn't scared of Edward when I seen him coming down the street like I was of his pa. He was the friendliest man I knowed next to Pop.

Respect for Edward continued to grow for the way he handled business. Customers searched him out at the bank, valued this young banker for the courteous ways he treated 'em when they walked through the doors of that establishment; made 'em feel like they was somebody. Edward, he seen the makings in folks and encouraged 'em to have faith in themselves, showed 'em what they could afford, how to budget and stick with it. He was a driving force to make people believe in themselves, convinced them to reach for a better way of living. Only a man on the up-and-up in them days could get through to people with ideas like that.

Being promoted to manager seemed to take only a short time, but Edward didn't change the way he done business. Like it was mostly done back then, he closed each deal with a handshake. It worked too. And if it got around town someone wasn't paying off the loan they took out with Edward, boy-oh-boy! A quiet but convincing kind of pressure was put on the guilty party who come to know it wasn't gonna be tolerated, and they better finish paying off their loan *or else*. Most paid off.

I never learned what the *or else* meant.

Grammy declared Edward woulda made a good preacher. He was a man of indisputable character, true to the core. (I loved it when I heard them big words; memorized 'em so I could use 'em some day).

May as well finish the story about Edward since it's been takin' so long anyhow. This way I won't have to come back to it later.

Edward moved up in the banking world, made good money. The time come when Walter worked with Fanny and Edward to design what house they wanted and needed since they had four kids by now. A fine brick house on a nice plot of ground it was, one of the nicest in Cedar Grove. A bedroom for each child, a big porch with round pillars and fancy rails that wrapped around the whole house, nothing too unusual about that, but this was the first house in Cedar Grove to have a porch - they called it a balcony - on the second floor off their bedroom. Identical rails like the lower porches was around it to keep the kids from falling off when the family gathered there on warm evenings to talk about their day before bedtime prayers and Bible reading.

Soon every new house in Cedar Grove and around had a second floor balcony.

Every Sunday morning - never failed - Edward'd be seen walking the six blocks to Sunday School and Church, Fanny on his arm and his four kids walking in front or trailing behind, all dressed up in their Sunday best. That family looked fit and happy as could be except for the littlest one. See, Stanley stayed little for his age, a mite sickly and pale. Often you'd see Edward pick him up when the little one started losing ground, falling behind; carry him on his arm Edward would.

No one knowed that the little fellow took after his daddy except he looked it and his dad didn't.

See, walking to work on a snow-blowing, cold winter morning - Edward liked to walk, said it cleared his brain so he could do his best work - well, without any warning Edward shocked the whole town by dropping over dead right there in front of the bank. Yep, died right there on the spot. Doc said it was a heart attack.

Funerals was still mostly held in the family's front parlor, but it was too much for Edward's widow and children to handle. Anyways it woulda never been enough room for all those attending. Adam and H.A. suggested the funeral parlor would be the best place for the funeral. Fanny and her kids - she included them, grief-stricken as she was, in planning for their pa's funeral and burial - agreed to that.

I gotta give Fanny credit there. If Mom maybe woulda left me in on things like people dying, it mighta been a little easier for me when I had to deal with my own grief.

The day of his son's funeral H.A. held on to his offhandedness even when the funeral parlor was packed to overflowing with flowers - wasn't enough room for them all - and people who was devastated beyond words. For the first time H.A.'s establishment wasn't near big enough to hold all the folks that come out to pay their respects to the rebellious young fellow that turned into an outstanding husband, father and businessman. From all around they come that sad, sad day! I was living with Bertha and Jack Detwiler then. They knowed Edward too. He helped 'em get a loan for their farm.

What a sight! We was all choked up as we stood in the freezing outdoors. The line snaked down to the end of the block and around the corner. Seemed everyone was there to view Edward's body and express our sorrow to his family, all the while thinking of all the good he done and how he'd be missed. His customers and friends couldn't picture how they'd get along without him; thought about their own loss as much as Fanny's and the kids.

We stopped at the coffin, couldn't believe our eyes. If we wouldn't of seen him laying there, we wouldn't of believed. Him there in the coffin, that made it real. We hugged Fanny and Kathryn, Suellen and Hilda, even Mrs. O'Rourke, shook hands with the four children who stood by their mom straight and tall through it all - except for Stanley. Menfolk pounded H.A. and Edward's brothers on their backs in sympathy, choking back tears one more time for this family, not knowing what to say.

You seen more handkerchiefs being used that day. Mr. Hostetter from the bank had this awful habit; after he'd blow his nose he'd hold his hanky in front of him and shake it out, fold it neatly and put it back in his pocket. Every time he done it all eyes watched. Even when all that came out was clear, it still made you queasy in the stomach. No one wanted to shake hands with him after they seen him do that. Such an outstanding businessman with such a coarse habit. Of course that wasn't as bad as some men who right where they was on the street, leaned over, put a finger over one nose hole and blowed out whatever was in the other one. That was worse'n spitting tobacco.

Why do the good die young? What will we do without Edward? Everyone wondered so.

H.A. and Adam held themselves back trying not showing their grief - they was the only ones, only Adam didn't hide it as good as his pa - so aloof he was you woulda thought he didn't rightly care for his youngest boy. Yes well, he was one of them men who didn't show much affection to their own kin, not never letting them know how much they was loved and wanted.

Pride, oh it sure harms them who can't let it go. H.A. was like most men, a Christian who read his Bible and went to church. Didn't he know that what the Bible said about pride was meant for him just like everyone else? Pap said to Grammy he hoped H.A.'s pride would loosen up before it brung about a greater fall in him, although what could be worse than this?

People didn't blame H.A. altogether for the way he controlled his family. That was the accepted way by most. Others figured his sternness musta been born in him from generations back - just like the Indian blood in David - cause his own pop and Edward sure wasn't never like that. Yep. Musta come from generations back.

Gotta give H.A. credit where credit is due though; he seen that his daughter-in-law and four grandkids was taken care of real good. Of course her parents did too. They wanted her to return to Harrisburg. They was getting up in years, liked the thought of their daughter and grandchildren moving in with 'em. Fanny couldn't; couldn't stand the thought of leaving the house that she and Edward made into a home.

Though wretched from losing her beloved husband, she was forced outta her sorrowful misery by her children. She pulled herself together and provided a fine home for them four. Never married again. Never got over the shock of Edward leaving her so sudden, dying in his prime. Never looked as striking as when Edward lived, but she still held herself accountable to be her best even when it didn't seem to matter no more.

The gossip around town was that Stanley, five years old, cried for three days straight after his daddy was put in the ground. The only thing that stopped him was a spanking by his oldest brother - not a real hard spanking, mind you, he was just at his wits end not knowing what else to do. Them kids was having a hard enough time missing their dad, they was. Now they was afraid Stanley was gonna get sick and die from his fretting over their misfortune; knowed their mom couldn't handle that now yet; or themselves for that matter. Stanley stopped crying after that licking but he never stop missing his dad.

Frail little Stanley was checked out by Doc Harrison with his brother and sisters after what happened to their dad. He was the only one outta them four kids who took after Edward that way, spent most of his life under a doctor's care. The rest married. Not Stanley. Lived with his mom. After his education he took a job his grandpa O'Rourke heard about with the government in Harrisburg. It was a desk job, didn't require no hard labor. Took wonderful good care of his Mom, and her of him.

Smart man, just like his dad. Respected too.

Soon after Edward's death, H.A. and Kathryn visited his younger brother in Kentucky where Edgar had a lumber yard and planing mill. H.A. noticed right off how rough it was for Edgar to keep his family from going under. He put in a big order for door and window frames that he needed, but better yet for Edgar, H.A. told him to move his family back to Pennsylvania, that the job of the manager at the furniture factory was waiting for him. It was growing faster than they knowed how to deal with.

H.A. never talked it over with his boys, just went ahead without telling them what he done. When they found out Edgar took up their pa's offer and was moving his family back to Cedar Grove in a brand new house built by - you guessed it - H.A. and his boys, it didn't go over too good with 'em. They believed their brother, Walter, was the best man for the job, him being the oldest and all. They got so riled up they was ready to up and quit on their old man. After all, they had some pride too. They was complimented time again, told that no one in the whole county built better houses or furniture. *So why did someone from the South have to come in and take over,* they complained. Family or not, he wasn't wanted.

In the end they come to see it was a sensible move. The furniture factory prospered with the good management Edgar brought to it. He was a jolly, good natured man with a considerate outlook. The workers liked him. He made the grimy, dusty gritty work bearable. He also took note how it was with H.A. and his boys so he drawed 'em in, talked things over with 'em, asked their opinions. It took 'em awhile to get used to being part of decision-making but Edgar encouraged 'em, learned what they was good at and made 'em even better. In the long run Edgar's patience helped bring the boys around to accepting him; molded them into a team that worked together even though they often rubbed each other the wrong way. Edgar was honest and fair like his pa, their grandpa Robert, except he had a better understanding of business dealings

Three long streets of Cedar Grove by this time was filled with houses and shops. H.A. decided it was time to sell off that business to a crew of fellas who worked for him so he could fully concentrate on furniture making and undertaking.

Life was settling down for the Briggs family. Fanny and the kids was coming along purty good. Edgar was making things work at the furniture factory.

Of course, nothing good lasts forever.

CHAPTER 27 - THE MAYOR

When I just think how things changed over the years, it's almost too much to take in. Take the county seat for instance. Mr. Wayne Gingrich was the mayor of York when York was next to nothing. It sure has growed a lot since then.

Mayor Gingrich and Pop was good friends. I knowed he was a good man the way Pop spoke about him and all the wonderful good things he was doing for the city.

Well, the mayor, he was the first man in the whole county to own an automobile. The first man! Can you imagine? Was a Ford. That didn't make John Miller very happy. He liked to be first in everything. He was the second man in the county to buy an automobile, but he told everyone he had something special put on it and that's why it took so long for him to get his. Phooey!

Anyway, Mayor Gingrich was proud as proud could be. He right away wanted Pop so bad to come see his automobile.

Now I can remember this just like it was yesterday. On a nice sunny day Pop hooked up Pet to the buggy. Him, Mom and me took off to York to see the mayor's automobile.

Albert wasn't along. He was with Lola. You'd almost believe them two was mother and child they loved each other that much even though Lola had plenty of kids of her own. Lola told Mom and Pop she liked having a little one around cause her bunch was growing up and not needing her so much no more. I guess Albert softened the hurt in her marriage, gave her something else to think about. Mom loved Albert, but he took so much tending being so sickly. Lola seen how hard this was on Mom with all her work. Besides, she loved Albert, wanted him to stay with her now and then. It gave Mom a rest since she was busier than ever with Dale Stuart who was just a baby; healthy, happy and content, all bubbly he was. He took after me. I loved Dale Stuart. Such an easy baby he was to take care of. But don't get me wrong. I loved Albert too.

Anyway, Mayor Gingrich arranged this meeting with Pop a week earlier. Grammy said she'd tend Dale Stuart for Mom. After we dropped him off we headed straight for York. Got to the court house where Pop tied Pet to the hitching post and went looking for the mayor. Mom and me, we sat in the buggy, enjoyed watching all the noisy goings-on of the city and its people. Next thing, here comes Mr. Gingrich bouncing down the court house steps so lively. He was proud as a peacock, ready to show Pop his new automobile. But first he come and greeted Mom and me so nice. Tipped his hat, shook Mom's hand, told her what a good man Ben was, wished he'd go into politics for he was truly admired the way he helped folks with their problems and how he could do a lot of good for the county. Mom turned red, got all *ferdutzed* with his kindly remarks. Her tongue got all twisted up so she stayed quiet, not knowing nothing about politics; just nodded her head in agreement. Then he looked my way and fussed over what a purty, young lady I was, called me a *schnickelfritz*. Again he turned to Mom and wondered how them two boys of Ben's was. Made us feel purty special that a high official took the time of day to comment to Mom what a friend Ben was to him, yet didn't forget to ask over the rest of his family. Since he appeared so friendly I was gonna tell him that I could sing and did he want me to sing him a song, but when the words started coming out, Mom shushed me with her elbow punching into my ribs. She knowed what I was gonna suggest. She didn't want no parts of me showing off.

I didn't mean it to show off, I just loved to sing. Sometimes people mentioned how purty I was and what a good singing voice I had. Of course Mom never said that about me so I didn't pay people no mind, except I was getting older and it felt good when somebody said something nice about me.

Pop always encouraged me to sing. Mom and me, we'd sing together when Pop got down his green mouth organ to play. But I guess I wasn't gonna sing for Mayor Gingrich today since Mom's sharp elbow gave me a dire warning to keep quiet.

After checking the automobile over inside and out, the mayor showed Pop how to start up the engine. With the thunderous, earsplitting noise from backfiring, poor Pet whinnied, jolted and strained at the hitching post. It scared Mom and me as we was being thrown around in the buggy, holding on for dear life. Between Pet and the mayor's new automobile, Mom and me thought we was gonna be throwed out and killed. Pop run over to where Pet was, grabbed her harness, calmed her down with his reassuring words and gentle touch. The mayor walked over to the buggy and wondered if Mom and me wanted to see his automobile. It wasn't hard to see how tickled he was with his new machine. He liked it when people gawked as they passed by, some stopping to ask him about it, others shaking their heads in amazement. Well, Mom heard enough, she didn't yet wanna see it! No way was she gonna step outta the buggy and get close to that dreadful, noisy, driving machine. She was more scared than Pet was. Even with Pop there, Pet was still purty skittish. Now me, I was ready to jump down real quick and walk over to see that wonderful new automobile. I could picture Mayor Gingrich and me riding down the street, hair streaming in the wind, waving to people as we rode by. Everybody'd look and wonder so who the purty young girl was, riding with the mayor, the owner of the first automobile in York, Pennsylvania.

But no, Mom held me back with the sleeve of my dress. It wasn't to be.

Mayor Gingrich wanted so bad to take Pop for a ride, but Pop, he wouldn't go on account of us and Pet. Disappointed, the mayor begged Pop to come back sometime for a ride.

As they said their goodbyes, I sat in the buggy and regarded this mayor and his admiration for Pop. You could see it in his eyes and the way he thumped Pop on the back.

He wasn't ready for Pop to go, but Pop figured it was too much commotion for Mom and Pet. It was time to head back home.

The men, walking to the buggy together, well, I overheard the mayor say a bit uneasy, "Ben, you look a bit peaked and worn out. Are you feeling ok?"

Pop said he couldn't be any better, just workin' hard at what he liked doin' best.

On the ride back, what the mayor said to Pop stayed on my mind. I seen the mayor and the way he respected Pop. He never woulda brought up about Pop looking outta sorts if he wasn't concerned about him. This worried me so. For the past couple months I seen Pop didn't appear as quick and as strong like he had been. But the thought of him not being healthy, oh my, it scared me outta my wits. I hadda think that nothing was wrong with Pop except he was working too hard. I'd fix that. I'd help him and Mom out even more so they wouldn't have to work so hard.

That settled that.

My thoughts was interrupted when Pop spoke up after Pet was well on her way, trotting back to Grammy's to pick up Dale Stuart. For awhile Pop had been quiet, deep in thought just like I'd been; only not over the same thing. After some reflection he just said over it, "*Ach vell* now, soon more people'll drive cars *un* soon there won't be so many horses."

I wiped with the sleeve of my dress what spewed outta Mom's mouth and hit me on the side of my face. She'd been taken by surprise with what she avowed was a dumb remark by Pop. She sputtered and stammered, "That ain't never gonna happen. Cars'll never take the place of horses."

"The day's gonna come when people'll fly through the air," Pop went on. That's just the way he said it.

"*Ach vell* now, don't talk so *dumm*! Don't be such a *dummkoff!*" said Mom.

This wondered me about people driving around in such noisy, cantankerous machines, but flying though the air, that

259

I couldn't grasp. My imagination went wild trying to picture people flying through the air.

Well, he didn't live to see it, but Mom and I did.

Pop, he never got back to visit the mayor and his car.

CHAPTER 28 - POP

Pop wasn't good but he wouldn't go to a doctor.

There was this doctor from York that come to go rabbit hunting on the first day with Pop every year. That afternoon they come back with three rabbits. When they walked in the house, this doctor said, "Estella, I never seen a man like yours. He's the durndest man I ever met. We walk along, that quick his gun goes off and there a rabbit lays. Why, I never even seen the darned rabbit!"

Then he went on. "But, when it comes to taking care of himself, he won't. Please try to get him to go to a doctor."

Turning to Pop he said, "If you don't want me, Ben, to give you an overhauling, go to another doctor. Please."

"*Ich* don't need none."

It was getting Pop couldn't do much of nothing no more. Him and the neighbors had always worked together. We only had Pet and the two mules, Bully and Kate. Just according what was to be done, why then Lance Mellinger'd come up with his two horses. They'd work together, them two. Pop went down to help him when he needed an extra hand. Other farmers worked together too. But it was getting Pop couldn't do nothing no more.

Pop wouldn't budge about a doctor even though he was getting worse. One day he went into the general store to get some things for Mom. He had to wait a good while, and well, his good friend, Frank Weaver, the store owner seen him stagger. It worried him so.

When he waited on Pop he urged, "Don't be so stubborn, Ben. Why don't you go see a doctor? There's something radically wrong with you."

"*Ach vell, du* too now yet!"

But he wouldn't go.

Frank couldn't get over the way Pop was that day, couldn't get it outta his mind. He didn't wanna interfere but he hadda do something. But what? He decided since Lola was such a nice, understanding lady and a good sister to Ben, he'd go and talk to her. When she heard Frank out, Lola went next day and got Annmarie. Together they come down to the homestead. When they seen Pop - the first in a long time - they realized how bad the situation was.

Annmarie wondered so to Mom why she didn't get him a doctor down. Mom told her right off, "*Du* know how stubborn Ben is. What can *Ich* do about it? The *dokder* from York was here not too long ago *un* begged Ben to let him give him an overhaulin' or get another *dokder*. He wouldn't listen to him, wouldn't have nothin' to do with it."

Annmarie was gonna give her brother a good scolding but she seen he wasn't up to it. Scared she got. So sick he looked! Much like their mom, the Old Lady her last days here on earth. She understood Mom's predicament but it wasn't good enough for Annmarie. She was ready to jump all over Mom some more, heap the blame on her as they walked out to the buggy. She hadda reproach somebody for her brother's sickness and she wasn't gonna hold him solely responsible. Mom was the likely victim. Lola seen her sister's intent and didn't want a big ruckus going on. She made up an excuse about having to get home while practically pushing Annmarie into the buggy and took off down the lane.

Pop couldn't climb the stairs no longer. Uncle George come out and helped Mom and me bring the bed down into the front parlor since it was the only room big enough downstairs. George filled in more and more for Uncle John who wasn't around much to help, not since Al Konhaus took him under his wing to learn him the cigar manufacturing business. Uncle John, he had a natural bent to it after making all them cigars in Pap's cellar. Al picked up on it, worked with John when he seen his own son, Howard, had his sights set on life beyond Cedar Grove.

While Uncle John was working hard at learning the ropes of the cigar business, he got sweet over Suellen Briggs, was always looking for her around town so he just might, as he'd say, "by accident run into her and shoot the breeze."

Grammy and Pap looked at their John with amusement over his infatuation with Suellen. They figured John and them wasn't good enough for her even though both families was on friendly terms. Boy-oh-boy! The day'd come when they'd change their minds about that.

Wasn't long till Pop couldn't breathe when he laid down; had to sit up all the time. How uncomfortable he was gasping for breath. Never complained though. Every now and then he'd quote from Genesis where an angel asked Abraham, *Is anything to hard for the Lord?* Then he'd gasp, "*Ich* can breathe a little bit better now. Maybe the *Goot Mann* is gonna heal me." But he didn't say it with the conviction like when he really and truly believed something good was gonna take place.

One day Lola come out by herself which we was always glad about. We wasn't never all that sorry when Annmarie wasn't along. Anyway, Lola seen the big, gilt mirror hanging in the front parlor where Pop could see hisself. She whispered to Mom about taking it down. "Ben's coloring isn't good. The color in his cheeks is all gone. I don't think he should look and see how bad he appears."

With his sickness he first got pasty white, then gray. Now he was yellow. Lola didn't want her brother to see hisself.

Pop overheard her and finally admitted to the truth, winded as he spoke, "*Du* ain't takin' the mirror out. *Ich* know when my time's up."

Lola went and urged Annmarie to come back with her - Annmarie wasn't never any happier to see us than we was to see her. But she was good at harping. She finally wore Pop down and got it accomplished that they got a doctor out.

"It's temporary *du* know," Pop told 'em.

Doc gave him pills and warned Mom, "Don't let him lay down anymore."

He was so short of breath that Mom and the doctor together made a strap. She padded it in the front that he could sit up to sleep. At first Pop balked. He didn't wanna use it.

"Try it Ben, for the kids' sake," Mom went.

So he did.

I was twelve at the time, Albert was six and Dale Stuart was just a mere baby.

Annmarie and Lola come more often after they seen just how sick Pop was. Between them they thought the doctor should treat Pop for yellow jaundice.

"*Nee*," Pop said. "It's the death look." He knowed what was ahead for him. Not me. I couldn't conceive of Pop dying on us, not when I loved him so much. We all needed him, sick or not. More'n that we wanted him to stay with us, sick or not. I didn't wanna live without my pop.

CHAPTER 29 - 1904

It was going on my twelfth birthday.

Myrtle Konhaus, Al and Annmarie's daughter, was at our house. She liked to be with her Uncle Ben and us kids and Mom. She just loved every minute at the farm. See, her mom was embarrassed about Myrtle being so big and heavy, the same way Annmarie's mother, the Old Lady was. She tried everything to get her girl to lose weight. She shamed and mortified Myrtle in front of people and sighed that she was at her wits end, didn't know how to get her daughter to shed them extra pounds. Nothing worked. It only made hard feelings between them two. Fact of the matter was, Myrtle had the build of the Old Lady and her Uncle Ben. It was her nature to be big-bodied. That plus she liked to gobble down everything in sight.

People's weight didn't bother us none. Lots of folks round-about was big and hefty. Nothing was ever said to Myrtle at the farm about how oversized she was so it was no surprise she appeared so happy and content when she was with us. She spent as much time as she could where she was loved just the way she was, and never made fun of.

The only problem was that coming here was a lost cause for Myrtle losing weight. Mom was the best cook around and had plenty of fattening things on hand that Myrtle couldn't resist. Mom and Pop didn't fuss at her cause they was getting bigger all the time, too. Me, I ate good but I stayed on the skinny side. All my life.

Every evening I had to see that the wood box was filled and chips was in the basket to start the fire next morning. Every evening after supper Mom pointed to me, then nodded at the wood box and to the door. It was time for me to get the wood in.

It was a cold, winter night. I slipped on my raggedy old coat, the one for chores, and started out to the woodpile that was stacked off the side porch. Myrtle said, "Alvernie, you go out and get started. I'll be out in a minute."

When she finally come out she sang over and over, "I got a secret, I got a secret." It was beginning to bother me some but I tried not to show it. I didn't like it when she - or anybody else for that matter - acted so snooty. Pop always said, "Have your fun but at nobody else's expense." I felt slighted. Was Pop and Myrtle having fun at my expense? I sure didn't like the idea that Pop might be keeping a secret from me but I was too proud to ask Myrtle or Pop what the secret was.

It appeared she read my thoughts for she went on, "I'll tell you sometime but not now." I had the basket filled up with chips, Myrtle loaded me up with as much wood as I could carry, then picked some up herself. The wood box was filled and I didn't worry none about this 'secret' business.

It was my twelfth birthday. I wondered so if anybody remembered. Myrtle was down again. Mom had pointed to me and the door. I knowed what she meant so I grabbed my coat and gloves and started outside to gather the chips and the wood.

Pop was just sitting there taking everything in. He gasped for breath then said, "*Kumme* here my right-hand-man." He always called me that since the time I stacked together his tools according to their kind. "*Kumme* here before *du* go out. *Ich* wanna show *du* somethin'."

Of course I went to him right away knowing it'd bother Mom that I didn't listen to her first off. I'd probably get a good smack later on for something she'd fault me with instead of the real reason that I listened to Pop instead of her. She'd be sneaky, not let onto Pop. But he knowed.

"Today *du* are got twelve years *alt*," he smiled as he gulped air.

"Yeah."

"Myrtle fetched something for me to give to *du.*"

Pop's hands was laying on his lap, swollen and blue. He turned his huge right hand palm up and opened his fist. There sat a little, blue, velvet box. Only ever seen others like it in store windows. He looked at me, nodded his head as if I was to take it. I looked at him hardly believing, looked at the box, then back at him.

Pop remembered my birthday. Oh, joy! I shoulda knowed he would. He looked deep in my eyes and I into his. I seen the same love that was shining through that first day we met in this very same farmhouse kitchen. "Take it," he wheezed. He used up all his energy to get them words out. It tore at my heart so bad I wanted to cry, but I held the tears back. I looked at him, pulled the old, dirty gloves off my hands and shoved 'em in my coat pocket. Then I slowly lifted the box outta his curled fingers that lay purply blue and still on his lap. He was so tired these days. Didn't have energy enough to lift his hand up and give the box to me.

My hands shook as I opened it. How nervous, how thrilled, how overjoyed I was that my pop, sick as he was, thought to get me a birthday present.

"Oh-h-h-h-h!" I gasped as I looked at the most beautiful finger ring I ever seen. It was a silver band with tiny purple stones that sparkled between shimmery white pearls. All around the band they went.

Oh, did he know he bought me the best present in the whole wide world? The stones and the colors, why they reminded me my doll baby's white and purple dress. Did he remember that. Or not? Was it only coincidence?

When I could get out the words I asked, "Is it really mine? Can I keep it?"

"Try it on," Pop said.

It was such a lovely ring, too big for my ring finger but it went on my middle finger.

"Are *du* want it now or *vait* till Christmas? Today is your twelfth birthday, but with me in *bedde, du* children won't have much of a Christmas."

"It's so purty! If I can have it now I'll keep it on my finger."

"*Ach vell*, all right, but promise that *du* won't take it off *un* give it to no one else."

"I won't," I promised him. And I promised myself that no one was ever gonna take this ring from me. No one, not even Mom. Not never.

"Thank you, Pop." I choked up, couldn't say no more. It was enough. Pop seen how much it meant to me.

Mom got huffy, stomped her foot. It was time to head out to the wood box. She didn't ask to see the ring but I walked over to where she sat. I wanted her to see it but she just shook her head in aggravation and nodded towards the door. She wouldn't look at my hand. Quick as could be I pulled on my gloves so the ring wouldn't get scratched. Myrtle went out this time to help me and asked, "Do you like it Alverna?"

"Oh yes. I like it. It's the best present Pop ever got me!"

Myrtle went on. "I was so *ferdutzed* about it. See, this was the secret I was singing about the last time I was here. Uncle Ben gave me money and said I should buy you a ring for your twelfth birthday." I said back to him, "For goodness sakes, Uncle Ben, how should I get a ring for Alverna with such skinny, little fingers like she's got when mine are big and fat?"

"*Ach vell* now, *chust* try," he begged.

"I was so excited when I helped you get the wood in that evening. I wanted to tell you so bad but I promised Uncle Ben I wouldn't. But, oh, Alverna, it was so hard. That's why I didn't come back till today. I was so scared I'd blurt out the secret and spoil your surprise."

"Did he tell you what colors to get?" I asked.

268

"No, he just gave me so much money and said to get the best it'd buy. In it are six - the jeweler called them amethysts. I have it wrote down for you - and six seed pearls. Twelve in all for how old you are.

So then. Twelve for each year I lived. Myrtle was so thoughtful. I thanked her, gave her a big hug. My goodness! She was a big girl. And warm. Even through her lightweight jacket.

And Pop, why, he gave Myrtle more money than he shoulda for my birthday present. I couldn't stop smiling. My heart was ready to burst with all this joy and happiness. Every day, one way or the other, Pop was letting me know how much he loved me.

That night in bed, why of course I couldn't sleep. I got to thinking how this was the *allerbescht* birthday present, the very best. See, Pop didn't know about the colors or how much they meant to me. Neither did Myrtle. That's what made the ring even more special. Why I figured maybe even the Good Man in heaven loved me and poured down a special blessing on my twelfth birthday. Yes, the more I thought about it, the more I was sure. The Good Man remembered the colors of my dolly's dress and pointed Myrtle to this ring. He never forgot my sorrow in losing my precious doll baby. I thanked the Good Man I believed in from when I was the littlest bit of a girl. Yes, I thanked Him from the bottom of my heart.

CHAPTER - 30 - BLACK SUNDAY

It was the Sunday after my birthday. Mom was busy making dinner. Pop was sitting on the rocking chair when the doctor walked in. I don't remember what Mom had on the stove but the doctor said, "Gee, something smells good in here." He was right. It always smelled good in the house from Mom's cooking.

I was setting the table, putting the plates and things around. The doctor went to Pop, looked him over and come back to Mom without looking at me or my brothers. He was steering clear of us. Kids ain't supposed to notice things like sickness and the like, but we noticed; couldn't help it. 'Twas right there in front of us, especially these last months. Albert, even little Dale Stuart, such a happy baby, had a worried look. Sickness, worry and fear was in the air. You could feel it. If anybody shoulda realized that kids ain't so dumb to not notice what goes on around 'em at times like this, it shoulda been the doctor. That's why he wouldn't look our way. He didn't wanna let on to us how bad Pop was.

"How's he doin'?" Mom wanted to know.

"He's all right, he's good," the doctor told her.

Hearing that gave me a little bit of hope, yet his voice didn't sound altogether sincere. I wanted so bad to believe him cause I wanted my pop to get better like he was before. Yes well, the mind can play tricks and mine did, but not quite. The truth about Pop was staring me right in the face every time I glanced his way. And what the doctor said made even me, who just turned twelve, wonder so. If Pop was all right, if he was good, why was he so tired and weak and sick all the time?

"*Du* are welcome to stay for dinner. It'll be ready in *ebaut* ten minutes," Mom said.

"No, I gotta go. I've got other calls to make."

After the doctor walked outta the house, Pop struggled from his rocking chair. It took all he had to pull hisself up. I wanted to run and help him, but big as he was he woulda knocked me over as he staggered and swayed back and forth. My heart ached as he tottered from the kitchen to the parlor and plunked down his bed. Mom said over it, "*Ach* now Ben! Can't *du chust vait* a little bit? *Kumme* over *un* sit right down at the table."

"*Ich* don't believe *Ich* want anything to *esse*."

The doctor headed back towards town. At the reservoir he run into Lenny Deller heading to Mass. This time Lenny was alone, purty unusual except that Rosemary had a new baby and wasn't able to get outta the house just yet. The Good Lord musta been watching out for us that day cause Lenny often had at least half of his brood tagging along with him. Lenny was a faithful Catholic and a good neighbor.

When Lenny asked about Pop, the doctor said, "You turn right around and go down there. He might be dead before you get there. She's gonna need your help."

When Lenny come to our door we had just put food on Albert and Dale Stuart's plates. He come in and right away asked how Pop is. When he told Mom what the doctor said she jumped up and run to where Pop was. So did I, Lenny right behind.

Pop looked at Mom, shut his eyes and that was the last.

I couldn't take it all in right then. Shock I guess. And to top it off, we seen how the doctor lied to us. Mom, oh, she was so put out. "If that doctor'd *kumme* in right now *Ich* wouldn't like to think what to him *Ich* might do," she said so bitter. "*Un* to *chust* think *Ich* invited him to sit down *un* have dinner with us."

For the rest of her life Mom struggled to forgive the two-faced doctor who lied to her face like that. I'm not sure she ever did. Only she knows for sure.

It was Pop's heart but he had water all through. That's why he couldn't lay down or the water'd go over his heart; called Bright's Disease back then.

Lenny helped us out so much. Right away he went after the doctor, the one who went hunting with Pop, to pronounce him dead. Mom said the double-dealing doctor'd never step inside her house ever again. From there Lenny stopped off at the funeral parlor to tell H.A. Both he and Adam come to the house. Oh! When I seen them come in it hit me full force that Pop was gone. I didn't wanna upset Mom or Albert or Dale Stuart but I started to cry. Just couldn't help myself.

By mid-afternoon, Grammy and Pap showed up with Purd to be there and help out. The truth that Pop was dead hit me again when I seen them three. I cried so bad. Grammy hugged me, then got busy. Purd and Pap went outside to do some chores.

I sat down in Pop's chair and went numb. I seen what was going on but I couldn't take it in, couldn't hardly breathe. It was like I had the breath knocked outta me. My feelings and my mind was cloudy like in an early morning fog when you know something's out there but you can't see it. My pop, he just couldn't be dead.

But he was.

Hope was gone.

Again.

H.A. and Adam, they knowed what a big man Pop was. They held him - Mom too - in high regard and wanted to do right by our family. They figured they'd both be needed to move Pop around and work on him. I heard 'em wonder so to each other that maybe they shoulda had Walter and David drive out too. Pap was there. And Purd. If they needed extra help to move Pop they'd use them two.

Kathryn Briggs, H.A.'s wonderful good wife always bought chickens, milk, eggs and butter, even garden produce from Pop when Mom had extra. When Pop went into town he made a point of stopping at the Briggs' big house just in case Kathryn wanted something. She bought him out most of the time. She and Grammy was so much alike - always had something on the stove to feed a big family plus visitors who was always stopping by. She trusted Mom and Pop, claimed they always sold only their best and that's what she wanted, the best. She was willing to pay even though everyone knowed money didn't come easy to her. H.A. was a bit miserly with her like he was with his boys. Bighearted with other folks, tightfisted with his own. Once in a while he handed over some extra change that she stuck away for when Pop showed up. Better yet, if H.A. was around when Pop was at their place - now Pop, he knowed how H.A. kept his money outta sight where his family was concerned - he'd step H.A.'s way and reach out his hand for him to pay the bill. My unflappable Pop made it appear it was only natural for the man of the house to hand over money. H.A.'d pull his change purse outta his back pocket that was overstuffed with bills and pay up. Made Pop and Kathryn both happy. It was a joke between them two but they never let on to anyone else. They wasn't sure how H.A. felt about it, but they had a purty good idea.

A good cook Kathryn was, one of the best around. The only complaint other ladies had about Kathryn Briggs was she never shared her recipes. Grammy understood this even though she never held hers back when asked. The way recipes was told was, *a pinch of this, a handful of that, or add just enough to make it moist but not too wet.* Grammy said about all Kathryn had she could call her own since she was so swallowed up being H.A.'s wife was her secret recipes. She wasn't about to pass 'em on and then end up being nothing or having nothing to call her own.

It's peculiar, but over the years I come to see that there might be only one thing in some people's lives that speaks for who they are, that sets them apart from other folks, and how hard they grapple to keep that little piece of themselves from getting taken away.

Yeah, I can see to this day how Kathryn understood her son Edward. She didn't fight the same way he did to be his own person, but she was fighting for the same purpose, to keep a part of herself that was her and nobody else. Isn't it strange that recipes could do that? But it worked for Kathryn Briggs. Recipes that was only hers, nobody else's. There was a lot more to Kathryn Briggs than she ever realized. There was so much good was in her. But she couldn't see it in herself. She was too busy tending after the needs of others.

Grammy admired Kathryn Briggs for her gumption in refusing to share her recipes. Wasn't easy. Sure made some ladies around town fuss something terrible.

Grammy and Pap hadda go back to Cedar Grove. They bundled up Dale Stuart and took him along. H.A rode along with 'em since Adam stayed into the night working. H.A worried maybe he didn't have a coffin big enough for Pop, but when he got back and checked, he found one. Figured he better have David right away hammer a couple more extra large ones. But first things first. David'd help deliver the coffin to the farm in the morning, then H.A., Adam and David'd get Ben Geesey into the coffin. H.A. wasn't even sure the three of 'em would be enough. Yes well, he'd worry about that when the time come.

After supper which none of us ate much of - we didn't have no appetite - Mom pointed to me and the door. I was to fill the wood box like I always done and get the chips in. I couldn't concentrate but I done my level best to help Mom out. Her cold silence laid over the whole house sorta like a black thundercloud that was about to break open any minute. She was still stinging with resentment towards the doctor while she was trying to keep things together for us. Hadda take her feelings out on somebody. I was hoping she'd not turn on me.

I was scared. I tried not to show it cause Albert was scared too. Cowered in his chair clinging to his baby blanket and sucking his thumb. Much too old for that he was but I wasn't gonna take what little comfort Albert had away from him. I was hoping Mom wouldn't notice. Albert and me, we was both wondering so what in the world would we do without Pop now that he wasn't no longer here to smooth things over.

I went to the corner of the house where the wood was, walking past the black crape that Grammy hung out front. It was fluttering in the cold, night wind. My-oh-my, Pop was dead in the room right in front of where I was standing. The window blind was down but hung crooked and made a narrow crack to see in. The wood coffin was there. H.A. had changed his mind and had David deliver it later that afternoon. A plain one. The lid was propped open. Earlier H.A and Adam had drug in their equipment, closed the door between the kitchen and front parlor and worked on Pop right there. Adam Briggs was in there right now. Them times the undertaker usually come to the house and done everything cause the funeral was held at the home. There he was. I could see him through the crack even though it was just a little one. I didn't wanna look but couldn't help myself. The truth of Pop's death hit me again. I froze to the spot. Couldn't move, couldn't get my legs working. There I stood. Finally I broke loose and scurried back into the house, crying with a broken heart over my pop. I knowed Mom'd be mad when I didn't bring no wood along back in but I couldn't help it.

What saved me was, this woman heard about Pop - news traveled fast - and had come with her girl to see if she could help out. Her and her husband was parted. They had three children. The two boys was with their daddy and she kept Molly. Them two lived in one room at Sadie Burkholder's boarding house. Cramped and crowded they was and she was only too glad to get outta there for a little bit and help Mom. Over that She said, "Molly will help you get the wood in."

And Molly did.

We walked across the porch. Molly took my hand as I shook and shivered. She took the basket from me, sat it down next to the woodpile. Before she started putting in the woodchips she turned to me and said so sorrowful-like, "My daddy ain't dead, but him and my brothers I don't get no more to see, so it's like they're dead and gone. I miss 'em and I know you miss your daddy."

I was a little bit comforted by Molly's reaching out to me. I woulda felt sorrier for her, but I was so wrapped up in my own hurt that I couldn't feel much for no one else right then. But it got through to me that Molly understood and cared, at least a little.

I closed my eyes and held my arms out. I said to Molly, "Pile them full so we don't need to come out here no more."

That's the way we filled the wood box then.

That night in bed the tears started and I cried so bad the bed shook. Then I scolded myself. I hadda be careful and not upset Albert. We slept together in the same bed. Albert was still sickly - always would be - and I didn't wanna make things worse for Mom.

Mom was gonna have the funeral in the front parlor but the preacher convinced her to have it at the church instead, even though Pop wasn't much of a church-going man. Besides, the bed and most of Pop's stuff was still in there. H.A. told Mom that she'd never have enough space at the farmhouse to hold all the people who'd come to the funeral.

On the day of the funeral Mom and me went with the undertaker to the church in his fancy carriage. Any other time I woulda sat up and noticed every little detail, asked questions till Mom woulda got all put out. Not this day. Nothing sunk in. Round and round in my head went, "Pop is dead, what'll we do? Pop is dead, what'll we do?" Over and over it went in my head; wouldn't stop. I wondered for the life of me how other people was going on as if nothing happened while my whole world crashed down on me till there was only pain and sorrow like I never felt before.

As soon as we got close to the church, the bell commenced to toll. It scared me so bad. I jumped and started shaking all over. Didn't bother the horses none. I guess they was used to it. Adam, the kindly undertaker, seen my distress, put his arm around my shoulder and told me that's what they do; as soon as they see the hearse they begin to toll the bell. Now I understood but I didn't stop shaking altogether.

H.A. Briggs was waiting for us. He took Mom and me up to the coffin. Pop, he didn't look so bad, looked more alive than he appeared in a long time. His cheeks was rosy again. Mr. Briggs took us to the front pew that had a fancy rope tied around it so no one else would sit there till we showed up. Tillie and Mary Godfrey was sitting with Myrtle Konhaus. All three was weeping their hearts out. They loved their Uncle Ben so much; only not as much as I loved him. There we sat, all the relatives together. We filled up one whole side of the church. The other side was filled with friends and neighbors. Albert and Dale Stuart wasn't along. We shoulda brought Albert along but I didn't dare suggest it to Mom. She wouldn't pay me no mind except to accuse me of thinking I knowed more'n she did, then swat me good. But, oh, I remembered about the Old Lady, how they kept it all from me; then when I found out, how it hurt so bad. Yes well, sometime I'd get Albert away from Mom and tell him just like Pop told me. And then I'd let Albert cry all he wanted to.

Then again, maybe Albert wouldn't listen to me, maybe he'd run and tell Mom what I said. Then I'd be in trouble all over again.

As cold and snowy as it was, the church was full. People from all over who thought so much of my pop was there to pay their respects. Even the mayor of York. He was one of the pallbearers. So was Frank Weaver, the general store owner. Allen Konhaus, Lance Mellinger, Bill Heindel, a couple school board members and Mr. Hostetter, the bank director - I was hoping he wouldn't have to blow his nose - eight in all with Pop being so heavy. Lenny Deller shoulda been but wasn't. Being Catholic he couldn't come to our church. That hurt him so bad. But he was a faithful Catholic, true to the teachings of his church.

Didn't hear a word the preacher said. Afterwards we filed out to the graveyard. Can you believe it, there was Lenny Deller standing way off to one side in a clump of bare trees so's not to be noticed. But I seen him. His bare head was bowed, his hat held against his chest with both hands. Looked like he was trying to hold hisself together, trying to not fall apart. I couldn't understand why his church was opposed to him coming, but now I knowed how much Lenny Deller thought of my pop.

"Thank you Mr. Lenny Deller," I said under my breath.

All I could think of was about what Pop said to me about the ring that I had on. I kept touching it to make sure it was there on my middle finger. Oh, my wonderful Pop! My wonderful good, *allerbescht* Pop, the man that started me on the right course for my life. Now he up and died.

After the service Ruby and Coral Heindel, Opal too, even Pearl was at the church and fixed food for folks to have something to eat before going home. Some traveled a purty good distance. This was always expected, always done. So many people there was. I helped wait on people. That kept my mind as well as my hands and feet busy for awhile. Only every now and then I'd wonder so how people could laugh and talk like they was so soon after the funeral. Me, I thought I'd never laugh again.

In the days afterwards I longed for my pop. I'd of gave anything to see his face and hear his jolly laugh that brought so much happiness to my life. Mom was indifferent to us kids except where we couldn't do without her. I didn't need no tending to like Dale Stuart and Albert. I done as much for them as I could. Most the time I felt deserted and alone.

Life was empty. Food made me sick in my stomach. I hardly ate. I was clumsy with my chores, but I got 'em done. Mom didn't have no patience. One day I stumbled and bumped her. She hit after me and hollered so that it scared Albert and Dale Stuart too. "Let me alone now yet! *Ich* have enough troubles without *du* gettin' in the way!"

That was easier for me to take than her being so shut up inside.

Wasn't long I got mad. It welled up inside of me, first of all at the doctor, but inside I knowed it wasn't his fault. Pop waited too long to get the help he needed.

I was gonna blame myself but I knowed I had no real power over Pop's health. He had been so strong and vigorous for his size, worked so hard, yet he got bigger and bigger, then growed weaker and weaker. Me, I worked hard, ate good and stayed little but strong.

Then I questioned what Pop shoulda done but didn't. Why didn't he take better care and see the doctor first off? Couldn't he grasp how he was hurting his family? It crossed my mind that maybe he didn't love us enough to take care of hisself, but deep down I knowed that that way of thinking was way off base. He loved all of us, he really did, so there hadda be other reasons.

Next I got mad at the Good Man in heaven. Time and again I wondered so how a loving God would cause so much suffering and pain. Our lives was ruined. If He was so good and powerful He coulda made Pop better. Why didn't He? Was we bad? Did we do wrong that God punished us so?

For all the pondering, the only thing I could figure out was that Pop seen when he powwowed what sickness could do to a body. He knowed his time was up and accepted it.

Thinking wore me out, but I hadda think it through. Pop was always there to help me before. Now I'd have to do it on my own.

I was still hurting and wanted to talk about my Pop. "Yes well," people'd say after they tired of listening to me go on and on. "You'll get over it. It happens to everybody."

It was like my pop wasn't even worth grieving over.

People get impatient when they're scared, and people are scared of dying. They prefer that people pretend they're ok. I shut up.

The only time I was happy was in my dreams. When I woke up it was like Pop was right there in the night talking to me. It made me feel so good. Them and the memories helped keep me going.

I guess the main reason I didn't go under was because of the way Pop helped me understand things, but most of all was the ways he showed me love. Pop's love was special and different. He made my life so much better than it woulda been without him. His love kept me on the right course.

I kept the ring on my finger that Pop gave me on my birthday. I thanked the Good Man for that. If I'd of said I'd wait till Christmas, maybe I never woulda got it. Nobody was gonna take that ring from me, not even Mom. She took my dolly, but she'd never get my ring, I'd see to that.

And she didn't.

There was Christmas and New Year with no school, just lots more chores. I done what was expected without no joy or enthusiasm. One day outta the blue it hit me that maybe I was cheating Pop. Behaving poorly I was. Pop wouldn't want me acting so bad. I comprehended it was up to me to keep making Pop proud of me. I knowed I'd never be good enough to please Mom, but Pop set the standard and I was gonna keep to it. My hurt softened day by day and I began to find some good now and then. Even Albert and I growed closer. He was still Mom's pet, but if he relieved some of her hurt that way, well, it was all right with me.

In time I seen how Pop left much of himself in me. He wasn't perfect, but nearly so. He was a wonderful good man, the *allerbescht* daddy a girl could have. Oh, how I longed to have him back. But that wasn't to be. I learned after the Old Lady died that dying meant not coming back.

So it came - only very slow; weeks, then months. I stopped asking the Good Man in heaven, *"Why did you take my pop away?"* Instead I thanked Him for bringing Pop and me together and the years we had. I considered over and over Grammy's stories about the Holtzapples and the two boys of theirs that died.

Yet even saying it now at more'n ninety years old, believe you me, the ache in my heart is still there, never went away altogether. I carry it with me today yet.

But thankful I am for the man I call Pop.

And now you heard my story. And I wonder so. What'll my granddaughter-in-law do with it? This much I do know. She promised to make copies and I'll pass 'em on to my kids, the ones still living. Hmm, I wonder if they'll even bother to read it. Oh, but I hope they do. I want 'em to know about this man I called Pop, and I hope they pass it on to the little ones about him. His kind seem so few and far between today. So much wrong in the world. That's why it's important, you know, to hear about the ones we call *allerbescht*. Yes well, that is important.

The ones we follow should be them that set the standard high.

I often wonder so. Has my life ever meant anything to anybody like Pop's life meant to me? Too often I fell short of the mark Pop set. But coming to the end of my life, well, I done my best to write this story. Probably wouldn't of done it if my granddaughter-in-law didn't keep pushing me. There's a little bit of hope in my heart it'll be worth something.

When I hand over the book to her I think I'll ask her, "Do you have a story to write about somebody you know, somebody who set their standard high and set you on the right course? Or how about your own story? What about yourself?

You reading this - maybe someday somebody'll wanna write a story about you. Will it be worth reading?

That's what I ask you and that's what I'm gonna ask my granddaughter-in-law.

My story's done. Guess I can die now.

Except, you know, I got so many more stories locked up inside of me. Maybe, just maybe I'll write down more.

If I live long enough.

PART II

CHAPTER 31- 1983

Wouldn't you know it, here I am already sitting down to write more of my story. Let me tell you why. A couple things happened these past weeks that're forcing me into it. The first thing has to do with my neighbor, Ivy. Remember her? At the beginning of my story? Well, she ain't my neighbor no more. See, a couple of weeks ago she called and asked did I wanna go and get my hair done when she goes. She needed a permanent, was tired of lookin' frowsy. I said, "Sure, I need a haircut." Ivy called Eva, our hairdresser, to set up an appointment. Eva always took us Mondays which wasn't her busy day. Sometimes she even come in what she calls her *spiffy red sports car* - it ain't all that spiffy though at one time it mighta been - to pick us up and bring us back home when the weather's bad and she don't have no appointments before or after us. Not many people have a hairdresser like that let me tell you. She is wonderful good, *allerbescht*. Ivy and me appreciated all Eva done for us. She liked us too. We three was good friends.

Eva washed, cut, put my hair in curlers and sat me under the dryer in between times when she was giving Ivy her permanent. When we was all gussied up we sneaked some extra money in Eva's curler drawer. See, she just don't charge us as much as her other customers and that ain't fair. Well, she seen what we was up to, pulled the dollar bills out and shoved 'em back down in our pocketbooks. Happens every time. "Holy Moses, girls!" she'd go on. (Eighty and ninety year old *girls*!) "Can't you let somebody do somethin' for you without you layin' out more money than need be? Now get outta here and go buy yourselves some supper. I'd go with you except I got another appointment in fifteen minutes. My feet're killin' me so I'm gonna sit down and prop my legs up here at the sink till she gets here."

Yes well, that settled that.

Ivy wondered if we should go out for supper. I knowed she wasn't feeling too perky but it felt good to get outta the house after being cooped up for more'n a week except for Mr. Smith picking me up for church. Supper at our favorite restaurant sounded like a good idea to me. Besides, it was only a couple blocks from our houses and Ivy wouldn't have to drive outta her way to get there.

We stepped inside and looked for our favorite booth where we always sat, knowing what was gonna happen right off. The waitresses wasn't busy, too early for the supper crowd, it was. As soon as they seen us they started in right away. "Good night's shirt!" one of 'em hooted. "Look at them two lovely ladies comin' in here, will ya?" Another chimed in, "All dolled up! Too fancy for this place. Get ready for the crowd girls! Before you know it we'll have tables filled with men comin' in pantin' after these two beauties. Get lined up and ready to serve the incomin' horde."

This went on till Ivy, in her raspy, hoarse voice from smoking all them years, told 'em to shut up and bring us menus. That was Ivy for you. Made everyone laugh with her crankiness. No wonder we always ended up there. The tables was clean, the food was tasty and the waitresses was always good for a couple of laughs. I ordered my usual; liver and onions, the liver rare with some blood still running. When business was slow like today, my order sent all the waitresses into a gagging fit. Yes well, that's the way I like it; more tender and juicy that way. With mashed potatoes and cole slaw. Ivy always ordered fish fried good and brown, with French fries and applesauce. "Gotta order something healthy," she'd say about the applesauce. Never ate it though.

Before we left the restaurant, Ivy was rooting in her pocketbook for heartburn medicine. She dumped out five different kinds of pills, all the time complaining that none helped.

"Come back soon, girls," the cook called from behind the grill as we paid the bill. "I can't wait to fry up some rare liver again. No one else orders it, Alverna. You're the only one." Then *he* gagged.

With gales of laughter from everyone in the restaurant, we walked out the door and hurried to the car so the wind wouldn't mess up our hair.

Next morning a knock come at my door. It was Ivy's daughter. "Alverna," she gulped then started crying as soon as she seen me. "They took my mother to the hospital on the hill last night."

"What did you say?" I asked not believing. "Come in and wait a minute till I get my hearing aids so I can hear you right."

Not wanting to miss a thing she said, I grabbed 'em outta the box where I stick 'em every night, jammed one in my right ear, hadda take it out and start over. No wonder it wouldn't go in right; upside down in the wrong ear. Such a squealing it made. Gosh darn it! That hearing aid company, they put a little red streak on the right hearing aid and a little blue streak on the left hearing aid to tell which is which. Wouldn't you think they'd know better? Most folks who need hearing aids, it might be their eyes ain't all that good to see them little colored streaks. But would a big company that makes hearing aids for thousands of customers think of making the whole back of the right one red and the whole back of the left one blue? Oh no! Just little streaks they put on. They just ain't got no common sense! I oughta write 'em a letter and tell 'em so. Think I will.

Finally got 'em in and Ivy's daughter said over it that her mom was in the hospital. Why I was so shocked I couldn't at first take it in.

"Oh no! Why? What happened?" But deep down I had a suspicion.

"She called me at one o'clock last night, gasped in the phone she was short of breath. I come out right away, called the doctor you took her to see that one time. Well, he said since he only seen her once and didn't know enough about her, we should take her right to the emergency room at the hospital. The ambulance took her in. Didn't you hear the sirens and see the flashing lights last night?"

Now come on! I just can't believe I never heard all that commotion at one o'clock in the morning. I never go off to sleep when I first hit the bed. Just lay there awake all night till about five in the morning when it's time to get up. That's when I'm ready to doze off, just when it's time to get up and moving. Honest to Pete, I never sleep, lay awake all night. And to think my bedroom window faces her house. Of all things! I just can't believe it. It can't be that I was already asleep. Hmm! I musta been deep in prayer.

Ivy's daughter went on. "She's in the heart unit; can't have visitors except family, but I'll let you know how she's doing. I'm going in to see her now. I stopped by to pick up some of her things and come over to tell you."

That was Tuesday. After the evening news on the television I tugged the rocker over to the front window so I could watch Ivy's house in case her daughter come back. When I'd see her I'd run out and hear how Ivy was doing. Sat there Tuesday night till way past my bedtime and most of Wednesday. My neck got stiff cause I couldn't get a good view of my television from where I looked out at Ivy's house. Turned up the volume to make up for what I couldn't see. Kept my hearing aids in so as not to miss nothing. Thursday morning I did the same after I had my diabetes shot and my breakfast ate. When I seen Ivy's daughter pull up out front, she was hardly outta her car when I was already out the door.

She took my arm and steered me from the wet sidewalk from all the rain we'd been having, back into the house. When we stepped inside she hugged me and let it out.

"Mom's gone" she sobbed. "But, Alverna," she said all bleary-eyed, "all the family, even her sisters who was on bad terms with Mom and didn't talk to her for years got together there at the hospital." (I understood how her sisters felt cause Ivy was hard to get along with. She told me how she come from the most miserable family and I always thought, 'And yes, Ivy, you're right up there with 'em.' Most people wouldn't put up with her. Me, well I just overlooked her bad parts, enjoyed the good.)

She went on. "Then Mom cried. She was so happy they was all together after so long. Just like one happy family. Soon after they left, her heart gave out. Died on the spot."

Eva, our hairdresser, come for me the day of Ivy's funeral. She said so proud how the undertaker called her to go to the funeral parlor to fix Ivy's hair.

"You be sure to do that for me when I go," I made Eva promise.

"Ok. But Alverna, don't forget to tell your kids that's what you want. If they don't know to tell the undertaker, he'll get somebody strange in to fix your hair and I tell you right here and now, you just won't look right. Then everybody'll gripe how Alverna just don't look like herself laying there in that coffin."

"I'll write it down as soon as I get back home so there's no mistaking it."

Boy-oh-boy, did I feel relieved that Eva'd do that for me someday. Maybe not too far in the future since the doctor hinted that I didn't have long to live. But what does he know?

Ivy's hair looked so nice. And her suit. 'Twas light blue, my favorite color. Something else for me to think about. The coffin, music, flowers. Ivy's girl done her mom good at the last just like she always done.

The waitresses sent a basket of carnations dyed blue.

Eva and me, we both cried during her funeral. The undertaker handed us a box of paper hankies.

I miss Ivy so much. How much, no one knows! Seems like I hardly get nowhere anymore. Wouldn't mind a little bit of her dangerous driving in my life right about now.

When my granddaughter-in-law come around to read my story I was down in the dumps about Ivy something awful. She said we should get outta the house and go for something to eat. We went to the restaurant Ivy and I always ate at so I could fill in the waitresses about Ivy's heart attack and funeral since they wasn't able to get off work. They'd wanna know how Eva went to the funeral parlor to curl her hair (the undertaker already had it washed, so Eva said), and how nice Ivy looked in her best blue wool suit with pearl buttons and a satiny white blouse and what for jewelry she had on. They wondered so if her diamond rings was buried with her. When I said I wasn't sure about that, they all wiped their noses and got back to work. Only I wasn't done talking. When I ordered the liver and onions - the liver hadda be rare with a little blood running out - the waitresses didn't go into their gagging fit today. Too sad just yet. Finished off my order with mashed potatoes drowned in gravy, and cole slaw for my second vegetable, then I got to telling my granddaughter-in-law about Ivy and how much I miss her.

She listened while I went on and on. When I was all talked out she said, "Grandma, you must have a good heart."

Did you hear that? She called me **grandma** instead of grandmother-in-law. Oh, glory be! I knowed it! I knowed all this time that she loves me. Yes she does. This proves it. Oh, I feel better already.

"I think I'm pretty good all through," I told her. "I got a strong constitution. The Old Lady said I'd go far, and here I am yet today. And Beulah, she told the preacher he didn't have no idea what a strong constitution I had. I don't know who I take after. I know I don't take after my mom on that. And not the man who gave me birth. He died purty young. I've got a pair of kidneys I'd donate but with diabetes all through me, maybe they wouldn't be so good after all."

"I don't think they take organs from people over sixty or sixty-five."

"They don't? That I can then forget. Yes well, I think I'm purty darn solid all through. Headaches - knock on wood - I don't know what a headache is, haven't had more'n one all my life. And let me tell you right now," I said pounding the table with my fists, "I'm gonna stay in my own home as long as I got two feet and can walk. When I go down to the county home to visit and see how many canes and wheelchairs and people in bed, why should I moan and complain? Why I got life purty good. And I think prayer helps a whole lot. You bet. Prayer helps a whole lot."

It hit me then and I almost jumped outta my seat. "I forgot my pills this morning. The doctor said I must take 'em every morning. Yesterday I forgot. That was the first," I said. "Have Ivy too much on my mind."

"We'll go back first thing after we eat," my granddaughter-in-law assured me.

We unlocked the door and the first thing I done was grab my pill container, the one my boy fills for the whole week. Then I wondered so out loud, "What am I gonna do with the ones I forgot yesterday? If my boy sees 'em he'll fuss and tell me he's gonna put me in the county home since I forget to take my medicine. Well, so I forgot one day and what happened? I didn't drop over dead. Not yet, anyway. I'll just flush 'em down the toilet so he don't know. Don't you tell him now, you hear?"

"I promise I won't," she said, then asked, "What are your pills for?"

After I made sure they was flushed away, I walked from the bathroom and said, "Just to hold me together. At my age I'm not gonna get better. The doctor did take my arthritis medicine away and gave me this bottle of pills. Said I could take four a day if I needed 'em. I think that's what he said. You know how it is. They make the directions on the labels so darn hard to read; such little words. Sometimes I think they make the print so small you can't read it right and take the wrong dose and kick the bucket. No, I guess that ain't true cause then they wouldn't have nobody to sell their pills to. They can't make any money that way, can they? Anyway, I won't take 'em unless I must. But them in the pill container, yes, them I must take ."

Missing Ivy so much I had got to thinking about others gone to their reward. I'd laid Mom's old photograph album out on the table for me to look over. When my granddaughter-in-law come she seen it laying there. Would you believe that girl? She pulled up a chair, made me sit down next to her and tell about every person in there. I couldn't pass one by, she made me tell about each one. Why, it made me think of when I was little and didn't let the man I called pop - but was Ben at that time - pass by a door in the big barn without telling me what was behind it. I wanted to know what was behind each and every door. Made him laugh, it did.

There was me with the big hair ribbon that covered my bald spot where I cut my hair right off. We got a good laugh over that one. There was Mom's picture - she was the purtiest of all the family members - and Pop's soon after they was married; so strong and good-looking. Grammy and Pap Farley. Every picture she wanted to know who they was and all about 'em.

Finally she said to me, "Now, Grandmother-in-law!" She was trying to get me riled up again cause I call her granddaughter-in-law instead of just granddaughter like she wants me to; but her being no blood relation, well, I just can't call her that. We don't get mad though, just keep our wits about us and go along with each other laughing and joking. But with all the carrying-on, I still see a little bit of sadness in her eyes that I can't get past the blood part. She loves me that much.

She went on, "Grandmother-in-law, you can't stop now. You must write your stories about what happened after your pop died. I can't pass on your stories if I don't know them. Why these little ones'll never know about what happened to you after your pop died because we haven't heard the stories. You just now talked about someone named Beulah who said you have a strong constitution. Why I never heard about Beulah. You have a story inside I wanna hear about. You must write your stories down so we can keep you with us forever. We'll all know you better and love you even more and talk about you often." And then she wore me down more by quoting from somewhere in the Bible, *"Our families will continue; generations after generations. . . ."* After which she said, "Now, Grandmother-in-law, since this family's gonna continue for generations and generations you might as well tell the ones coming on all about you."

Well, putting it like that, I'd sure like to keep a part of me with 'em always. Can't do it by giving my organs away so I might as well give 'em my story. But not all of it. When I get done with this part it's over and done with. And I mean it. Anyway, I'll probably be dead by then since that's what the doctor thinks. He figures I don't got long to live. He don't know what a strong constitution I have. But this I do know. It's wearing out. I can feel it.

My kids keep telling me that my great-grandchildren won't remember me so why write? I gave it up till this one come along. She won't let up on me. And you know what? I'm glad. Even though the rest thinks she's butting in too much and oughta mind her own business, I'm gonna do it. Besides, if I quit doing this they'll just find something else to gripe about. But if they read my story, they're sure gonna be surprised at what they find out.

Guess I better get started since according to the doctor I don't got long to live. I'm just not too sure about him. Then it hits me and I scold myself. "Alverna, don't start coming down on other folks. Doc's only doing his job. Now you do yours and live the way Pop wanted you to. He always said, "Have your fun but at nobody else's expense. Remember, my right-hand-man, the *Goot Mann* sees deeper'n others do. He sees what's in your heart."

Can't say I have much pain these days. I don't dwell too much on what pain I do got. Writing takes my thoughts past my pain. And it makes the time go fast. When I get tired I watch my stories on television or play solitaire or work long division. Them things keep me occupied when my kids forget to come by. Keeping busy helps about Ivy too. But I'll never get over missing her and not having her around to take me places.

Yeah, I made up my mind, I'm gonna forge ahead and write some more.

CHAPTER 32 - LEAVING THE FARM

Life was too hard for Mom on the farm to keep after. Come spring she knowed in no uncertain terms we'd have to leave. At first she was thinking about maybe moving back in with Grammy and Pap Farley but there wasn't enough room. Uncle Will had married and set up housekeeping for the time being with Grammy and Pap since he was following in Pap's footsteps, working with him in his carpenter shop.

What happened was, the February after Pop died Will come by with some terrible bad news. Grammy was in pitiful shape. Will said he and Pap was in the shop when they heard this loud shriek, rushed outside to where it was coming from. Horror-struck they found Grammy laying on the cold ground outside the privy, its door swinging back and forth. Grammy, was a purty hefty person. Even though Will was burly and well-built and Pap was purty strong, they hadda half-drag, half-carry her into the house. They managed to prop her on the horsehair davenport in the front parlor. Purd run to get the doctor who come right away. Grammy, she was coming to her senses and moaned over and over that some man come from behind and hit her on her head when she stepped outta the privy. After the doctor checked her over he said what really happened was she had a stroke.

Soon after that Grammy lapsed into silence, couldn't talk. All that come out was babbling noises, then they soon stopped. Will's new wife, much as she liked Grammy, didn't wanna spend her whole life taking care of her mother-in-law, so Lilliemae, her man and young boy, Lester, moved in. The big bed was brought downstairs and the parlor now come to be Grammy's sick room. Pap took the wonderful good flower painting that Charlotte Hoff left Grammy in her will and hung it on the wall opposite where Grammy lay so she could see it whenever she looked up. We wasn't sure Grammy could see it; her eyes looked awful dim, getting covered over with black just like Pet's was. It didn't matter. I loved Pap all the more for doing that. It showed just how much he cared about Grammy.

I didn't get to visit and help out there too much since I was needed on the farm them months till we moved, but Grammy's sickness hit Mom and me awful hard; Pap and all the rest, too. And now with Pop gone, well, sorrow lay heavy on all our hearts. How I pitied Dale Stuart; he'd never get to know his grammy like I did. It was almost too much to bear.

People said to me, "Be strong for your momma and your brothers." Well, boy-oh-boy, I wanted to be but I wondered so how could I be strong for them when it seemed I didn't have no strength for myself? I felt like any minute a bolt of lightning was gonna hit me and I'd break apart into a million pieces. But it never happened. Day after day I made it from morning to night. Then one day I realized that I made it through all these sorrowful times and was now yet alive, strong enough to do my part to see us through. Life goes on in spite of pain and suffering, I discovered. Sure wished I wasn't handed so much right then, though.

With Lilliemae and her family at Grammy's, and Will and his new wife still there even though they was looking for a place of their own to live, it was just too crowded for Mom and us kids, so my uncles helped find a place for us to live.

There was this little row house in a nearby town. See, towns was springing up, one right after the other'n for some time now. Wherever there was a farm on a road that was purty well traveled, it sometimes - more by accident than anything - come to be a stopping place for weary merchants and travelers who didn't make it as far as they first thought, or loggers and farmers whose wagons broke down. More often than not the farmer's family was willing to put people up for a night or two, even provide meals. Of course the travelers mostly offered to pay for their lodging and food. After a time when it was happening more'n more, these folks seen they could take in some extra cash along with farming. If they was smart they put in goods to sell that boarders might have a need for. Before you knowed it, folks who lived nearby stopped off for provisions instead of traveling all the way into the city. What was once only a farmhouse now become a hotel/boarding house and dry goods store. Next thing it become a dropping off place for the mail. The farmer was turning a profit and didn't need to farm all his land, so he sold acreage that butted the road for houses to be built. Just like that a village was born around the farm that turned into a hotel, dry goods store and post office of sorts.

In this part of the county, one town ran right into another till there was a string of villages along the main pike. One wasn't much different from the rest except for their names. Cedar Grove was different, tucked all by itself about a mile off the road to York. Cedar Grove was where we woulda liked to move, close to Grammy and Pap and the rest, but wasn't any houses to rent right then. Mom hadda take what she could get.

Besides our clothes and personal things and the stuff we needed for housekeeping, Mom packed one trunk she wanted to keep of Pop's, things she didn't need, just wanted; a leather harness, a couple tools, his powwow book, some almanacs where he had wrote in the margins, his Bible, a set of his clothes, things like that. I wished she didn't lock his Bible away. Maybe reading from it woulda made us feel Pop closer at hand. She locked the trunk, wore the key on a chain around her neck that she tucked under her chemise. That meant she didn't intend for others to see what was inside. It was all she had left of Pop and she wanted it to herself.

It surprised me as I watched Mom sort and pack this trunk of Pop's stuff. It was hard to think of Mom having a sentimental bone in her body, but now, a better understanding of her was coming to light. I seen how she had hid the real feelings she had for Pop, her true feelings that she hardly never showed. Now that he was gone she missed him but it was too late for her to show him how much she cared. I took this knowledge and figured in my mind that if Mom had shut off her true feelings about Pop, then she sure must love me too. Mom, long ago, musta shut off her true feelings for me, just like she done with Pop. That settled it. No matter what Mom said to me, no matter how she scolded or swatted after me, Mom loved me. I accepted the gist of the matter right then and there, and no matter what happened between us I never wavered from it. A big burden fell from my heart when I come to understand Mom a little bit more and believed she really and truly loved me with all her heart even though she didn't let me know.

I was hurting to see how hard it went for Mom at the farm. After my grief let up a little, I stayed in the background, always near to help however I could. The day come she started selling stuff off. There was this man, he bought Pet. When he come for our horse that was like family, Mom was wary, didn't wanna sell her to him but she didn't have no other offers. Guess not too many people was interested in a blind mare. She took Pet around the neck and said, "Pet, *Ich* hope *du* get a *goot* home."

"She'll have a good home," the man said grudgingly as he handed Mom the cash, "but she'll plow too."

I didn't like the sound of his voice. It rang with an underhanded threat. It troubled both Mom and me. But what could we do?

"Please see she gets *goot* care," Mom begged. "Pet never plowed by herself, just when Ben harrowed *un* used her with Bully *un* Kate, the two mules," She sure was hoping the man paid attention to what she said.

It was a sad, sad day when we said goodbye to Pet.

School was something I always looked forward to, even as crowded as the classroom was the year we had to sit three on a bench not made for three. Opal Heindel sat with me and Susie. See, Opal was purty big. Portly she was. If she started squirming, us on the end got pushed off onto the floor, not intentional, but Opal couldn't sit still too long. Her plump body let out lots of heat and she couldn't manage being cooped up between two skinny classmates. Susie and I took turns sitting in the middle but it was awful miserable getting stuck in there. Sweaty, smelly. I put up with it because after all, Susie was my best friend. For her I'd allow myself in the middle to get stuck.

When we was yet on the farm, once in a while when Albert - a momma's boy - was more sickly than usual, Mom kept me home from school to help with him and Dale Stuart. I couldn't hardly keep up tending them two besides my chores and farm work. So much to do there was. I loved school and I cried when I had to miss. I tried not to cry; Mom didn't like it. But now that I think of it, maybe I wasn't crying all that much about school. See, I didn't have no trouble catching up with my lessons. Opal'd stop in on her way home and show me what we studied that day, then I'd go over it when supper was over and my chores was done. Didn't take me long at all to catch up with my classmates.

I think maybe what I was crying about was how much I missed Pop, only I wasn't allowed to cry about that, so I was using my tears about not getting to school as an excuse. That way I spilled out some of my grief without letting on. Mom accused me of being a sissy for crying over such a little matter like school. That was alright. At least I could cry. But not too long.

It was good of Opal to help me out that way except I think she done it for selfish reasons like staying at our house for as long as she could get away with it instead of going home to do her own chores. She liked Mom's cooking too, but Mom didn't put up with Opal hanging around too long. Sent her home purty quick, she did.

The Heindel bunch was at our house a lot. One time we was sitting around the big table and Ruby was saying how she had this dream. There was money all around her but every time she'd reach out to pick some up, it'd turn to dust.

Her mother told her that whenever she thinks about the dream she's to turn her apron inside out and wear it that way. That'd bring her riches.

Mom frowned when Pearl went on like that. Later she'd say, "That's all Pearl ever thinks about. Money, money, money!"

Pop didn't say nothing when Pearl blabbered so, but after the Heindel's left, he'd turn Mom's scow into a wide grin by rolling his eyes and raising his eyebrows till they was hidden in his hairline. Then he'd wiggle them bushy brows and say, "All that glitters ain't gold." Mom couldn't hold back then, try as she might. She'd throw her arms in the air and laugh out loud. That was contagious. I laughed too. Oh, how happy I was when we could laugh together.

Once Opal got sick, turned into croup it did. Now it was her turn to miss school. Too sick she was to even study her schoolwork. Pearl sent word down with Coral about Opal. Pop had Mom put some stuff together for Pearl to mix up and plaster on Opal's neck and chest to loosen the cough. He mixed some herbs and other stuff into a cheesecloth bag to hang around her neck. Pearl was to lay it on Opal's chest to loosen up her lungs. He sent me to fetch it to the Heindel farm along with school lessons that Opal missed. Although the snow was deep I was happy to be outside trudging through the field in the beautiful white snow that lay white much longer than it does today. As I walked I remembered a school book with a picture of a nurse. I started making-believe that I was that nurse in a gray uniform with a red cross sewn on my right sleeve, a crisp, starched, white nurse's cap pinned on my head. Over my nurse's outfit I wore a warm, red woolen cape that swung in the winter wind. Matching red woolen gloves warmed my hands that held my nurse's kit with medicine for Opal inside. I was Alverna the nurse, journeying forth in my long, gray woolen stockings that itched something terrible, and shiny gum boots. I was plowing through the snow to heal the sick.

Pearl seen me coming and wondered so why I was wearing such a broad grin. I didn't dare tell about my make-believe nurse. No, just said I liked being outdoors. She left me visit with Opal for just a couple minutes.

As I walked back to the farm I thought to myself, "Well, Opal hasn't changed any." See, she just couldn't believe that she was the one that hadda be sick and I was the one walking around. Laying there in bed and coughing all over me, she twisted and turned and moaned so bad you woulda thought she was gonna die except I knowed it was a big put-on. "It just ain't fair that I'm the one so sick I might die and you're the healthy one," she whimpered in self pity.

That was Opal for you. She never changed. Oh, I could tell you one story after the other as we growed up.

But not right now. Don't wanna die talking about Opal Heindel Miller.

We moved the summer after Pop died. Purty sure the year was 1905. Anyway, come the new school year I hadda go to a different school, one that was not long before built. It was bigger, had more'n one classroom, more pupils and teachers.

My teacher in the one room school I left told me - now it wasn't a graded school but I had all fifth grade books, all but the big geography book - she told me I better say to the new teacher that I'd been in third grade.

That's what I done. When asked what grade I'd been in I said, "Third grade."

That's where she put me. I liked my new school except the schoolwork was too easy. I'd learned all that stuff before.

It didn't take me long to make new friends. That I could do without no trouble - or so I thought. I knowed my new teacher too. Miss Viola went to church where we went. She was a good teacher, strict, yet fair.

One Friday it was near recess time.

"Alverna," Miss Viola said. "I want you to stay in at recess. I need to talk to you."

"All right."

Most kids woulda been scared about that but I knowed I didn't do nothing to get punished for.

I sat straight in my seat when the other kids went out on the schoolyard to play. Miss Viola went to the blackboard and put this great big arithmetic problem there that could be worked two ways. She didn't say I was to work it so I just sat, figuring it in my head. Soon Miss Emily, the fifth grade teacher showed up. Miss Viola had been waiting for her.

"What in the world's going on here?" I wondered to myself.

The classroom door was open. The kids come to the door and peeked in. "Alverna, why don't you come out?"

Miss Viola said, "Alverna's all right. I asked her to stay. She didn't do anything wrong that I made her stay in. Go play."

She told me to **try** to work the arithmetic problem. I went to the blackboard and they seen me work this problem two ways in no time.

When I was done - didn't take me long at all - Miss Viola wanted to know, "Whatever in the world made you say the third grade?"

"My teacher said I better say that."

"Well, she oughta have her head examined! Monday you will go into Miss Emily's fifth grade class."

That Monday when I walked into the classroom there was only one empty desk way in the back. There I sat. When it was time to give a definition and no one raised their hand to answer, Miss Emily would ask, "Alverna, what is your definition?" I'd give my definition. That made the kids who I thought was my friends wonder so what this new girl was up to getting moved up two grades so soon after school started.

They looked at me sorta strange and backed off from being so friendly. They wasn't so sure about me no more.

For one whole week there was snickering and spiteful looks wherever I was. I felt lonely and left out. Then it started full force. Anywhere I went on the playground I was teased and called names. The other kids said I was acting uppity because I was the only one called on who knowed **all** the answers.

I wasn't acting uppity and they knowed better. They was just downright jealous.

They didn't let me jump rope or play games with them. When before the girls walked home with me, now no one would. None of the kids wanted anything to do with me. It got so bad I'd go home bawling every day. If I'd go out on the front porch after school, kids come up and stuck out their tongues or made faces when they seen me. I took it for all them months. No use saying nothing to Mom or the teachers. They hadda see what was going on but I guess they didn't wanna butt in.

When school started in the fall I wasn't gonna take it no longer. I told Mom, "I ain't going back to school." She didn't scold. It didn't matter to her.

When I didn't show up the principal come knocking on the door. "Estella, you're making a great big mistake not sending that girl to school. Right now she could take the eighth grade examination and she wouldn't flunk a thing except Algebra, and that she never had. Why, someday she'd make an excellent teacher. She could go far."

Mom told 'em how I'd been teased and made fun of.

"I'm going to see about that!" he promised.

When he come back and said he talked to the teachers and my classmates, I knowed that was only gonna make things worse. In my despair I determined that I wasn't going back to all that meanness and teasing. If only there maybe woulda been just one girl there to take my hand like I did for Liza Peters with all her warts, or stand up for me like I stood up for the Hartmans who was Dunkards, maybe then

I'da stuck it out. But no. Not one classmate done that. Oh, how I missed Susie! And Rachel.

Mom didn't put up no fuss. I think she welcomed it. That way I could help get Albert off to school and then tend Dale Stuart.

During the summer and fall on days Mom didn't need me at home, I pulled my express wagon loaded down with vegetables from the garden to sell from one town to the next. Albert coulda went along to help out, but he was lazy and didn't wanna and Mom didn't push him to it. I'd pick wild strawberries, or raspberries, mulberries, cherries, apples, whatever I'd find was ripe. I loved being outdoors; made me think of the good times I had with Pop. Mom's jelly, baked goods, anything I'd come across to help her out I'd load in my wagon and pull it for miles if need be, stopping at one door after another, hoping somebody'd buy something. Some houses I passed without knocking cause they didn't look too friendly. Never stopped at that one house where curtains was always pulled across mud spattered windows and the front porch was caving in. Junk was all around. Heard tell an old witch lived there and nobody bothered him except them who wanted a curse put on somebody, or a spell removed. That was one place that scared me so much, why I'd cross to the other side of the street instead of going past that rickety old house that looked evil. I was afraid the witch'd come out and snip off some of my hair and put a dead spell on me. And if I didn't sell much one day I'd think maybe I didn't get by that house quick enough and the ugly, old witch put a bad-luck spell on me from his window.

One summer day after I'd gone purty far down the road, Rachel Deller seen me and asked if she could walk along.

"Sure," I said, glad for her company. I liked Rachel. When we moved, me and her was in different schools. It was good to see her again.

I wondered out loud sometimes about places to stop for people to buy things. As we went past the nuns' home I thought maybe I should stop - them ladies in there needed food. Why maybe I could empty my wagon in one stop. Rachel, she looked at me like I was off my rocker. Being Catholic, she told me no, that other people took things there for them to eat, they was too poor to buy.

I didn't know. As we walked past I prayed a little prayer that they'd have enough to eat. If I coulda, I woulda gave 'em my whole wagonload of produce. On second thought, I knowed that wouldn't go over with Mom. So we walked on.

A couple months after we moved, Lance Mellinger stopped by on his way to York.

"I wish you'd see Pet!" he fretted.

"Wass iss?" Mom asked.

"She's nothin' but skin and bones. That was one man that I hoped would never buy that horse, but he did and he's workin' her like crazy."

That sent Mom into a fit. Ended up with a headache that lasted three days.

I sure liked Susie's dad, but while I was pitching in for Mom who took to her bed, I wondered to myself that if he knowed that was gonna happen to Pet, why didn't he buy her? He coulda used Pet on his place and she woulda been treated good. Got a little suspicious of Lance Mellinger, wondering if he was all talk and no action. Later in the day I come to my senses and scolded myself for thinking such mean thoughts. Everybody's got their own load to carry.

I was purty vexed about Pet and the awful treatment she had to endure, but was too busy taking care of Mom and my brothers and the house; I just didn't have much time to fret with so much to do.

Mom kept us together by taking whatever work she could find. (See, John Miller somehow or other took over selling the farm. Mom sure lost out there, but she figured John Miller musta raked in a big bundle for hisself. She wouldn't put up a fuss or go to Al Konhaus about it, though.)

Life was purty hard, but helping out Mr. and Mrs. Wagner's a day or two every week gave her some extra money. Besides, it got Mom outta the house. That way us kids was outta her tight grip for at least part of the time.

Mom didn't take any of us with her except for the time the Wagners wanted to meet us. It was all right with me that I didn't never get back there again. Mrs. Wagner appeared so different from Charlotte Hoff when I had went there with Grammy. See, I didn't much like Mrs. Wagner that first and only time I met her. She was a frail, little lady - she couldn't help that, but the whole time we was there she was so down and out. She grumbled how she couldn't do nothing no more, needed help with cooking, washing and cleaning. "I'm no good for nothing. Might as well do myself in," she complained with a self-pitying whine, wringing her hands together as she went on and on.

Anyway, they said what they'd pay Mom if she'd help 'em out.

Mom said she would.

The days Mom was gone, I stoked up the stove and washed a bucket of Dale Stuart's diapers first thing every morning; got Albert dressed, gave him breakfast and sent him off to school with a lunch, not much. He never ate much. Next I hung the diapers out to dry, washed the other clothes and ironed 'em with the big, heavy sad irons; took care of the house, cooked, baked and cleaned, tended Dale Stuart all day long. That was the best part. Dale Stuart was such a happy baby. Didn't fuss much at all. I played with him and taught him what I learned from Pop and from school. Having to wash his diapers everyday I made up my mind for him to learn to use the chamber pot and the privy by the time he was two instead of taking after Albert who'd still been in

306

diapers at four. The place Dale Stuart learned best to not pee in his diaper was on the back porch where he aimed for the flowers. Didn't matter to me. All I cared about was not having to clean and wash all them diapers.

I was twelve years old, going on thirteen then.

Mr. and Mrs. Wagner, they both took a liking to Mom and the way she worked for them. Mom purty much enjoyed going there too. Mrs. Wagner always looked forward to the mid-morning cup of tea Mom made her. The older woman insisted Mom had one with her though she woulda rather had coffee. Mom thought Mrs. Wagner perked up after her tea, not so much down in the dumps. Maybe the way Mrs. Wagner was, that's why she never got much company. She was always thinking about herself and her problems.

Mrs. Wagner and Mom, they talked then and come to be good friends in spite of their age difference.

This went on through the winter. Mom was there two and a half days a week, sometimes three. One frosty, spring day when Mom went - she always knocked, then opened the door and called so Mrs. Wagner knowed it was Mom for sure. Mr. Wagner was gone, as usual. He was one of the old men that didn't no longer work; hung out with his cronies at the general store indulging in a cigar from the factory of Al Konhaus or a cud of chew while playing card games or checkers or batting the breeze around the old pot-belly stove.

When Mom called, Mrs. Wagner always let out with a small, shrill, bird-like *hello*. But this time Mom didn't hear nothing. Being a bit wary she went inside, shut the side door and looked around for the old woman. She searched all around downstairs. No Mrs. Wagner. Opened the cellar door and called down, but she was sure Mrs. Wagner wasn't down there. She wasn't strong enough to climb down the dark, narrow, cellar steps with only a wobbly rail dank with mildew to hang on to. All that was left for Mom to do was climb the stairs to the second floor. She called as she climbed, nervous as all get-out, thinking how her Mom - years before - climbed a ladder and found Charlotte Hoff dead in her house.

No sound come from anywhere. Mom was uneasy, ready to jump outta her skin.

When she snuck a peek in the bedroom, it was almost too much to take in. Mom was dumbstruck, felt her knees give way! Couldn't believe her eyes at first - they almost popped outta her head, so she said. What a terrible sight! As her legs turned to water and she started to go down, she grabbed onto the doorsill to keep from falling.

Mom, flustered as she was, run right away to the bed post and cut Mrs. Wagner down, wondering how in the world this feeble, little old lady could do herself in like that. Here what happened, right after Mr. Wagner left the house, his wife musta clambered up on her bed, tied a long cotton stocking around the bed post, stuck her neck through the loop and stepped off the high bed. The loop tightened and that was that.

Mom seen she was too late to help Mrs. Wagner. She lay on the floor, dead as a door nail.

Letting her lay where she landed, Mom run outta that house all the way to the general store where she figured Mr. Wagner was and broke the news as best she could. Didn't say his wife was dead, only that something was wrong and for him to go home right away.

Mr. Wagner knowed; it only took one look at Mom for him to figure out something terrible happened. Besides, Mrs. Wagner threatened over and over she was gonna do herself in so he was purty sure what he'd find. But when he seen how she accomplished it, he too, was befuddled. Where in the world did his sickly, little wife find the strength to climb and stand up on the high bed, tie the stocking around the bed post and take her life?

The doctor told Mom how the stocking stretched when off the bed Mrs. Wagner stepped which made it take longer for the end to come. "If she wasn't so sickly you mighta yet found her alive." Doc said every time he sees tragedies like this it stupefies him to think how people use such peculiar ways with unbeknownst vigor to take their lives once they get determined.

Mom couldn't blame herself for not being there. She showed up on time that morning like she always done. But she felt bad just the same.

That took its toll on Mom. Another headache put her in bed till the funeral. Things just wasn't going good for her at all.

We lived in a four row house. The privies at the end of the yard sat back to back.

Evie Myers, the next door neighbor, she come with her two boys one Saturday morning. She walked with Mom to catch the train to York to do some shopping. They did this together every month or so. I was sitting on the front porch tending Albert and Dale Stuart.

"Alverna, you take good care of my boys and I'll bring you something nice when I come home. You can stay out front, but don't let the boys run up and down the street. Sit on the steps or stay up on the porch."

I smiled as they walked off, wanting to take her at her word but knowed better. She went on like this every time, telling me the same thing. The **something nice** always turned into something much of nothing. Not that I minded. I didn't ask for nothing. A couple more boys to watch didn't mean anything to me. I'd of done it for nothing. It was just the way she went about saying it that made me hot under my collar. And to think she said not to let them run about but to make them sit still! Four boys sitting still; all day long! Ha! I laughed out loud when her and Mom was out of hearing range. Then I let it pass. I didn't hold grudges. Took too much energy I needed for other things. Well, not too many grudges.

Maryellen, a girl a little younger than me lived down the street and she come up to talk while I was watching the boys. Maryellen didn't have nothing to do with me when other girls was around. Some of the girls from school come to me one day when they seen me by myself and said I got 'em in trouble when I told on 'em; they heckled me and made fun.

They sure was brave being all together like that.

I didn't stand up for myself, knowed they wouldn't believe it was the principal that come to my house and not me who went and told on them. They said they made a pact; they wasn't never gonna play with me or talk to me again, stuck out their tongues and made faces at me then walked away. I went in the house and cried that day. Dale Stuart, he seen this and he cried too. I hadda stop before Mom heard and got mad at me.

This morning the coast was clear so Maryellen come up. She thought we should go out back where there was a yard for the kids to play. I went along with that even though I knowed she didn't wanna stay out front and get caught being seen with me. It'd be easier to keep outta sight in the back yard. I thought to myself how nice Maryellen was when we was by ourselves and how mean she was when other girls was around. Well, Pop taught me different and I wasn't gonna be mean just cause they was. I sure did crave a true friend though.

Anyway, while we was out back a young neighbor fella come out his back door that was next to ours and went up to the privy. When he went up, Maryellen said she hadda go to the privy too.

I scolded her. "You just wanna go up because Matt went up."

"No, I believe I must go - I believe I'm getting. . . ." Now how did she call it? I can't remember. It won't come to me right now.

"What do you mean?" I asked.

"Now, Alverna, don't tell me you don't know nothing about it cause you're older than what I am. You know what it is."

When she explained it to me, I got flustered and said, "Oh, Maryellen."

Then I told her how it had been with me when Albert and I was strippin' tobacco.

And I had never knowed. See, Mom never told me.

Maryellen made one beeline outta the back yard and down the street to blab to her mother.

Maryellen's mother waited till Sunday, then she come up. Did she give my mom the dickens.

That done it. Mom gave up. She figured she couldn't handle nothing no more and she gave up housekeeping.

CHAPTER 33 - SEPARATED

Mom started looking for a place to live. She read an ad in the newspaper that a Mr. Fred Fry had in. He was a farmer looking for somebody to help with his children. All they hadda do was cook, keep house and things like that. He had five kids besides a baby nine months old when his wife died. One boy worked away and come home on weekends, one boy was old enough to help work the farm, three was in school, then was the baby.

When Mom talked to him about her taking over that work, he said right off he didn't have room for all of us, him having six kids of his own.

The way it would go at hard times like this, family or friends stepped in and helped out. Lola, she always wanted Albert, begged Mom to let him live with her till Mom could get herself together and take him back. Her husband, John, grudgingly went along with taking Albert but he didn't want me. Said so right in front of me. Lola didn't want me either. Or so I thought. She liked me and all but she only wanted Albert.

Mom agreed to this.

I went to live with Aunt Jemima Brillhart, Pop's oldest sister, and her husband, Earl. It was arranged for me to live there and help 'em on a farm they worked. They didn't own it, just worked it. It was purty far from town but within walking distance if need be. When I first went there that's how I got places - by walking.

They had a grown son, Clyde, that lived and worked the farm with his pop. Then there was Tillie and Mary Godfrey who had lived there for a time but now was out on their own. Jemima needed help; I was picked to provide it.

The first week I was there, Aunt Jemima told me how when Clyde was born they coulda put him in a quart tin and put the lid on, he was that little. "I almost died when Clyde was born," she said. "Doc said I'd never live through another birth. Earl was upset about almost losin' me, didn't wanna go through that again and declared I'd never have another'n by him."

I relished the way Jemima told her stories. The way she spoke of Earl's love for her, why it was a real-life fairy tale with real-life characters, only these people had warts and all, not perfect like I'd see in story books.

Little as he was first off, Clyde growed up big and strong.

"We never had no more kids; managed the farm with Clyde's help and them like you that stay with us every now and then."

Mr. Fry grudgingly left Mom keep Dale Stuart with her since me and Albert had some place else to go.   M o m shoulda kept looking for a place to live, but no, she took the first one that come along. After moving in she seen how his farmhouse was big, woulda held all of us. I guess it coulda been worse. Maybe I was better off with Jemima and Earl than with Fred Fry.

Not wanting to take the trunk of Pop's things to Fred Fry's, Mom asked Jemima if she'd let the trunk be stored in her attic since I was gonna live there anyway. Jemima said yes and that's where it was put; way back in a corner in the attic. Mom kept the key with her.

Aunt Jemima was big and heavy, just like her mom who was the Old Lady I'd loved with all my heart. Uncle Earl was little, sorta scrawny, but them two got along better'n alot of folks. It did my heart good to see how they worked things out by talking them over with each other and Clyde. They was a real family. They did their durnedest to make me part of their family too. It was the best place for me to be since I couldn't be with Mom. Yet, oh, I missed her and Albert and Dale Stuart so much.

Jemima, she didn't get to church too often because of milking, but she encouraged me to go every Sunday. I took classes at the Reformed Church and joined there. I loved to go to church, as much for the singing as anything. I wasn't too particular about which church I went to. I'd of went to almost any church. That was an important part of life back then, partly cause there wasn't too much else to do around these parts, and most important, we was taught about God and Jesus. The Reformed Church I'd joined at that time didn't have no Sunday evening service, so us young people who belonged to different churches would often get together and visit them that had one. Of course, Rachel Deller never invited her friends to her Catholic church nor did she ever attend one of ours.

I had a purty good singing voice from little on up. I'm not bragging, that's what people told me. Sometimes a bunch of us girls got together and practiced singing hymns. I was in glory then. Singing and new friends helped me fill the aching loneliness from not living with Mom and my brothers. We sounded real good. Once in awhile we'd be asked to get up and sing a couple hymns during the evening service. We did. It soon come to be a regular occurrence for us girls to sing somewhere almost every Sunday evening.

When I moved in with Jemima and Earl, it wasn't that I went there expecting to be handed everything. The way it was, I was actually hired out. I was expected to do so much in exchange for room and board and maybe some pocket change if I was worth it.

Aunt Jemima was a wonderful person, much like her brother, my pop. The work on the farm was hard, yet small as I was in build, I learned how to get the work done and done right. Uncle Earl was pleased with me, said I done my share; even more'n my share. Them two made me feel good about myself. I was more happy than I thought I ever could be. Part of that was my own nature, part from Grammy, lots from Pop, and now Jemima and Earl.

Sometimes we wasn't so busy. With Grammy Farley being purty sick, Jemima and Earl would shoo me off to go and spend a day or two at Grammy's so I could help Aunt Lilliemae with all she had to do. She had kept her good humor and flair for acting-out in spite of the back-breaking work she done. I stepped right in and joined her carrying-on. Oh, the two of us, we had lots of good laughs to mingle with the sickness and sadness in that household. Pap worked long hours in his carpenter shop with Lilliemae there to take care of Grammy, but with Will working alongside of him, he come in at lunch to spoon-feed Grammy and linger awhile. What I would have given to see Pap eat peas with his knife just one more time. But, no, his spark for teasing was either gone or buried deep with Grammy being so sick.

Lester was a joy to all. He'd sit next to Grammy, her eyes wide open but unseeing, her mouth hanging down with drool running out. Didn't bother him at all. A rag was there for him to wipe her off if need be. Lester pointed to pictures in his story books thinking maybe she could see, reading and making up stories when he didn't know the words. He done the same at night with Pap. Lester, he had some of his mom's acting talent. Watching him made me think how me and Pop sat and read together so long ago.

As I watched, it made me so homesick for Pop and the farm and my family. Nevertheless, I was happy for the way Lester was with Grammy and Pap, glad for all Lilliemae and her man done in that sickroom and house.

One day I was hanging up the wash for Lilliemae and I seen this young girl walk by the house. She walked back and forth, kept looking in like she was searching for someone or something in particular. She looked familiar yet I couldn't place her. I was certain I'd never before seen her. I mentioned this to Lilliemae when I went back in. She tugged at my dress sleeve and pulled me outta hearing range of Grammy.

315

"That girl might be looking for you," Lilliemae said. "The reason she looks familiar is because you and her look alike. You look more like your real daddy every day. That's your half-sister, Lawrence and Miriam Holtzapple's girl, Sallie"

Nothing more was said about it, but it made me wonder so. That evening I was sitting on Grammy's front porch, tired as all get-out after a long day's work. I just got done with the supper dishes after helping Lilliemae give Grammy her bath. I was all sweaty, sitting there to catch what little breeze was blowing, my head back on the porch rocking chair with my eyes closed wondering how in the world Lilliemae could do all she was doing and still keep her good humor. I just about nodded off when I heard someone clear their throat. I opened my eyes to see a younger me staring me in the face.

"You're Alverna Holtzapple, ain't cha?" she asked soft and quiet with a shy, backward manner.

"Yes, but I don't know you."

"You should. I'm your sister."

By that time Lilliemae come out on the porch and said, "Sallie, does your mom know you're here?"

"No, and I'll get a lickin' if Momma finds out, but I don't care. Alverna and I belong together. We're sisters."

She kept her eyes glued on the dirt road in case her mom come outta the house looking for her. She stepped onto the porch, then waited to see if Lilliemae'd scold her. When she didn't, Sallie moved in and leaned against the house so she'd be hid from her mom's sight unless she come walking up the road looking for her.

"When you're here helpin' with your Grammy, I'm gonna sneak away and come see you," she promised.

She cried then. "Things could be a lot better if only we'd get to know each other more. You're the only sister I got."

Right then Miriam's loud, piercing shrill was heard as she yelled for her daughter. For a few seconds my thoughts went back to when I was eight years old and heard Miriam shout like that at Lawrence.

Sallie pulled up her skirt, wiped the tears from her eyes, leaned over and touched my arm so tender-like but quick, then ran off to her momma.

I thought of Sallie. Who was she like? Surely not her mom with that awful noisy, earsplitting voice. Sallie was quiet. She didn't fire back at her mom when she mighta. I seen her being brave and courageous in spite of her fear of getting caught, so she wasn't like her dad who run away like a coward that day so many years ago. No, Sallie was bold to come to where I was, knowing she'd get whipped if she was found out.

I liked Sallie. I pitied her for what she had to live through. I never seen Sallie again to talk to.

I was at Jemima and Earl's going on two years. One time at an evening service where us girls was to sing there was a youngish preacher preaching that night. On the one side of his head he had little white spots of hair mixed in among his thick, black hair. Just the one side mind you. It looked so strange. It made us giggle. The girls I was with made fun of him. Whatever got into me I don't know, but I went along with 'em and called him Spotty; not in front of him, of course.

How could I forget what Pop told me about having fun at other people's expense? He always said over and over again. "Have your fun but at nobody else's expense." Well, that night it was like the devil got a hold of me. I knowed I was doing wrong. My conscience flared up but I didn't stop.

Two weeks later we was invited back to sing again. That was the night my whole life changed again. This time for the better.

I told Aunt Jemima about it when I got back to the farm after the evening service, told her how I joined in with the other girls and made fun of Spotty. Then I went on. "When he preached - I never heard a preacher preach like that. He walked from one side of the church to the other, paced up and down the aisle as he spoke; filled with conviction he was. He said how there's two powerful forces at work in the world and in our hearts. He warned us about the devil, how he prowls around like a roaring lion to scare and confuse us, how he sets out to deceive every child of God. 'He'll catch you off guard if you let him; he'll pick away at you till you're fit for nothing but the lake of fire.' Oh, Aunt Jemima, why I could see the flames leaping up around me. It was scary as all get-out. My skin crawled with goose-bumps."

Jemima just sat and listened.

"Then he talked about how Jesus died for sinners and if we confess our sins he'll forgive us, blot 'em out forever. He told us to obey God and to stand firm against the devil. He made everything so plain, plainer than I ever heard before. Aunt Jemima, he presented the same ideas my pop and Grammy and Pap used to talk about, only this time it was so wonderful clear what he said."

I went on. "He invited everyone to come to the mourner's bench, to confess our sins and repent and be born again. Some folks went up but I didn't even though I was pricked in my heart for the awful way I made fun. After we left the church, here the other girls felt the same way. We talked about it. Susie said we should take hands and do what the preacher told us to do; confess our sins - like making fun of the preacher - and promise to change and obey. It wasn't maybe proper the way we prayed but we went around and each one promised Jesus from now on we'd serve Him instead of the devil. As we stood there outside the church holding hands, a wonderful good feeling washed over me. My goodness! I never felt like that before. When I opened my eyes and seen the way Susie and Lydia looked, well, it was the same with them too. Before we could change our minds we all hurried back into the church to tell the preacher how we was so ashamed of making fun of him. We was sorry and promised never do it again. Would he forgive us?

Why he didn't even get mad or scold us. Instead, mind you, he told us how happy he was for us, said tonight we was born again. But he admonished us to read the Bible every day so we could grow and keep strong in the Lord; and to come to him if we had any questions or needed help. We told him we would."

That's what I told Jemima. Oh, it was so good to tell someone who listened. I said that my best friend Susie said in front of us and the preacher how all her life, from little on up, deep inside she wanted to be a missionary when she growed up; never could understand where them longings come from cause she didn't even know a real live missionary, only read about 'em or heard about 'em at church. Now she said that was what she was gonna aim for cause she knowed it was Jesus who put them thoughts in her heart all that time. Susie said she never told no one about that before and wasn't sure what her momma and daddy'd think about it. But no matter what anyone said, her mind was made up and she was gonna carry it through.

Aunt Jemima was overjoyed at what we done. She gave me a big hug. Oh, my! Do you know how long it was that a hug I got? My heart felt like it was gonna burst with joy.

I wondered so what Mom would say when I'd write and tell her. See, we wrote letters every week. She one week, me the next.

After I was done telling Aunt Jemima about our experience, she and I went to bed. Uncle Earl had went earlier.

Sometime that night - I was sound asleep - Aunt Jemima come through my bedroom with the coal oil lamp. I woke up.

"Alverna," she said, holding the lantern up to me, "are you all right?"

"Yes. Why?"

"I thought I heard you."

"No, I didn't say nothing."

When she seen I was ok she went back to bed. It took a long time for me to get back to sleep. I heard her and Earl talking far into the night, only I couldn't make out what they was saying.

The next day Aunt Jemima was showing me where to plant some of her flowers. She liked around her house for things to look bright and colorful. She couldn't hardly bend down no more so I was glad I could help her out this way.

She was more quiet than usual. I said nothing cause I wasn't sure what went on during the night. I was wondering so about this when finally she broke the silence. "Alverna, you always had a good singin' voice, but I never heard you sing as beautiful as you done in bed last night," she told me.

"Is that why you come in my room?" I wanted to know. All this still puzzled me.

"Yes. Your singin' was like it was comin' straight from heaven."

"What did I sing?"

"*In That City, Bright City.* I thought maybe you was thinkin' about your pop, but then maybe you was thinkin' about what happened with you and Susie and Lydia and Joyce."

"I think about Pop every day, so maybe that was it. Maybe too, it was what the preacher said. It was wonderful what he preached."

"Well, that musta been on your mind."

And I didn't even know I was singing in my sleep.

With Joyce, it had been altogether different. She made the same promise the rest of us did but she didn't feel no different; all the same she was determined to stick to her promise. Joyce told us what happened as soon as we got together the next Sunday to practice our songs for the evening service at her church. That Wednesday she was wearing down. Her little sister kept pestering her and she was sick of it, had this strong craving to holler back at her and hit after her. She started after her, ready to grab and shake her. Then it come to her about her promise; she reminded herself that she'd be giving into the devil, so she told herself, "Don't do it. Stand firm for Jesus." The second she said it, why it was like a thunderclap of pure joy inside. Now she understood what us other girls was talking about.

After that our singing just got better and better cause we done it for Jesus, not just for us.

As excited as I was and as much as I wanted to, it was hard to tell most people about my new experience, sorta like when Pop died and people didn't wanna listen to me talk about him. Struggling to describe what happened that night, well, my thoughts was all jumbled up and my words come out hither and thither. I had trouble finding the right words to match my feelings. Some people just didn't understand. I got lots of blank stares and was put off most the time. Same thing happened to my girlfriends. So, we put our heads together and had a talk with the preacher. He said maybe the best way to share our new faith was through our singing; that when we sing together, make sure we're singing to praise God and not ourselves.

I suppose that's why my songs and recitations and readings appeared to touch people's hearts. When I got in front of people I always told the Good Man that what I was doing was for Him, not me. Then I just let it come from deep in my soul. When I was done, why sometimes I'd see a head nodding in agreement or hear a sniffle in a hanky that showed me people was listening and their hearts was touched. And I was glad.

Aunt Jemima was so much like the Old Lady in the way she showed she cared about me. Uncle Earl was too, but especially Jemima made me feel good about myself after having to leave Mom and my brothers. I thrived on her kindheartedness and the way she made me feel useful. Being so busy and tired out with the hard work around the farm kept me from falling apart, missing Mom and Albert and Dale Stuart so much.

Even though I worked hard, Jemima and Earl was never mean in their demands. I could hear Jemima's affection for me in the way she talked. Her and them Sunday evening services sure helped see me through.

Remember Maryellen and what happened that day in the back yard? Well, one day it all come to a head. Poor Aunt Jemima seen one day how dumb I was about such things that I shoulda knowed long before this. See, the first time I got my sickness that young girls get every month was when Pop was still living but not too good. Albert and I was sitting in the shade of our front porch stripping tobacco. I felt I hadda go to the privy and when I stood up, why here the whole bottom of the bench was full of blood. Oh my gosh! I couldn't believe what I seen. I had no idea what this was. I got scared to death and started to bawl.

Albert, when he seen this he begun to holler and cry, "Is Alverna gonna die? Is Alverna gonna die?"

"No!" Mom scolded, looking outta sorts. "Alverna ain't gonna die."

But she wouldn't tell me. She never told me what I could expect - never!

She sent me upstairs then fetched me water for me to clean myself up and rags to put on.

I was scared outta my wits, had no idea what was happening. In spite of Mom saying I wasn't gonna die, I was sure I was gonna keel over dead.

I didn't wait till bedtime to pray that day. Right then and there, if ever a child prayed that this would go away, it was me. I prayed as hard as I knowed how that I'd never get it no more. And by golly! I didn't. Not till I was sixteen. That was the day we was picking big stones in the field to clear for plowing. I felt this wetness between my legs. It was good that we just about hadda full load of stones to empty where the stone fence was. When I got outta the wagon, my clothes was wet with blood. Aunt Jemima saw this, took me in the bedroom, told me what this was and showed me how to make pads to wear. The first I understood what this was all about was when I was sixteen years old.

CHAPTER 34 - ST. JOHN'S CHURCH PICNIC

I was happy at Aunt Jemima's. There was lots of chores and work - hard work - but that's purty much all I knowed anyway. That woulda been anywhere I lived. I missed Mom and Albert and Dale Stuart, but Jemima gave me freedom to be with friends after my chores and work on Saturdays and Sundays. My friends had mostly the same kind of work to do too.

After church one Sunday, Lydia's boyfriend Rob said that next Saturday is St. John's Church Picnic. I heard it was a fine picnic. Lydia vouched for it.

Rob said, "I'll have the wagon cleaned out and put in fresh, clean straw and see how many we can get to go. But it'll cost $1.00 a piece."

The news spread and ten of us with Rob driving went. We was to meet in front of Weaver's general store except those Rob picked up on the way. We all made it through our morning chores and met on time. Filled up the wagon we did.

There was hardly anybody at the picnic grove yet when we arrived early on. Rob pulled the team up and tied the horses. We was sitting there in the wagon under a shade tree. After a minute or so I just said, "What do you go to a picnic for if you don't get some ice cream?"

"We just got here," Lydia said.

"Well, I don't care," I shot back. "I can eat ice cream anytime."

Charlie, Susie's brother, reaches in his pocket, pulls a dime out, hands it to me.

"Hey, I don't need your money, I got my own money. I can get my own ice cream."

Willie was sitting there. He just broke up with his girl and was eyeing me up. "If she wants ice cream I can get it for her."

Now I liked Charlie but I liked Willie better, only I wasn't too sure about him yet just breaking up with his girl.

"Can you believe it?" I thought to myself so surprised. "Them two fellas wanna buy me ice cream!" I wasn't gonna take their money so I pulled out my own dime.

Charlie barged in. "I dare you to go ask for ten cents worth of every kind of ice cream they got. You know, a little bit of every kind to make ten cents worth."

I climbed outta the wagon.

Rob whispered to Lydia, "Is she really gonna do it?"

I walked up to the fella in the refreshment stand, the only one working there yet. He seen 'em in the wagon laughing and asked me what it was all about. He thought maybe they was making fun of him.

"No, they're not laughing at you. They dared me to ask for ten cents worth of all kinds of ice cream."

"I'll go 'em one better," he said. "and you'll get your ten cents worth."

He dished me out every kind of ice cream. My goodness! So much it was I couldn't hardly believe my eyes. We both laughed at the joke on them in the wagon. I handed him my dime and started back towards my flabbergasted friends. I wasn't more'n a couple steps gone when he called, "Hey little lady, come back here!"

I went back thinking maybe he'd want more money.

"How many of youse is there?"

"Ten with me."

"Ok," he winked. "You got your ice cream. All right, you go back there, sit down and enjoy it."

I went to where the wagon was, climbed in while holding my dish of ice cream for dear life, sat down, began eating the different flavors of ice cream. The whole bunch was quiet, didn't know what to make of this.

"Ain't you gonna offer us any?" Charlie finally asked. I shook my head, smiled, licked the spoon and went on eating.

I sat facing the refreshment stand and seen the man had took the lid off one of the cans of ice cream, then wiped it out. He dished nine scoops of ice cream in that lid. I counted 'em as he was dishing it out. He stuck a spoon in each scoop. You can imagine how high it was piled! He come down, sat it on the wagon seat. "Now, go ahead. Help yourselves," he said with a good-natured grin. "All I ask is for my lid back and my spoons."

Walking back towards the stand he turned and said. "That's some spunky girl you got in that wagon. Give her credit for me dishin' out this ice cream and not chargin' youse. And, by the way, don't youse dare tell anyone else what I done. I'll run myself outta business if youse do."

I can see it all now. Me with my dish of ice cream and the other nine crowding around the lid to eat their scoop of vanilla ice cream. Such laughing and fun we was having about our good fortune. While we was eating Lydia avowed, "I told you! I told you! When Charlie dared her, you can't back Alverna down. Don't you dare tell that girl to do anything. I know she'll do it."

She was right except I wouldn't never do nothing wrong or hurt nobody. Pop taught me that much. "Have your fun, but at nobody else's expense," he'd say; and the preacher's sermon reminded me how I slipped that one time.

We all ate the ice cream, my scoops of every kind being the biggest. The lid and spoons was returned with Rob laying money down he collected from all nine for the generous man at the refreshment stand. It's good we got there early that day, for soon after that incident, people arrived in droves. Why the fellow got so busy he never woulda had time to dish out ice cream for us like he did earlier.

That started the picnic off just right for us. To top it off, Lydia and Rob won a cake during a cake walk. Coconut. We said how we shoulda had that with our ice cream.   We all had one grand and glorious time at the picnic the whole afternoon.

Rob took us back to where we met like he promised, but he stopped at his place first. He was worried about his cow. "Millie'll wonder what happened that she ain't been milked yet."

Lydia said, "I'll stay here and milk her while you take the rest home."

And she did.

Maybe Lydia had more'n one reason to milk Rob's cow cause she sure had a soft spot for him. Rob, that is, not the cow. It was natural for most of us to help out each other when help was needed. That's the way we was and that's the way we done things.

By golly! What a grand and glorious time we had! Such good, clean fun.

CHAPTER 35 - TAKEN BY SURPRISE

My-oh-my, such memories. I laugh easy and I cry easy. That's why it's hard to tell some of these stories. Especially this one. I'll cry for sure. And to think this is the first anyone'll hear it from me. Even my own kids. They never before heard how it happened.

It was a cold, December Saturday. I was seventeen years old, still living with Aunt Jemima and Uncle Earl on the farm. Aunt Jemima was by now so heavy she couldn't hardly get down to milk, so Uncle Earl and I done the milking. I worked hard, done practically everything that needed done. Done it because of the way I was raised and my love for Jemima and Earl. They was good to me; in return I wanted to do right by them. There wasn't nothing much I couldn't do except the heaviest outdoors lifting. Yet there was this one time in particular when I left 'em down. The way it happened was this: The church never had any entertainment for Christmas but this year there was eleven of us asked to put on a Christmas play. Some folks didn't like the idea of a play in church but the preacher said it was just one more way to get the Christmas message across.

This particular Saturday evening a gang of us girls went to Susie Mellinger's house. It was purty far from Jemima and Earl's to the Mellinger's so Earl gave me permission to stay all night since he knowed her family good and how Susie and I was best friends. Sunday morning Aunt Jemima'd help with the morning milking, then when they come to church I'd meet 'em there and go home with them. That way I wouldn't have to walk the long distance in the cold.

After church, Susie said to Earl and Jemima, "Alverna can't go home now yet, they're all coming to my house to practice for the Christmas play. Please let her stay."

Uncle Earl said I could go back with Susie but be home in time to milk.

Well, it began to snow right after we got to Susie's.

"I'm gonna start walking home," I said. "It's gonna get deep and no one'll come to practice."

By then two brothers arrived, then two more. But only two of the four was in the play. We was talking and having a good time but no practice. The snow worried me.

"I'm going home. If I don't get started Aunt Jemima'll have to go out and milk again tonight. I don't want that."

Charlie said, "Stay. Later I'll take you home and I'll explain everything." Just then some more showed up and talked me into staying. The snow got deeper and deeper. Seeing how worried I was, another one of the young fellas said, "I'll see that you get home." I thought his friend would go along and then them two would walk on home to Cedar Grove. Only it didn't happen that way. Just this one fella went out with me.

When we got to Jemima and Earl's we was almost froze. Us girls wore long dresses at that time. My dress and petticoat and winter coat was weighted down with snow and ice above my knees. While Aunt Jemima filled the stove, the fella who walked me home tried to explain how worried I was about the milking and everything. He was telling all this to Aunt Jemima so she wouldn't be mad at me. She ended up pitying him more'n me, made him take his shoes and stockings off and put 'em in the oven to dry. Aunt Jemima told me go upstairs right away and put dry clothes on.

It was nine o'clock, a little bit after. Uncle Earl had went to bed. I come down after changing my clothes and hung the wet ones on a line near the stove. Now it was time for Aunt Jemima to go to bed. She was wore out.

I checked his shoes and stockings. They had already dried so I said to him, "You're fully dry. Now you can go."

I finished hanging my wet clothes and turned to see him to the door, but he come up behind me, grabbed me and pulled me to him. He took me by surprise. I was *ferhoodled*. I didn't understand what he was doing.

"Oh, you figure you're gonna get rid of me that quick? I want paid back for walking you home."

And I often wish to God, how I often wish that I coulda pulled away from him and went to bed and left him there. But it didn't happen that way.

That one time, and I was in a family way, and that was that.

Jemima and Earl was getting up in years and wasn't able no longer to keep after the farm. Earl got a job in the cigar factory and they was packing up to move to town. They wanted me to go with 'em but I reckoned I'd be more bother than worth, so I said no. Uncle George come and took Mom's trunk to Pap Farley's attic where it'd be safe till Mom was ready to keep it with her.

By this time Mom was married to Fred Fry and had a girl by him and another baby on the way. Fred said I could stay there and help Mom with her work and the kids, but after I had my baby I'd have to go. Fred wasn't no dummy. He seen how both me and Mom worked good and hard and knowed that when we done something, we done it right. He figured to get as much outta me as he could with Mom being in a family way and needing extra help. When I wasn't no more use, Fred, he'd send me on my way.

Never mind. I was glad to be with Mom if only for a little.

It was a pleasant, sunny, Spring Saturday. The door was open to let in the fresh, clean air. I was washing the dinner dishes. See, what is lunch to most folks is dinner to us Dutch, and what other people call dinner, we call supper. I was putting the dishes in the cupboard when I heard someone out front. I went to the door and looked out. It was the fella that got me in a family way. I wondered why in the world he was showing up here at Fred's.

"Hello," he called and looked in. "How are you?

"I'm good. Will you come in?"

"No. The rest are at the end of the lane waitin' for me. We're goin' to the church picnic at St. John's. It's the first one this season, you know."

Before anymore was said, Fred heard this, went after him, grabbed him at his shoulders and gave him a good shaking. "You rotten son-of-a-gun! You think more of goin' to the picnic than bein' here with your girl. Why, I oughta give you a good lickin'!"

"She ain't my girl!" He jerked outta Fred's grasp, turned and run down the lane to catch up with the gang and go have his fun.

Since this was the second man that run away from me, Lawrence Holtzapple being the first, I wondered so if that was gonna happen all my life. Seems like people got outta me what they wanted, then run away. For a minute I considered that's what Pop done - run away by dying on us when we needed him so much. Scolded myself. Not Pop. Anyway I never woulda married this fella. He had a wonderful brother just a year younger. His sister wasn't much. And then there was a five year old brother, retarded. At church this little boy would always look for me. "You're my girl, ain't cha?" Every time he seen me he asked.

"Yes, I'm your girl," I'd tell him back and give him a hug. The way that little boy clung on to me I could tell he loved me.

When I went to stay with my mom and Fred, I didn't get to that church no longer. The little retarded boy missed me something terrible. His brother, the nice one, told him that I didn't get to church cause I was gonna have a baby, but he didn't tell him their brother was the daddy.

It was late August. I'd been out in the potato patch all day in the sweltering heat. After I made supper, cleaned up the kitchen and hauled clean water in for to get washed up,

I was worn out. It was dark by the time I crawled into bed. Something didn't feel quite right. I got outta bed to use the chamber pot but it wasn't that. Here my baby was on the way. I called Mom to come help. Fred grouchily roused from his sleep and sent his oldest boy who come home for the weekend, to go fetch the doctor, then went back to bed. In no time, with only Mom right there with me, my tiny little baby girl was born.

Mom had washed her up and wrapped her in a blanket, was cleaning me up when Doc come. He seen how things was and said with a good-humored chuckle that he shoulda knowed to not bother coming, that between Estella and Alverna things would turn out ok. He was right.

All night, long after Mom laid her beside me, I couldn't take my eyes off of this fine-looking little girl baby. I looked at her round head, just a little pointy, covered with reddish blond fuzz, her squinty eyes, flattened nose and red, wrinkled face. It didn't matter that she looked like her handsome daddy instead of me. To me she was perfect.

I lay there pondering in my mind how hope comes in all sizes and shapes, sometimes when you're not in the least bit expecting it. I remembered the doll baby with a flocked lavender dress named Hope. She was hope unfulfilled. Yet, in many ways, hope reached out to me; many a time it was my pop who gave me hope; Grammy too. One time hope come when a preacher preached about how our only real hope is in the Good Lord.

I considered naming this wonderful little girl Hope; she gave me a fresh batch of it, but I didn't have to make a quick decision. There was plenty of time. The doctor said a week at the most. Then he'd need a name for the birth certificate. Yes, I'd take my time.

A couple days later Lola come with Albert to visit. So dressed up in expensive, fine clothes they was. Albert looked peaked, was that way all his life, yet he was healthy enough under Lola's care to live a long life. Mighta not been that way without her constant attention. He was now living in a different world. I seen by the awkward way he looked around at the place and us that day, well, although he was happy to visit us, he never woulda wanted to come back to our plain way of living. Yes well, he never hadda.

Wouldn't you know, Lola and Albert had their hands full of presents for everyone. Poor Lola. I pitied her so, but maybe she didn't need my pity. She wasn't able to have the kind of life with her husband she dreamed of when she was starting out years ago but she done her best with what she had. Somewhere along the line she stopped being afraid of John's tightfistedness and learned how to spend her husband's money for the good of others. All the store owners there-abouts knowed who Lola was. They was glad to see her come into their shops. A good spender she was. Whatever she bought, she said just put it on John Miller's expense account. What could John do but pay the bills when they come in? She had reasoned if he ridiculed her about everything else, money was only one more thing for him to fault her about, and in her eyes what was one more thing on top of the others? So what could he do? Nothing. To tell the store clerks to not let her charge items would only show how stingy with her he was. So, Lola spent John's money without hesitation. Matter of fact, I think it gave her real pleasure.

When Dale Stuart seen 'em he was his bubbly, happy self. The couple months I was at Fred Fry's I spent as much time with him as I could, teaching him about things Mom wouldn't, being so closed-mouth, busy and all. Right off he directed everyone into the bedroom to see his new baby. He then went to say how he wanted a boy to play with but shucks, Alverna went and had a baby girl when there was already enough girls here. Everyone laughed and so did Dale Stuart. Albert come over and looked at the baby. "Glory be, Alvernie! Glory be! She sure is a purty one."

Just the way Albert said *glory be,* it made up my mind what to name my baby. I'd name her Gloriann after the *glory be* that come outta Albert's mouth and the Ann after Mom's middle name. Eliza after Grammy. Gloriann Eliza Holtzapple.

I gave her my last name, not her daddy's. No indeed, she wasn't gonna get his name. She might look like him but it ended there. She wasn't gonna get his last name since he didn't want nothing to do with her. Matter of fact, I was happy about that cause it made it easier for me to determine that no one was gonna come and take this little girl from me like my doll baby and my baby sister that was taken from me so long ago. But I didn't say nothing then about her name. I'd wait awhile, do it in my time.

Lola got Albert to hand out the presents, things we never before had. There was a story book with bright colored pictures and a real, store-bought toy for Dale Stuart, a cast iron, bright red fire engine. He'd spend many a happy hour playing with it, his little half brother and sisters wanting to help. Bighearted as he was, he'd share it with 'em. There was shirts for all of Fred's boys, even the one that come home only on the weekends, handkerchiefs and a straw hat for Fred that'd come in handy all summer and fall. Two dresses for Mom's girl, pretty they was but practical. They hadda be or Mom never woulda never dressed her little girl in 'em; and white cotton stockings. For Mom was a new apron and lots of brand new kitchen utensils to replace the old, worn-out ones she'd been using ever since she moved in here. Knowing Mom, she'd probably tuck 'em away till the others fell apart to nothing and she couldn't use 'em no more. That was ok. Lola knowed Mom was like that. She wouldn't use 'em till beyond a shadow of a doubt she needed to. Besides, it was comforting to have something never-used and shiny stored for a rainy day.

They was all handed out except mine and the baby's. Albert handed me a big brown sack. Heavy it was. "For you Alverna," he said so proud. First I pulled out a bolt of material to make me a new dress. Oh, how purty it was. There was matching thread and lace trim and buttons, everything. Oh, I just couldn't believe Lola went to all that trouble. I was so admiring it when Lola broke in. "Now Alverna, I know you won't have time to sew up a dress for yourself so I wanna take one of yours that fits you and take all this back to Esther Prowell for her to make you a nice dress for church. Do you like the color and pattern of the material? If not I can exchange it for something you like better."

"Yes, oh, yes! It is so purty." I started to say that it was too much for her to do for me but Lola brushed me off and took the items and put 'em in a cloth bag she had emptied other presents out of, walked over to the peg on the wall and took down one of my dresses hanging there. I told her that yes, that one fits me fine so she put it in the bag with the other stuff. But that wasn't the end. "Get out your other present," Albert insisted.

There was more? For me? Oh, my! When I pulled it out I just couldn't believe it. Never before in my life. . . . I always hadda borrow someone else's. Oh, I couldn't of wanted anything better'n this. There lay in my hands a Bible of beautiful, soft, white leather - white, mind you - with my name on the front in gold letters underneath a set of gold praying hands. Then I hadda cry. Lola, she was so good. She sat down next to me, looked me in the eyes, said in a quiet, loving voice that was meant only for me in the room full of people, "I couldn't take you when I took Albert, Alverna. I love you and I wanted you only it wouldn't of gone over with John. I hadda pretend I didn't want you so he wouldn't hurt you - or me - with more spiteful, heartless words that's hard to get outta our minds once we hear 'em. But you made do with where you've been, what you've done and all the hard things you've been through. You keep on, Alverna. You read that Bible and keep growing strong in the Lord. You're gonna need it and that's what'll get you through."

The rest was impatient by this time to see what was for my baby. How was I gonna open her present when my eyes was blinded with tears? I blowed my nose and got on with it. It was in an oversized box at the bottom of the brown paper sack. I lifted the lid and there lay a dress of shiny silk, so light and feathery it looked like it was gonna float away; a long, white baby dress like I'd only ever seen in magazines.

335

Little buttons the whole way down the front that'd take the smallest button hook to close; satin petticoat underneath. There was tiny white stockings and shoes; and a bonnet. Everything brand new except for the dress. I looked at Lola.

She explained. "This dress was my Mabel's when she was a mere baby for when she was baptized and her first picture. It's been in the chest all these years. No use laying there getting all yellow with the material rotting away to nothing. I thought maybe you'd like it for your baby to have her picture taken and when she gets baptized. Why maybe you'll have more babies someday and you can use it all over again, then pass it down."

My heart overflowed with joy and happiness. Lola's gifts was so thought out, so wonderful good. She wouldn't of hadda give us nothing but she couldn't of given us anything better. She and my pop - her brother Ben - was so much alike. For all the good things they gave, their best gifts was that part of themselves that they was always so generous with.

Gloriann Eliza Holtzapple. My precious little girl baby. Mine to love and care for. And to rock. I never got to rock my baby sister or my doll baby after that first day, but Gloriann, I'd rock her as much as I wanted to.

Oh, how we sometimes believe we have control of maybe even just little pieces of our lives and we're happy and satisfied with just that much. Then the day comes when we find out that no matter what we think or do or plan, it don't hardly never turn out that way.

CHAPTER 36 - THE DETWILER FAMILY

Everyone wondered where in the world did I get that name.

"Never mind," I'd say. "Her name is Gloriann."

Mom had another girl towards the end of October. With Fred's big family I wasn't able to keep up with all that needed done. Fred asked two neighbor girls to help. They was the middle ones in a family of eight girls. One evening when we all sat down at the supper table, they got to talking about their family and how two of their older sisters had married the Detwiler brothers some years before and together them four lived on a big farm, working it together.

That gave Fred an idea. He got in touch with these people to see if they needed help. They did. In the spring my little girl and I moved to the Detwiler farm where I was hired out. I was there only two weeks when I figured everything would go all right.

Dottie and Beulah was the sisters. Dottie was married to Oscar Detwiler, Beulah to Jack. Beulah and Jack, they had a girl, Bertha, not in school yet. Dottie and Oscar didn't have none, but what they done was take children whose parents couldn't keep 'em due to a rash of bad luck. If things got better for the parents and their luck changed, then they'd come back after the kids. If not, Dottie and Oscar said they'd raise 'em till they was eighteen, then give 'em fifty dollars. If they wanted to leave they could leave; if they wanted to stay they could stay and work on the farm. The ones they had was good kids. Dottie and Oscar got so attached to 'em they was hoping their parents wouldn't come back to get 'em,

I tell you, we worked on that farm. We worked long and hard. Mondays we done the washing and got the things ready for Beulah and Jack to go to market on Tuesdays. Then Tuesdays we got for Dottie and Oscar to go Wednesdays.

Then Wednesdays we got for Beulah to go Thursdays. It all depended on what they had, you know; eggs when the chickens laid, milk and butter from the cows, vegetables in season, pies, cookies, cakes. Of course Fridays was the baking and churning butter, cleaning the churns and the milk pails and all that there plus getting ready for both of 'em to go to market Saturdays.

It was too far for me to get to the Reformed Church I joined when I was with Jemima and Earl, so I went with Beulah and Jack to their Lutheran and Reformed Church which was one building, two congregations. See, Reformed services was one Sunday, then the next Sunday was the Lutheran service. Jack didn't like it that when the Reformed preacher preached, the Lutherans didn't show up; after all, when the Lutheran preacher preached, the Reformed members was there. It made him mad so they started going to the United Brethren Church.

The United Brethren preacher heard me singing one Sunday morning. He come and told me he wanted to start a choir and would I join. He'd talk to the song leader, Jacob Ziegler, thinking he'd be the director of the first choir.

When the preacher approached him, Mr. Ziegler huffed, "You can start what you want but I won't be the leader of it."

"Why, brother Jacob?" asked the preacher.

"Because the devil always sits in the first seat of the choir to fill them people up with pride."

The startled preacher, after some thought, come back with, "Well, brother Jacob, if you think the devil sits in the first seat of the choir to puff who's singing there up with pride and self-importance, maybe the devil hovers around the song leader to convince him into not letting anyone else stand along side of him because too prideful he is to share the attention."

Probably don't have to tell you that the preacher's come-back pricked the pride of brother Jacob. The United Brethren Church hadda look for a new song leader but held off on starting a choir till the uproar settled down.

That preacher encouraged church members to take part in the service, something not practiced too often back then. See, some preachers couldn't let go. They hadda take charge of everything. Their way of thinking was that no one could do it as good as them so they'd do it all themselves. Not this preacher. He was a humble man. Some members fussed that too many changes was taking place, but other members liked it and took part if they felt they was gifted and called to serve.

That congregation, even though they knowed I had a baby and wasn't married, well, most didn't hold it against me. Jack and Beulah knowed most the people there. Them and my singing helped get me acquainted with folks purty soon. Four or five of us girls sang a hymn or two purty near every Sunday evening. If the rest didn't show up, I was called upon for a reading or a solo or recitation. But not Sunday mornings, only Sunday evenings.

Even though I didn't transfer my membership right away my life went smoother because of that church, its preacher and its members. They encouraged me to take part. They was to me like a church should be, a family.

It was my turn on the farm to make supper. One evening I'd make supper, one evening Dottie made supper, one evening Beulah made supper. Before we went to the field that morning we filled the stove up with wood and put on a whole kettle full of soup beans.

"Now," Dottie said, "When you get in to make supper the beans'll be purty soft."

Mid-afternoon I'd come in from the field to start supper. I was supposed to slice the potatoes to fry, and there was always plenty of meat there, you know. The first thing I done was look at the beans. Oh, my! The whole top of the kettle was full of bugs! I didn't know what in the wide world I was to do, so I picked up the heavy kettle, took it out back and poured it in the chicken yard. I wondered so, "Hey, what in the world am I gonna make now yet?"

Over this then, someone come driving across the bridge, tied up the horse at the hitching post, walked up the steps and come right in without knocking.

"Who might you be?" he asked.

"Holtzapple," I said.

"Holtzapple! That's as Dutch as sauerkraut!"

He looked around but mostly looked at me. "You mean to tell me you're gonna make supper?"

"Sure, don't you think I can?"

"If you make supper, I'm staying."

"I don't care!" I said, but he got me all flustered up.

This man with a long beard all the way down to his chest was a preacher friend of the Detwiler family, but not their preacher. He stopped around every now and then.

Back outside he went.

I sat the table wondering about what to make for supper. "Well, I know how my mom used to start off when she wanted to make - we always called 'em johnnycakes. And I knowed there was always a lot of flour and corn meal there at the Detwiler's. I stirred up a couple and tried it. Tasted alright. So then I went to work and cut ponhaus yet. Fried the ponhaus, the potatoes and made the johnnycakes. I purty much had everything cooked up and ready.

Then, Dottie come in. "What made you stir up johnnycakes?" she wondered so.

I told her about the beans.

"Oh my gosh! Them beans'll have to be gone over before we try to cook anymore. What did you do with 'em?" Dottie wanted to know.

"Fed 'em to the chickens."

She nodded sharply then walked away. I didn't know if what I done was right or not. I wasn't sure cause of the way

Dottie acted. She didn't say. It flustered me all the more but I managed to finish supper and get it on the table with Beulah and little Bertha's help.

They all got around the table; Beulah, Jack and Bertha; Dottie, Oscar, the two they was raising and the preacher; and of course, me. My baby was asleep.

Well, this preacher man appeared purty nice, but still. . . . After he prayed the blessing he looked at Oscar and asked, "Do you think we dare trust to eat this stuff she made?"

"Well, I don't know."

Jack butted in. "Anything she makes you can eat."

They went deviling back and forth that way for so long.

Bertha put her two cents in. "Alverna's smart. Why, she can say the ABC's backwards faster'n I can say 'em forwards. Learned that when she was just a little girl like I am now. She's teaching me to say 'em like that."

"I don't believe it," said the preacher. "Let's hear you go through 'em, and you better not get any mixed up."

I was all *ferhoodled*. Got red in the face. I thought, "What if I get tongue tied and get 'em outta order? Then they'll laugh at me all the more."

Under my breath I asked myself if I was gonna let 'em have a good laugh on me. My back stiffened with determination and I said in my mind, "Holy heck! They can laugh all they want but not cause I done wrong. They'll laugh cause I said 'em right."

And laugh we did. I laughed right along with everyone else. All together we had the best time.

It felt like Pop was smiling down on me right then and there cause he taught me them things and how to reason 'em out. My reasoning worked that time. My wonderful good pop. He was *allerbescht*!

Beulah chimed in, "Now that's enough. You got the girl so flustered up she don't know what she's doing."

The preacher said, "Yes, I know, but I just have to torment her a little bit."

Before he left that evening he handed me a piece of paper he pulled outta his pocket. "Now, I want you to recite this for me the next time I come around."

I looked at it. "Why, it's in Dutch!"

"Not anymore Dutch than you are."

I took it along in the little back room that night and read over it before I outened the coal oil lamp. Never did take me long to learn anything. I remembered Dutch from long ago. See, when I was little I knowed more Dutch'n I let on. That way when Mom and Pop and the Old Lady spoke Dutch thinking I didn't understand too much, I knowed more'n they woulda ever guessed. Not Grammy and Pap. They figured I knowed more'n I left on.

The preacher man, he never did get around no more. They put him in another church.

On Sunday evenings I was invited to recite the Dutch poem at different churches. It was beautiful, filled with lots of religious meaning. People loved hearing it in Dutch since sermons wasn't no longer being preached in the German language no more; only English.

Today I still know that Dutch poem. I recite it every now and then so I don't forget all the Dutch. I have an awful time translating it, but I do know it talks about *himmel*. *Himmel* means heaven.

I liked it so much at the Detwiler's.

But then Dottie got her backside up.

My little girl and I was at the Detwiler's two years. It went along all right although Dottie griped and complained how nobody done their work as good as her. She hadda have a hand in everything - after it was over and done with, that is. Then she'd look back and say what we done wrong and how she woulda done better. See, she never gave nobody credit for their hard, back-breaking work. According to Dottie, she was the only one on the whole farm who did any work worthwhile. Another thing, if you said *black* she argued it was *white*. If Beulah said it looked like rain, Dottie insisted the sun would shine. She'd complain something terrible about a person behind their back, then nice as could be she was to their face - sometimes! At other times, face to face she'd tear you apart. Knowing how she was, we all purty much put up with it, that is till they planted a peach orchard, maybe eight or nine trees. Jack and Oscar planted 'em. Every time it was any grubbing to do around 'em Jack done it. He was the one to hunt around the roots for grubs and borers. Oscar and Dottie done the spraying, Well then, after the peach trees come in and they began to bear, that's when the fussing started. See, Dottie was gonna claim all the peaches even though it wasn't too many to begin with.

Beulah had it up to here, rightly so. She was always getting the short end of the stick. "I knowed that's the way it'd go!" She spoke up for a change. See, stuff like this was going on from the day they moved to the farm together. They was supposed to divide up the produce and eggs and such, but Dottie always appeared to have more on her market days. It was suspected that Dottie checked the nests the morning when the eggs was to be for Jack and Beulah to take to market, then hid some so she'd have more to sell on her market days. Jack only had the one cow there so they only got that much butter to take. Dottie claimed all the others. Things wasn't equal and Beulah, so vexed, couldn't take it no longer.

Jack, he was different. He didn't say nothing. It was Beulah and Dottie's daddy who seen they got this place and he didn't wanna cause no trouble. He just wanted peace. He was willing to give up them peaches and blow off all his hard work getting the trees to bear so the fussing would stop. Beulah knowed the fussing would never stop. She had all she was gonna take.

When Beulah and Dottie's pa heard about how his two girls was hammering away at each other, he come out. Beulah just said, "Pop, if you know of a farm that we can get, just help us get it because we can't endure it here no more."

He said, "I know of a wonderful place I can get cheap for you. A little bit hilly but it's reasonable and it'd be a wonderful place to raise things to take to market, but you'd have to start everything over."

"Better that way than with Dottie's fussing all the time," Beulah said.

So that's what they done.

Their pop made sure some strawberry plants and things from the farm went with Beulah and Jack. Dottie didn't much like anything leaving **her** farm, but she knowed just how much she could get away with around her pa. She couldn't get away with as much from him as she could with other people.

Me and Gloriann stayed behind with Dottie and Oscar. It didn't go too good. Dottie had it in for me cause she knowed Beulah and I always worked together in peace and accord, and on top of that we exchanged letters now yet. When she'd come from market, Dottie'd right away snip at me, "Well, had a letter from Beulah today?" She was so snappy and mean, ugly, you know. But I could take that from her.

"No. No letter from Beulah," I'd answer back, sometimes wanting to snap back at her but I remembered what Pop taught me. Then, too, I promised I'd serve the Lord. I couldn't honor Pop's memory if I snapped back, and you don't serve the Lord by being mean and snappy.

Beulah told me that anytime I couldn't take it from Dottie, I got a home with her and Jack.

Two times when I was living with Dottie and Oscar I got away to help Mom out. That was when she had two more babies, not much more'n a year apart. Both girls. When I went to Mom's them two times, Dottie insisted Gloriann stay with her and Oscar since I'd be so busy with Mom and her kids. I didn't like it but I couldn't argue my way outta anything with Dottie.

When Mom had her babies Lola'd bring Albert to visit. In spite of the good care she poured out on him, Albert's health wasn't good. He growed up short and scrawny, looked pale and underfed, but with Lola we all knowed he got the best care. She doted on him and he appeared content. He mighta died if he stayed with Mom when she went to Fred's. Of course Dale Stuart was growing big and tall. Looked just like Ben Geesey, his dad, my pop. It was so good to be with all three of 'em again.

Lola still brought nice gifts for everyone and the new babies. She even remembered Fred and his boys so they wouldn't feel left out. Lola, she knowed how to butter Fred up so he didn't mind when she'd come with Albert to visit.

Fred wasn't a bad sort, not like I first thought when he didn't let Albert and me live there cause he said he didn't have enough room when all the time he did. I guess he was suspicious of Mom moving in with her family. He mighta thought after she moved in she'd not take care of his children and the work that needed done. He got a better woman than he ever expected with Mom. On top of that, when he seen how much I helped out and how hard I worked when Mom needed me, he woulda let me come there and stay. Only by then I was content where I was. If only Dottie woulda just let up on me a little bit.

One thing though, Mom wanted me with her when it was time for her to have her babies. She never had an easy time giving birth. The last one, well, the doctor thought he might lose Mom and the baby both. So after this little girl was born and Mom almost didn't make it through again, the doctor got a grip on Fred, backed him against the wall, looked him in the eyes and asked, "How many kids do you have, Fred?"

"Fred hadda use his fingers to count."

"Don't you think you done your duty? Now listen to me, Fred. It's time to quit! The way Estella is now, I'm warning you, she'll not make it through another."

Before he left the doctor sighed and went, "At least now that Alverna's here, I know it'll be all right and Estella'll get in the pink again."

And she did.

That was her last one. Mom had no more children. That was good. She was getting wore out from having babies.

Dottie was acting awful strange, worse'n before. If Oscar wanted to do something, Dottie wanted to do it with him. It was like she didn't trust him.

The men would get together still and go coon hunting. One night when they planned to go, well, Dottie wanted to go along.

Oscar, he never called her Dottie like the rest of us. "Now DotDot," he said so patient as he patted her hand. "Tonight you can't go. Just me and Hen and Jack and George are goin'."

Well, Dottie just throwed herself into a fit and got sick over it. So sick she hadda go to bed and we hadda get the doctor for her. Oscar seldom stood up to her but this time he went anyway. That didn't go over so good with Dottie. We all paid for it, but she took it out on me more'n anyone else.

Oscar seen how more and more Dottie was being ruthless towards me. He come to me one day when he was mixing feed to take to the mill. "Alverna, I want you to help me put the feed in bags." That was the first time he ever asked me to do anything like that. Dottie looked at him and me in a strange way but said nothing.

When we got out to the barn he handed me a bag to hold for him to fill. "I guess you think it's funny I asked you to come out here," he said.

"Yes, but Oscar, I think I know what's what."

"I just hate to see how DotDot devils you about every little thing. I just can't take it no more the way she's always jumping on you about everything you do around here in spite of you being the best help we ever had. She just won't let you alone. Besides, she don't like the way you and Beulah get along so good."

He began conjuring up excuses for the way she was acting. "You know, Alverna, DotDot, she ain't good."

But he knowed it wasn't Dottie's health. She was always spiteful to most everyone except with the kids she took in. She demanded hard work outta each one but she wasn't nasty or unkind to any of 'em. With me it was her jealousy from the way her sister, Beulah, and me got along so good together. Almost like real sisters we was even though Beulah was older'n me. I never brought anything up when Dottie was around about Beulah, even tried to put her letters outta sight, but Dottie had eagle eyes and searching hands; she seen the letters and this was eating away at her.

"Well," I went. "It don't make that much difference to me. I can take it."

"No, I want you, if you feel like you wanna go to Beulah and Jack's, you go. But, Alverna, your little girl stays here.

"Oh no, Oscar! Where I go, Gloriann goes with me."

He looked at me, then away. Tears come to his eyes. "If you take her from DotDot it'll kill her. Me too."

That quick his voice changed like he was scolding me. "Hold that bag up so I can shovel more feed in it."

I figured Dottie was sneaking up on us and he seen her coming. We worked together. Nothing more was said. After awhile Dottie slinked back to the house.

That's how fond they was of my little girl who was almost three years old now. I was there with them from soon after she was born. Dottie was all wrapped up in the child. And no wonder. A happier little girl you couldn't find. So cheerful, so curious, so full of life she was. Maybe I shouldn't brag, but she was so purty, too! Why, she gave joy to everyone around with her blondish red curls bouncing and her green eyes shining the brightest as she lived life to the fullest. And that's the way I was letting her grow up. Little as she was she had her chores to do, but never did I take away her cheerfulness from her. Not never!

Anyway, Dottie made it worse'n worse for me; finally I packed up to go live with Beulah and Jack. Of course Gloriann went along. Beulah come for me in their wagon on one of Dottie's market days.

First thing Dottie done when she come home and seen we was gone was to sit down and write me a letter cursing me out like I never was cursed before.

Beulah and Jack welcomed us like real family. Their girl Bertha, was in school now, but how she had missed her little playmate. She thought the world and all of Gloriann. Together again, Bertha drug her all around the little farm while they done their chores. After supper Gloriann crawled up at the table while Bertha done her school work and I cleaned up the supper dishes. Bertha took to being the teacher, taught Gloriann what she learned at school. Smart as a whip my little girl was, soaking it all up.

I felt cherished when I moved in with Beulah and Jack. With them and Bertha and my little girl, we was one happy family. And now I could start back at the United Brethren Church with them. Let me tell you, that church was just like another family. And that's the way I was treated. Gloriann, too. I changed my mind from when I first said I wouldn't join another church. Now I was more'n ready to transfer my membership to the church that welcomed me right where I was in life - and helped me grow through thick and thin.

CHAPTER 37 - LOSING HOPE

I can't fully describe the way some folks is. It's not in my vocabulary. The Bible says it best: *"His speech was smoother than butter, yet war was in his heart; his words were softer than oil, yet they were drawn swords."* I read that in Psalm 55:21 once and it hit me that that's the way it was with Dottie. She could be nice as apple pie one minute but when things didn't go her way, watch out! So truthful, so reasonable she sounded that even at first I almost got caught up in things she said except there was just something about the way she said it that made me leery. Something about her just didn't add up, but most people didn't pick up on it till they got burned by her. She was so sly that she had people believing her gossip and outright lies about innocent folks.

If you don't know anyone like this, you won't understand what I tell you next.

Dottie was fuming that I went to live with Beulah and her family. She spread all sorts of gossip about me; Beulah too; even Jack and Bertha. How we was lazy, didn't do our share, took things that didn't belong to us. Then she said how I wasn't a good momma, was mean and nasty to my little girl; all sorts of wicked stories. She said I didn't just up and leave, that she kicked me out cause I wasn't no good. Some people around there didn't know me all that good and musta wondered so about me; was I as bad as Dottie made out? They shoulda knowed better being around Dottie like they was. I guess some only wanna hear the bad and spread the gossip. Dottie planted suspicion about me everywhere she went. What little I heard, why of course it hurt, but mostly I didn't pay no mind. Wasn't much I could do about it. Besides, Gloriann and I was happy with Beulah and Jack.

Lots of people wasn't all that aware of what went on for years between Beulah and Dottie. Jack and Oscar never said nothing beyond their front door. They got along good in spite of what was between their wives. Beulah and Dottie kept the fighting between themselves purty well hid from others till they separated. Of course Dottie ranted about Beulah then, so people was hearing a side of Beulah they never heard before. Guess they didn't know what to believe.

As much as they didn't want nothing to do with us, Dottie and Oscar was homesick for Gloriann. One evening they come in their horse and buggy down the hill. Bertha was done with her lessons so Gloriann crawled down from the table and went out on the porch to wait for me to get done with my cleaning up after supper. See, this was our special time of the day, just us two, alone together. Wiping my hands on my apron, I was ready to step out on the porch. Gloriann seen the buggy before anyone else and who was in it. She called out, "Pappy, Pappy, Pappy!" That was what she called Oscar. She off that porch lickity split before I was able to get out the door and grab her. She run down the steep hill and slid right under the buggy. I screamed in horror. I was sure she got run over.

Somehow or other Oscar got the horse and buggy stopped before the wheel hit her. After the first shock wore off, I run down to the road when Dottie jumped outta the buggy that quick, pulled Gloriann from underneath, bellowed and cursed at me for not looking after my little girl any better. "We're takin' her with us where she'll get proper care. Don't you dare try to come after her, you wicked momma, you!"

She lifted my little girl into the buggy. Gloriann wasn't paying no attention to Dottie, she was just reaching after Oscar, her beloved pappy. Dottie's voice carried to where I was standing and into the kitchen where Beulah and Bertha was. She demanded Oscar to pull away on the spot. My little girl leaned over Dottie's lap and waved at me like we was playing a game. She didn't know she wasn't coming back.

I did.

Gloriann was gone.

I lost hope.

Again.

You scoff at me and say, "You shoulda fought to get her back."

You think I'm a coward, don't you, a momma who didn't want her little girl enough to fight for her. I only can say, deep down inside - I can't explain it - something told me I couldn't whip Dottie and get my Gloriann back. She made up her mind she'd do whatever damage it'd take to keep this little girl for herself, and I knowed it. And Oscar'd back her up. This I knowed deep down in my miserable, suffering soul.

I slumped down on the edge of the porch, leaned against the banister.

The rest was in the kitchen talking this over. To me there was nothing to talk over. Gloriann was gone.

I just sat. Didn't move. Couldn't move. My body stopped working. Beulah come out, throwed a blanket over my shoulders and sat with me. Took my hands in hers, held 'em. Didn't say a word. That was good; there was nothing to say. I couldn't of stood to listen to anything just then. Never in my life did I know what a headache was; now my head throbbed so bad I was sure it was gonna explode and the rest of me with it. Every part of my body hurt as needles of pain shot through me. From head to toe I hurt so bad I wanted to scream. But then, the screams in my heart stopped. It was like my heart froze over. But not enough to stop the hurting.

Hours later Beulah stood me up, drug me into my bed, laid me down, took off my shoes and covered me up. I laid there, two, three days, I don't know. It coulda been a week, maybe more. It didn't matter. I slipped in and outta a daze so deep my throat closed and I couldn't speak. Couldn't hardly breathe. When I opened my eyes it was like I was blind; didn't see nothing. It didn't matter. I didn't care if I went blind.

The only thing that come into my consciousness them days was I heard a rocking chair moving back and forth, back and forth, slow and steady. Nothing more except now and then a quiet voice, soft and hushed. Couldn't make out any words. Didn't wanna. Didn't care. That, and every so often someone squeezing water from a wet cloth onto my parched lips and into my mouth, then laying the cloth over my forehead and eyes.

When I finally come around, Beulah cleaned me up and the room like I was a baby. At first they didn't ask nothing of me. Just let me grieve. I got my Bible and started to read in Job, the man in the Bible our preacher called the suffering one. When I come to where it said, *"My days are spent without hope"* (Job 7:6), I wondered so whether a man named Job knowed what I was going through. I closed my Bible and laid it down. Couldn't read no more just yet.

Beulah and her family was so patient with me. Got me to doing little things at first. "Set the table just this once," she suggested. Another day it was, "Weed just one row in the garden, that's all I ask." "Fetch some butter from the spring house." Or, "Go with Bertha to gather the eggs since Jack is busy in the barn."

I did what she said but didn't have no desire of my own to see things got done.

One day the preacher we called Spotty - his real name was Luther - stopped by with my best girlfriend, Susie. I looked at the white spots in his black hair and thought of how I made fun. Now the tables was turned. In three weeks my hair turned from dark to white. Was I being punished for making such fun of him that one time? After all, I knowed better back then. In hindsight it was more likely from the shock of losing Gloriann. Maybe both.

He sat down next to where I was, asked how I am.

"As good as can be."

He just sat there for ever so long, said nothing. When I looked his way I seen tenderness and concern in his eyes. After while he said. "Alverna, some people hate the good in people so bad that they'll do anything to crush it. A wicked person laid a snare for you, lied about you. Trouble and anguish have overtaken you, ain't that so?"

"Yep." He wasn't telling me something I already didn't know. I even knowed where he was getting them words. Right out of Psalm 119. I answered him right back, *"I am small and despised. My soul melted for heaviness. I have seen an end of all perfection."*

"But you got a strong constitution and a powerful faith. God is your hiding place. Hope in His word. You will get better. "

I didn't answer him back. Didn't know if I wanted to get better.

At least Luther didn't make promises about getting my little girl back, promises that'd never get accomplished. He didn't keep harping away at me to get over it. Instead, he squeezed my hand in encouragement and said, "You're not alone, Alverna. God goes before you to prepare your way. He who is in you is greater than He who is in the world. Stand firm."

"Easy for him to say," I thought, but said nothing. There was nothing to say.

Luther, he just sat there for awhile, so quiet, head bowed like he didn't know what more to say, almost like he was in prayer. Finally he stood up, squeezed my shoulder, stepped outside and left me and Susie alone

"He can just up and walk away," my heart cried out. "Me, I'm living with hurt that I'll never be able to walk away from. Not for the rest of my life." Yet he sounded sincere and understanding. Maybe life dealt him some deep sorrow I didn't know nothing about. Then I stopped thinking. It made me tireder all the more.

Susie come and sat down next to me. She didn't say anything at first, just put her arm around my shoulder. After a long pause she said, "Alverna, Luther's right, but it'll take a long time for you to come around. Two things are in your favor. You're in good hands with Beulah and her family; and you know the Lord."

"Yeah, I'm in good hands. That I know."

"These folks love you so much and they want to help you get better."

"Yeah." The thing was, I wasn't sure I wanted to get better.

Another long pause, then she asked, "Can you take some good news about me?"

I looked at her for the first time since she come in. I seen how sad she was for me, but there was something more, something coming from deep inside. She was aglow with joy. Something wonderful good happened to her, I could tell.

"I can try."

She bubbled over, attempting not to be too happy since I was so heartbroken, but she couldn't hold back. "Alverna, ever since that evening we got convicted in our hearts from Luther's sermon, I've been going to his class to learn more about the Bible and about China. Do you remember about that?"

"Yeah." Susie was attending Wednesday night prayer meeting and Bible study conducted by the preacher after us girls had that religious experience. She hadda deep interest in the Bible, wanted to learn all she could. She said what a good teacher Luther was.

"Well, Luther asked me to marry him and I said yes. He's much older'n me but we love each other and we love the Lord. We're just now training for mission work in China. We'd like for you to be happy for us. When we get to China I promise to write to you every week if I can work it out. Promise you'll write back to me. Oh, please, Alverna, promise you'll write. I need to keep in touch with my best girlfriend ever. I'll need to hear how things are back here and how you are."

Susie was smart. So much she got accomplished in just a short lifetime; finished school, got convicted, learned her Bible, fell in love, was getting married and planning to go to China with her husband-to-be as missionaries. Just what she always wanted.

Susie, she sure done a lot in her few years..

Her dream was coming true.

How could I not be happy for my best friend since little on up? I was glad, really and truly glad.

"I'll write," I said, happy for Susie.

Their visit helped. And Beulah, oh, how she helped me. Don't know where she got the strength.

I started to eat some, pushed myself after I seen how this was eating away at young Bertha as much as Beulah and Jack. They missed my little girl, too. They was worn out with worry and extra work. Now just think! How many people woulda put up with me as long as they did? I pushed myself hard to help with the work again. I done my best to act normal. By and by it got better, just a little bit better.

We didn't talk much about what happened till one day I worked up my nerve enough to ask Beulah that when I'd been in bed, the only sounds I remember was a rocking back and forth, and a hushed, quiet voice, and now I was wondering what that was all about.

"We took turns sitting with you, Alverna. You was never alone. We sat by your bed and we rocked. Me, Bertha, even Jack. Why even Clyde brought his mom from town one day. Jemima, she sat and rocked for eight hours straight."

I thought I'd smelled Jemima's comforting and assuring presence then, but nothing was coming through real clear.

"How did your work get done?"

"People come, offered their help, brought food. They purty much know how Dottie is, except never figured something this evil'd come outta her. They know this gotta be hard on you. They wanted to help. We took 'em up on it so one of us would always be with you."

"Even Jack?"

"Yeah, even Jack. He didn't mind. Wanted to. Bertha too. We wanted you to not be left alone, not for one minute."

Then I wondered so, "Not always, but now and then, a hushed voice, so soft and quiet, I heard."

"Yeah. That was me."

"Was somebody else there who you was talking to?'

"Yeah."

"Who?"

"God. I kept telling Him how much we love you and want you to get better, body and soul. Alverna, you got so much living to do now yet."

Beulah, she took every measure to help me get well - and I did.

And that was that.

CHAPTER 38 - WILLIE

I was with Beulah and Jack two years.

Willie was a member of the United Brethren church where I joined only I didn't see him there much, just once in a while on a Sunday morning. When he found out I was going to church there, I become aware that he was there more often. Lydia said she told him that I was one of the girls who got up and sang on Sunday evenings. Wouldn't you know, before long he was showing up Sunday evenings now too. He kept eyeing me up. I pretended not to notice but I did. One evening the girls I sang with wasn't there. We was invited to sing at another church but I didn't wanna go and miss seeing Willie in case he showed up that evening. Of course I didn't give that for a reason. For that matter I didn't let anyone know how I felt about Willie.

That evening the preacher asked me to sing a solo; *Rock of Ages*. I did.

After church on that brisk, fall night, Willie walked over to where we was getting ready to get in the wagon to head for home. He said something to Jack; Beulah piped right in and said that of course it was alright if Willie took me home in his buggy. When he lifted me rather than helped me step up into the buggy and held onto me just a couple seconds longer than need be, I felt how strong his arms and hands was. No one ever lifted me up like that before. I ain't kidding when I say a tingle went all the way through me. That was something I never before felt. I blushed and hoped he didn't notice, but I think he did.

He steered the horse to trot the back way home which took longest to get there. I was purty flustered. It took all I had to think of something to talk about. Then we got on how he was one of them that years before offered me a dime to buy ice cream at St. John's Church Picnic. How we laughed and talked then.

"Yeah, I broke up with my girlfriend right before the picnic and tried to sit next to you in the wagon but you wouldn't have nothin' to do with me."

"Yes well, I thought maybe you was trying to make her jealous and I didn't wanna get caught in the middle and make trouble between you two."

We was quiet for a minute. Then Willie said, "Look at us here now. That was a long time ago and we're both still not married."

"Yeah."

He reached under the seat of the buggy and pulled out a package, wrapped awful awkward in brown, waxed butcher paper - he musta done that hisself - and handed it to me.

I put it on my lap. Wasn't sure what to do with it.

"Open it."

When I tore the butcher paper off there was this beautiful pink box decorated with crepe paper flowers of all colors. Why I couldn't at first believe what a purty box it was. I didn't even think about lifting the lid to see what was inside.

"Boy-oh-boy! This musta cost a lot of money," I thought.

I sat there wondering so. Had he worked this out ahead of time and bought this box and what was inside thinking I wouldn't turn him down the first time he offered me a ride home? Well, if that was what he figured, he was right.

I blushed at the idea, then remembered my manners. "It's so lovely."

"Look inside."

I lifted the lid. There was chocolate covered candy, each piece decorated with little sugar flowers of all colors, miniatures of the crepe paper flowers on the outside. I couldn't believe my eyes! Never seen nothing like it.

I guess I musta gasped in surprise while Willie all this time was looking me over.

"Take a piece," he laughed.

"It's too purty to eat," I said back.

"Well," he said reaching into the box for a piece he snatched and popped in his mouth. "It's not too purty for me to eat," he said as he chewed.

I took out a piece, passing over one I'd spied first off. It was one purple blossom of hard sugar painted with little dots of white - so small they was almost invisible. It made me think of my doll baby's dress of long ago. If this whole box was mine to keep, I'd look at that piece closer when later I got by myself. Sad thoughts I didn't want right now to break in on this wonderful evening. I put the lid back on real fast.

I never tasted anything so sweet and delicious in my whole life.

"Is this whole box for me?" See, I never got much of nothing for myself except for the ring Pop gave me, the doll baby and book bag from Sim, and Lola's presents.

"Yeah. It's all yours." He went on. "I bought it from Jenny Prowell at her candy store and bake shop."

"I haven't seen the Prowells in years. Does Jenny's brother, Lee, still help her out?" I asked.

"Yeah. He manages it. Special orders the boxes that are made for Jenny's candy. People like to collect different ones. Her pies and cakes are put in regular boxes since they get all messed up with icing and pie filling, but her candy boxes are special made."

Willie went on to say that Tim, their older brother, and David Briggs was building a room onto the Prowell's house. Just about finished they was.

"It'll be a place where people can sit inside to eat some of what they buy. Candy, cookies and donuts, rolls and muffins, pieces of pie and cake too. They'll have coffee, too. Whatever people want. Lee is gonna bring in ice cream and soda. Said maybe he'll put in a Victrola or player piano for people to put in a nickel or dime and play some music while pumpin' pedals or windin' up the Victrola. It'll be called Jenny Lee's Snack Shop. They think up in their heads one idea after the other. Right now they're tryin' to convince their mom to quit her sewin' and make sandwiches so they can call it Jenny

Lee's Snack and Sandwich Shop, but Esther too much likes to work with her needle."

I told him about the dress Lola had made for me by Esther. I was saving to wear it for something special. When the time was at hand, I'd know.

It was good to get caught up on news about people in Cedar Grove from Willie since I hardly ever got back there. I was enjoying the ride home with this handsome young fella. In my eyes he was handsome, yes he was. Not too tall to tower over me who was small and short, but his body was strong and well-muscled. His dark, wavy hair he combed into a pompadour that kept falling down over his forehead and into his eyes. He had this habit of brushing it back off his forehead with the hand where was a crippled, little finger; but his hair never stayed. His crooked grin was lively; no teeth was missing that I could tell. All his parts fit together real good except his ears, that is. They was sorta small for his large head, and his nose stopped a bit short of where it shoulda. And I noticed when he walked towards Jack's wagon that evening that his legs was slightly bowed, but only just a little. And that one little finger was crippled, all bent outta shape. I seen that for the first time when he brushed the hair outta his eyes and later when he handed me the beautiful candy box wrapped in plain butcher paper, and wondered so how it happened. Maybe some day I'd find out. Yes, overall, he cut a fine figure.

When he pulled up to the house it was getting late so come along in he didn't.

I was almost ready to jump down from the buggy when he hopped down and come around to help me get out. I waited then. A bit breathless I managed to thank him for the candy and the ride home.

"Maybe I'll come next Sunday night to hear you sing again," he mentioned.

Was that his way of saying he wanted to see more of me?

"A Dutch poem I'll be reciting next week instead of singing." I said.

"Then I'll be sure to be there."

When Beulah seen the candy box she gave a broad grin and made a clucking noise just like a mother hen, the way women do when they smell romance in the air. I hurried to the little back room I shared with Bertha. I didn't offer the Detwiler family no candy that night. I was so scared one of 'em might go for the piece with the purple flower covered with them tiny little white dots. That woulda broke my heart. I wanted to look at it closer. I could hardly believe how after all these years I'd still find things that reminded me of my dolly's dress. I lifted it outta the box with great care and clutched it to my heart. Afraid the chocolate and the flower might melt, I wrapped it in a little piece of the butcher paper I tore off, then tucked it in the back of the one bureau drawer that was mine alone. I hadda hide it just in case anybody come upon my box and sneaked some. I wouldn't care but for that one piece. Not after the way this family was to me.

That one piece of candy, it might sound silly to you, but it gave me just a little bit of hope. Even with Gloriann gone.

The next evening at suppertime I sat a piece of the decorated chocolate candy at each plate. One for Beulah, one for Jack and one for Bertha; and a piece for me. It was gonna get ate all too fast. I wished I could share some with Mom and Albert and Dale Stuart, even share a piece with Lola to let her know I was glad she took such good care of Albert and the way she showed us she cared. But not John if I had my way. What he said still stung. If only John woulda just said they'd take Albert and left me out of it altogether. Why did he have to say, "Albert can come but we **don't want** Alverna." I knowed that upset Lola too, but she dared not say nothing to him about the way he made it sound, like there was something wrong with me, like I wasn't good enough for him or his family.

Well, wasn't long before Willie was driving me back to Beulah and Jack's after Sunday morning and evening services. He ate Sunday dinner with us, too. Never invited me to his Mom's house for dinner. I wondered so about that but didn't ask over it.

It went on like this through winter and into spring. Willie gave me three more boxes of candy, each lid different from the one before. I kept 'em all.

It was towards the end of May. Willie was driving the buggy back to Beulah's after morning service. The spring air, fresh with plowed fields and plantings made me feel lighthearted and gay as I sat next to my fella. When we got on the main road Willie appeared lost in thought. I didn't mind. It was alright to be quiet. Then he started getting fidgety, kept looking down at my hands. I wondered about this but said nothing. Finally, with a jerk of his head towards my right hand, he said in a sharp voice about the ring I was wearing on my finger. It was still on my middle finger, still too big for my ring finger. See, other'n Sundays or special days, I knotted a narrow black ribbon around the precious ring Pop gave me, then tied it around my neck to protect it from the dirt and grime of my house chores and farm work. I always kept it with me. I kept it on my body one way or the other, fearful if I didn't, it'd get lost.

He didn't sound real pleased about it, sorta come out in a jealous tone.

When I told him how Pop gave me the ring, I heard come outta him a deep sigh.

He cleared his throat. "I thought maybe it was from the daddy to your little girl and you still had strong feelin's about him."

"I never had strong feelin's about him." I snorted. "I never consented to the way he forced hisself on me. This ring has nothing to do with him. Pop gave it to me and I'll never part with it. I'll wear it till the day I die! And I want it to go with me when I'm laying in dead in my coffin. "

He reached over, took my hand and said, "Maybe someday I'll buy you a ring."

Next he said, "What do you think? Maybe we oughta get married." Just like that he said it.

I said, "Ok".

I told Beulah and Jack. By golly, they was so happy, said we could live with them till we got our own place. I'd help there like I done for the past two and a half years, Willie'd keep his job at the quarry.

Beulah and I was cleaning the front room. "Alverna, what are we gonna do with all these empty candy boxes?"

"Burn 'em I guess. All but that one. No. That one I'd like to keep. It was the first one I got. I might have a girl someday who'd like to play with it."

Then Beulah said maybe Bertha'd want the rest to play with and I said "Sure. I'd rather she'd have 'em than have 'em get burned."

At that then Reverend Barnes come in. He said, "What did I hear?" Then we told him. He was just like one of the family, often stopping at the farm and helping out Jack when he needed an extra hand. Jack paid him for his help when he could. I think Reverend Barnes didn't earn too much as a preacher and liked the hard, physical work and extra pocket change.

"Can I tell you something?" he wondered.

"Sure, but I don't know whether I'll listen," I teased.

"If you marry that Seiple fella and you have any children, I'm afraid you won't have any girls. They'll all be boys."

I looked at him. "Why?'

"He's got a stronger constitution than you."

Beulah laughed out loud. "Reverend Barnes, you don't know for what a strong constitution our Alverna's got! You just don't got no idea!"

"Well now. We'll just have to wait and see, won't we?" he chuckled back.

Willie's mom was in the garden picking early peas. He went in where she was.

"Mom, I'm gettin' married on Saturday."

She figured it was coming but she didn't like it. "Well, you're old enough," she grumbled. She thought because I had that little girl, well, she was leery about me.

CHAPTER 39 - THE HAPPIEST DAY OF MY LIFE

The day come for us to get married. It was a beautiful day full of sunshine, hard work and promise. I was so happy inside. In the early morning I helped pick seven crates of strawberries, got the eggs and other things ready for Beulah and Jack to take to market. They got on their way, then all of Saturday's work was ahead of me.

I told Bertha, "You go out and see whether there's any eggs in the chicken house."

She come back empty handed. "No, but there's two chickens on the nest."

I got down on my hands and knees to wash the floor up. Soon I heard a chicken cackle.

"Bertha," I called. "Would you go look and fetch the eggs in?"

Bertha come back with one egg. "The other chicken's still on yet."

"Well, this one'll be alright."

"What do you want with one egg?"

"Never mind."

I started heating the stove up. I handed Bertha money and told her, "Now you go up to the store and get me a pound of sugar and a pound of icing sugar." The other stuff I could use of the Detweiler's.

And, of course that other chicken didn't lay that egg. I had just one egg. I stirred the cake up and honest-to-goodness, the layers raised so nice with only that one egg. I was so happy the cake come out so good.

Bertha still wondered why I wanted a cake. "Why, you just baked pies yesterday."

"We're getting a lot of company tomorrow and a cake will go good too." That's all she knowed.

When they got home from market, I was helping put the market things away when Beulah smelled the cake. "A cake!"

she smiled. Then Bertha began to tell how I run her after the eggs. They knowed what was going on but Bertha didn't.

"You know what!" Beulah scolded me. "I have a notion to kick that rear end of yours."

"Why?" I wondered so at her words.

"You got the eggs ready for market. Why didn't you keep four out?"

"Beulah, I know that you have customers for your eggs and I wasn't gonna do that."

Yes well. So. That was that.

Of course I wanted Beulah and Jack to go along to the preacher's that day, but she said no, they'd stay home.

For my wedding I wore the dress Lola had Esther Prowell make for me some years earlier. I wore it once or twice before to church, but I always knowed the day'd come when it'd be a special time for me to wear. Today was the day. I'd saved and bought myself brand new underwear and stockings. My old shoes hadda do but I polished 'em till they shined.

After we had left, Beulah said to Bertha to help her clean the bed off in the little room way back.

"Why, Mom? Why are you gonna clean that bed off now?"

Beulah told Bertha that I was getting married, and now she would sleep in the little bed they were cleaning off in the room that was more the size of a closet - only we didn't have closets back then; not yet. Bertha began to cry. "I always slept with Alverna before and I wanna sleep with her now yet."

We rode to the parsonage the back way, just the two of us. Willie said we didn't want nobody to know about us getting married till after it was over - except for his mom and Beulah and Jack who already knowed. That direction took us past the grove where the gypsies set up camp every summer. We could always rely on them showing up cause they never missed a summer to visit where the old gypsy lady lay buried in the graveyard, thanks to H.A. Briggs who seen to all that back then. This year they was already there, much earlier than usual. I looked amongst the crowd for the gypsy girl close to my age that I'd seen every summer when I was at Grammy's. I wondered so that if I spotted her, would I recognize her after all this time. Probably not. It was going on many a year that I didn't get by the grove when the gypsies was there.

The first time this gypsy girl and I caught a glimpse of each other was when we was just young girls. I was looking out into the camp from behind a tree and she spied me. When no gypsy come to chase me away and no one pulled her away as she stared at me, we stood and waved to each other. She moved a little closer. I got brave and said to her, "Hi. My name's Alverna."

She paused, then repeated my name. "Alverna. Never heard that name before. Mine's Maribella."

Just then Purd yanked me away. He said it was time to go before the gypsies stole us away. But I think he was jealous because I made contact with one and he didn't. I told him that ever since they buried the old gypsy lady in the graveyard, they was so grateful to H.A. Briggs and the town that they'd never do nothing like that. That's what I heard Grammy say and I always believed Grammy who never spoke nothing but the truth - except that one time to the witch lady, and that was because her life depended on it.

Every summer the gypsy girl and I played this game of searching each other out, me hiding behind the exact same tree as always, she keeping an eye out for me. When I was able, I got away from the other kids who stuck together as we approached the gypsy camp. I never left anyone else in on our game and she never did neither that I know of. We never talked except to say hi and call each other by name.

367

I woulda liked to but was scared to get any closer, so I just waved. By then we had our own peculiar wave. It was like a secret signal between us.

Willie slapped the reins to make the horse trot faster. I was glad the horse didn't pay much attention to him.

Wille said he didn't like gypsies, didn't trust 'em. He woulda if he knowed 'em better like I did. I was telling him about the burial of the old gypsy lady, but he didn't appear convinced. I figured I better just let it go.

I craned my neck towards the camp, and then, oh! I was sure of it. I seen her! Glory be! Or was it my imagination? If only Willie wouldn't be pushing the horse faster. See, there was this young gypsy woman bending over the campfire. As she stood up and stretched, rubbing the small of her back to get the kinks out, she musta heard the horse clopping along and looked out to the road. She was taller and older than I remembered - why, of course she'd be - but she had the same features of the Maribella I waved to summers of long ago. I stared. She turned back to the fire, then, like a bolt outta the blue, as if she recognized me that instant, she turned and looked my way again.

I called, "Maribella!" She took a couple of steps towards the road and stared back. I was right. It was her, it was! A smile broke out on my face and I waved, the same secret signal we used every year from behind the tree. Her face lit up. Then, O, lordy!

"Alverna!" she hollered. She waved and signaled back. It was her for sure. It was Maribella. She broke into a little jig that made her bright, colored skirt puff out all around. The bracelets on her arms and ankles jingled in merriment. Then, that quick, we was outta sight.

But, boy-oh-boy! My heart spilled over with happiness. Honest to Pete, I ain't superstitious - at least I don't think I am - but I took this as a good omen for my wedding day. No, I decided it wasn't an omen. That sounded too much like a witch's spell. I turned it around and made it a blessing, a blessing from the Good Man who lived in heaven. That made it sound better. Oh, how I wanted to think my pop was standing right there with the Good Man watching all this and sending me his blessing too. Then I told myself to believe it, and I did.

But I didn't tell Willie. Somehow or other I didn't think he'd understand the wonderful good, happy way I was feeling. He didn't hold to the same way of thinking as me about gypsies. I didn't want that moment spoiled so I didn't say nothing to him. It was a secret between me and the gypsy girl to this day. And now, after all these years, me writing this down, well, for the first time, somebody else besides me and Maribella knows. I don't expect you to be crying like I am as I'm telling my story, but maybe you can at least feel how happy I was and be happy too.

The preacher's wife opened the door and said, "Oh, Henry, look who's here!"

We went in. He come to the hallway and said, "I'm surprised to see you two."

Willie handed him the marriage license.

"Oh, I see." Then he wondered whether we had witnesses. I told him I wanted Jack and Beulah to come along but they didn't.

"Well, Emmy's here. She'll be your witness."

That suited us.

Yes well, we was sitting there an awful long time not saying much of nothing. Finally, he married us.

After we left, Willie asked, "Do you wanna go right home, or how about goin' down to Jenny Lee's for some ice cream and pie now yet?"

Well, nothing coulda pleased me better. I said that pie and ice cream was a good idea, that we should go.

"It'll soon be time for Jenny to close down, but maybe she'll make an exception this *onct*," Willie said.

As soon as we walked into her shop and she seen us, Jenny come running. She sure had come to life after all them hard years of trouble with her dad, the blacksmith.

She was several years older'n me, but I was pleased to see she remembered me. "Alverna?" she laughed. "Why I haven't seen you for years. But Willie! Now he's a different story," she said, not taking her eyes off me. "So, you're the one he's been buying my candy for. I ask him every time he comes in for a box who it's for, but he'll never say. And look at the two of you. My, but you two look nice this evening. For goodness sakes Alverna, is that a dress my momma sewed?"

I told her it was and how Lola had it made for me!

"Well you look just beautiful. If I can find Momma I'll have her come to see how good the dress looks on you."

It was getting late in the day, so wasn't many people there, but she spoke as if we was the only ones. She made me feel so special, so welcomed, so glad to see.

Willie just said over it, "I made her mine tonight."

There was only five or six people there besides us, but Jenny drawed in her breath, so surprised she was that she almost choked. Taking hold of herself she shouted all over the shop, "Willie and Alverna just went and got married." She hugged me all over again with such gladness and cheer.

I wondered how Willie was taking all this. For myself it felt so good for someone to be happy for me on my wedding day. I don't know last when I was so overjoyed with so much good coming my way.

Lee come out from the storage room looking *ferdutzed*.

"Jenny, what're you up to? What's goin' on?" he wondered, hearing the happiness in his sister's voice.

"We got married this evening," Willie said.

"All right! Congratulations! The ice cream's on the house. All you want."

As we was talking there together Willie just said, "Now, Lee, I made her mine tonight and if she don't behave I'll smack her rear end real good and hard."

Lee come back right off the bat. "If you ever lay as much as a finger on her and I find it out, you'll have me to worry with. We ain't seen much of Alverna here in Cedar Grove these past years, but we remember the way the Farley family done for us. Even now, the news of how Alverna treats everybody so nice - even them not so nice to her - comes back here about her. She was the best girl not taken this part of the county ever had and don't let me ever find out you hurt her in any way!"

"My goodness!" I thought to myself. "Willie's only joking and Lee sounds so serious. He's gotta know Willie's just teasing."

Over that, Tim come in with David Briggs. Them two got to know each other at the furniture factory where Tim loved working but David didn't. All he wanted was outdoors jobs, liked working alone the best of all. A couple of months ago he quit his job at the factory. Now he was doing what he enjoyed more'n anything else which was fixing up houses or adding on a room - like Jenny Lee's Snack Shop. Tim, good with finishing work, helped David in the evenings.

Jenny Lee's Snack Shop had been open for business for a couple of weeks but they was putting on some finishing touches here and there. They wondered so what was going on in here with all the hooting and hollering. Jenny told 'em about us getting married and what Willie said about smacking my bottom if I don't listen.

Tim, thumbs latched onto his pants pockets, swaggered over to Willie. "Listen here Willie. If I was the marrying kind, you'd of hadda hustle to get Alverna. I never wanna get married, but she's the one girl that I woulda wanted outta all the girls in these parts. She and the Farley bunch was one of the few who never turned their backs on us when other folks did. They never said a mean word about us when we had all them troubles with Pa."

Tim went on. "Matter of fact, we never heard her say a mean word about nobody, not never. So, you better watch that mean streak of yours and what you do and say with

Alverna. If I hear about any harm you do to her, you'll have me to answer to."

Well my goodness! I never knowed they remembered how Grammy and Pap insisted that the Prowell family be treated like everyone else in spite of their pa. Why that was second nature to us, behaving towards people like we wanted to be treated. I never coulda been mean to them after what they was going through with their drunken daddy. "Live by the Golden Rule," is what Grammy taught us. Pap too.

"Why in the world are they talking to my Willie like that?" I wondered so. "He was only teasing. I never seen him hurt nothing or nobody."

"Stop!" I admonished them. "You're making me blush,"

"You and your family helped us through, and we never forgot it, never," Tim looked and me and said.

All three of them congratulated us with good wishes, shook our hands, then went back to their work.

When Jenny brought the pie and ice cream to our table, she sat down and talked to us, bringing the good mood right back in. She wondered all about me, then teased Willie. "You better not stop buying Alverna candy now that she's yours. Why, I'll go outta business if you stop now," she joked. It done my heart good to see all she went through to come out so good natured and cheery.

It was getting late. The hour was past for the shop to close. All the other customers had congratulated us and left. Jenny just said over it not to worry and just went on talking. While Willie went to the privy, Jenny asked me if I ever get to see Opal Heindel.

"No, I never get back there."

"Then you didn't hear she married Chance Miller?"

"You mean Lola and John's only boy? Oh, my! No, I didn't hear."

"John was upset, didn't think Opal and her family was good enough for the Millers, threatened to disown Chance if he went through with the wedding. Rumor is Chance didn't love Opal, he just got sick and tired of his pop lording over him. Figured it'd go against his pa's grain if he married her, so that's what he went and done. Didn't tell anybody till it was over and done with. Oh, Alverna, what an awful way for Chance to reach out and try to hurt his pa. That man is past beyond being hurt by anyone, so hard-hearted he is. But if Chance don't truly love Opal, both of 'em'll be hurt, not John."

Jenny wasn't done talking yet. "Anyway, Opal likes my candy, stops in often to buy some. Never wants the decorated boxes, just the candy. She's still awful heavy you know. Anyway, Opal said how I charge way too much for my candy, that it's a shame how some people make out so good by taking advantage of others. Then she went on how I must be pulling in all kinds of money. I wouldn't say this to anyone else but I think she's jealous. She forgets all the years of hard work me and my family done. Believe you me, Alverna, it was awful hard to be nice to her - you know how they say the customer is always right - well, thank goodness she got away before I blew my stack. After she was in here last time, I heard she come up with some ideas of her own and put it in Chance's head to go into the restaurant business right down the street from here. She figured she'd make lots of money selling hot meals when people'd stop here for baked goods. It sounded like a good proposition to me, would bring me in more customers too. They put a lot of money into fixing up a big dining room and kitchen in that old house half way down the block. But you know Opal, how she thinks of herself before anybody else. I heard she was so mean to her employees that all of 'em quit after a couple days. Me, I wanted to believe she had better business brains than that so I stopped in one day to congratulate her and Chance. I thought maybe she'd order some pies and cakes from my shop for her desserts. Oh, my; the new cook didn't show up that morning and she and Chance was standing there in the middle of the restaurant arguing loud and clear. He wanted her to put on an apron and cook. She flat out said no. Six weeks later they was closed down. They still live above the restaurant. Chance is gone most of the time with his salesman job. Last I heard, Opal's saying she wants to adopt a girl like Pearl and Bill took her in so she can train her to work good and hard just like she learned."

We giggled about that. Pearl tried to teach Opal, but how successful she was, was a matter of opinion.

When Willie come back in I was thinking, "After all these years and Opal still hasn't learned what it takes to be happy."

We was afraid of holding Jenny up, but she kept on talking, so happy she seemed.

"Oh, I'm so excited, Alverna. Willie, can you stay long enough for me to tell you one more thing?"

Willie nodded, mosied around the shop. I seen he was restless, ready to go, but after all he agreed. I was having such a good time. I sat back down.

"Don't sit down. Come over into Momma's shop. I wanna show you something."

She took my arm, then grabbed Willie's and pulled us through a doorway.

Here, oh my goodness, was hanging two of the purtiest dresses I ever seen in my entire life. I looked at Jenny again. Now I knowed why she was so happy. One was a dress for her marriage, the other'n musta been for her mom to wear on Jenny's wedding day. Jenny and her mom together was sewing the most beautiful dresses I could ever imagine. One dress was light purple. I looked to see if there was white flocks on it, but no, there wasn't.

I looked at Jenny. "Who's the lucky man?"

"He was just in with Tim. It's David Briggs. Oh, Alverna! I went about five months ago and asked him to draw up plans for a new shop for me and Lee. He come by almost every evening for a week, sat down with us and worked out the plans with us step by step. Such a gentleman he is. Over time we come to know each other, first working together on a business transaction, then friends. Wouldn't you know, we fell in love. We'll be married in September. It'll be at the church with just our families. If we'd invite others it'd have to be all our customers and I'm afraid it'd get outta hand. David doesn't want that and neither do I. He's gonna build a house for us on the big lot right behind the house and snack shop. That way I can keep the shop going with Lee's help. Being right on the main street here in Cedar Grove, we have lots of people coming in right from the factories and general store and the bank. David teases, says he might have to build rooms for Mom and Lee and Tim in our new house because we keep taking up more space here for our businesses. And can you believe this? David's brothers said they'd pitch in and help him in their spare time. They don't build houses no more but I think they just wanna try it and see if they can accomplish it without killing each other. Remember how they used to squabble? They seem to be getting along much better, at least right now. Oh, Alverna, I'm so happy - and now for you and Willie too."

So much for David Briggs being a loner. Well, he was older so he should know by now what he wanted. I'm sure the whole Briggs family was happy about David and Jenny.

We left then. Jenny gave me one more hug while warning Willie to not forget and stop by for candy now and then for his new wife.

Such a time like this day was. I couldn't of asked for a better wedding day.

When we got home Bertha went right away to Willie. Bertha liked Willie. She'd always take his hand and say she wanted to see that crippled finger. He'd let her hold it and look.

Beulah took me aside and said that her and Bertha cleaned off the bed in the little room way in the back. Then she warned, "Bertha is cross."

After Bertha come over to me I said, "The way your mother told me, I didn't think you'd wanna see Willie."

She pouted, "Well, I was cross, but I can sleep with you when he ain't here, can't I?"

And that was that.

The next day was Sunday, when all the company come. Beulah set a big table. Her mother and dad was there, and two of her sisters - Dottie wasn't one of 'em - and their boyfriends; six besides us.

And, of course, after dinner, Beulah, well, she hadda say something about the cake.

"Boy-oh-boy!" I just went. I knowed I was in for a teasing.

Bertha told them how I made her run back and forth to the chicken house.

How they deviled me that whole Sunday!

Such good fun!

CHAPTER 40 - SETTING UP HOUSEKEEPING

Willie and I, we stayed with Beulah and Jack almost a year. He still didn't much take me along when he went back to his mother's.

When he was there once his mom told him how she wanted to get rid of the people that lived in the old homestead just a stone's throw from the big farmhouse where she lived with her other son, Ken, and his wife, Lucretia. The renters was letting everything go to pot and she wondered whether we'd move there. See, she knowed how all this time she wasn't nice to me, never welcomed me into her house, said bad things that wasn't true, tried to pit Willie against me. She musta thought she could work Willie over better if he was closer. She put on her best act and whimpered to Willie that she reckoned I wouldn't wanna move that close with such a hilly yard and garden to keep after. She never said what bad shape the house was in and how we'd be expected to help on the farm, but she knowed.

This one day when he come from her place, he said what his mom told him.

"My golly days! Does your mother think I never worked in hills? Why, that's all I ever knowed."

"Maybe we better not go back there. That's where my old buddies now yet live and where we raised Cain together," Willie said looking away from me. I sorta detected a side of him he was warning me about what I didn't know of yet.

"You got a whole different life now. You don't have time for to go out and make trouble."

We left Beulah and Jack on good terms. Beulah and Bertha both shed tears; me too; even Jack. His jaws was set tight, only he couldn't keep back a choked sob as he sent us on our way to set up housekeeping.

Beulah and I promised to write to each other the way we done when they moved off the big Detwiler farm and I stayed. We'd visit too - and see each other at church.

Willie's Mom was right about one thing; the little old house, first on the property built, sure was run down. Willie was working long days at the quarry and had little time to fix it up. After we was there awhile and I seen how bad things was, I didn't know if we'd be able to stay through the wintertime with all the loose cracks and broken boards and other damage. I suggested maybe we should talk to David Briggs and see if he'd come and do some fixing up, something temporary, you know, just for over the winter. Willie said something to his mom and she come back so mean, "Who does she think she is? Does she think we're made of money? If Alverna can't handle living there maybe she ain't worth the room she takes up." That's what Willie told me she said.

Well, I figured it was no use to say more. I took what rags and newspapers I could and stuffed 'em in the biggest cracks. Even nailed some boards to keep the outside out. The kitchen, smaller than most kitchens back then, was the warmest room and that's where we lived. Kitchens was big in the old days, but not this one. I made room for two rocking chairs at the one end for us to use in the evenings. I closed off the upstairs and all the other rooms except for our bedroom which was freezing cold, but that was alright with us. Willie worked outside all day so he was used to the cold.

Come spring - and it couldn't come too fast for me but I didn't complain - Ken stopped in. Willie's older brother wasn't used to having things perfect neither - he and his wife lived on the big farm with his Mom and worked it - but when he seen the way the house was, I seen he was shocked real bad that family of his was living like that.

He got up nerve and talked to Willie, forced him over to their mom's for a talk. She was a tyrant. They was both afraid of her. Willie, he didn't like standing up to his mom.

378

What Ken said, to this day I don't know but he musta come down hard on Willie and his mom both, cause before long them two brothers was working together every spare minute - and there wasn't many of 'em - to fix up the house, inside and out. And me, well I worked right along side of 'em.

That summer I carried a share of my garden produce - all cleaned and ready to eat - to Willie's mom. Just cause she didn't come see me it didn't keep me from going to her. More often than not I'd make extra for our supper - I had a meat and potatoes man. I'd dish out piping hot portions for - I called her Mother - and Ken and Lucretia. That gave Lucretia more time to work the farm when she didn't have to cook supper. Willie's mom was to make supper but she wasn't reliable that way and left Lucretia in a bind day after day not knowing what she'd find when she come in from the fields late afternoons. Many a time she hadda make supper after working outside all day.

What I gave 'em, first off the older woman turned up her nose, throwed her share out for the pigs. Finally it got the best of her when she seen how Ken and Lucretia enjoyed it. The time come when she gave in and ate some. That loosened her up a bit. I knowed she forgave me for marrying her boy when once she asked me how come my meat always tasted a lot better'n hers. I said I didn't think that was so but that I always salt my meat before I brown it. She sputtered to think something so simple and easy could make meat taste so good. But she tried it and said it was so.

After she got to know me she asked me hundreds of time, "Alverna, can you ever forgive me?"

"Mother" - I called her Mother - "there's nothing to forgive."

"Yes there is. See, Ken was his dad's boy and Willie was my boy. I didn't wanna give him up so I talked about you because you had that little girl single. I was mean, thought maybe he'd give up on you and I'd get him back. The way I treated you when you come around with Willie was wrong. Why, you are better to me than anybody ever's been. Can you ever forgive me?"

"Yes, Mother, only there's nothing to forgive."

Me and mom exchanged letters every week. One time I got this letter, such a surprise. But that's what life is, full of surprises. Mom wrote, "You couldn't guess what happened if you'd guess for a hunnert years. Lawrence and Miriam was here on Sunday. Miriam got religion and now she come and wanted to make everything right with me. She was hopin' you'd be here too so she can make it right with you cause she knows what a wrong she done you."

Never got a chance to talk to Miriam. She died within a year after she was at Mom's. Purty young she died. Lawrence soon followed after.

Can't say I felt awful bad about them not coming to see me. But I wondered so about Sallie.

Willie never liked school. In fact he hated it. It was only after we was married I come to learn he couldn't read or write except for his name. One thing he knowed good was work. Hard, back-breaking work. Couldn't find a better worker anywhere. He could handle a pick and shovel on the job and he wasn't afraid to use 'em either. He was made boss of a ten man crew not long after starting at the quarry. He was a good boss. When he told his crew what to do and how to do it, they knowed he was telling them the right way cause that's the way he done it.

One day he come home and said, "What would you say if we moved again?"

"What? For goodness sakes, why?"

"My boss told me he thinks I'm the man to run the whole quarry operation out near Pittsburgh."

Well, I knowed that'd never go; so did he after he thought it over. But it was a good thing to be asked. The reason we knowed it'd never happen, see, Dan Holtzapple, one of the Willie's crew members was his right-hand-man at work. Right there Dan was whenever Willie needed him. And Willie needed Dan. See, Willie knowed where each man's name was on the ledger book, but more'n that he didn't know. Dan was always there to help him out with the figures regarding hours and wages.

Willie, he never knowed Dan come to me when he heard about the promotion. Dan waited till Willie wasn't home.

How good it was to see Dan Holtzapple. When you're young and know all these folks you think they'll always be around, only it's easy to get outta touch.

He shook my hand - so formal and respectful he was. After all, I was the boss's woman he was speaking to, not the little girl he used to carry on with. I didn't invite him in. Instead we stood in the shade of the big maple tree out back. A twinkle come into his eyes and the creases in his face turned up in a smile. "Alverna, I remember when you was just a little baby and you'd come to our house with your Grammy. I'd pick you off the floor and throw you in the air and swing you all around, You'd holler and laugh and want more. If I coulda been, well, I wanted to be a daddy to you when my brother Lawrence was too weak-willed to step in and own up to what was his. Of course, that never woulda worked."

We brought to mind a couple more memories, then he got down to business. "Alverna, Willie's a good boss. A lot of older men won't say that about the younger ones comin' in, but they respect Willie. He knows what's what. If he could read and write he'd go far. Besides bein' my boss, Willie's my friend; a good man he is. It's only natural for me to help him out with the figures and the ledger work. We calculated how to accomplish what needs done with the two of us working together, only without makin' it appear what we're doin'. And I'm glad to do it. All this time we're doing it and think that Lenny Deller, the big boss, never figured out what we're up to. Or else he don't care.

"So Lenny Deller's the big boss now at the quarry? I didn't know."

"Yeah, and a good one too. But I tell you this. If Willie goes to Pittsburgh, Alverna, he'll kill you with the work he can't do."

He went on to tell me how the one time he got sick was why Willie brought this big ledger book home to me. In it was ten names, the names of his crew. That was when I hadda fill in behind their names what he told me. Though I tried to teach him - my, how hard I tried - Willie never could get words or figures straight on paper. He said everything looked all jumbled up. I did this for a month. One day he took the book along with him and I never seen it again. Dan said that was when he got over his sickness and was back on the job.

Dan, he figured Lenny had an inkling of what was going on after Willie took the ledger book home that one time but he never pursued it to find out for sure. It didn't matter to him that Willie couldn't read or write as long as the work got done. Lenny knowed how Willie and Dan worked together so he didn't say nothing because Willie was a good boss and Dan was a good worker.

After speaking his mind about what he come to say, Dan left then. He didn't wanna start any gossip by showing up at the house and maybe bring trouble between him and Willie, or me and Willie. "You know the way people talk about things that ain't true," he cautioned as he started down the lane.

I didn't worry none about that. If Willie's mom or Lucretia seen this and wondered about it I'd just say it was a Holtzapple relative passing through and he stopped in for a minute before he went on his way again. And that was the truth.

What it come down to was, Willie told Lenny Deller he didn't have enough education so he had to turn the job down. We stayed right where we was. Maybe that was the best, maybe not. Who knows?

Willie's mom wasn't easy to get along with. Ken and Lucretia was at the end of their rope, couldn't hardly put up with her no longer. We talked it over. It was decided she was to stay with Willie and me for three months then go back with Ken and Lucretia for three months. Well, when it was Ken's turn to take her back, Lucretia said she wouldn't. Ken come to me and begged, "Alverna, if you take her for me I'll pay you $50.00. When I told Willie this he just said over it, "We'll take her for sure but we won't take no $50.00. We have room enough. Besides, she'll be able to help you out with some of the work.

"Well," I thought to myself. "She's too old and much too cantankerous to do any work, but that don't matter to me. We'll get along as is."

So that settled that. I loved having her with us.

Wasn't long till our family got bigger by one. Clyde Brillhart, Jemima and Earl's grown son was moving to Harrisburg. He was involved in a new business venture of some sorts, I can't remember what. That meant Uncle Earl hadda walk to work at the cigar factory, a purty good distance. Earl said he didn't mind, he'd just up and do it till he couldn't no longer.

Clyde moved and was working hard to become successful. Things seemed to be going ok. Then, a couple months later Uncle Earl was walking to work. He hadda leave when it was still purty dark outside yet. Well, one of them newfangled automobiles that we was seeing more and more of, went by. It passed him by so close that his coat, which was blowing out in the wind got caught in the door handle of this automobile that drug him along till it got wrenched off from bearing Earl's weight. Earl went down. The automobile driver rode away, never stopped to help him. Earl was found bloodied, bruised and dead along the road by a man walking to work around daylight. His coat was all twisted around him. Inside was found a door handle off an automobile. Everybody wondered so how many door handles could be missing off a newfangled contraption that we still wasn't used to. People all around was on the lookout for a damaged automobile door. Was only two days later, we heard that John Miller drove his automobile that same day all the way to Philadelphia. Come back driving a new one. It was never proved who killed Uncle Earl. Didn't matter. Everyone knowed. It was John Miller and his automobile. He was never brought to justice for this terrible crime. Still, everybody knowed.

Clyde was besides hisself, just didn't know what to do with his mom. There wasn't no room where he was living. Besides, he was gone from early morning till late night working hard to get his new business off the ground. After Uncle Earl's funeral, which was conducted by Adam Briggs who was still single - we figured he was so busy in his work he didn't have time to find a wife - Clyde come and asked if me and Willie'd take her. If only we just had one room for her he'd put her bed and some furniture in and pay us so much every month for her keep. Willie was agreeable, said we'd take her. Clyde sent the money to me every month. I handed it over to Willie and never seen it again.

Willie's mom was downright mean to Jemima. Jemima flat out refused to take part in her contrariness and helped me out best as she could even though she wasn't good. Her legs was so big she had an awful time just getting in and outta her chair. Besides, she was hit hard with the way Earl left this world. They was so close all the years they was together. She didn't complain, but you could see her struggle every hour with her grief.

I guess when Willie's mom seen Jemima wasn't gonna take no part in fussing and fighting, she bent a little; before long them two was getting along just fine. They talked long hours away, neither hearing much what the other said cause they was both talking at the same time. While I worked in the kitchen, which wasn't too often cause I was working the farm with Ken and Lucretia, I hadda chuckle at them two, dear old souls. They reminded me of Aunt Lilliemae and her dramatic way of talking. Now and then I thought they coulda taught Lilliemae a thing or two the way they went on, one trying to outdo the other. I listened to their stories, relished each and every one. Willie's mom took up her needle and thread again while Jemima crocheted a bedspread. Said it'd take her a good part of a year. After that she said she was gonna start knitting. Jemima made the most of every day while looking ahead to what she was gonna do next.

I was just getting over a summer cold; it mighta been the flu, I'm not sure. There was a bad epidemic of that going around. A lotta people was dying. Such a coughing and going on I was. Finally I was feeling good for the first time in two weeks; a little weak but a lot better.

Two mornings later Willie asked, "Alverna, can you take the three horses and roll the field since it looks like rain is comin' later on today. Then the two boys down the road can take care of some other work that needs done."

"Why sure," I said. "I'll do what I can."

Before I went out to roll the field I said to Willie's mom - I called her Mother - to holler for me around three o'clock. See, I had no idea what I was gonna make for supper that night and I needed time to come in and get it started. All day I worked. I had one more round to make, but according to where the sun was in the sky it was near three o'clock. Only Mother didn't call me in so I finished the last round.

When I come in I realized it was getting awful late. I got the horses and equipment away, washed at the pump, went into the kitchen. Something smelled so good. I wondered so why Mother didn't call me in. When I asked her, she went, "I got a piece from the smoked hams that're hangin' in the attic and I made boiled ham potpie."

I asked if she made ham potpie before.

"No, but there wasn't nothin' else here for me to make."

Well! Never in my life did I hear of making pot pie with ham. And Willie was sneaky, that he was. I was purty sure he wasn't gonna like that potpie. Well, glory be, that night at supper we ate that ham potpie with cabbage slaw till it was all gone.

When the Dutch finish their meal there's nary a scrap of food left on the plate. If you sit at the table of the Pennsylvania Dutch, when you push away on your chair, your plate better be clean. A piece of bread'll wipe up the leftovers a fork can't get. Why, the plate looks so clean sometimes you can't remember if it was washed or not. If not clean, the cook'll think you didn't enjoy your supper. *Waste not, want not*, is something we live by. Our plates was clean as all get-out that evening.

It was time to wash up before bed. We all washed outta the tub in them days. Willie's mom washed, then Willie. Jemima only sponged herself down. She didn't get too dirty not being able to get around too much since she was so heavy. Next it was my turn. It was late. Almost nine o'clock. Five o'clock in the morning would come around too fast.

I had just put my leg in the tub and I felt the baby coming out that quick. I called to Willie and he come running, grabbed me and the baby hanging down my leg, put us on the bed, washed himself off, then went through the heavy rain that started right after supper to fetch the doctor.

After the baby was born - not before - I got such pain I didn't know what to think. When he got there and I told him this, the doctor said, "You might have another one in there."

After awhile he said no, no second baby, just the afterbirth.

I had a baby girl, the first of a large family for Willie and me.

I was hoping soon to see the preacher who said I'd never have a girl baby, that they'd all be boys. I was gonna rib him about that!

Each baby that come along, boy or girl, didn't matter, each one got a Bible name.

These are the ones that today don't want me to tell my story.

Well, write my story I did. When I hand it over to my *granddaughter*, I'm done for sure. I won't butt in and tell my kids' stories. Let 'em do it on their own. I'd like to read 'em if they do. But you know what the doctor said. He said that I don't got long to live. I still ain't too sure about him though. Been living longer than he calculated.

But I tell you for sure, after all I've been through, whether I live or whether I die, I still got a little bit of hope. That's what I'm gonna tell my *granddaughter*, the one who pestered me to write my story. I'm gonna tell her that her name's been added to the list of people who gave me a little bit of hope.

ABOUT THE AUTHOR

Phyllis Plowman, a life-long resident of Pennsylvania Dutch country, created her first novel after years of writing stories for family members.

Formerly a licensed funeral director, Phyllis is owner of Trinkets & Doodads, a business in which she buys and sells estate jewelry.

Phyllis acknowledges with gratitude her three special families and their importance in her writing endeavors; her immediate family and relatives, her community of friends, and the family of First United Methodist Church, Hanover, PA.